Avail
from
Spec

From ... orever
by Karen Templeton
&
The Family He Wanted
by Karen Sandler

Baby By Surprise
by Karen Rose Smith
&
Daddy by Surprise
by Debra Salonen

A Kid to the Rescue
by Susan Gable
&
Then Comes Baby
by Helen Brenna

The Sheikh and the Bought Bride
by Susan Mallery

A Cold Creek Homecoming
by RaeAnne Thayne

A Baby for the Bachelor
by Victoria Pade

The Baby Album
by Roz Denny Fox

BABY BY SURPRISE

"What does the baby feel like when he moves?"

Francesca's green gaze locked to his. In that moment there was a spark of understanding in her eyes that he needed to be part of this pregnancy. "Do you want to feel him when he moves?"

Before he could think better of it, Grady answered, "Yes."

She closed her eyes for a moment, and then laid her hand on the right side of her tummy. "You can feel him move here."

She was wearing a long-sleeved, purple maternity sweatshirt with matching knit slacks. He told himself he just wanted to feel the baby. There wouldn't be anything intimate about his touch.

But when he laid his hand where hers had been, when he could feel the heat under the material and then the flutter of movement, he knew touching her this way was *very* intimate.

DADDY BY SURPRISE

"So, if I wanted a tour guide, you'd be the one to hire, right?"

Jack watched Kat carefully for her response.

"I've never done that before."

"Would you be interested?"

"Do you mean I'd drive you around in my car?"

Jack shook his head. "On my bike. You could give me a running history of the area and tell me where to go."

Kat frowned slightly, as if thinking over the proposition. "When?"

"Tomorrow? If it doesn't rain."

"Well, I don't have my kids tomorrow…so I suppose I could. But I couldn't do it free."

"Of course not." He did some quick maths. Eight hours. Forty dollars an hour seemed fair. He quoted her the price.

"Seriously? Deal." She flashed a bright smile, then continued with what she'd been doing.

He wasn't an impulsive kind of guy, but in two days he'd made some impulsive gestures. So far, he was pretty satisfied with them. He only hoped this would prove equally smart.

After all, there had to be worse things than riding around the mountains with a beautiful blonde on the back of his motorcycle.

First published in Great Britain 2010
Harlequin Mills & Boon Limited,
Eton House, 18-24 Paradise Road, Richmond, Surrey TW9 1SR

ISBN: 978 0 263 87981 0

23-0710

Harlequin Mills & Boon policy is to use papers that are natural, renewable and recyclable products and made from wood grown in sustainable forests. The logging and manufacturing processes conform to the legal environmental regulations of the country of origin.

Printed and bound in Spain
by Litografia Rosés S.A., Barcelona

BABY BY SURPRISE

BY

KAREN ROSE SMITH

DADDY BY SURPRISE

BY

DEBRA SALONEN

MILLS & BOON®

BABY BY SURPRISE

BY
KAREN ROSE SMITH

Karen Rose Smith has seen over sixty-five novels published since 1991. Living in Pennsylvania with her husband – who was her college sweetheart – and their two cats, she has been writing full-time since the start of her career. She enjoys researching and visiting the West and Southwest where this series of books is set. Readers can receive updates on Karen's latest releases and write to her through her website at www.karenrosesmith.com or at PO Box 1545, Hanover, PA 17331, USA.

For Suzanne and Sydney – May the future bring you many blessings and much happiness.
Love, Karen

Chapter One

Francesca Talbot barely registered the lines of wind turbines in the fields as she headed out of Sagebrush toward the hospital in Lubbock, Texas.

A wave of dizziness washed over her, leaving her suddenly weak. Over six months pregnant, she'd ignored her thirst for the past few days, attributing it to takeout food. As a neonatologist she should have known better. But she'd planned to discuss it with her doctor at her monthly appointment at the end of the week.

The road pitched and bent—

She quickly swerved back to her lane, blinking against the gray dots dancing before her eyes. The blurriness grew worse. Dizziness enveloped her. She felt bumps, a huge jerking motion that threw her against the door, then she sank into unconsciousness.

* * *

Six hours later, Francesca found herself in an unfamiliar position at the hospital where she worked—that of a patient! She tried not to panic at the diagnosis her doctor had given her—gestational diabetes. The condition would probably resolve after her pregnancy, but she had to handle her diet carefully. Everything else looked good with the baby, and…

She now knew she was having a boy.

A boy.

Grady should know.

Francesca had been talking and singing to her baby ever since she'd learned she was pregnant. She laid her hand on her rounding tummy awkwardly due to the cast on her arm. Even after more than six months, she vividly remembered her out-of-character one-night stand with Grady and, more important, her decision to experience her pregnancy on her own to give herself time to consider how Grady would fit into their child's life.

"I don't know what will happen when I call your daddy," she murmured to her son. "He told me he wanted to be involved in your life after you were born. Maybe we'll have to include him *now* just to make sure you'll have a backup."

Tears burned in her eyes. She had two very good friends, Tessa and Emily, who used to be her housemates. She hadn't called them yet, either. She was sure they'd come running to help. So why did she feel as alone as she had when she was a child, cowering in her closet to stay safe?

The phone was one stretch of the fingers too far. Francesca looped her index finger around the cord, pulled the receiver off and grabbed it. She punched in the numbers for Grady Fitzgerald's saddle shop.

To her relief he picked up himself. "Sagebrush Saddles."

His deep baritone rippled through her as it had the night they'd met. They'd attended a reception for a lawyer opening offices in Sagebrush and had bumped into each other periodically during the evening, feeling the buzz of attraction, each time having something new to talk about. With the party stuffy and crowded, Grady had invited her to the building a few doors down where he worked. They'd had a glass of wine, sat on his couch—

Erotic pictures flashed on her mental screen and she switched them off.

"Grady, it's Francesca."

He must have noticed something in her voice because he asked immediately, "What's wrong?"

"I had an…accident this morning. The baby's fine," she rushed to add. "And it's a boy. I had a sonogram."

Silence lay heavy between them for a few beats. "Are you okay?"

The concern in his voice washed over her. She hadn't expected him to ask that. She'd expected, "What caused the accident? What happens next?"

"My arm is broken, but that's not the problem. I have gestational diabetes. It caused blurry vision and dizziness. That's why I had the accident."

In the silence, Francesca pictured Grady's ruggedly

handsome face, the sweep of his black hair, the intriguing depth of his blue eyes.

"That's something I'm not too familiar with. Explain it to me," he said.

Nervous about calling him, she blurted out the medical explanation. "Pregnancy hormones produced by the placenta can block insulin. As the placenta grows larger, more hormones are produced and insulin resistance becomes greater. When the pancreas makes all the insulin it can and there still isn't enough to overcome the effect of the placenta's hormones, sugar builds up in the blood and gestational diabetes results. It can happen without much warning."

"But you and the baby are okay?"

He really was concerned. That knowledge made her heart hurt. She sucked in a big breath, seeking to escape to facts rather than her emotions. "We will be. At thirty-seven, I'm at a greater risk than someone younger. The diabetes usually clears up as soon as the baby's born."

An awkward pause settled between them, neither of them knowing quite what to say. She added, "I just thought you should know. Especially that we're having a boy. And..." This was so hard to get out. "And I guess this changed the way I'd been looking at the future... I just want to make sure our baby has another parent to rely on if need be."

She did know Grady had come from a big loving family and looked at family differently than she did. To her, family ties had only hurt.

"When are you being discharged?"

"This evening. My doctor will be making rounds around seven."

"Do you have a ride home?"

"I have friends. I haven't called them yet."

"Don't. I'll take you home."

She thought about facing him again, fighting the pull toward him, riding in his car— "Grady, that's not necessary."

"I think it is. We have a few things to discuss. I'll be there by seven unless you find you're being discharged sooner."

She'd kept away from him the past few months for more than one reason. Her last relationship had taught her she wasn't over her past. She'd chosen the wrong man. After a long-distance relationship, which had lowered her defenses, she'd moved to Lubbock to begin a life with Darren. But after he convinced her to move into his condo with him, he'd changed, becoming a man like her father.

After she'd made love with Grady, she'd been afraid to take a risk again. However, now they had to figure out how to be parents *together.* "All right. I'll see you at seven."

"Seven," he repeated, and clicked off.

Francesca took the phone from her ear and just held it in her hand. She'd learned early on fate wasn't kind. Each decision she made mattered.

Had she made the right decision in calling Grady Fitzgerald?

Grady rapped on the hospital door. He'd decided to bide his time with Francesca. Look what had happened.

He'd never expected an automobile accident. But as

he'd learned before, life was made up of unexpected surprises. Some nice, some not so nice. One thing he knew for sure—this baby was his main priority and he'd do whatever he had to to protect him.

A boy. Francesca had said they were having a boy.

He heard a sweet "Come in." The first night they'd met, her voice had been easy, pleasant, almost hypnotizing. She'd been so interesting. And she'd been curious about him…about his family. Her voice that night had wrapped around him like perfume, arousing him.

He pushed open the door and stepped inside the room. Francesca was standing beside the bed, dressed, only—

She was wearing a light blue maternity sweater that looked soft and lay enticingly over her. He hadn't seen her since she looked…pregnant.

"Hi, Grady." Her greeting was hesitant, her eyes searching.

"Hi, yourself. How do you feel?" His gaze went to her arm in the cast. The sleeve of her sweater came just below her elbow where the cast began. She looked pale and he was worried about her. Worried about his baby.

"I'm better now."

He couldn't keep from approaching…from standing in front of her…from touching the bruise on the side of her cheek.

She backed away from his hand and joked, "Better than my car."

The car was inconsequential. Her pregnancy wasn't. "How long are you taking off of work?"

Suddenly a physician swept into the room. He was wearing a white coat over his suit and a stethoscope hung around his neck. He was as tall as Grady, fit and good-looking.

He responded to Grady's question. "I told Francesca she should rest for a few days…at least." The man gave her a wink and then extended his hand to Grady. "I'm Jared Madison."

Francesca spoke up. "Jared, this is Grady Fitzgerald."

Jared looked from one to the other. "I'm going to give Francesca some instructions. Maybe you should step out."

"No, it's okay," Francesca told him.

Grady could sense the familiarity between the two of them.

"Jared married my former housemate, Emily," Francesca explained.

Grady felt himself relax a bit and his snap-buttoned shirt collar didn't feel quite so tight. "Is Francesca really okay?"

Jared arched a brow at Francesca, and she nodded. "She is right now. She will be if she can control her sugar. She's going to have to be more strict about her diet, exercise and get more rest."

"Would it be better if she had someone with her for a few days?" Grady asked, a plan forming in his mind.

Francesca's "That's not necessary" was overridden by Jared's "It wouldn't be a bad idea." He continued. "We don't want her getting dizzy again and falling…or worse. Maybe Emily or Tessa could stay with you."

"They have kids," Francesca protested.

"She can stay with *me*," Grady insisted without thinking twice about the decision he'd just made.

Silence fell over the room.

Finally, Francesca responded, "I'm not going to impose like that, Grady."

"You won't be imposing. There's nobody there but me and a few horses. Your friends have their responsibilities. My employees in the saddle shop can work whether I'm there or not."

"The two of you should discuss this," Jared said, obviously feeling the tension between them. "I'll send in one of the aides with the paperwork to get you discharged. My receptionist will make you an appointment with the diabetes specialist to go over diet and any questions you might have."

Then Madison put his hand on Francesca's shoulder and gave it a comforting squeeze. "You already have your next appointment set up with me. I'll see you through this, Francesca. You'll have a successful labor and delivery."

"I wanted Emily to be my midwife," she protested.

"I know you did. But she's only taking on low-risk pregnancies. She can coach you, though."

Grady had seen the story in the papers about Emily Diaz Madison and her past. But apparently she was going to practice as a midwife again. And if the "Tessa" Madison had mentioned was Tessa Rossi, Grady knew the pediatrician and her new husband, Vince. When Tessa was a little girl, Grady and his dad had delivered her first saddle to her. And Vince— He had worked at the saddle shop while Grady was in college.

Madison extended his hand to Grady once more. Grady shook it; then the doctor exited the room.

Immediately, Francesca began, "Grady, I don't know if it's such a good idea for me to stay with you."

"Why not?"

She reflectively glanced down at her stomach, and he did, too. Their gazes met.

He felt a zing to his midsection.

Damn, if there wasn't still chemistry between them. He'd let Francesca cut off personal contact after she'd told him she was pregnant and he'd stipulated she e-mail him with a doctor's report after each visit. He'd had the sense she'd run if he demanded more. He'd also realized the two of them were very different. However, every time one of her reports arrived in his e-mail, he could picture her sleek, long, brown hair lying across his sofa, her body under his, and the way his desire had gotten out of control. In spite of that, he'd kept his distance.

He *wouldn't* let a career woman make a fool of him again. He wouldn't let someone whose values didn't match his play a significant role in his life.

But Francesca Talbot was carrying his child. His son. That meant he had to watch over her. That meant they would be connected for a very long time—if *he* had anything to say about it.

From their first meeting, Grady had guessed Francesca was an independent woman. Having someone take care of her was a hard pill to swallow. He had to tread carefully now or he suspected she'd stubbornly walk the other way.

"We have to put the baby first, don't you think?" he asked.

She worried her lower lip, and he suddenly had the urge to take her into his arms and kiss it.

After studying him for a few long moments, she replied, "If I consider staying with you, I don't want you to hover."

Independent was right. "You have a cell phone. I have a cell phone. I can spend most of my time in the barn. But at least I can get to you within minutes if you need help. Speed dial is a great technological advance."

A small smile crossed her lips at his wry tone. "Do you cook?"

He shrugged. "*Cook* is a relative term, but I told you I come from a big family. My mother or sister drops off meals once or twice a week. I do know a saucepan from a frying pan, though. Most men these days do."

He saw remnants of emotion in her eyes. Memories of men who didn't?

He kept his voice gentle as he would with a spooked mustang. "I know this isn't something you want to do, Francesca. I get it. So why don't you just try it for a couple of days and see what happens? I promise not to wait on you hand and foot. But I'll be close by if you need something."

She sank down onto the hospital bed and he was by her side in an instant. "Are you okay?"

"I'm just tired." When she looked up at him with those big green eyes that packed so much punch, he almost wished he hadn't issued the invitation.

She said simply, "I don't depend on anyone, Grady. That's not me. I wanted to see this pregnancy to its finish on my own."

"I know you did. But this is *my* child, too."

"That's why I called you."

"I'm glad you did."

She stood again, but when she picked up the pharmacy bag on the bed and stuffed it into a larger one on the bedside table, he noticed her hand trembled. Still, as she moved the rest of her toiletries into the bag one-handed, he didn't offer to help.

She explained, "One of the nurses brought me supplies since I didn't know how long I'd be here when this first happened."

"We'll need to stop at your place and pack a suitcase," he suggested.

She raised her gaze to his, and he saw doubts once more.

Stepping toward her, he took her hand from the bag and held it. Her hand was cold. "This is going to be simple, Frannie." He had called her that once before and it had seemed so right. "You're going to stay in my guest bedroom, and I'll be a holler away. That's all there is to it."

"I don't trust easily."

He searched her eyes to find out why, giving her the opportunity to tell him. But she didn't.

"You can lock the door on your bedroom," he kidded. When a guarded look came over her, he added, "I have a great border collie who'll be your watchdog. Will that make you feel better?"

"You really have a dog?"

"His name is Shadow."

"Shadow?"

"I found him alongside the road. A car had hit him. After I took him to the vet and brought him home, he never left my side."

"Tessa didn't tell me about Shadow," she murmured.

"But she told you other things?" Grady arched a brow.

"Not much." Color came into her cheeks because her comment had told him she had asked.

He wasn't going to let this go. "Not much, such as…"

"She told me her dad bought saddles from your father, that you're close to your family and spend a lot of time with them."

"*I* told you that."

"I know, but it made me feel easier that she…confirmed it."

So it was true Francesca didn't trust easily. Not even herself. Why was that?

Did he *need* to know? Did he want to get personally involved with the mother of his baby? It was a ridiculous question, but they certainly could stay removed from each other just like divorced parents did. They were going to have to figure out how they wanted to play this. He had to figure out how *he* was going to play this.

The aide came into the room with the discharge paperwork and Grady was glad for the interruption.

He had a feeling he was going to be spending a lot of time in the barn.

Grady pulled into the driveway that led to a detached two-car garage beside the old Victorian where Francesca lived. He spotted a jewel-toned light shining in the foyer. "Is that on a timer?"

"It is. I set it up after Tessa and Emily moved out."

"How long have you known Tessa?"

"Since Family Tree opened. We consulted on a case and became friends." The Family Tree Health Center in

Lubbock—which offered the best health care in West Texas—housed many professional offices including Tessa's and Francesca's. But the two-story Victorian they'd shared was located in the small town of Sagebrush about fifteen minutes from Lubbock.

Suddenly Grady wished he knew a lot more about Francesca than he did. "How long did Emily live with you?"

"About nine months."

Vince had told him the three women were as tight as sisters. He knew about sisters. His tried to poke into his life when he let her.

Grady opened the door to his truck and came around to Francesca's side. After he opened her door, he extended his hand. She accepted his help until her feet were firmly planted on the ground.

"Are you going to live here by yourself?"

"I'm not sure."

They strolled up the walk, Grady slowing his pace to hers. The early December wind blew and he noticed she shivered.

"You need a heavier jacket," he said gruffly. The light wool jacket she wore wasn't insulated enough for the colder weather.

She turned toward him, her gaze locking to his. "I know that. But when I left this morning, I didn't realize a cold front was moving in."

In the sudden silence he realized he had to back off a little and corral his protective instincts. "Point taken."

After they reached the door, Francesca used her key to unlock it. They stepped inside and the Tiffany light illuminated the foyer.

Grady immediately focused on the steps. "I suppose your bedroom's upstairs?"

"I can handle a flight of stairs," she said absently, as if the thought of them fatigued her more. She might even still fear a miscarriage.

"I know you can. But Madison told you to rest. Tell me what you need and I'll go up and get it." He didn't want her getting dizzy again or feeling weak and falling.

She smiled. "It's not that simple. My suitcase is in the closet. I've got sweaters in one drawer, jeans in another—"

"You have your cell phone, don't you?"

"I do."

"Good. And I have mine. I'll program my number in. You sit on the sofa and call me. You can tell me exactly where everything is you want me to bring down. This doesn't have to be a big deal, Frannie."

She hesitated, then said, "I've never had a nickname."

They were standing close in the small foyer, the heat of the house chasing away the cold. Or was his proximity to Francesca chasing it away? This was the woman who'd set him on fire with a desire he hadn't experienced in years!

Studying her now, he saw she was still pale and the smudges under her eyes were becoming even bluer. She'd had a long, exhausting, traumatic day and he just wanted to get her back to his ranch.

He cleared his throat. "So how about the phone?"

Making up her mind, she slipped her phone from her coat pocket and handed it to him.

"I'll be done in ten minutes tops. Then you can sit in

my favorite recliner with Shadow at your side and I'll bring you whatever you want."

"I'm going to need lots of vegetables," she murmured.

"No problem. I've got a freezer full. They'll only take a few minutes to steam. How does that sound?"

"That sounds great."

He programmed his number into her phone, then handed it back to her. Taking his from his pocket, he jogged up the stairs and at the top called down, "Ring me."

She did. For the next few minutes, their system worked pretty well. Until…

"In the second drawer in the chest I have some—" Francesca hesitated "—some underwear. Just grab a few of the blue and pink ones."

He couldn't help but tease. "Should I ask what the other ones are?"

"They're my nonpregnancy underwear."

He laughed. "It's okay, Frannie. I promise I won't look at them. I'm just packing a few into the suitcase, stuffing them under a sweater." For the most part, he *didn't* look. He knew he had to gather everything quickly or she might change her mind.

Grady was on his way back downstairs when the front door opened and two women spilled in. Tessa Rossi he recognized right away. He supposed the other woman was Emily Madison. They both took one look at him and stopped short. Then they aimed their gazes at Francesca, who was sitting on the sofa in the living room.

Rushing toward her, they gave her hugs.

After a few moments, Tessa released her. Her friend's gaze assessed Grady and the suitcase he was carrying.

"When Francesca called to tell me she was being discharged, she said she's going to your ranch with you."

"Her doctor doesn't think she should be alone." Grady felt defensive, not exactly sure why.

Emily assured Francesca, "On the way here, Tessa and I talked about taking turns staying with you."

"You both have kids to take care of. I'm not going to steal you away from them. Grady insists I won't be any trouble, so I thought I'd try it at least overnight. We'll see how it goes."

Grady saw the way the women exchanged looks. He figured Tessa and Emily knew what had happened between him and Francesca, down to the failed birth control. That made him uncomfortable.

As if sensing that, Tessa left her friend, crossed over to Grady and extended her hand. "Do you remember me?"

"I remember exactly how your eyes lit up when you saw your first saddle."

She smiled. "Vince mentioned you're going to take one of the mustangs he brought back from the sale."

"I sure am. Vince may be able to bring one over this week. I'm looking forward to it."

"She's going to take time," Tessa reminded him. "These horses are used to being in the wild and are not at all happy at being penned up."

"I have a stall ready and the pen outside, too. It'll be okay, Tessa. I'll take good care of her."

Emily had wandered over and now Tessa introduced her. "Grady Fitzgerald, this is Emily Madison."

"You're Dr. Jared Madison's wife?"

Emily nodded and shook his hand, her black, very

curly hair bobbing around her face as she did so. "Yes, I am, though I'm still getting used to the name. We married about six weeks ago."

Grady turned his focus back on Tessa. "And you and Vince married in August?"

"Yes, we did."

Francesca levered herself up, using the arm on the chair. They all could see she looked exhausted.

Emily went to her and gave her another hug. "If there's anything you need, anything at all, you call."

When Emily was finished, Tessa moved toward Francesca and dropped her arm around her. "You know we both mean it."

Francesca nodded. "I know. Thanks for…being here."

Tessa dismissed the thanks with a wave. Her blond hair falling over her shoulder, she followed Emily to the foyer and out the door. They called, "Good night" as they left.

Minutes later, Grady heard a car back out of the driveway. "They really care about you."

"Yes, they do. They're my family now."

"You don't have any family in Sagebrush?"

"I don't have any family at all."

When she said it, he heard pain in her voice. Was that from losing them? Or some deeper reason?

"Come on. Let's get you to my place. After you have something to eat, you can try out my guest bed and sleep as long as you want." He knew she'd made arrangements while at the hospital with the other doctors in her practice to cover for her.

"I can't remember the last time I slept without setting the alarm."

"Tonight, you don't have to set an alarm. You can sleep as late as you want."

When she looked up at him, he saw gratitude in her eyes. And he almost…he almost kissed her. But he knew better than to tangle up their lives any more right now.

He knew better than to become involved with a woman who backed away from emotional intimacy. He'd been deceived and betrayed by a woman who didn't know the meaning of love. He wouldn't risk his heart again.

Chapter Two

Francesca rubbed her damp palms on her pant legs and worked to slow her pulse rate, telling herself to *calm down.*

Grady slanted a glance her way as he drove. "What's wrong?"

"I…I don't think I should have come."

"Are you going to chicken out on me?"

"I'm not chickening out!" Her tone was louder than she intended and she felt her shoulders square.

"That's better. That's the Francesca Talbot I met the first night. You're not any different than you were then. *I'm* not any different than I was then. We obviously got along, so let's just see if we can't get through at least one night."

At that, he pulled into the driveway of a stone and clapboard ranch house and parked. She hurriedly unfastened her seat belt, opened the door and slid out before he could try to help her. But it was a long way down. He was there as she landed unsteadily, his hands at her sides, holding her. "Are you okay?"

"I'm fine. It's just been a while since I maneuvered in and out of a truck."

"Or off of a horse?" he asked with teasing lights in his eyes. They sparkled silver under the floodlight that lit up the front of the house.

"I've never ridden a horse. I've only been around Vince's lately."

He let out a low whistle. "Well, after this baby's born, you're going to have to learn. Our son will be riding a horse by the time he's three."

"Three? Are you out of your mind?"

"With supervision, of course. But let's get you inside."

She wasn't sure if he was trying to rile her on purpose or tease her. The night they'd met, she'd liked his sense of humor. Why didn't she appreciate it now?

As Grady unlocked the door, a big black-and-white dog shot through the opening before Grady could open the door the whole way. The canine rounded Grady's legs three times, then sat down in front of him.

Grady leaned down to pet him. "Hi, boy. I brought someone to meet you. I'd like you to spend a little time with her so she feels at home here."

Shadow cocked his head at her. She'd like to be friendly with Grady's dog. She loved animals almost as much as children.

Slowly she extended her hand. Shadow came forward cautiously and sniffed her fingers.

She didn't make a move to pet him, waiting to see what he'd do next.

Shadow went through the same antics he had with Grady. "Can I pet you now?" she asked as he finally sat blinking up at her, feeling herself relax a little. She leaned down and gently touched his head. He rolled his head to the side as if he wanted more.

"I think he likes you," Grady decided with a chuckle, and pushed open the door the whole way. He switched on a few lights. "I'll go get your suitcase."

Francesca stood in the entryway, thinking the place didn't look at all like a bachelor pad. There were curtains at the windows in the living room—a burgundy-and-navy plaid—the same material as the sofa. There were two navy, corduroy recliners by the native stone fireplace, braided rugs in tan and navy and wood side cabinets and shelves that housed a collection of hand-painted horses. Framed photographs lined the length of his entertainment center.

When she glanced to her right into the kitchen, she spotted clean, off-white counters, maple cupboards and an oval table big enough to seat six.

"Don't look so surprised," he said with an amused expression as he came in with her suitcase. "What did you expect? A sink filled with dishes? Coffee rings on all the tables? Newspapers scattered about?"

"I didn't know what to expect. I don't know you, Grady, and I'm still not sure I should be here."

He looked at her curiously. "I never thought you'd be this jumpy about it. We slept together. How much more personal can that get? Spending the night here shouldn't be a big deal."

Grady might be perceptive sometimes, but he didn't know her. He didn't realize how hard it was for her to trust. That she still bore the effects of a past that she was trying to shake off and didn't know if she ever could. Her turmoil must have shown in her eyes.

Approaching her slowly, he rested his hand on her shoulder. She was supposed to feel comfort. But there was more...a zingy pull toward him that had affected her since the night they'd met. She backed away, unconsciously trying to create enough distance so she could think.

But he clearly took it for something else. "You've had a difficult day. More than difficult. I'm surprised you're still on your feet. Come on, let me show you to your bedroom. If you do want to leave tomorrow, we'll think of another plan."

We'll think of another plan.

She absolutely wasn't used to teaming up. Sure, Emily and Tessa were around for support. But she made up her own mind and made her own decisions. She'd done that since the night she'd had to defend her mother from her father—one very big decision that had changed all of their lives.

Reflexively, she touched her left ear. She'd lost some hearing in that ear because of that night. But only Emily, Tessa and Vince knew that. Somehow she manufactured a smile. "I promise I won't look for scattered newspapers or coffee rings along the way."

He didn't return her smile, just looked troubled. Maybe he was realizing having a stranger in his house wouldn't be easy. They really *were* strangers, no matter how intimate they'd been.

His gaze locked to hers, and she felt an elemental tug toward him. But he turned and headed down the hall. She followed him into the guest bedroom.

Grady settled the suitcase on the black metal-and-wood bed. "That door leads to your bathroom. You can reach it from the hall, too. I've got one in the master suite so you don't have to worry about being interrupted. And all of the doors *do* lock."

In some ways she felt foolish about her reluctance to stay, in others she just felt totally off-balance. She took off her jacket and laid it on the patchwork quilt next to the suitcase. "Thank you for offering me a place to stay tonight so that I'd have someone close by."

His penetrating blue eyes searched for the truth in hers. "I want you to get some rest. I want our baby to have the best chance at life."

He was only doing this because of his son. She'd better not weave anything else into it. "I've been talking to this baby ever since I learned I was pregnant. But now that I know he's a boy, our conversation might change a little."

Grady smiled. "You're going to discuss football with him?"

"I don't know. I'll have to think about it." She laughed.

A few feet separated them, yet at that moment, Francesca felt closer to Grady than she had all evening.

The doorbell rang.

Grady groaned. "I told her not to come over tonight."

"Who?" Francesca asked.

"My mother. I phoned her about the accident."

"You told her I'd be staying here?" Francesca couldn't keep her voice from rising.

"You're already pregnant. It's not as if anything else is going to happen," he offered wryly as he left the room and went to answer the door.

Francesca wasn't sure what to do—hide and unpack her suitcase or go and face Grady's mother. She was exhausted. But this woman would be her child's grandmother. Didn't she want her baby to have a loving family in his life?

Loving. Maybe Grady's mother wouldn't even like her. Maybe Grady's mother was going to disapprove of this whole situation.

Francesca couldn't help but go to the mirror over the dresser and take a peek at herself. She wished she hadn't. She looked as if she'd been in an accident. If only she could just drop into bed. And yet she couldn't. She had to check her sugar with the meter and supplies the pharmacy had sent up before she left the hospital and make sure she ate something—the *right* food.

Life had gotten way too complicated today, and she knew that wasn't going to change any time soon.

As Francesca walked down the hall to the kitchen, she smelled cooked food. She wasn't sure what kind, but her stomach grumbled.

An attractive woman who might have been in her sixties, with reddish-brown, chin-length hair laced with gray and rimless glasses turned her way.

"Aren't you going to introduce us, Grady?" mother asked son.

This was an awkward situation in so many ways, but Francesca shored up any energy she still possessed and walked right into it.

"Mom, this is Francesca Talbot. Francesca, this is my mother, Maureen Fitzgerald. When I told her I was going to bring you here, she decided to load up the refrigerator."

Maureen gave her son a jab in the ribs. "Don't be ridiculous. I know you can cook. But I also know you're busy. And having a guest—" She stopped. "Well, I just thought you both might like something homemade." She studied Francesca. "Did you have supper?"

"There was a tray in the hospital around five, but I wasn't very hungry."

"No, I guess not. Not after the day you've had. Grady told me you have a sugar problem, so I grilled lean ground beef patties and cooked brown rice. There's a tossed salad and broccoli with cheese that's still warm. We can zap it in the microwave if you need it hotter."

His mother searched his cabinet for serving dishes.

"Mom, please."

Maureen stared at him. "What?"

"I asked you to wait until tomorrow to come over, didn't I?"

"Yes, you did. But I thought you'd need supper tonight, and obviously you do."

Grady looked exasperated. "Francesca needs to get her feet up and turn in. She's not going to want to eat a heavy meal."

Shadow had come along with Francesca and now sat beside her at the table, glancing between Grady and his mother.

Francesca was afraid Grady had hurt his mother's feelings. "Actually, Grady, maybe I could just have half of one of those patties and a few stalks of broccoli. Everything smells delicious. I'll wait for a while after I eat before I turn in."

"You won't be able to keep your eyes open."

She gave him a look and Maureen saw it. His mother also seemed to notice the way Shadow stayed by Francesca's side.

Before Grady could protest further, Maureen took a dish from the cupboard and a serving spoon from the drawer. Then she cut and slid half of a patty and a serving of broccoli onto a dish. She set it on the table.

"Did *you* eat?" she asked her son.

"Yes, I did."

"Good." Maureen snagged a glass from the cupboard and a jug of milk from the refrigerator. Pouring it half-full, she handed it to Francesca. "So…Grady tells me you're a neonatologist."

"Thank you. Yes, I am. With this arm it's going to be hard to doctor for the next month. But I'll figure out a way."

"Maybe you could take some time off," Maureen suggested.

"I'm going to take a few days, but then I really need to work. There are several preemie babies and we're going to be short-staffed. One of the doctors in my practice is going out of town."

Although her mind was sluggish due to her fatigue, Francesca made a stab at continuing the conversation. "Grady told me he has an older brother, a younger brother and a younger sister. Do they all live in this area?"

"Yes, they do, and I'm so glad of that. It gives us all a chance to get together often. Liam lived in Amarillo for a while when he was married, but since his divorce he's back in Sagebrush. Do you have family here?" Maureen asked as Grady leaned against the counter and crossed his arms over his chest.

"No, I don't." Francesca didn't say more.

"Do they live somewhere else in the state?" Maureen pressed.

"No, actually I don't have family. My mother died a few years ago before I moved here. We lived in Oklahoma then."

"And your father?"

Suddenly Francesca wasn't hungry at all. She didn't travel this route often. "My parents were separated when I was a child."

"And you didn't continue to see your father?"

Francesca made it as simple as she could. "No. We moved away, my mother and I."

"But he was still—"

Grady cut in. "Mom, maybe we'd better cut this short."

Maureen examined the two of them, then agreed. "I guess we should. I was simply concerned this might be my only chance to talk to Francesca. You've told us about her, but this is the first glimpse I've had of her. She's carrying my grandchild."

Whatever Grady had told his mother had apparently caused her some consternation. "Mrs. Fitzgerald, if you'd like to talk to me, I can give you my number."

That seemed to surprise Maureen. "You'd do that?"

Francesca's eyebrows arched. What *exactly* had Grady told his mother about her? "Yes, I would."

Maureen seemed to relax a bit. "Well, that would

be nice. Maybe you could join our family for dinner some Sunday."

"Mom," Grady warned, as if they'd had a conversation about this, but she wasn't sticking to the script.

How comfortable or uncomfortable would dinner with the Fitzgerald family be? Francesca felt as if she'd just landed on a foreign planet and was treading her way very carefully. "I'll certainly think about that."

His mother didn't look satisfied, but she didn't look altogether put off, either. She nodded to Francesca. "You go ahead and eat. I'll leave. I would appreciate having your number."

With a grunt Grady said, "I'll give it to her." He scribbled something on a piece of paper and handed it to his mom.

Francesca took a bite of the broccoli and said to Maureen, "This is very good. Thank you for bringing it over tonight."

Grady's mother smiled at her. "You're welcome."

After Grady walked his mother to the door, they stepped outside together and had a few moments of conversation. Francesca couldn't overhear. It was probably just as well.

When Grady came back in, he shook his head. "I'm sorry about all that. She's a strong-willed woman. And my sister is just like her."

Francesca laughed and it felt so good to do it. "She meant well." Francesca took another bite of the broccoli, then asked, "What did you tell her about us? About how this happened?"

Grady ran his fingers through his hair. "I didn't say

much. I just told my family that you were pregnant and that we were giving each other some space until the baby was born."

"They thought we were involved?"

"I was vague."

If she had family who cared about her, would she have told them that she'd had a one-night stand? She didn't know why she was even wondering. Having family had only ever hurt her.

"Does your family interfere in your life often?"

Shadow bumped her leg, as if he wanted to share her supper, or the remains of it. But she didn't know if she should feed him.

The question she'd just asked Grady apparently caused him some annoyance because he was scowling at her. "What's that supposed to mean?"

"You said you asked your mother not to come tonight, but she came anyway. Don't you consider that interference?"

"Would you have considered it interference if your mother had stopped by?"

She wasn't touching that question with the proverbial ten-foot pole. "I thought only lawyers answered questions with questions."

Digging his thumbs into his hip pockets, he paused for a moment, then responded, "My mother likes to look after her family. It's as simple as that. She does what she thinks best. I don't always agree with her and I tell her that."

After Francesca finished her milk, she set down her glass. "It *was* very kind of her to bring over dinner."

That seemed to take the wind out of Grady's annoyed sails. He glanced at her empty plate. "I think you really *did* like it."

She motioned to the food on the counter. "Do you want help stowing that away?"

"No, I'll take care of it. You put your feet up. That's what you're supposed to do."

"I'm going to take a shower first. Do you have something I can wrap around my cast?"

After rummaging in a bottom cupboard, he pulled something out of a box. "Here's a plastic bag. Do you need help taping it on?"

She shook her head. "I'll be fine. I have to take off my clothes first."

That brought a look into his blue eyes that she'd seen the night they'd had sex. It was an intense look that told her maybe he was imagining that night all over again.

Before that movie could play in *her* head, she had to make her getaway. She said, "I'll see you in the morning."

Without waiting for a good-night, she hurried down the hall. She didn't know why she was so skittish around him. Sure, he'd seen her naked. Sure, they'd talked a few hours, sexual tension bumping back and forth between them. The problem was, she still got butterflies when she looked into his eyes. And that would never do. She didn't want a relationship with Grady. She didn't want a relationship with anyone...except her baby. And Tessa and Emily, she added as an afterthought.

Francesca decided to wait to test her blood sugar until after she was out of the shower. But she was suddenly more tired than she'd been before. Maybe it was the warm food in her stomach. Maybe the day had finally just taken her to the end of her rope. The cast on her arm made everything more difficult, especially dressing and undressing. It took her much longer than she planned, and when she was finished she almost felt like crying. That was ridiculous. She didn't cry.

Hormones?

Sure.

Attaching the plastic bag around her cast wasn't easy, either. Stepping into the shower, using one hand to turn on the water, bathe and soap her hair took more energy and ingenuity than she thought she had. Finally, when she was finished, she stepped out of the bathtub, toweled off and realized she hadn't packed a nightgown. She hadn't really packed. Grady had. She'd simply forgotten about the nightwear.

Wrapping a towel around herself, she tucked it in the best she could, then searched through her suitcase to find something to wear to bed. Panties and a bra she couldn't hook? A sweater?

Finally she sank down onto the bed and dropped her head into her hand, her wet hair falling along her cheeks.

She heard scratching at her door. A knock followed.

She groaned. She was not up to more conversation.

"Francesca, Shadow wants to come in to say goodnight. Do you mind?"

"I'm not dressed," she called.

"He won't mind."

She actually almost laughed. "Will you be coming in with him?"

"Only if you want me to."

"Let Shadow in. Maybe he can help me find something to wear to bed. I forgot to list a nightgown in the items you were picking up."

There was silence. Then the door opened and the border collie barged in. He didn't even hesitate, but jumped up on the bed and licked her face. She put her arm around him and felt real tears burn in her eyes.

Seconds later she felt a male presence. Lifting her head, she saw Grady towering over her. "Am I going to have privacy staying here with you?" Her voice trembled a bit and she hated that.

"You'll have your privacy. But right now I think you need this more." He handed her a white, button-down silk shirt.

"This looks like a good dress shirt."

"I don't have any weddings or funerals in the near future, so wear it. Do you want Shadow in or out?"

"In is fine." She didn't want to admit to Grady that his dog seemed to understand her. How odd was that?

"Do you need help getting that bag off your arm?"

She had taped it the best she could, probably with more tape than was necessary. Pulling it all off could take a while.

Although she hadn't answered him, he sat down on the bed beside her and started ripping tape from the plastic. It took him no time at all. "I had my arm in a cast once. It's no picnic, especially when it still hurts."

"When I get settled and stop moving around it will be okay."

His fingers edged the top of the cast first. Then he

slid them down and touched her fingertips sticking out from the bottom of the cast. "You're cold," he said.

"I just got out of the shower."

"Did you say you had to test your blood sugar?"

"Yes."

"Do you want me to be here when you do?"

She looked over at him. "You want to be part of that, too?"

"Your health is important to the life of our baby. I should know what's going on."

She sighed. "Give me five minutes to get into your shirt."

Grady returned five minutes later. She'd dropped her towel, donned his shirt and finally managed to roll the cuff above her cast. At least she was buttoned from neck to thigh. The material of the shirt wasn't much different from a nightgown, and it molded to her when she stood.

After reading the meter instructions, she'd laid out everything she needed on the bed and prepared the lancet.

Grady pulled the rocker up to her so he could see what she was doing.

They were knee to knee, tantalizingly close.

She moved her leg away so it didn't brush his. She was much too aware that he'd probably shaved before he'd picked her up. His jawline was clean. She was also aware that he'd slapped on cologne, an outdoor scent that reminded her of trees and woods and places she'd never been.

Grady watched intently as she inserted the test strip into the machine, used an alcohol wipe and pricked her finger to collect a drop of blood.

She studied the readout. "High-normal. But it hasn't been two hours since I ate, so that makes sense."

Changing his position on the bed, Shadow crossed one paw over the other and settled his head on his paws. When she stood and crossed the room to set the meter on the dresser, she looked in the mirror and saw Grady watching her.

"What?" she asked, knowing the bulge of her tummy was evident under the soft shirt.

"You look better in that shirt than *I* ever did."

"Are you trying to flatter me?"

Now he didn't keep his distance. He walked right up to her and stood very close. "You're a beautiful woman, Francesca. I don't know many men who could see you like that and not want to look."

"You looked before," she murmured, knowing her cheeks were flaming.

"That was different."

"Different, how?"

"You weren't carrying my child then. Now it makes a difference." He lifted a wet strand of hair away from her face. "You didn't have wet hair then, either."

"I don't have the energy to dry it."

"Let me do it for you."

"Oh, Grady..." she whispered.

"I brought you here to help you. What good is help if you won't accept it?"

Emily and Tessa told her all the time that she didn't know how to accept help, that she took on too much all by herself and felt she had to do it all. She was so sleepy right now, she wouldn't mind falling asleep with wet hair.

But Grady was insistent. "Do you have a brush?"

She gestured toward the bag on her bed, knowing the one the nurse had bought for her at the pharmacy was somewhere inside.

After Grady moved the cane-backed rocker over to an outlet, he motioned for her to sit in the chair and plugged in the hair dryer that he'd brought from the bathroom. She hadn't remembered *that,* either.

"Grady, you really don't have to—"

He switched on the hair dryer, ignoring her protest. She expected just a quick ruffle and brush through and they'd soon be finished. Damp hair didn't matter to her. But that wasn't the way Grady did it. He was careful, oh so careful. In fact, he wasn't simply careful. Each brush-stroke felt seductive. He took his time, brushing her hair away from her face, making sure the air didn't hit her eyes or her mouth or her nose. With each stroke she sank deeper into relaxation. With each stroke, she remembered the touch of his callused fingers on her skin—

When he switched off the dryer, she looked up at him. "I don't think I can move a muscle."

"You don't have far to go, though I think Shadow's going to take up half your bed. Are you sure you want him here?"

"I'd like him to stay." It was on the tip of her tongue to say, "I'd like *you* to stay." That was absolutely insane. She was only here because she needed a little bit of help.

The idea of a bond or an involvement or a relationship with Grady Fitzgerald terrified her. When she was small she had often hidden in a closet to be safe from her father. The day she'd found courage to protect her mother from him, he'd hit her, drawn blood and caused her hearing loss. For the most part she'd worked through her childhood over the years. Two years ago, when she'd decided her fear of relationships was foolhardy, she'd chosen the wrong man.

No, she wasn't ready to take even a few slow steps into a relationship. Her focus now was her baby. Nothing else.

Rousing herself from the fatigue and exhaustion that had finally caught up with her, she stood and moved to the bed—away from Grady's hands…away from his strength…away from anything that would tempt her heart.

Shadow gazed up at her when she slipped under the covers.

Grady laid the hair dryer on the dresser. "If you need anything, I'm across the hall."

She nodded. But she knew she wouldn't. Not from him.

Grady exited the room and closed the door behind him. She turned on her side, placing her hand on Shadow's warm coat, totally aware of Grady's shirt against her skin.

Chapter Three

When Francesca awoke the following morning, she was disoriented for a few seconds. Then she realized where she was—at Grady's ranch.

She patted Shadow on the head and he barked. Shortly after, there was a rap on the door. "Francesca—are you up?"

Hearing his master's voice, Shadow jumped off the bed. Making sure she was covered by the sheet, as well as buttoned to the neck in Grady's shirt, she called, "Not quite. But you can come in."

Grady opened the door and stepped inside. He was wearing a many-times-washed T-shirt today, jeans and the ever-present boots. She didn't think any man had ever looked sexier. Quickly she pushed that thought away as Shadow trotted into the hall.

"Do you need anything?" he asked. "Tessa's dad and Vince are bringing the mustang over, so I'll be heading to the barn as soon as I grab a cup of coffee."

"I'm going to scramble myself an egg," she said, knowing she must look a mess. "I could make more than one if you're interested."

His blue eyes were more than interested as they locked with hers and she felt a little tremor ripple through her. How could she be attracted to him when her life was a mess right now?

"I'll scramble the eggs," he offered, "as soon as I let Shadow out. You're supposed to be resting. Remember? That's why you're here."

Granted, that was the reason for her being here, but she couldn't let him do too much for her. She couldn't become dependent on him. She'd taken care of herself all of her life, and she wasn't going to stop now.

Instead of keeping a bit of distance between them, he ambled into the room and loomed over her.

Her chin came up and she straightened her shoulders.

A puzzled expression crossed his face as he lowered himself to the bed, right beside her hip. "You haven't told me yet why I spook you."

"You don't," she protested quickly, as if that would answer his question.

He shook his head. "You've changed since the night we met."

Sure she had. That night, he'd been an attractive man she'd met in the crowd. That night, she hadn't been pregnant with his child. That night, she hadn't been scared to death of feelings for him that had taken root a little deeper each time they'd talked. That night, for once in her life, she'd simply let go.

Look where that had gotten her!

"You've changed, too," she answered, knowing she had to go on the offensive. "You weren't protective and hovering. You weren't trying to tell me what was best for my baby."

"Do you think that's what I'm doing now?" he asked without getting angry, and that surprised her.

"I don't know, Grady."

"If you were staying with Tessa, would you mind if she made you breakfast?"

She thought about that and easily knew the answer. "No, I suppose not."

"At least you're honest." His tone was wry.

"I try to be."

He nodded to her arm. "How does it feel?"

"It aches a little, but nothing I can't handle."

He rose to his feet. "There isn't much you can't handle, is there?"

"Do you want me to answer that, or was it a rhetorical question?"

"It was rhetorical. I'll make those eggs and then get out of your hair for a while. Maybe you'll relax if I'm in the barn."

As Francesca watched him leave, she breathed a sigh of relief. Maybe she *could* relax if he was in the barn. But she doubted it. Because she was still carrying his child.

Francesca saw the horse trailer roll in. She heard men's voices and recognized Vince's and Walter McGuire's.

She'd only met Tessa's dad a few times, but she knew his history with Vince. When Vince fell in love with Tessa in high school, Mr. McGuire had disapproved. After Tessa had gotten pregnant and decided to marry Vince, her father had disowned her. Later in her pregnancy, she'd lost her baby and almost died. She and Vince had gone their separate ways until this past spring when he'd returned to town with his best friend's baby and they'd fallen in love all over again. He and Tessa were married now, and as happy as could be, raising Vince's little boy as well as adopting a little girl. Besides that, Vince and Tessa's dad seemed to have found some common ground and were putting the past aside.

It was hard for Francesca to remain still and rest as her doctor had suggested. But she'd do anything for this baby. So she sat on the sofa, making notes for anyone who covered for her at the hospital this week.

When the door opened, she expected to see Grady. Instead, her gaze landed on Tessa's husband.

Vince grinned at her as he came in the door. "Hey there, I told Tessa I'd stop in and see how you were doing. I think she and Emily are planning to come over tomorrow."

She could use her best friends' company, but was glad to see Vince, too. Since she'd gotten to know him over the summer, he was almost like a big brother.

"I'm glad you stopped in. I'm supposed to rest and…" She grimaced. "I'm not used to doing that."

Vince sat on a chair across from the sofa and petted Shadow. "Hi there, boy. Are you keeping Francesca company?"

The dog cocked his head, gave a little bark in answer and then settled his head on his paws again.

"I can imagine resting for the sake of resting is a headache," Vince said.

"So you brought over a mustang?"

"Yep. Grady wanted one. It's quite an adjustment for those horses, captured from the wild, being hauled off to auction. But they make wonderful companion horses once they're gentled. They're good workers, too."

"How many horses does Grady have?"

"You haven't been to the barn?"

"I've never been here before, Vince."

His face darkened a little. "I'm sorry. Tessa keeps her friends' lives private. I thought maybe you'd spent some time here."

"No. After I found out I was pregnant, I thought it was better if Grady and I kept our distance. It would help us both to figure things out."

Vince's brows arched. "When two people share a child, they've got to tell each other what's going on in their heads."

"You know why I might be reluctant to do that."

Tessa had known Francesca's background soon after they'd moved in together. But one night this summer, when Francesca had visited the couple, she'd felt comfortable enough with Vince to fill him in.

His eyes were gentle as he said, "I know you've had a rough time with men. My father was an alcoholic—thank God, not a violent one—so I understand a little bit of what you went through. And that doctor you got involved with, I know he was more of the same."

"Darren isn't an alcoholic."

"No, but abuse is abuse."

Francesca remembered her relationship with Darren all too well. She remembered the day she'd left him—for all the right reasons.

"I don't know what happened the night I met Grady. I don't know why—" she waved at her tummy "—this happened. It was so out of character for me."

"Maybe you were just tired of guarding yourself so well. Maybe you sensed Grady was a different kind of man."

"Is he?" She sought her answer in Vince's eyes.

"When I worked at his dad's saddle shop, he was around now and then during school breaks. I've got to admit, I was jealous of his relationship with his dad. They worked together like a father and son *should.* They talked. They joked. They seemed to enjoy each other's company. Grady was older than I was, but he never ordered me around. He taught me what needed to be done and he was patient."

She thought about what Vince had said. "He and I are very different, Vince. Not only our backgrounds, but who we are. You know how much time I spend at the hospital. You know those babies mean everything to me."

"But now *your* baby is going to mean the world to you."

"Yes, he is. I'll figure out a way to work and take care of him. I don't know if I want to share those responsibilities. I already love him more than I've ever loved anyone, so when I think about handing over my baby to someone else, even for a couple of hours—

What if Grady demands joint custody? What if he wants equal time?"

"Whoa! You're getting ahead of yourself. Do you want some advice?"

Vince was a good guy and he wouldn't steer her wrong. "Sure."

"Watch what Grady does, rather than thinking about what he doesn't say."

Advice was one thing, a riddle was another. "Am I supposed to know what that means?"

"I think you'll figure it out. The important thing is you can understand the measure of a man by his actions. Watch Grady—with you, with the horses, with Shadow here, with Tessa and Emily if they come to visit. Watch him until this baby is born, and then decide whether or not he's going to make a good father."

"That makes sense."

"Good." He reached out and patted Shadow's head again. "I'll tell Tessa you're already on the mend." He rose to his feet.

"Thanks, Vince."

He reached down and squeezed her shoulder. "No thanks necessary. We're friends. Friends look out for each other."

Grady entered his house, not knowing where he'd find Francesca. She was supposed to be resting, but she had a mind of her own. He had to wonder just how much she wanted this baby. After all, an unexpected pregnancy could mess up a career woman's life. His resentment of Susan's actions still caused a bitter taste in his mouth.

He was surprised to find Francesca asleep on the sofa, curled on her side, Shadow on the floor close at hand. When he saw his master, he came running over to him.

Grady hunched down, scratched the dog behind the ears and said softly, "So you've been watching over her? Does she give *you* a hard time, too?"

Grady had checked his cell phone about every fifteen minutes to see if he'd missed her call, if she'd left a message because she needed something. But she hadn't. He noticed the list on the coffee table, the medical terms in her pretty handwriting.

Her long, dark hair glimmered with red highlights in the afternoon sun streaming through the window. She was so beautiful. He almost felt as if he were awakening a princess.

He crouched down beside her. "Frannie."

Her eyes opened and she stared up at him in bemusement for a moment. Then reality hit. She hiked herself up and rubbed her face with her hand. "Grady. I must have dozed off. What time is it?"

"Almost one. Did you have lunch?"

"No. I was thinking about getting up and decided to close my eyes for just a little while. I guess I fell asleep. Did Vince leave?"

"A long time ago. I've been doing chores in the barn, getting the new horse settled."

He was making conversation when all he wanted to do was sit down on that sofa and take her into his arms. There was no defiance in her eyes now, or rebelliousness. This was the woman he'd seen the night he met her. This was the woman who had captivated him so. He wondered how long it would be until she brought back the emotional armor.

"What would you like for lunch?" he asked. "We have leftovers from last night. I also stopped at a deli before I picked you up, so I have sandwich fixings, too."

"Leftovers sound good."

Before she became that guarded woman again, he had a question that had been nudging him. Now was as good a time to ask her as any. "What does the baby feel like when he moves?"

Francesca's green gaze locked to his. In that moment a spark of understanding flashed in her eyes—that he had a role in her pregnancy…that he was asking out of more than idle curiosity. He had no idea what she'd say or do.

Unexpectedly, she answered his question with one of her own. "Do you want to feel him when he moves?"

Before he could think better of it, he answered, "Yes."

She closed her eyes for a moment, and then laid her hand on the right side of her tummy atop her sweatshirt. "You can feel him move here."

He told himself he just wanted to feel the baby. There wouldn't be anything intimate about his touch.

But when he laid his hand where hers had been, when he could feel the heat under the material and then the flutter of movement, he knew touching her this way was *very* intimate.

"What was it like the first time *you* felt him move?"

"I was brushing my teeth," she responded with a smile that aroused him even more than touching her had. She went on, "And I felt this little wave, a little rustle, and I realized my baby was moving!"

He didn't correct her by insisting this was his baby, too, because he suddenly realized every woman carrying a child must feel that total union. No man could ever fully understand pregnancy…carrying a life…bringing a miracle into this world.

He didn't move his hand away. He couldn't. He wanted to feel his child's life again. "Have you given any thought to names?"

"I have. A doctor I worked with in Oklahoma—he was my attending and mentored me—was a member of the National Guard, and he was called up and deployed to the Middle East. He was killed there. His name was Joshua. I like the name. But…" she hesitated. "I imagine you have some suggestions, too."

Before her accident, had she decided to share the naming process with him? Could they compromise? He was sensing that they were both strong-willed. What did that mean for the chance of them parenting successfully together?

One step at a time, he told himself. "I like the name Michael. It was my grandfather's."

He knew he had to stand, move away from her, make them some lunch. But his hand stayed on her stomach. He felt their baby move again. They seemed to lean a little closer to each other.

Then she leaned back and took a breath.

He took the signal for what it was—her defense mechanisms shifting into place. His had better do the same.

Withdrawing his hand, he stood. "I'm going to wash up, and then I'll get us that lunch."

She lowered her gaze to Shadow, slid her fingers into

the ruff of fur at his neck. "I'm going to call the hospital. I need to check on one of my patients."

"Fine," he replied, and walked away.

He had to walk away for now…until their baby was born. Then he'd be in Francesca's life, whether she wanted him there or not.

Francesca took the last sip of her milk and set down the glass. Conversation had lagged over lunch and she wasn't sure how to pick it up. "How many horses do you have?"

"We're not on a date, Frannie. You don't have to make conversation if you don't feel like it. I'll go back to the barn and you'll have your privacy again."

"No! I mean, this is your house. You should feel comfortable in it. And I'm not just making conversation. I want to know."

He gave her an I-don't-really-believe-that look, but answered her. "I have four horses now—with the mustang."

"What kind are the others?"

His gaze narrowed a bit. "I have a quarter horse, one part Arabian and one part Tennessee walker."

"Have you had them long?"

"There's not a simple answer to that one. Dad always had horses. When I took over the ranch and the business, I kept them."

She absorbed that, not knowing if she should ask any more personal questions.

"What?" he asked.

"You grew up here?"

"Sure did. And I couldn't let mom and dad sell the

ranch when they moved to the retirement community in Lubbock."

"Do they like it there?"

"They do. Mom babysits a lot for my sister, Laurie, and my older brother, John. They've also made friends there who they can socialize with. Dad's on the hospital board and still comes to the shop a few days a week."

"Your mom mentioned a younger brother—Liam?"

"Yes. He moved back to Sagebrush about six months ago. He lives in town."

She remembered the names from the stories he'd related that first night. He'd also told her he spent every Sunday with his family. She could hardly imagine what it was like to sit down with a family, have a peaceful dinner with everybody actually wanting to be together. She and her parents had lived in a vacuum in California. Her father had had his drinking buddies, true, but he had isolated her mother. Her mother had been scared to death to even go to the store without asking her dad first. And after she and her mother had fled to Oklahoma, they'd kept to themselves.

"You mentioned you lost your mom," he prompted.

He was leaving the subject open for her if she wanted to talk about it. She didn't, but she couldn't go completely quiet on the subject or he'd ask more questions later. "My mother died four years ago."

"And that was in Oklahoma."

"Yes."

"So what brought you to Sagebrush?"

This conversation had started because she'd asked

him about his horses. She wished she could go back to that subject.

But since Sagebrush was small, residents could have long memories. She might as well tell him something about Darren. "I met a doctor at a medical conference. We had a long-distance relationship for a while. He was from Lubbock and he asked me to move here."

"So you did."

"Yes, I did. But it didn't work out. I moved in with Tessa, and the rest, as they say, is history. We shared the house together for a year before Emily moved in with us."

"And now you're there alone."

She didn't respond.

Pushing his plate away, he asked casually, "Have you decided what you're going to do about working after the baby's born?"

She became wary. "Not yet."

He leaned forward and placed his hand over hers. She was at once electrified and scared by the feeling. But she didn't pull away…no man's touch had ever made her feel the way Grady's did.

His eyes seemed to become a deeper blue as he assured her, "You don't have to make all the decisions yourself."

"I've made decisions for myself for as long as I can remember."

He leaned back and his jaw set. "I told you before I want to be involved in my son's life."

"I understand that. But all this is very new to me and I'm taking each step carefully. Right now, all I'm concerned about is my baby's health. Surely, you can see that."

The look in his eyes gentled a bit. "I can see it. That's one reason why I think you should stay here through the weekend to make sure your sugar is stable, your arm is healing and you don't overdo it when you shouldn't."

If she stayed, she might find out who Grady really was…what kind of father he might be. She had to know if custody became an issue. "If I'm not in the way, if I don't interfere in your life too much, I'll stay until Sunday."

Somehow she had to figure out how to let Grady help her while maintaining her independence. If *that* wasn't a dilemma!

All she knew right now was that Monday she'd be returning to work.

After all, her career was her baby's future, too.

Dressed in Grady's shirt that night, cold with the early December wind blowing against the house, Francesca went into the bathroom and retrieved her meter from on top of the sink. She wasn't sure whether to hate the little device or be grateful for it. Every time she used it she thought about everything that could go wrong. On the other hand, using it protected her baby's health, as well as her own. After washing her hands, she inserted the test strip into the device, pricked her finger and let the drop of blood flow onto the strip.

"Does that hurt?"

Francesca smelled leather, damp flannel and man. Mixed with all of it was Grady's unique scent. She remembered nuzzling his shoulder—

"I use a different finger each time. It's not bad." The silky shirt had molded to her as she'd prepared materials and used the machine. Now Grady was staring at her tummy under the fabric. His gaze on her was like a caress.

She tried to keep her tone light. "I'm going to have weight to lose after the baby's born."

"Not much. You haven't gained weight anywhere but at your stomach."

Where he'd laid his hand this afternoon. Yes, he could tell where her weight was and wasn't.

She checked the meter readout.

"Good or bad?"

"It's good. Your mom's cooking must be just what I need."

"If I tell her that she'll be here every day, so I'd better do some cooking and see how we do."

Francesca started putting everything away, but he stilled her hand. "I know you're determined to go home Sunday. But will you be able to take good care of yourself? How can you cook with one hand?"

"You'd be surprised what I can do with one hand," she teased.

They both must be remembering the same pictures because she could feel her cheeks heat up and she thought he looked a little flushed, too.

"I promise you, Grady, I'll continue to check my sugar levels. I *will* take care of myself. This baby means everything to me."

"You aren't thinking of asking for sole custody, are you?" He released her and held up his hand. "Before you answer that, you should think about the benefits of having me share care of our baby, and of having an extended family who will love this child, too."

The idea of an extended family panicked her. Would they be judging her? Would they be waiting for her to mess up so Grady could have more control?

"Hey, what did I say?" he asked, looking at her curiously.

"Nothing."

The bathroom was small. Grady was close.

"We have to be honest with each other, Frannie, or we'll never have a good chance to be parents together."

"I can't tell you all my thoughts."

"Just the important ones," he prompted.

What to say and what not to say? "You and I see family very differently. Besides, I have the feeling that yours could all gang up on me to persuade me to see their way—your way."

"I wouldn't let them do that."

She searched his eyes, looking for the truth, hunting for what she'd never found before. The moment was fraught with memories of that night on his couch, the hunger in his kiss, the sensual magic of his touch. She couldn't be seduced by chemistry, or a roughly handsome face or gentle hands that could easily turn not quite so gentle.

He leaned in closer and she would have backed away, but his words were as seductive as everything else about him. "I won't hurt you, Frannie. I won't hurt our baby. And I certainly don't want to get hurt myself. We don't have to jump into anything. We can just take it as it comes."

With that, his lips settled on hers, gently nibbled, then claimed a real kiss. Soon her good hand was on his shoulder, her other at her side. But he wouldn't let her be awkward about it. He slipped his fingers around her waist, pressed her growing child against him and tasted Francesca thoroughly and well.

Francesca felt dizzy. The kind of dizzy that could make her lose her good sense…and her perspective…and her heart. She knew she should run in the other direction. But Grady's hands held her, gently but firmly. His kisses promised passion that she already knew was red-hot. But that one night had been an aberration. She didn't talk to strange men for an evening and then have sex with them. Maybe what she'd been trying to prove to herself that night was that she was still a woman in every sense of the word…that a man other than Darren could desire her.

She hadn't counted on that night affecting her so. She hadn't counted on ever seeing Grady again. But now here she was, pregnant with his child, staying at his ranch. His attitude could turn in a minute and his concern for her could change to a need to control. She had to watch for it. She had to make sure she wasn't sinking into a situation like that again. Not with her baby involved.

For one thing was true. She would never stay with a man like her father. That's why she'd broken off her relationship with Darren. That's why she had to watch Grady carefully.

This was always the awkward part, ending desire too soon.

Even before she'd pulled away, Grady had let go. He didn't turn away to catch his breath. He didn't look down on her as if she were the one with something lacking. Rather, he said, "You really don't want to be here, do you?"

"No," she admitted.

"And you really didn't want me to kiss you."

"That one's not so easy."

He looked surprised her answer wasn't definitive. She was surprised, too.

"Then I didn't read the signals wrong."

"You read confused signals," she responded with a sigh, turning away from him and the sink, thinking about running, yet knowing she had to stay and explain. "I'm attracted to you, Grady. That's obvious." She turned from him.

But he was quick and caught her before she entered her room. "You can run for a while, but eventually you're going to have to tell me what's going on in your head."

"No, I don't have to tell you. That's the point. We have separate lives. We're going to *live* separate lives. The baby might bring us together every now and then, but we probably won't know each other any better then than we do now."

"You're wrong about that." There was an edge to his tone. "I intend to learn everything I possibly can about you. By understanding you, I'll understand our child."

She was startled by his insight and she didn't like it. Yet she knew he was right. "Don't try to close me in, Grady. I'll just work that much harder to break away."

"Is that a threat?"

"No. That's just the way I am."

Shadow had padded into the bathroom when he heard them talking. Now he looked from one of them to the other. When Francesca went into her room, he followed her inside.

She crouched down on the floor with Shadow and wrapped her arms around his neck.

When Grady finally turned and left, she felt like crying.

Shadow licked her chin and she held on to him tightly. When she left, she was going to miss him.

Chapter Four

All night Francesca had tossed and turned, thinking about Grady's kiss. If she was honest with herself, she hadn't just been thinking about it—she'd been reliving it.

The smell of coffee and toast, the sizzle of eggs in a frying pan wafted into her room as she opened the door after her morning routine. She was going to feel awkward with Grady, no doubt about that. Then she thought about the fact that she wasn't wearing a bra because she couldn't hook it. Thank goodness she'd had Grady gather sweatshirts. There were so many things she still couldn't do for herself. But there were so many things she *could* do, too. She could manage.

Shadow had slept with her again last night, and early this morning Grady had opened her door to let him out. She'd pretended to be asleep.

When she'd shared an apartment with Darren, living together hadn't been like this. At the end of their relationship, any time they'd spent together had been fraught with tension. But it was a different kind of tension than she felt with Grady…because *here* she almost felt at home.

That feeling practically panicked her. From experience she knew sharing a home with a man eventually hurt. Sharing a home with a man always came to an end.

When she stepped into the kitchen, Shadow woke up from his nap in front of the fireplace and came to meet her. After she bent to pet him, she straightened. Her gaze collided with Grady's and neither of them seemed to be able to turn away. Then the eggs in the cast-iron frying pan began smoking.

"I hope you like your eggs well-done," she joked.

He grimaced. "I like them over easy, but not black on top. Are you interested in one?" he asked with a wiggle of his brows.

"Do you know how to make poached?" she teased.

He scowled. "I understand eating healthy, but you're eating for two."

Yes, she was. "That's why I'm going to have yogurt, granola and fruit."

"And maybe a scrambled egg?" he suggested.

He was trying so hard. She had to admit she liked that. She liked *him.* She hadn't had many people in her life who had pampered her. Not until Tessa and Emily had come along. And now Grady.

"What are you thinking?" he asked, his voice going gentle.

"I'm thinking that you're being good to me."

"Why wouldn't I be?"

She was saved from answering by the chime of the doorbell. The caller didn't wait for Grady to come to the door to answer it. It opened and a beautiful young woman, possibly in her late twenties, pushed it open wider with her knee, her arms full.

"Hi," she called brightly, making her way into the kitchen as if she knew the house well. She looked at Francesca and then smiled even brighter. "I'm Laurie, Grady's sister. I brought some things I thought you might like—my own trail mix that's all natural and a cranberry-apple fruit salad." She looked shyly at Francesca. "I also brought photo albums. There are some good shots of Grady."

Grady's sister really was a beauty, her wavy black hair tied back in a ponytail, her crystalline-blue eyes lighter than her brother's. She was wearing a yellow down jacket, and white acrylic fur framed her face.

"Did Mom send you?" Grady asked, sotto voce.

"Of course not. I wanted to meet Francesca myself." After she laid everything on the counter, Grady's sister came over to Francesca and extended her hand. "It's good to meet you," she said, sounding as if she meant it. "Grady hasn't told us very much, so we have to see for ourselves. I don't want to make you feel awkward or anything, but the whole family is interested in you and your baby. We want to help however we can. That's what we're here for."

Francesca absolutely didn't know what to say. This was a stranger offering her help.

"I think you've shocked her," Grady suggested, half joking, half serious. He set the platters of food on the table and motioned for them all to sit.

"Is there enough for a third?" Laurie asked.

"Sure is. I always make more, hoping Francesca will eat it."

"Is the baby very active?" Laurie asked, sitting at the table.

Francesca took the chair across the corner from her. Shadow settled at her feet as she answered Laurie's question. "He seems to be getting more active every day. Maybe it's because I'm a neonatologist, but all the charts I've always used, the sonograms I've seen, all the explanations I give to parents mean so much more to me now. At this stage he's already a little person."

"I have two little boys, three and six," Laurie explained. "I still take out their sonogram pictures and look at them. I like to compare what they were then and who they are now. That's why I keep so many pictures around, I guess. Mark, my husband, can't quite understand it. He thinks the albums are good enough. But I want to memorize both of them at every single stage and never forget. Do you know what I mean?"

"I know exactly what you mean," Francesca assured her softly. "In theory, anyway. You want to keep the happy times in a special pocket and pull them out whenever you need them. And the photographs aren't just for you, I'm sure. They're for your kids, too. They need those pockets full of fun pictures. Every child deserves to have too many happy moments to count."

Grady was studying her curiously and she was afraid she'd said too much. "Grady told me you live in Sagebrush in one of the new sections over on the east side."

"We're in a town house for now. Maybe in a few years we'll be able to buy a house."

"I told you if you need a down payment—" Grady began.

"You know Mark and I want to do it on our own. After Seth goes to kindergarten, I'll see if the optometrist I used to work for still needs help. Mark works at the post office," she told Francesca. Then she glanced over at her brother, who was almost finished with everything on his plate. "Did your mustang arrive yet?"

"Sure did. Vince brought her over yesterday."

"Do you know Vince?" Francesca asked Laurie.

She nodded. "There was a storm when he was chief of police here. He helped coordinate cleanup in our neighborhood. He did a great job of it. I got to know him a little bit then because we had a power line down in our yard. I take my kids to his wife, Tessa. Since you're a doctor you probably know her."

"I used to live with her," Francesca replied with a laugh. "She and I were housemates, and then Emily Diaz moved in with us. But since Tessa reunited with Vince and Emily married Dr. Jared Madison, I'm alone there. That's why your brother offered to give me some help for a few days." She didn't want Laurie to think this was a permanent arrangement.

Laurie leaned closer to Francesca. "I was really surprised when he said he was bringing you to the ranch. He never invites anybody but family here."

"Laurie…" Grady warned.

"Well, you don't."

"It's not as if I have a lot of spare time."

The two women exchanged a glance. Laurie was the one who piped up, "Men don't need a lot of spare time to have a little fun. At least that's what *I've* heard."

Francesca told herself not to look at Grady. Don't look at him. Yet her gaze skidded around the table, right to his plate and up to his face. He was staring at her, too. They were both thinking about that night in the saddle shop. Had they had fun? Or had there been too much heat, too much passion, too much intensity to call it fun?

Laurie must have realized she'd insinuated something she shouldn't have. "Oh, sorry. I didn't mean to set my foot in it. I don't know anything about how you met, or how—" she waved her hand in the air "—you got pregnant."

Grady pushed his plate back and stood. "And you're not going to know. That's private." He glanced at Francesca. "The problem is, my family doesn't understand the meaning of the word *private.* They think they can poke their noses in wherever they like. Since you're here today," he addressed Laurie, "is John coming tomorrow? And maybe Liam the next day?"

"Don't be silly. Besides, Liam's having all that fun. I'm sure he wouldn't even think about making you trail mix."

Grady laughed. "I'm sure he wouldn't. But he and John both will want to see the mustang."

Francesca could tell Grady might complain, but he loved his family. How would it feel to have a family like that? She simply had no idea.

"Let's go over to the sofa and look at the albums," Laurie said to Francesca, heading there herself, albums in her arms.

Francesca realized she'd eaten more than she usually did as she'd listened to Grady and his sister. "I'd love to look at the pictures. Especially any you could blackmail Grady with."

Both of them chuckled as Francesca followed Laurie to the sofa. Francesca made sure Laurie was on her right side so she could hear her better. Shadow, coming over to join them, hopped up next to Francesca, though he did look over to his master to see if that was acceptable.

"You're going to go wherever she goes, aren't you? There's no point in my protesting," Grady decided.

"He's not allowed on the furniture?" Francesca asked.

"He wasn't allowed on the furniture until you came. I'll just have to make sure he washes off in the pond a little more often."

Laurie bumped Francesca's good arm. "He's kidding you. He gives Shadow a bath once a week. You should see him in the old washtub out in the barn."

"That could be fun to watch."

"No one watches when I give Shadow a bath. If anyone wants to be there, they have to help me and end up all wet just like I do."

Francesca held up her cast. "I can't get this wet. I'll have to take a rain check."

Laurie giggled and opened the first album on her lap, pushing it over so Francesca could see it, too.

Twenty minutes later Francesca had laughed herself silly at Laurie's stories, as well as some of the pictures.

Grady's sister was full of anecdotes of how the boys had always gotten into trouble and how she'd wanted to join in, but they wouldn't let her. As they went from photo to photo Francesca realized what each represented…a happy family with two loving parents and children who adored them. She saw pictures of holidays—Thanksgiving, Christmas, Valentine's Day, Easter, the Fourth of July, even Halloween. There were many in front of a local church that the whole family attended. There were also photos from school programs, recitals and graduations. No one in this family missed anything.

Francesca's father had missed her whole life. Her mother had only started truly living a few years after they'd left him. But her living had been on a very small scale. She'd always been afraid to try something new, always afraid they wouldn't have enough money, always afraid Francesca would blame her for not having a father. Francesca didn't blame her mother for that. But she did blame her for not helping her feel safe. She blamed her for not acting more like an adult than a child. Francesca had always felt *she* had to be the adult. *She* was the one who had to make the decisions. *She* was the one who had to make sure they were okay. At the end of her mother's life, Francesca had been the caretaker, just as she'd always been. She had been the advocate, the one to hold her mother's hand and tell her it was okay to let go.

These family pictures were affecting Francesca in a way she hadn't been affected in a long time. Doors to her heart began to creak open. She usually didn't think about her past. She tried to dwell on what *was* rather than what used to be. That's how she'd gotten through her childhood and med school and sitting by her mother's bed when she was dying.

Laurie closed the last album. "We have a big gap in Grady's pictures. He was away at college and then lived in Chicago.

"Chicago?"

"I worked there for a number of years before I came back to Sagebrush."

Francesca's gaze sought his. "What did you do?"

"I worked in an investment banking firm for a while."

She felt as if she'd had the wind knocked out of her.

Laurie grinned. "He doesn't seem like the type, does he?"

Francesca remembered the silk shirt. He must have lived differently in Chicago. Light-years from his life here. "Why did you leave it?"

"I'd had enough."

If that didn't cover a world of reasons, she didn't know what did. He'd had enough of Chicago? Enough of banking? Enough of a woman, perhaps? That would be something to ask Laurie when she had her alone.

On the other hand, she could just ask Grady.

"Do you want me to leave the albums?" Laurie asked.

"No," Grady grumbled while Francesca answered, "Yes."

Laurie laughed. "Well, that's a consensus. I'll leave them until the family dinner on Sunday. You can bring them over then." She turned to Francesca. "How long are you staying?"

"Sunday."

Laurie looked down at her arm.

"I know everything I do is going to be limited," Francesca admitted. "Especially at the hospital. But at least I can give instructions if I'm there. I can monitor the newborns with problems, keep an eye on their charts and vital signs. I can do more than just call and find out how they are."

"Can you drive?"

"My car is being repaired. For the first week or so I'll catch a ride with someone if I can."

"Well..." Laurie looked from one of them to the other. "I think I've worn out my welcome for today. I'd better get home to the kids. Mark has some errands he wants to run and it will be easier without Mark Jr. and Seth tagging along." She smiled at both of them. "I'm glad I stopped by today."

Grady didn't respond, but Francesca answered, "Me, too. It was good to meet you."

Laurie actually looked as if she might want to give her a hug. But they really didn't know each other. They weren't family and they weren't friends, although Francesca suspected they could be. On the other hand, maybe Laurie was just friendly because Francesca was carrying her brother's baby. Maybe the family wanted to have no doubts that they would have time with the newest addition to the Fitzgerald family.

Crossing to her brother, Laurie stood on tiptoe and kissed his cheek. "I'll see you Sunday," she reminded him.

He gave her a hug. "Tell Mom I might be later than

usual. I want to spend some time with the new horse. She's going to need a lot of gentling."

"I'll tell her," Laurie said as she opened the door. Then with a wave she was gone.

Grady shook his head. "She comes on strong. I'm sorry about that."

"She was great. Besides, how else would I have gotten to see you in a diaper when you were six months old?"

When he came toward her, she patted the seat on her right. Shadow was still settled in on her left.

Grady lowered himself beside her. "You know, our baby might have your brown hair and your green eyes."

"That never entered my mind," she responded.

"Because he's a boy?" Grady asked.

"I guess." She ran her hand over one of the albums on the coffee table. "Your family looks so happy."

"You sound amazed. Families always take pictures when they're happy. That's why you only see smiling pictures in the album."

She leaned back a little. "You mean you weren't happy?"

"I'm not saying that. I'm just saying the squabbles aren't in there. The arguments aren't in there. The I-hate-yous and the I-never-want-to-see-you-agains aren't in there."

"But none of that matters if you come together again. If you make up, if you see each other's differences and if you're still friends after all that—besides being brothers and sisters—that's because of how your parents raised you."

He must have heard the weight of the sadness in her voice. "Are you going to tell me about your childhood?"

"It wasn't like yours. I don't talk about it. There's no point."

"Frannie—" He lifted her chin with his thumb. "There *is* a point to sharing. When you're ready."

She knew he wouldn't understand. He'd think she was partially at fault. He'd think they should have stayed together as a family and somehow worked it out. He'd think so many things. And that would get all muddled up with the idea of them having a baby.

"What's bothering you?" he asked.

Bothering her? She didn't let the past bother her. That's why she worked so hard. "Nothing's bothering me. I'm glad your sister came over. But now do you know what I'd like to do?"

"Do I want to guess?"

"I'd like to see the mustang."

He studied her for several long seconds. "All right, but bundle up. It's cold out."

When she rose to her feet, he rested his hand on her shoulder. "I realize you changed the subject. Someday I hope we'll have a talk about *your* past…someday when it will mean something to both of us."

If she told him about her past, she'd be giving him a part of herself. She definitely wasn't ready for that. Maybe she never would be.

Francesca took her down jacket from Grady's closet, but then realized she couldn't zipper it one-handed.

"What's wrong?" he asked, ever observant.

"Nothing's wrong. I'm ready."

He was wearing a ribbed red thermal shirt with a navy insulated vest on top. His Stetson and boots added appeal she'd never felt for a man before. As he approached her, her breath hitched.

He took the bottom two ends of her jacket, threaded the zipper into its track and zippered it up to her neck. His fingers were so very close to her chin. "You don't have a hood. Do you have a hat? We're going to be outside to see the mustang and the wind has some bite today."

His voice was husky and she wondered if his breath hitched when he was close to her, too.

Digging into her pocket with her good hand, she produced a green knit cap. But then again, putting it on one-handed could be a problem. As she tried, it slipped to the side and almost fell.

Grady caught it. "Just *ask,* Francesca." His eyes twinkled with amusement as he set it on her head and pulled the sides down over her hair. His fingers seemed to linger a bit and slide to a few other strands. If she leaned forward, her lips would be mere inches from his.

She remembered the happy family pictures she'd examined earlier. Everything about Grady was so magnetically appealing—from his very blue eyes to the dream of the family she'd never had. But the sheer seduction of all of it made her even more afraid to get involved with him.

Leaning away, she took a deep breath. "Let's go see your mustang."

After they left the house, Shadow running ahead of them, they strolled down the walk, crossed the gravel lane and headed into longer grass near the barn.

"Watch you don't turn an ankle. We have jackrabbit holes."

Francesca was indeed careful as she walked. She didn't want to have to grab on to Grady. She certainly didn't want him to carry her back to the house. Her dependence on him was going to come to an end sooner rather than later.

"Look at her," Francesca marveled as she spotted the pinto pony running across the field.

"Since Vince brought her over, she runs and runs. But she doesn't try to get out. I think maybe something's telling her there's safety here, as well as captivity. She nuzzled one of the other horses through the fence yesterday. That's a good sign."

Francesca could see that the mustang's pasture was fenced off from the one beside it.

"She came within three feet of me this morning," Grady confided. "I'm hoping later today, or maybe even tomorrow, she'll come a little closer. Once she trusts me, I think we'll be great friends."

The wind whipped Francesca's hair around her face and she knew Grady wasn't just talking about the horse. "Trust is precious, but it's such a fragile thread. Once it's torn, it's hard to weave it back together again." She felt Shadow against her leg, quietly watching the horse, too.

"Can I ask you something?" Out here in the wide-open spaces with the wind tossing anything it could, Francesca felt a freedom she didn't feel when she was enclosed in a room with Grady.

"You can ask. Depending on what it is, I might decide not to answer," he replied.

She felt her cheeks start to heat a little, in spite of the cold beginning to numb the rest of her. "When I told you I was pregnant, you said the condom you used had been in your wallet for a long while."

"Yes, I did," he agreed warily.

"Did that mean you hadn't been with a woman for a while?"

Grady kept his gaze on the mustang, one hand on the fence. "That's what it meant."

"So…that means one-night stands aren't a habit?"

Now his gaze left the mustang and settled on her. "No, they're not a habit. Are they for you?"

"No! I told you, I hadn't been with a man for a year." She wished she knew why Grady didn't take her at her word.

The wind ruffled leaves on the live oaks. Tall grasses bent to it. After a few prolonged silent moments, Grady asked, "This is the guy who asked you to move to Lubbock?"

"Yes. I was living in Oklahoma when I met Darren Whitcomb at a medical conference. We dated long-distance for a few months and had lots of phone calls. Eventually I moved here and in with him."

"Why didn't it work out?"

"That's water under the bridge," she decided, turning to watch the mustang again. The horse had stopped running and was aware of the two of them standing at the fence. Her ears were perked up and she was listening.

Grady's hand cupped Francesca's elbow. "Why don't you want to tell me?"

Facing him again, she asked, "Are you going to tell

me every detail of your last relationship?" Her instincts were good and she knew he wouldn't.

He blew out a breath. "No, I guess not. But on the other hand, you have seen pictures of me in a diaper."

Grady had a way of using humor to get past her defenses.

The mustang suddenly ran toward them, stopped abruptly and threw up her tail. Grady stood perfectly still and so did Francesca.

"What's she doing?" Francesca asked.

"Trying to make up her mind about us."

Francesca stood fascinated as the horse trotted closer, spun away, ran in a circle and then faced them again. Her dance of sorts continued until she was about seven feet from the fence. Francesca was almost as intrigued by Grady as she was with the mustang. He was perfectly still, not moving a muscle.

Then she heard him say gently, "Come on, girl. I won't hurt you." He slipped something from his pocket and held it out in the palm of his hand.

The horse eyed Francesca.

"What should I do?" she asked quietly.

"Nothing. Just stay still. She's probably afraid if she comes close to me, you're going to toss a rope around her neck."

Holding her breath, Francesca watched as the horse came within two feet of Grady, eyeing the piece of carrot in his palm. Then with a toss of her head and a whinny, she spun away and ran across the field once more.

Francesca was disappointed for the horse. Instinct told her Grady would take good care of her.

Grady stuffed the carrot back into his pocket. "That was closer than before. I'm making progress."

"Will she come inside if the weather turns nasty?" She could see the mustang's corral narrowed, led under the barn's overhang and into a stall.

"She'll come in eventually. She'll let me near her eventually. It's just going to take some patience." After he watched the mustang streak across the pasture, he asked, "Do you want to see the others?"

"Sure."

He studied her face to see if she meant it, then nodded and took her arm to guide her through the tall grass and stones that led to one of the barn doors. It opened with a loud creak.

Francesca was so aware of his arm in hers, aware of his height, aware of his broad shoulders, aware of everything about him. She made conversation to distract herself. "Do you take care of all of this?"

He chuckled. "No. The son of a friend works here after school. Liam helps with any repairs that need to be done. Since John lives in Lubbock he doesn't get out here much, but if I need him, he comes. Laurie rides, so when she can, she exercises the horses with me. Dad used to drive out here more, but I think being here makes him sad because he can't run the ranch himself now."

When they stepped into the barn, Francesca watched Shadow trot down the walkway. She inhaled musky, damp smells of horses, years-old wood and hay. Grady led her to the walkway between the stalls where Shadow sat waiting.

Grady stepped up to the stalls and introduced three horses to her.

Francesca reached out and let the pewter-gray horse smell her fingers as Vince had taught her, then rubbed the side of her neck.

"She's getting her winter coat. I need to let them out for a run and then groom them."

Although Grady hadn't given a hint of it, Francesca knew she was taking up a lot of his time when he should be working or doing chores.

"I can go back to the house on my own." She turned to go.

He caught her good arm. "You don't have to leave yet."

"If I weren't here, what would you be doing?"

"I'd probably be in at the shop. This break is kind of nice. I'm getting things done around here I've let go. I've got a pile of wood that needs to be split. I'm going to tackle that this afternoon."

She could imagine him splitting wood, his face to the sun and his muscles moving under his shirtsleeves.

"I have another question for you," she said softly.

He turned toward her, all of his attention focused on her. "What?"

"Is your sister naturally that friendly?"

"I don't understand."

"I'm carrying your baby. Would your family be interested in me, or even stop by, if I weren't?"

After a few moments of thoughtful consideration, he answered, "You *are* here because you're carrying my baby. But if you're asking if my family would want to meet anyone I was involved with, the answer is yes.

Laurie wasn't pretending interest. She's not like that. Neither is Mom." He paused for a moment. "I'd like to know why the idea of family caring is so foreign to you."

She could deny his conclusion. She could tell him why. But ever since the accident, ever since he'd picked her up at the hospital, ever since she'd felt almost comfortable in his home, she'd wondered if she'd fallen down a rabbit hole. She'd wondered if she was trying to make fantasies become reality. She had to go home, get her life back and look at all of it realistically.

So to Grady she said, "Not today." If he was really patient he wouldn't push her. If he cared, he'd try to develop a bond of trust between them.

Did she really want that? Did she want to get closer to Grady?

He had a question of his own. "Is this a test?"

When she didn't answer, he added, "Because I don't like tests. I like games even less. You and I have to understand each other if we're going to parent together."

Parent together. That's what he cared about. He cared about his son. Well, so did she. "No games, Grady. But sometimes a test or two is necessary before trust can develop. And sometimes trust takes years."

She left him in the barn with that thought, knowing even time couldn't heal some wounds. She might feel the pull of family here. Yet she couldn't forget Grady's main focus was his son.

Their son.

Chapter Five

Late Friday morning, Grady swiped the grooming brush over one of the horses—Avalanche—glancing Francesca's way. Her cell phone beeped, echoing in the stone and wood barn. She'd been restless and, he supposed, feeling cooped up, so he'd suggested she come out to the barn for a little while. She was ensconced in an old captain's chair, a saddle blanket tucked around her for additional warmth, Shadow on a hay bale close by.

Avalanche sidestepped in his stall as her cell phone beeped again.

Grady was glad for the interruption. Having her watch him work had become distracting!

She managed to pull the phone from her pocket and checked the ID. "It's the hospital," she explained.

He unabashedly listened as she answered the call.

"What's up, Josie? Give me the details," Francesca requested a few moments later.

Grady realized Francesca was now in *doctor* mode.

As she listened, he finished grooming Avalanche and left his stall.

Francesca checked her watch. "I'll find a way to get there. Call me on my cell if anything changes."

"*How* are you going to get there?" Grady asked as soon as she closed her phone.

"Can I use your truck? If not, maybe you could drop me at Tessa's and she can drive me. I'll call her—"

Suddenly he was worried and stopped her before she could call her friend. "You can't drive the truck. What if your control with one hand isn't as good as you think it is?"

"Grady, they need me there. The doctor who's covering for me can't be there. His wife is sick and his daughters need him. But there's a preemie with jaundice who's also having breathing problems. What if that were *our* baby?"

"That's not fair," he grumbled.

"Life isn't fair. But I want to make it just a little better for this boy and his family."

"You are one stubborn woman," he announced, half in frustration and half in admiration.

Francesca drew herself up to her full height, letting the blanket fall. "If I were a man, you'd be calling me confident rather than stubborn." She turned and headed for the barn door, Shadow jumping off the bale to follow her, before Grady could make further objections.

If she thought he was going to let her drive herself, she was mistaken. He strode after her and caught up to her as she was putting her cell phone to her ear. "I'll drive you to the hospital."

She closed her phone and stared at him a few seconds, obviously gauging what she wanted to do. Without her cap her hair blew in the wind. The urge to run his fingers through it, to take her to his bedroom and keep her there was so strong that he clenched his hands at his sides.

Finally, she asked, "There's no point in my saying you don't have to drive me, is there?"

"Nope. No point at all."

"Thank you," she acquiesced, giving him a soft smile that aroused him so fast he felt as if his blood was on fire.

He was suddenly grateful winter had come early.

Grady cut a glance at Francesca as he drove her to Lubbock. His overwhelming desire to take care of her was making him crazy. He'd never felt quite this way about a woman before.

He couldn't forget watching her at the fence with the mustang yesterday. She hadn't been around horses much, yet she'd understood the type of stillness that was needed to encourage the wild horse to come close. Most people wanted to reach out to the wilder ones and thought the animals should understand their eagerness to be friends. But Francesca had apparently realized that no amount of reaching could entice such a creature to her. Only stillness and time and patience could establish a bond.

Francesca had been patient with the mustang. And he had to be patient with her. She was very much like that wild horse, although he hadn't realized it the first night he'd met her. She put on a good show, but underneath she was afraid of getting close.

He eyed her again. She was staring out the side window, a distracted look on her face.

"Do you worry about each of your patients this much?"

She glanced at him. "I have to. I have to give them a chance to take their next breath, or beat an infection or develop normally so they can live a full, healthy life. The infant mortality rate in this country is way too high. I try to do everything I can to bring it down."

Infant mortality rate. That phrase sent a chill through him. He knew he'd taken this pregnancy way too lightly up until now. Maybe it was time he faced reality and the risks, along with what he and Francesca had to do to parent this child together. He'd thought taking one day at a time was enough. But maybe it wasn't.

He was as distracted as she was on the rest of the drive to the hospital.

Ten minutes later he pulled up under the portico, quickly got out and went around to her side to help her down.

Before she took his hand, however, she said, "You don't have to stick around. This could take a while. I'm sure I can get a ride back with someone."

"I'll wait."

"Grady, it could take hours!"

"I'll give my dad a call. He can drive over and maybe we can have coffee. As a member of the hospital board, he's here on and off. Don't worry about me. I won't get bored."

She eyed him as if she didn't believe him. Then, apparently deciding there was no point in arguing, she placed her hand in his and let him support her until she stepped to the ground.

They were very close...within kissing distance. Heat spread through him again. Their interlude together on the sofa in his office flashed in his mind. Something about this woman sparked his libido.

In Chicago, his ex-fiancée had been all about her career. She'd been so passionate about it, she'd been unfaithful to him. Not only unfaithful, but she'd betrayed him. She'd slept with their boss to get a promotion Grady had been working for for two years. The worst part of it had been she'd expected him to take it all in stride. As if what she'd done was a matter of course. That's when he'd known he wanted to return to Sagebrush and its small-town values, to a family that was loyal no matter what. He'd suddenly gotten a different perspective on his high-powered career. Sexual attraction had led him to believe there was a connection between him and Susan. But they hadn't put any time into the relationship. They'd just conveniently slept over at each other's places. They hadn't faced life—the low points and the high points—together. Their lives had been mutually exclusive.

It hadn't been easy to leave Chicago without looking back. And now, five years later, at age forty-four, he'd gotten his priorities straight. But that didn't mean he'd forgotten how deceptive a woman could be. That didn't mean he'd forgotten how all-consuming a woman's career could be.

Although he was so tempted to pull Francesca closer and kiss her, he restrained that impulse. Stepping back, he said, "I'll come up to the neonatal unit in about an hour to see how you're doing."

Her cheeks flushed a bit—as if she'd been as aware of him as he was of her—and she nodded. "Just stop at the nurses' station. They'll tell you where I am."

When Francesca disappeared through the sliding glass doors into the lobby of the hospital, Grady stared after her in turmoil about the path ahead of them both.

Grady had been at the hospital for two hours when he spotted Tessa at the NICU nurses' station. "Are you back to work?" he asked, surprised, because Vince had told him his wife wasn't going to return until February.

"Not officially," she replied with a smile, pushing her long, blond hair over her shoulder. "But the doc who's taking my place had some questions about one of my patients who has recurring problems. I stopped in to look over the chart."

"And ended up here?" Pediatrics was in another wing.

"The mom of one of my other patients just had a preemie."

"You doctors are addicted to work, aren't you?" He was beginning to see how Francesca's work could have an effect on their child's life.

Tessa frowned. "No, we're not addicted to work. My children are at home. Mrs. Zappa returned from her visit to her son's, and now she'll be there when I need her to help me with them."

Rhonda Zappa had been Vince's housekeeper before

he married Tessa. She'd taken care of his little boy. Grady knew the couple trusted her implicitly.

"I guess I can't compare this to an investment banking job," Grady admitted.

Tessa laid her hand on his arm. "I don't know. How much did you care about your clients? There are doctors who put in their hours, go home and don't think about their patients. But Francesca and I aren't like that."

Both of their gazes shifted to the double doors of the NICU.

Tessa added, "Francesca cares about each one of those babies as if they were her own. She saves their lives, Grady. Each one of those infants has a hold on her heart."

"She's supposed to be resting," he grumbled.

"I think she's had enough of resting. I spoke with her last night and she's restless to go home."

"She doesn't realize how difficult that will be with her arm casted."

"I think she does. She's already arranged for a ride to the hospital on Monday with Gina Rigoletti."

After a long pause that became awkward, Tessa asked, "How much do you want to be a dad?"

"I think I've been waiting my whole life to be a dad. I called my father this morning. He came over and we had coffee. He talked about raising us, the difference between raising boys and girls. He's been a great role model. I've also watched my brother and sister with their kids. I've got to admit I've been a bit envious at times."

Tessa's blue eyes twinkled. "So now you'll have *your* chance at it."

"I hope so. Francesca and I have to work that out."

"You will, especially if you put your baby first. It will help if you and Francesca can agree on the basics."

"We haven't really settled on the kind of custody we'll have."

"Then there are all the little things, too. Can you stop in whenever you'd like or are you going to adhere to a strict visitation schedule? If *you* have the baby, can she call and ask if she can put him to bed with you? Do you want to start a college fund? Will she consult you if your little boy needs braces?"

He had to admit he hadn't thought of any of the concerns Tessa had mentioned. "I guess a lot of what we do depends on what kind of relationship we have."

"I guess it does."

Tessa was studying him curiously and he felt uncomfortable. He wasn't sure himself what kind of relationship he and Francesca had.

Suddenly the doors to the NICU slid open and Francesca stepped out. Spying the two of them, she crossed to the desk. She and Tessa embraced and Grady could again sense the strong bond between the two women as they began to chat animatedly.

"I can leave now," Francesca said. "Dr. Saxby will be here shortly. And Dr. Martin will be back from his vacation tonight."

"Did everything go okay?" Grady wanted to know.

"For now, but it's still touch and go."

"How about some lunch at the Yellow Rose Diner before we go back to the ranch? Tessa, you're welcome to join us." He thought it might be interesting to hear what the two women had to say when they were together.

Tessa shook her head. "No, thanks. I promised the kids I'd watch a Christmas movie with them. I'll be heading home, too." Tessa returned the chart in her hand to the stand behind the desk. "I'll see you two around. Have a good lunch."

After Tessa headed down the hall, Francesca asked Grady, "Did you get hold of your dad?"

"Yep. We were in the coffee shop for about an hour. He was going to drop in on the chief of staff."

"He knows Dr. Gutieras?"

"They went to school together. I think that's how Dr. Gutieras corralled Dad to be on the board. He wanted a commonsense person."

"That's your dad?"

"Most of the time."

They walked down the hall together to the elevator. When they reached it, Francesca pressed the button for the lobby.

"So, what about lunch?" Grady asked again.

"You really don't need to be anywhere?" she asked, looking worried.

"The saddle shop's doing fine. Christmas orders have come in so everyone's working steadily. I'll have time to exercise the horses and do some chores this afternoon. A half hour for lunch won't throw a wrench into those plans."

She studied him for a few seconds.

"What?" he asked, feeling a bit unsettled.

"Do you always take everything in stride?"

"I had about fourteen years of running like a rat in a maze. When I returned to Sagebrush, I decided I was never going to live my life like that again."

"That was one huge life change."

"Yes, it was, but it was worth it. I'm always going to make time to be a dad, Francesca. You should know that."

He wasn't sure if that statement pleased her or worried her as the elevator doors opened and they stepped in. He still didn't know Francesca, did he?

Maybe he never would.

The Yellow Rose Diner was a Sagebrush landmark. When Francesca had moved in with Tessa, she'd found it a gathering place for everyone, from the town's lawyer to its patrol officers. The restaurant bustled as usual as Grady escorted her inside. Christmas wreaths heaped in a stack by the row of windows threatened to topple onto the pile of red ribbon rolls in the corner.

Grady hung his Stetson on one of the hat holders on the wall, then helped Francesca out of her jacket and pushed her chair in for her. She looked up over her shoulder to murmur thank you and found her face very close to his. She swallowed hard.

After a moment of heart-stopping awareness, he straightened and went around to his seat. He ran his hand through his hair before he settled in across the table.

Francesca remembered running her fingers through his hair. What had happened to her that night? What had happened to Grady? Why had they felt free to be that intimate with each other? Now the tension was ratcheted to such a level between them she could hardly catch her breath. Maybe because the stakes were much higher.

"It looks as if they're decorating for Christmas,"

Grady observed, obviously trying to make conversation. "I usually put up a tree."

"Do you?" That surprised her. Most bachelors wouldn't bother.

"My nieces and nephews tell me it's not Christmas without a tree. They believe Santa might not stop by if he doesn't have a place to put the presents."

She laughed. "Christmas *is* all about children, isn't it? And the stars in their eyes. Tessa and Vince will have a wonderful Christmas this year with Natalie and Sean. Emily showed me the Cinderella coach ornaments she bought for their twins when they were at Disney World for their honeymoon. Courtney and Amy are going to love them."

Grady gave a crooked smile. "Children do make it special. My dad still reads *The Christmas Story* every Christmas Eve. It's a tradition. With his grandchildren gathered around him, it seems to have an even deeper meaning."

Francesca wondered if she'd see Grady over the Christmas holidays. Maybe when she left his ranch, they'd go their separate ways again until the baby was born. Wasn't that what she wanted?

Francesca's favorite waitress came hurrying over to them then, looking harried. Mindy lifted her pencil from its perch in her auburn hair and stood poised to take their order. "Hi, Francesca. Grady. What can I get for you?"

Francesca realized that today the waitress didn't have spare minutes to make small talk. She ordered turkey salad and a glass of milk. Grady ordered a beef club and cheddar cheese fries.

As Mindy rushed off, he studied Francesca for a few moments, then asked, "When you were growing up, did your family decorate much?"

She knew he was trying to see into her past and in a certain sense, she was still ashamed of it. That scared little girl inside would never forget the weight of her father's disapproval, the resounding harshness of his yelling, her mother's cowering fear.

Chatter in the busy restaurant swirled all around them. Maybe Grady thought conversation would be easier here than when they were alone together somewhere. But her past wasn't easy conversation no matter where they were.

"We had one of those electric candles you could plug in and set in the window. Mom put that out every year."

"You said your parents separated?"

"My mother left my father. They never actually divorced."

"Did you see him after you left?"

"No."

Grady stayed quiet as if he were attempting to get a handle on her childhood.

To keep him distracted from the subject of her past, she offered, "I decorated for Christmas with Tessa. That was a lot of fun in the Victorian. We even hung strings of lights outside."

His gaze told her he knew her change of subject was deliberate. He took their conversation in a different direction. "I know you'll be going home Sunday. But how would you like to have dinner with my family first? When I had coffee with Dad today, he said he'd like to meet you."

Dinner with Grady's family. Her curiosity about them, about the dynamics between brothers and sisters and parents had only swelled in the wake of his sister's visit. "Who will be there?"

"Everyone," he answered with a grin.

Everyone. Did she have the courage to take on the Fitzgerald clan?

Sure she did. "What can I bring?"

"Just yourself."

Somehow she'd manage to make a cherry cobbler. She should be able to handle that.

Much easier than she might be able to handle Grady's family!

On Sunday, Francesca's heart thumped hard as she walked into the Fitzgerald one-story condo attached to another on the side street of a fairly new development in Lubbock. Cars spilled from the driveway along the curb. When Grady opened the door, the aroma of baked goods wafted out ahead of a wave of chatter from the inside.

Francesca glanced at Grady. How many Fitzgeralds *were* there?

He leaned close and whispered in her ear, "None of them will bite. I promise."

She'd tried to hide the fact that family made her jittery, but wasn't very good at it. In fact, with Grady she couldn't seem to hide much at all.

There were three women in the kitchen, all involved in some aspect of the baking process. Maureen was rolling out cookie dough on a pastry cloth. Laurie was removing cookie sheets from the oven. Another woman, pleasantly plump, her hair styled in a pixie cut, was mixing water and confectioner's sugar in a small bowl.

Grady's father, a ruddy-faced, tall man with black hair like Grady's but with silver at his temples, pushed himself up from his recliner and came to greet them. "You must be Francesca," he said with a hint of gruffness in his tone.

"Yes, I am."

Two little boys ran from the hallway and wrapped their arms around their grandfather. Francesca wondered if they were Mark and Seth, Laurie's sons.

"Hey, everyone. This is Francesca." Grady waved a hand at her and pointed to the man at the left side of the sofa. "That's John." He pointed to a younger man at the other side of the sofa. "And that's Liam. Jenna, John's wife, is stirring the icing."

Everyone gave Francesca a nod or smile except Liam. He sort of shrugged and cocked his head, examining her as if she were an alien. At least that's the way Francesca saw it. Grady's brothers hadn't stopped by to see the mustang as he'd expected. Because they didn't want to intrude?

Maureen called from the kitchen, "Come help us with this last batch."

"Let her get her coat off, Mom, before you put her to work," Grady teased.

His mother took it in stride and just gave him a grin and a wink. "Put her jacket in on the guest-room bed with everyone else's."

Francesca felt like a deer in headlights. She handed

Grady the cherry cobbler, shrugged out of her jacket, then traded with him.

A little girl of about five, who had been drawing at the coffee table, came over to Francesca now and looked up at her expectantly. "Are you Uncle Grady's girlfriend?"

Francesca dropped down to her eye level. "I'm your uncle's friend. What's your name?"

"Marly."

"It's nice to meet you, Marly."

The small child eyed Francesca's rounding figure. "Daddy told Mommy you're going to have a baby."

"Yes, I am…at the end of February." Francesca smiled at the blue icing on Marly's chin and a streak of yellow on the front of her T-shirt. "Were you helping to make the cookies?"

"Yep. But I got tired of doing that. But maybe I can show you how to do the angels' wings."

"Maybe you can. Let's go ask your grandma." Francesca stood and followed Marly into the kitchen.

There she handed Maureen the cherry cobbler. While Grady had spent most of the day at the saddle shop yesterday, she'd baked. "I wanted to contribute."

Maureen said, "Thank you. We can always use more dessert. Beef barbecue is simmering in the slow cooker. I didn't add brown sugar since you were coming. We thought we'd be further along with the cookies by now, but cookie-making can't be rushed."

Francesca felt awkward, unsure of what to do or say. But then Laurie piped up, "Francesca lives in Sagebrush in an old Victorian. Tessa Rossi used to be her housemate."

Laurie went on to explain, "Tessa was on call at the hospital one time when Mark Jr. fell off his skateboard. I liked her and started taking the kids to her." Turning to Francesca again, she added, "My Mark and Seth were the two hooligans who ran to Gramps when you came in. Marly belongs to Jenna and John. Their two boys are in the garage trying to fix an old bike."

Jenna offered Francesca a bottle of food coloring. "Do you want to mix the colors?"

"Pink for the angels," Marly piped up. "White for their wings, blue for the bells and yellow for the stars."

"She has it all planned," Jenna said with a smile. "Life's choices are a lot less difficult when you're five."

Francesca smiled back. "I suppose that's true." She picked up one of the small dishes of icing and shook in a couple of drops of blue food coloring. She'd never decorated cookies before. This might even be fun.

After a few minutes of silent work, Maureen commented, "Grady said you went into the hospital on Friday. How did that go?"

Francesca decided if Laurie and Mrs. Fitzgerald had been bluntly honest with her, she could be with them, too. "It felt great to be back. But it was frustrating. Without two hands, I couldn't do what I usually do."

"I can only imagine," Jenna sympathized. "I broke my arm in a biking accident two years ago. I work in the office at the denim factory, nothing like you do. But it was such a relief when I had that cast off and I could feel useful again. I hated not being able to button the kids' shirts or tie Marly's shoes. I can only imagine how you felt at the hospital."

"What do you do at the denim factory?" Francesca asked, eager to move the conversation from her to Grady's family.

"I'm an account manager."

The conversation seemed to roll easily after that. Francesca found she liked decorating Christmas cookies with Marly's help. Maybe Christmas traditions were something to think about planning for the future.

When Francesca glanced into the living room, Grady was cross-legged on the floor with his two nephews, playing some kind of board game. He looked up and his gaze met hers. Was he thinking about how she fit into the Fitzgeralds's Christmas traditions?

Dinner itself was noisy and informal. Mr. Fitzgerald set up a card table for the kids in the living room. Francesca had never experienced anything like this. The adults just fit around the dining-room table. They all held hands and said a prayer before they ate.

She did notice the only one who didn't participate as much in the conversation and laughter was Liam. Grady had told her he'd been divorced recently and she wondered if that was why. Grady definitely favored his father. Liam, with his reddish-brown hair and freckles, favored Maureen.

Since Grady's dad was on the board at the hospital, he and Francesca had much to converse about. They were just discussing the merits of an expanded cardiac rehab facility when Liam asked Grady, "So when are you and Francesca getting married?"

Silence blanketed the table. Even the children in the living room were quiet for the moment.

Not for the first time since she'd met Grady, Francesca wasn't sure what to do. Maybe the best thing would be to let Grady discuss whatever he wanted to discuss with his family without her present. Marriage *wasn't* on the table. Her father had forced her mother into marriage when she'd told him she was pregnant. Francesca had vowed that would never happen to her—no man would ever control her life.

Pushing back her chair, she stood. "Please excuse me. I need to use the ladies' room."

She left the dining room and went down the hall, knowing that the powder room would be her sanctuary for at least ten minutes. That should be enough time for Grady to deal with his brother.

When Francesca did emerge from the powder room, Grady was standing right there outside the door. "Are you all right?"

"I'm fine. I wanted to make sure I didn't interrupt anything when I came back in."

"There was nothing to interrupt two minutes after you left."

She told him the truth. "This family stuff is foreign territory for me, Grady. I just didn't want to interfere."

Grady stood toe-to-toe with her, his voice low. "I'm not making excuses for Liam's rudeness, but he isn't in the best of moods these days. When his wife asked for a divorce, he didn't see it coming. She didn't want to try counseling because she'd met someone else. He's still licking his wounds and that's why he's… bristly."

"I understand," she said quickly.

"No, I don't think you do. I love my family. I wanted them to meet you. But what happens between you and me, that's *private.*"

She wasn't sure why, but she did feel some relief at his words. "What did you tell your brother?"

"I told Liam my relationship with you is none of his business."

"I don't want to come between you."

"You won't. He and I have had healthy disagreements all our lives. He's the youngest. There's twelve years between us. He's never wanted to take my advice."

"But you've always wanted to give it?" she asked with a small smile.

"For the past few years I've finally learned to keep my mouth shut. Anyway, I know you've probably had enough of my clan for now. I just happen to have a Christmas tree in the barn. Would you decorate it with me?"

"Tonight?"

"Sure. We've got all evening. I'll get you home in plenty of time to turn in early. What do you think?"

Her hand went to her tummy. This was her last evening with Grady. Decorating a Christmas tree with him could become a tradition with their son.

A tradition. She hadn't experienced many of those. "Yes, I'd like to decorate a tree with you."

Grady's blue eyes darkened. His woodsy cologne invited her closer. A burst of laughter came from the living room and he shifted that way.

No matter what Grady said, his family was important to his life. Would they be important to hers?

Chapter Six

When Francesca stared at the tall, broad evergreen Grady had set up in his living room and the low fire burning in the fireplace, a multitude of feelings washed over her. She realized gratitude and appreciation for today superseded them all.

Grady brought in the last heavy box from the guest room closet and set it on the coffee table. "That's it. Now we can unpack the ornaments and get started."

Get started. She'd begun a process when she'd called Grady from her hospital room. She hadn't realized how involved and complicated that process was going to be.

Curious about the type of ornaments stored in the box, she rose to her feet and went to it as he flipped open the lid. "Are these your family's or yours?"

"They're mine. As you could see, Mom still puts up

a gigantic tree. She kept most of the treasured ones from when we were growing up. Mine are a little more primitive. Many my nieces and nephews have made for me, others I found on travels or were gifts. See what you think."

She peered into the box. The first ornament she lifted out was a miniature angel with a crocheted skirt. The delicate white thread wound about her in rings and was obviously starched. Her wings were the same delicate threading. Her face was a painted wooden ball and her halo was made of gold wire.

"Where did this one come from?"

"The wife of one of my customers. I had a display set up in my shop for her to sell a few of them before Christmas."

"It's wonderful." She lifted out another. It was a leather boot with a gold bell for a spur.

"One of my employees made that one."

Grady was near to her now, near enough that their hips bumped. As they bent over looking into the box, their elbows brushed. Neither of them moved away, and Francesca knew she should.

Taking the angel ornament by its little red string, she crossed to the tree and hung it on one of the branches. This could be the start of a Christmas tradition. Emotion lodged in her throat.

Grady must have been watching her and saw her bite her lip.

Suddenly he was at her shoulder. "What is it?"

"Hormones," she replied with a small, forced smile.

Grady hesitated for a moment and then wrapped his

arm around her shoulders, turning her toward him. "You can only use that excuse once a month for me to buy it."

"First time this month," she joked.

His hand went to her stomach, startling her. "Honesty—for the sake of the baby. Remember?"

Oh, she remembered. Gazing into his very blue eyes, she felt so many emotions. Emotions she'd never had before, never let herself *feel* before. Because of the baby or because of Grady?

"I didn't have a pleasant childhood," she began, the softest way she knew how.

When he removed his hand, she realized how protective that simple gesture had been.

He tilted his head and studied her. "You're going to try to sugarcoat this, aren't you?"

"Most people can't deal with it otherwise."

"No sugarcoating. Just tell me what happened."

"Grady…"

Perceptive, he asked, "Why don't you think I'll understand?"

She studied the angel for a few moments. "Because your family is loving and connected. You grew up with a mom and dad who loved you and protected you. That is absolutely huge."

"Neither of your parents protected you?"

For him to understand, she'd have to paint a picture. "What's your earliest memory?" she asked him.

He considered her question. "I was about three when my dad put me on a horse for the first time. We have a picture, so I don't know how much my memory comes from that or from the event itself. But I recall things that aren't in the picture—the feel of his hand on my back, the way he held the reins, the coarseness of the horse's mane as I held on to it."

She could tell Grady still appreciated every aspect of remembering. She also knew memories were the most vivid when emotions were high. His that day had been the sheer excitement of a new adventure.

Hers today would be the lingering scent of Grady's cologne, the soft feel of his flannel shirt and the intense look on his face as he studied her now and asked, "What was yours?"

"Like you, I was about three. I was hiding in a dark closet as my father yelled at my mother."

Grady stayed silent and she guessed he was hoping she'd go on without his prodding. "I have a lot of memories of hiding in the dark in that closet until I was eight."

His hands slid from her shoulder to her hand and he tugged her over to the sofa.

After they were seated, he said, "He abused your mother?"

"Yes."

"When he came home drunk, you went and hid because you knew what would happen."

"Yes."

"Did it go beyond black eyes and split lips?" His voice was as grim as his expression.

"Sometimes. Sometimes she'd lie in bed for a day or two and I'd crawl in beside her. The one thing I remember most besides the dark and the fear is how helpless I always felt. I wanted to make her pain go away. And not just the physical pain. I saw her tears, and when I was really young I thought they were from the physical hurt. But as I grew older, I realized she was suffering in her heart. Somehow I thought that by putting my arms around her, by staying close, I could help."

"Did he touch *you?*" Grady asked gruffly.

"Not as long as I stayed in the closet."

She didn't know why, but telling Grady about this, about her, was much harder than it had been to tell Tessa, Emily or Vince. Maybe because she didn't want pity from him. She did *not* want him to feel sorry for her. She was past it all now and on to a different life.

"You don't talk about this, do you?"

"No. There's no reason to."

He looked dubious. "There's more to it than what you've told me. You said your mother left your father. How old were you?"

"I was eight."

"What made her finally leave?"

He was still holding her hand and he rubbed his thumb across her palm. Grady was the father of her child and she didn't want to keep secrets from him. She knew secrets damaged relationships and didn't build them.

"It was a Saturday night," she remembered all too well, keeping her gaze on his strong fingers holding hers. "We heard my father come up the steps unsteadily. He fell once and swore. He started yelling before he even reached the apartment door. It was 10:00 p.m. but he said his supper had better be on the table."

She shivered, all of it rushing back although she'd tried to erase the sights, sounds and feelings for years. She went on as if a play were unfolding in front of her eyes. "As soon as my father opened the door, I headed for the closet. But that night I didn't *stay* in the closet. I thought his voice seemed fiercer than usual. When he got louder, I heard something fall. I was afraid it was my mom. I came out of the closet into my room."

She could remember the heat of the floorboards under her feet, the scent of jasmine floating through the open windows, the little bedroom that had been a refuge. "My room was small, only big enough for a single bed. But I had that closet. Two doors between me and my father had always seemed to be better than one. That night, though, I suppose I was tired of hiding. I felt like a coward when I hid. I felt like I should do something to protect my mother."

"You were only eight!" Grady protested, sounding as if just the thought horrified him.

"I was old enough to know the consequences of talking back. My mother had become more passive over the years. If she didn't fight him, she didn't get hurt as badly. But that night, for whatever reason, I couldn't be passive. I couldn't let him hit her again."

Francesca closed her eyes as if that would blot out the pictures. But she knew better. "I watched through the keyhole. When he went for her I flew out of there, yelling for him to keep away. But he came after me instead of her and backhanded me across the face, then again across my ear. I ended up on the floor seeing stars. My mother always had a teapot on the stove. She grabbed it, threatened my dad with the hot water, pulled me off the floor and took me to her bedroom, where she locked the door."

The memories were still so real when she summoned them up. "I expected him to break it down, but he didn't," she went on. "He shouted at us, and then left. When my mom examined me, she saw I had hit the leg of the table when I'd fallen. I had a cut across my temple that needed stitches. My ear was hurting and I couldn't hear on the right side. She dragged a suitcase from under the bed, packed as many of my things and hers as she could shove into it, took money she'd been hiding away from a jar under a floorboard and hurried me outside. We ran a couple of blocks until she flagged down a taxi to take us to the hospital. The doctors treated me and sent us to a shelter. A week later we were on a bus to Oklahoma and a new life."

Grady's expression was filled with so much compassion, Francesca could hardly stand it. She expected the usual questions like, *Did you ever see your father again? How difficult was it starting over? How did your mother handle it?*

Instead, he asked, "How long was it until you stopped being afraid?"

Maybe he *did* understand. "I was in my early twenties. I had taken two self-defense courses in college. That helped. In my late twenties I decided to find out if my dad was still in Salinas. I learned he had died two years before and knowing that wiped out most of the fear."

But she knew there was still a residue. Sometimes it kept her from taking risks.

Grady's voice was gentle. "I'm sorry for what you went through. You're right, it's hard for me to imagine it. I guess anyone who hasn't gone through it can't truly understand it." They sat in silence together, his hand still covering hers. "So has it been hard for you to have serious relationships because of all of this?"

She knew what he was leading up to—and she might as well get this over with all at one time. "I know it might sound crazy, but for a long time I didn't even realize my background was the reason I didn't want to date. I made the decision to become a doctor when I was in high school. I was all about getting good grades, winning scholarships, putting all my energy into my career so that I could make my mom's life better, too. Then in med school I hardly had time to breathe, let alone get involved with a man. But I had that mentor I spoke of—Joshua—who was so kind. He was the first person I told about my childhood. When I did, he warned me not to be too careful because that could lead to mistakes, too. I didn't know what he meant then, but I found out."

"With this Darren you were involved with?"

"Yes. I *was* careful. As I said, I met him at a medical conference. Maybe because I was on my home turf, maybe because I was missing my mother—she'd died the year before and I felt a little lost without that connection—when he asked me to show him around the city on a break, I agreed. We'd had several professional conversations by that point and I liked him. He was charming…without coming on strong. He said he didn't drink. I couldn't find any similarity to my father."

Grady's intelligent blue eyes sparked and he made the connections. "But he was like your father in some way?"

"I didn't see it at first. We had lengthy phone calls

long-distance for a few months. He told me about the Family Tree Health Center opening in Lubbock and said the hospital where he worked was looking for a neonatologist and offices were available at Family Tree. It would be a risk for me to start a new practice somewhere I'd never been, so I came down to visit for a few days and he showed me around. Sure there was some arrogance about him, but I've found that's often the case with doctors, so it wasn't surprising. There was…an attraction." Though nothing like she felt with Grady! But she wasn't about to tell him that right now. Everything was too raw and vulnerable for her to be even more vulnerable with him.

"So you packed your bags and moved here?"

"I did. I became friends with Tessa almost right away. We consulted on a case, had lunch and I…connected with her. Thank goodness I did. As soon as I moved in with Darren, he began becoming more possessive. When I wasn't working, he wanted to know where I was every minute. He didn't give me Tessa's phone messages if she called the condo. I started having nightmares again, nightmares like I hadn't had in years."

"Nightmares about being locked in a closet?"

"Yes. Then I realized why. I was starting to feel trapped, as trapped as I'd felt as a little girl. With our work, Darren and I didn't have a lot of time together. We snatched dinners when we could and managed to get away one weekend. But when I returned, I had a new little patient who was hanging on by a thread. I was at the hospital day and night for a week. Darren understood his own dedication, but sometimes I don't think he understood or believed in mine. Whenever I mentioned I was interested in learning about neonatal units in other hospitals—which could involve traveling—he shut down the conversation completely."

She saw Grady's frown, but he didn't interrupt her. Now she just wanted to finish. "One morning, Darren told me he wanted to go to dinner with me that night and he'd made reservations. I explained I'd already made plans with Tessa. His reaction was over the top. He got angry, took me by the shoulders and shook me, telling me I was having dinner with him. I was so shocked, I couldn't say a word. Then he left, slamming the door behind him. As soon as his car sped out of the driveway, I packed my bags and moved in with Tessa. I swore off ever getting involved in a relationship again. I turned my back on dating and poured everything I had into my little patients."

After a long pause, Grady said gruffly, "But then you went to an open house."

Yes, she had. When she'd met Grady, she'd felt giddy and excited, forgetting everything that had gone before. "I really don't know what happened that night, Grady. My life was in gear again. I was happy…busy. I was living with two good friends and had everything I needed. I wasn't looking for—"

"For a roll on a denim couch? No, neither was I."

"Then…why me?"

"Have you ever looked at yourself in a mirror?" he asked wryly.

She felt heat suffuse her cheeks. "I'm sure there are lots of pretty women around here."

"You were more than pretty. You were smart. You

didn't try to make me notice you. We just started talking. Every time we ran into each other that evening, we talked some more. You were easy to understand. You knew how to listen. You didn't seem to like that crowd any more than I did. But I never expected what happened in my office to happen, either. That wasn't my motivation for asking you to go there. I mean, sure, I was thinking maybe I'd like to take you to dinner sometime. But whatever flared up between us caught us both by surprise. It was too hot to escape."

Just sitting here like this with Grady, she could feel the heat again. She could feel the buzz of electric attraction every time she looked at him, every time he touched her, every time they exchanged a word.

Now when he leaned closer to her, their chemistry together tempted her, enticed her, coaxed her to believe this man was different from all the others. His lips on hers were gentle until the heat took over once again. It consumed them both.

Grady's mouth was so sensually teasing. His arm was strong and muscled as it circled her. What was it about him that made her want to jump out of her own skin into his?

She hardly noticed when his hand slipped beneath the hem of her top. But she definitely noticed when she felt his callused fingers on her side. With a fleeting thought, she was so glad she wasn't wearing a bra so there was no impediment when his hand moved higher, when he cupped her breast and his thumb circled her nipple. She moaned and pressed into him, needing more, yet at the same time, she wanted to give more.

Grady's hand on her breast urged her to reach for

his shirt and pull its fabric from his jeans. The growl in his throat when she touched bare skin led her to fumble with his belt buckle. In no time she had it open along with his fly. Sliding her hand inside his briefs, she caressed him until he broke their kiss and held her face between his palms.

"Frannie!" His voice was deep and husky. "Do you know what you're doing?"

"The same thing you're doing," she returned, the sensual haze between them lifting a bit, though their breathing was still short and shallow.

"I don't want to take advantage of you."

Were her defenses down because of what she'd told him? Had his kiss been full of pity and compassion and she'd thought it had been more? How could she have just tumbled into this with him again?

She slid her hand away from the intimate contact. She let her defenses once again weave their fingers around her heart. Physically, as well as emotionally, she withdrew from him.

"Don't look at me like that," he protested.

"Like what?"

"Like you're sorry you told me anything."

Maybe she was. Because now she felt more vulnerable than she ever had before. Sometimes secrets were terrific insulation against the risk of loving and the pain when everything fell apart.

When she leaned away from him, his hands dropped from her face. She straightened her sweatshirt, took a deep breath and didn't look at him again until he asked, "You *are* sorry, aren't you?"

She wasn't getting into a revealing conversation again. Just because Grady was a good listener, just because there were sparks between them, didn't mean he really cared about her. He cared about his child, but that wasn't the same thing at all.

"Maybe I should go home now. Gina's picking me up tomorrow morning at seven-thirty."

"How are you going to get home from work?"

"I have several options. Don't worry about me, Grady. I'll be fine."

His gaze was penetrating as he studied her. He must have realized he couldn't persuade her to take more time off. Without embarrassment or awkwardness he zipped up his fly and rebuckled his jeans. "You have my number if you need it." The tightness in his tone was not lost on her.

She would call him if something happened that involved his child. Otherwise, she wouldn't be calling Grady until she went into labor.

As Francesca opened the front door of the old Victorian a half hour later, Grady was right behind her, carrying her suitcase. She was vitally aware of his physical presence. She had been since they'd almost made love in his living room.

Silently, he followed her inside. She went in, turning on lights as she went.

He stayed in the foyer. "Should I leave your suitcase here?" he called.

Seeing that everything on the first floor was still as it should be, taking in a breath of the old house and the light cinnamon scent of potpourri, she returned to the foyer. "Yes, just leave it there."

His brow furrowed. "I *could* carry it upstairs."

Yes, he could. But her dependence on him was over. "It's okay. Really."

He shoved his hands into his pockets.

Francesca knew she had to slice through the tension, but wasn't quite sure how to do it. "Thank you for inviting me to your house this week. The truth is—I've never had anyone look after me that way."

As he studied her, the lines around his mouth didn't cut quite so deep. "I guess that's why it was so hard for you to relax."

"I relaxed," she protested.

"When I wasn't around."

He really *was* on the mark. They couldn't seem to be around each other without generating…something—something that was incendiary and dangerous and she knew would eventually hurt them both. They had no basis for a relationship beyond their attraction and this pregnancy.

He added, "I'd still like you to let me know how you're doing, how you're feeling. Will you do that?"

"I will," she assured him, knowing now he really cared about her welfare.

He proved that again as he moved toward the door and asked, "Do you have food in the house?"

"Enough. I'll get some groceries tomorrow."

To his credit he didn't ask how she would get those groceries.

Her phone rang.

"You'd better get that," Grady said, and stepped outside.

"Thank you," she called after him.

But he just tipped his hat and strode to his truck.

Her phone rang again. As she closed the door, she turned to answer it. She swallowed around the lump in her throat. Was she upset because Grady was leaving?

She was startled to see Darren's number on the caller ID. Why would Darren Whitcomb be calling her at home?

Anxiety tapped at her chest as she picked up the phone and told herself there was nothing to be afraid of. She'd left Darren. It was over.

"Hi, Darren."

"Hi, yourself. I tried to call earlier. I heard about your accident and I wanted to know how you were."

Did he know about the baby, too? Probably. Hospital scuttlebutt was faster than Amtrak. What he didn't know was whose baby it was. No one had known that except for Tessa, Vince, Emily and Jared.

"It was kind of you to call, but I'm fine."

"I heard one of the nurses say you came in Friday to take care of the Vasquez baby, but that you weren't returning to your own house."

Why would Darren care if she was at her own house? "I stayed with…a friend. My physician thought that was better after the accident. One of my arms is in a cast for at least a month and I'm getting used to that."

"But you're coming back tomorrow?"

"I'm going to see how it goes."

"You're always the conscientious one, aren't you?"

His voice was too familiar, as if he knew her better than he did. "Aren't all doctors?"

"Not in the same way. You know that."

She kept silent, waiting for the reason for his call. They hadn't ended their relationship on friendly terms. He'd been angry she'd left. She'd just been so relieved to be away from someone who wanted to control her, someone like her father, that she hadn't cared if they remained friends or not. But they did work in the same hospital—although on different floors and without much direct contact—so they should take a stab at being civil. Was that what Darren was doing?

"I have a case I'd like to discuss with you, a young pregnant woman with tachycardia. Would you have time to have coffee with me sometime tomorrow?"

"Darren, why aren't you asking Dr. Saxby or Dr. Martin?"

"Because we work in the same hospital and I think it's time we get over what happened. There's no reason why we can't be friendly colleagues."

Francesca hated the fact that she was suspicious, but she didn't believe that Darren did anything without good motivation. What was his motivation for this? Or was she just being paranoid? Still, she wasn't a coward and if he wanted to have a face-to-face meeting she would do that, though it might be their last.

"I'll have to assess my day when I get in in the morning. Can I give you a call around nine?"

"Nine is fine. Then we can set up a time to meet."

If she set up a time to meet—

Her doorbell rang. Had Grady forgotten something? Her heart started an excited little patter.

"Is that your doorbell?" Darren asked. "It's getting late for visitors."

That was his "I know what's best for you" tone. She'd better get off the phone before she said something she shouldn't. "Yes, it is, so I'd better see *who* it is. I'll give you a call in the morning. Have a good rest of the night, Darren."

"I'll talk to you in the morning," he agreed, and hung up.

Francesca thought over the puzzling conversation as she went to her door, looked through the peephole and spotted Tessa standing on her stoop. Her arms were filled with two bags.

She called, "Let me in before I drop these."

Francesca laughed and opened the door. Tessa hurried to the kitchen and set the bags on the eat-in counter. "I thought you might need supplies. Or did Grady take you to the grocery store?"

"No. I was going to shop tomorrow."

Something in Francesca's voice must have alerted Tessa as to her distraction. "What's wrong?"

"What's wrong? You mean besides having an accident, gestational diabetes, being taken care of by Grady for almost a week, meeting his entire family and then getting a call from Darren?"

"Darren? What did *he* want?" Tessa started emptying the bags. She knew where everything went.

"I'm not sure. He says he wants to meet for coffee to talk about a case."

"But?"

"But he and Dr. Saxby have been colleagues longer

than he and I have. And Dr. Martin is back from vacation. Darren and I haven't spoken since I left him."

"Maybe he wants closure."

"Maybe."

After Tessa stowed milk in the refrigerator, she studied her friend. "So how did the week go?"

"I saw you on Friday."

"Yes, you did, but we couldn't talk with Grady there."

This was Tessa, her friend. She didn't have to watch her words or worry about their meaning. After she took a loaf of bread from one of the bags, she put it into the bread keeper. "He confuses me, Tessa. Everything that happened before and is happening now between us confuses me."

"Why?"

"Because there's too much feeling attached to the air when he's in the same room!"

Tessa laughed. "And that's a bad thing?"

"That's a bad thing if neither of us wants to be personally involved."

Tessa's eyes cut to Francesca's baby bulge. "I think you're beyond personally involved."

"You *know* what I mean. Beyond being parents together. I'm not even sure I want to do that. I'm not sure about anything except that I love this baby already and I only want to do what's best for him."

"That will probably mean having Grady in his life."

"I suppose so. It's just that we're so very different. You know what I came from. He's satisfied to be back in Sagebrush and doesn't want to live anywhere else. I've always wanted to see more of the world. Just because I have a child doesn't mean I can't do that." She paused, then added, "Tessa, I just… I don't trust him. I can't."

"You don't trust men in the generic sense. Grady is one man. One awfully rugged, handsome Texan, don't you think?"

Francesca groaned and dropped her face into her hands, with her elbows on the counter. "I don't believe in fairy tales, remember? So don't start weaving one."

"I think Vince and I, and Emily and Jared, have found our happily-ever-afters. Why don't you think *you* can?"

"Because there are too many obstacles to overcome, too many memories I'd have to wipe away, too many doubts that are always with me. No man would want to take them on. And Grady? I think he has walls of his own. Even with that terrific family of his."

"Do you know anything about his life before he settled in Sagebrush again?"

"Not much. Just that he was an investment banker in Chicago. His sister told me he was all set for a promotion and then something happened."

Francesca raised her gaze to Tessa's again. "He gave up that life and now he could really focus on raising a child. Maybe he's being nice to me just because of the baby. I have to be careful about that."

"You don't think he'd try and take physical custody away from you?"

Francesca's heart practically stopped at the thought and a chill crept up her spine. "You never know. I don't want to give him grounds. But I also want to live my life in a way that's best for me and the baby. I don't want to have to worry about his approval or disapproval."

Tessa crossed to her and put her arm around her. "You don't have to make all the heavy decisions tonight."

Francesca glanced sideways at her.

They both smiled. "No, I guess I don't," she said.

But she knew she was going to have to make major decisions…very soon.

Chapter Seven

Francesca sat across from Darren in the café at the Family Tree Health Center the following afternoon, comparing him to Grady in spite of herself.

Both were good-looking men, both had an air of confidence about them. But after that the comparisons ended. Darren's hair was cut short and neat. His curious gaze now even held some interest. She didn't want that interest.

They'd talked about one of his cases for a good fifteen minutes, but now he pushed the folder aside. She realized the conversation was going to shift to the personal when he said, "You're looking good."

"I'm feeling good. And if we're finished talking about your case, I really have to be going."

"Important date in the middle of the afternoon?"

He'd tried to keep the question light, but there was

an edge behind it. She'd learned how to read that edge. It took root in the fact that he wasn't in control and he didn't like it.

"If by a date you mean an appointment, yes, I'm going to look at day-care facilities."

"With the baby's father?"

She could shoot back that that information was none of his business, but she kept her tone neutral. "No, with a friend." She pushed back her chair.

"Tessa Rossi?"

As she stood, she felt defensive and she replied bluntly, "Darren, it's really not your concern."

He acted nonchalant. "Just trying to make friendly conversation."

She thought about all the friendly conversations they'd indulged in at the beginning of their relationship...even the first month she'd moved in with him. But then friendly had transformed into these questions with the edge underneath. He'd been suspicious of where she'd gone, what she'd done and with whom she'd done it. Their comingling lives had become about *his* schedule, *his* cases, *his* upward climb at the hospital, *his* likes and dislikes from movies to restaurants. She'd found she was losing herself. Finally when he'd laid his hands on her in anger, the scared little girl inside her had pushed out of her closet and run for dear life.

Suddenly Darren seemed to realize he'd reverted to an old pattern. "I just want to know how you are, Francesca. When I heard you were in an accident, I was worried. Just because we split up doesn't mean I stopped caring."

When Darren was his charming self, he *always* wanted something. She didn't know what he wanted now, but she wasn't going to wait around to find out.

"Thank you for your concern, but I'm fine, really. And I have to be going."

With another forced smile, she rose and headed past the ledge lined with pothos ivy and a bird-of-paradise potted plant…out of the café. She was escaping again. She knew that. But wasn't that the best route to take?

At the doorway she turned left and practically ran headlong into Gina Rigoletti. "Gina, I'm sorry. I was distracted."

"You *look* distracted. Actually, I was searching you out. Somebody told me you'd come down here. I wanted to make sure Emily was still picking you up and you didn't need a ride home."

"She's still picking me up."

Gina studied her. "Are you okay? You look a little pale."

Everybody was asking her if she was okay. She appreciated their concern and their kindness, but all of it was becoming a little unsettling. So she told the truth. "I just had a consultation with Darren Whitcomb about a patient. But he and I were involved once and it was a little unnerving."

The two women had started walking along the sunny yellow walls. Gina stopped in a small alcove with two leather chairs that looked out a plate-glass window over the grounds. "Even the thought of exes can be unnerving," she said solemnly.

Francesca gave her a questioning glance. She knew

Gina had moved back to Sagebrush not so long ago, and she was staying with her parents.

"Do you have a few minutes?" Gina asked.

"I have about fifteen unless I'm paged."

That morning Gina had seemed distracted on their drive to Family Tree, but Francesca hadn't asked questions. They'd had several conversations and were becoming friends, but she didn't want to poke into private areas.

Francesca took a good look at Gina now. She was a beautiful young woman with black curly hair. Head of the baby development center, she was an expert in her field and mostly spent her time working with children who were developing more slowly than they should be.

Gina looked hesitant now. "I wondered—are you looking for a housemate? I just love your Victorian house. I know you had housemates who moved out."

"I didn't think anyone would want to live with a new mother and an infant!"

"I work with infants and toddlers. I love them. I wouldn't mind that at all."

"Even the interrupted sleep?"

Gina laughed. "Well, let's just say my dad snores and my mom has insomnia. My sleep has been interrupted since I returned to Sagebrush."

Francesca liked Gina. She also missed Tessa and Emily.

"I'd understand if you need to think about it—" Gina ventured.

Instinct made the decision. "I don't need to think about it. When would you like to move in?"

A grin broke across Gina's face. "I brought up the

subject with Mom last week about finding my own place. She and Dad would really like me to stay through the holidays. So why don't we say the first week in January?"

"That sounds great." Francesca checked her watch. "I think my fifteen minutes are up. We can talk about this more tomorrow."

The unexpected happened more often than not. As she and Gina went their separate ways, the possibility of finding a new friend in Gina made her smile. She'd have to introduce her to Tessa and Emily.

On Friday afternoon, Francesca waved to Tessa as she drove away from Laurie's duplex. Grady's sister had phoned her and asked if she'd be interested in baby furniture her kids no longer needed. Francesca had told her she'd stop by after a doctor's appointment with the endocrinologist Tessa had driven her to. Laurie had offered to drive her home.

Francesca hated depending on others. But that concern was miniscule compared with what the diabetes specialist had reminded her of. Gestational diabetes could lead to premature delivery or an overly large baby. She had to take care of herself down to the letter. More exercise for one thing. She was going shopping for a treadmill tonight even if she had to do it online!

To her surprise, before she could even ring the doorbell, a truck pulled up to the curb. It was Grady's!

She waited to push the bell. As he approached, she asked, "What are you doing here?"

"Laurie called me. She thought you might need someone to lift and carry."

Was his sister playing matchmaker? Had Grady told Laurie that Francesca might push him out of her life?

Instead of ringing the bell or opening the door, he commented, "I heard you were visiting day-care centers."

"You heard? How?"

"Sagebrush is a small town. One of my customers saw you going into Wee Care Day Care."

"And he or she ran back and told you? How did they even know you were the father?"

"I'm not keeping it a secret. Are you?"

"No, but I've always kept my private life private. I don't put it onstage for the whole world to see."

And they both knew why that was. She'd learned the lesson well from her mother.

"Frannie, my customers have been my customers for years. Many of them are friends."

Whenever he used her name like that she felt all warm and melty inside. Then she thought about her conversation with Darren on Monday and how their relationship had ended so differently than it had begun. Why would she think Grady would be any different? Wasn't he demanding some sort of control now?

"Did anyone also tell you I went to Little People's Day Care and Rainbow Day Care in Lubbock, too?"

He frowned. "No. Why so many? Why any at all? If we had talked about this I could have told you—" He stopped when he saw her expression. "What?"

"I scouted out facilities because I knew they might have waiting lists, and they did. Do you expect me to discuss my every step with you?" She knew she sounded defensive. She knew she might even be picking a fight.

But she didn't want to feel trapped, or watched over and especially not controlled.

Grady gently took her by the shoulders and looked into her eyes. "Whoa. I don't know what you're thinking, but I suspect it isn't good. If you had told me, I could have mentioned that Laurie knows the woman who runs Rainbow Day Care in Lubbock. She has great credentials. But she doesn't take on babies until they're at least six months old."

"I know. That's why I'm also looking at other options. Vince and Tessa's housekeeper/nanny, Mrs. Zappa, is wonderful. Vince found her through a service. I was thinking of maybe going that route." The heat from Grady's hands warmed her through and through. Maybe he didn't want control. Maybe he just needed to be involved.

"I have another suggestion." His face wasn't very far from hers. "My mother said she'd consider minding our baby if you went back to work."

Francesca didn't know what to say to that. Grady's intense blue eyes staring into hers stirred up deep emotions, and she still didn't know why.

"Taking care of a baby would tie her down," she murmured.

"I don't think she'd care—she offered. But you can talk to her yourself about it if you're interested."

Was she interested? Did she want to become even more entangled with Grady's family?

"I know what you're thinking. You don't know if you want me or my family in your life."

She'd never thought she was so obvious. But with Grady— He saw behind the walls and the excuses.

"We can't act as if we're a couple, because we're not," she protested, leaning away.

He released her shoulders and stepped back. "No, we're not. And I can see your point. But if you want to go back to work, you have to find someone you can trust."

"I want to think about it."

"That's fair." He put his hand on the doorknob.

Impulsively, she clasped his arm. "Grady…I told you about my background and it wasn't easy. At some point I'd like you to tell me about yours."

He dropped his hand to his side. "You already know how I grew up."

"I do. But I don't know other things. Were you involved in serious relationships? If you want to be a dad, why haven't you ever married?"

He tipped down the front brim of his Stetson and she knew what that meant. He was uncomfortable and would rather not talk about it. He hedged. "This isn't the time or place."

"Will there *be* a time and place?" she asked quietly.

"We'll see."

Yes, they *would* see. Because she wouldn't let it go. She felt transparent with him, as if she'd given a lot more than he had. She needed to know Grady's romantic history. She needed to know what had kept him from becoming a family man before now.

"Did you ask her?" Laurie targeted her brother.

"No, I thought I'd let you do that."

Laurie lived in a town house. As soon as Francesca and Grady had walked inside, she'd thrown her question at him.

Seth, Laurie's three-year-old, came running toward Grady full-bore and wrapped his arms around Grady's knees. "Uncle Grady! Uncle Grady! Let's play horsey."

He picked up his nephew and held him high in his arms. "Just a minute, cowboy. I might have to do some talking first."

The little boy wrinkled his nose at him, gave him a kiss on the cheek and then squiggled in his arms to be let down.

Francesca had to smile despite the trepidation. The talking would likely cover his mother babysitting. Maybe both he and Laurie were going to try to convince her.

"Grady told me your mother offered to babysit," she said to Laurie, wanting to be up-front.

"Oh, he did? Well, I guess Mom's disappointed because I decided to stay home with Mark and Seth until they're both in school. Jenna did the same with Marly. I think Mom would have liked to have her own family day-care center."

Laurie glanced toward Seth, who was occupied in one corner of the living room with LEGOs. "No, this isn't about babysitting. I have some baby clothes besides the crib, play saucer and swing. The kids were in and out of them before I hardly had a chance to wash them. They grow so fast."

Francesca had to start thinking about saving for a college fund, and she still had school loans to repay. Everything would change with this baby, especially if she took time off. She'd saved money wisely over the past few years, but that wouldn't last forever.

"Yes, I'm interested. I'd love to see what you have."

"The crib, the saucer and the swing are in the shed out back. They should fit in Grady's truck if you want to take them along."

"I'd like to pay you for them."

"Absolutely not. When you're finished with them, maybe you can find someone else who can use them. If not, I'm sure I can. As long as they're in good condition, we'll just keep passing them on."

"I like that idea."

Laurie motioned to her to come sit on the sofa. "Do you have time to look through the clothes and see what you want and what you don't?"

Francesca's eyes met Grady's. He shrugged. "I have time."

Making time for what he felt was important seemed to be easy for him. Would he do that for his son?

"Those are deep thoughts," Grady said when she hadn't spoken for a few moments.

"Not so deep." She ducked her head to the box and opened the flaps. But Grady wasn't going to let her get away with that.

"We'll talk later."

That was either a promise or a warning.

A small smile played on Laurie's lips as she took in their interchange and opened a second box.

While Grady let Seth climb on his back to play horsey, Laurie went through the clothes with Francesca. She looked through terry cloth play sets, footed pajamas, even a winter bunting that would be just right for the time when her baby would be born. She held up a little shirt decorated with a helicopter and the blue jeans to go with it.

"Not only does Mom like to babysit, she likes to buy baby clothes. I thought I'd warn you before the baby's born, because she'll have a few gifts," Laurie said.

Francesca was absolutely amazed by the generosity of this family. The way they thought about each other and others, the way they worked together, was a stark contrast to her parents and their attitudes and what they'd had and didn't have. "Your family amazes me."

"Because of our sheer numbers?"

Francesca laughed. "Yes, but…also just by who they are. I didn't have a lot growing up, and my mother didn't reach out to others very much. So your generosity just kind of bemuses me."

"*You're* generous."

"Excuse me?"

"You are. Look at the field you've gone into—saving newborn lives."

Francesca ran her fingers over the embroidered duck on an infant shirt. "There's something about a baby that makes the rest of the world good again. I have to do whatever I can."

"I think Grady's afraid to believe you are what you seem," Laurie confided in almost a whisper.

Francesca kept her voice low under little Seth's laughter. "Why?"

"He'll have to tell you that. He's a good guy, Francesca. Being a guy, he can be a little arrogant and patronizing and impatient sometimes. But he's a good guy."

He'd been patient with her. But the uncertainty of visitation rights loomed. Were they the reason he was putting his best foot forward?

That same question continued to nag Francesca an hour later as she stood in the guest room that she'd chosen for the nursery and waited for Grady to bring up the crib.

When he carried it into the room, he stopped and met her gaze. Her breathing came faster. An electric charge filled the air.

"Are you going to leave the walls yellow?" he asked, trying to make conversation.

"I thought I would. I could hang little boy decorations on them."

He chuckled. "You mean like baseballs and footballs?"

"I have some photos of horses and a few catalogs with more ideas. I just haven't gotten serious about decorating yet."

He let that comment hang in the air as he propped the crib against the wall, then went to the tool belt he'd brought up earlier that was lying in the corner.

"Can I help?"

He took a Phillips screwdriver and a wrench from the belt and then approached her. "You can hold on to these. I'll need them once I open up the crib."

She took the tools from him, their fingertips grazing. Her breath caught and maybe so did his, because he froze for a few seconds and then moved quickly away.

Ten minutes later the crib was angled in a shadowed

corner of the room. Francesca stood by, ready with a set of pale blue sheets and a navy-and-white spread. Grady lifted the mattress from its position against one wall and plopped it into the crib. Francesca shook out the cotton sheet.

He watched as she fitted it on the mattress. But she had trouble with the fourth corner.

Without a word, Grady rounded the crib to stand beside her, took hold of the material and yanked it into place. The side of his body was practically smack against hers. She could feel his heat, his muscled tautness as he straightened and didn't step away. She held her breath.

"It's hard to believe that in a few months our baby will be sleeping in this crib." His voice was rough and she could tell the thought affected him deeply.

"Sometimes it doesn't seem real to me, either. But then I just put my hand on my tummy. I'm connected to this little person in a way I've never felt connected before. I feel as if the future has opened up in front of me. Each step will be a new adventure."

"Sometimes I can feel your joy," he surprised her by saying. "It just radiates from you."

She wasn't aware of that. She just knew that at moments she was completely happy and content. Maybe that's what Grady could feel.

He was facing her now. When his arms came around her, she automatically slipped her arms around him. No matter what her doubts were, they were sharing this adventure. This baby was his, too, and she was realizing more each day that she couldn't cut him out of her life.

Standing with her like that, he gave her a slow smile. "The baby's getting bigger."

She felt her cheeks heat. "So am I."

"Not really." He ran his hands slowly up and down her back, sending shivers up her spine. "Your breasts are fuller."

"Grady—"

"Well, they are. I notice things like that, especially since I remember exactly how they looked before."

"Stop," she protested softly.

"Why? It's not as if we haven't been intimate."

Physically. But how connected were they emotionally? She pondered the question. Yet as Grady's head bent to her and his strong arms grew a little tighter, as she leaned into him more, letting their baby press into him, she knew she was becoming connected emotionally to a man—really connected—maybe for the first time in her adult life.

That realization careened against the walls around her heart. Yet fear hardly had a chance to start because when Grady's mouth captured hers, she felt something much different. Something more than a simple connection. One that could lead only to heartache.

Yet didn't she deserve something more than fear and separation? Didn't she deserve to see a dream in the distance and hope one day she'd find the right road to lead her there?

Grady's hands slid from her back to her waist. He grasped handfuls of her maternity top and lifted it until he felt her skin. She wanted to feel his, too, yet—

What if this attraction was only that for him—an

attraction? What if physical satisfaction was all he was seeking? What if this was simply a means to keep her and the baby close? Did she dare take a chance?

He must have felt her hesitation because his hands dropped away from her midriff…and the baby. His tongue stopped probing and his lips clung only a second before they separated from hers.

He gave them both a few moments to cool down and then he asked, "What are you thinking about?"

"Why you came back to Sagebrush. I also want to know why sometimes you mistrust me almost as much as I mistrust you."

"Maybe you want to know too much," he replied tersely.

"Maybe. Or maybe I have the right to know who the father of my baby really is."

Grady began to unpack the play saucer.

Francesca felt as if the road to her dream had just grown much longer.

Chapter Eight

"That's the last box," Grady said fifteen minutes later as he plopped it on the floor.

Looking up, he was surprised to see Francesca hanging framed photographs of horses on nails she must have hammered in. When she turned, he felt that sucker punch that was becoming all too familiar. Her eyes had the power to do that to him and he didn't like it. He liked it about as much as the personal questions she'd been asking.

"Did you take those?" he asked. "In fact…" He studied the photographs more carefully. "Aren't they Vince's horses?"

"I have a digital camera. It doesn't take a genius to do something like this now. I sent them to be printed in eight-by-tens, found mats and frames and here they are."

"So you were serious about the horses?"

"I'm living in Texas now. Why wouldn't I be serious about horses?"

Maybe he had hoped for a different answer. Maybe he had hoped *his* horses and *his* ranch had something to do with it, because their son would be spending time there.

She was studying him, and he didn't want her to skip from one realization to another. "You need a rocking chair."

"Actually I found one at a yard sale two months ago. Tessa knew someone who refinished furniture and I've been using it in my bedroom. I guess I just wasn't ready to put this room together yet. But now I think my nesting instincts are kicking in. I'll have to buy a chest and a changing table, diapers and bottles, stroller and car carrier. Goodness. I guess I'd better get started."

Now he remembered a rocker in her room. He hadn't paid attention to the furnishings when gathering her clothes for the stay at his place. "Maybe Santa will bring some of the things you need."

"I've never written a letter to Santa."

"Are you serious?"

"I never thought he could give me what I needed. I wasn't interested in toys. I was interested in a real home."

Francesca seemed to be as genuine as a woman got. He was finally learning about the feelings and fears and the hell she'd been through as a child. "Why don't I go get that chair? You can decide where you want it."

"My room's a mess. I wasn't planning on a visitor."

He just touched his hand to the side of his hat as if to say, "That doesn't matter," and headed for the Wedgwood blue-and-white room.

He stood in the doorway this time, having more than a few minutes to take it in. She'd told him she'd brought her furniture from Oklahoma. It was plain, with straight lines and a beautiful wood grain. The room might seem like a mess to her, but it just showed him the evidence that she lived here. Sweatpants and a T-shirt lay over a corner of the bed, running shoes at its foot. The bed *was* made, however. The dresser held a jewelry box, a mirror and a framed photo of an older woman he presumed was Francesca's mother. Other than that it was uncluttered. The white ceramic lamps and white trim around the doors and baseboard lent a pristine aura to the space.

He spotted the rocking chair over by the window. Unlike the rest of the furniture, it was a bit more decorative, with its tall, rounded back and staves for support leading from the top down to the seat. The arms were solid wood and sturdy with spokes leading to the seat also. The planks on the seat were molded in such a way that they looked almost comfortable rather than stiff and unforgiving. The rockers were large and would give good motion. It was an interesting chair, as interesting as the woman who had chosen it.

He lifted it, carrying it to the nursery. He had to decide which of the rooms in his house he would turn into a nursery. Did he want Francesca's input or would he rather do it on his own? He might keep the horse theme, but in a more primitive way. Liam was great at drawing. Maybe he could paint a little cowboy with a rope on one wall and a horse on the other. The more Grady thought about it, the more he liked it.

Bringing the chair into the nursery, he set it by Francesca, who was standing at the window, staring out into the yard. "We'll have to look at swing sets. They have baby seats now that that you can attach to them."

"And a jungle gym for when he's older. Boys like to climb and explore."

She turned. "Girls don't?"

"Oh, no. I'm not stepping into that one!" He examined the room with a critical eye. "Where are you going to find a chest and a changing table?"

"I'm not sure, but I still have time."

They gazed at each other, more quiet than they'd been since she'd asked him her questions.

"I could use something to drink. Got anything in the refrigerator?" he asked.

"Sure. Soda, juice, beer for when Vince visits and wine for Jared."

"A bottle of beer sounds good."

She looked around the room again and smiled. "I'll have to write your sister a thank-you note. This has really helped me get started."

"You don't have to write her a note. Everybody's coming to the ranch this Sunday. I'm going to play Santa. You're welcome to join us. You can thank her then."

"I don't know, Grady. I often work Sundays."

He knew when Francesca was going full tilt she might work seven days a week. "You can't get away for a few hours?"

"Let's see what the weekend brings."

Did she want to see what the weekend brought or did she want to see how much he'd give of himself? He hated talking about the past, and especially about what had happened with Susan, because he felt like such a fool.

A short while later they'd gone downstairs. Francesca poured herself a glass of milk and brought him a longneck beer. They sat on the sofa, silent at first, and awkward together in that silence. They'd been intimate, but not really. They were friendly, but were they really friends? She kept her guard up with him and his past few years of not wanting to get involved with anyone kept him from becoming involved with her. At least in a real way.

He knew why *she* was hesitant. She'd had a rough road. He guessed the worst part of it was that she didn't trust her own judgment now. She was sharing more and he wasn't. The least he could do was to be as forthright with her as she'd been with him.

He didn't know how to start, so he just jumped in. "You asked why I'm not married."

She didn't say anything, just gazed at his face and listened. Her complete attention did something to him. It loosened words that had been stuck in the back of his mind.

"When I went to Chicago, I decided I wanted a life outside of Sagebrush. I'd grown up here. I wanted to make my mark in a big city…see more of the world. And I did. Or at least I'd started to. I was willing to travel and it helped me move up in the firm. I saw Hong Kong, Amsterdam, Geneva, Paris and even New Delhi. A colleague and I started an affair. I thought it was going somewhere. I thought it would lead to marriage and children and a life in Chicago, different from the one I'd seen in Sagebrush, but with the same family values."

"And she shared your values?"

"Well, that's the thing. I thought she did. I thought everyone looked at marriage the way I did, the way my parents did, the way my sister and brothers did. But then the opportunity for a promotion came up and we were both in line for it."

"It's hard to compete with someone you love," Francesca said with understanding.

"I think we could have handled the competition. *I* could have handled the competition. But apparently she felt she needed an edge. She slept with our boss to get the promotion."

"Grady, I'm so sorry." After a pause she asked, "Did she get the promotion?"

"Yes, she got it. The worst part of it was she didn't think she'd done anything wrong. Afterward she told me sleeping with him was just part of the game. It didn't mean anything. I remembered all of the nights we'd spent together and wondered how much *they'd* meant to her."

"How did you find out she'd slept with him?"

"One of my 'friends' told me. He'd seen them together in the boss's office late one night. I didn't want to believe it. I asked her why she'd been there that late, and she admitted that's how she'd gotten the promotion. She didn't just sleep with him once, either. They met at a hotel two or three times, nights I thought she was out with friends or working late."

"You must have felt so betrayed by both of them."

"Betrayed...deceived...used. So I confronted him. As long as that was the way he did his business, I was quitting. The whole thing left such a bad taste in my mouth, I came back here. After I licked my wounds for a few weeks, I decided Sagebrush was where I belonged. I missed my family. I missed the ranch. I missed loyalty, honesty and forthrightness."

"But you lost your ability to trust a woman."

"I absolutely didn't understand how she could say she loved me in one breath, then tell me she slept with a man to get ahead in the other. Those two concepts just don't work side by side. That's when I realized our values were very different."

Francesca was studying him curiously.

"What?"

"But there must have been good parts. Do you ever miss your life in Chicago?"

"People talk about the advantages of big city life, the cultural events, the stores, the employment opportunities. But I don't see it that way. I can find anything I want in Sagebrush. Just give me a good horse, a loyal dog, work I like and my family around me and I'm satisfied."

Francesca bowed her head and looked down at her hands in her lap. She picked up her glass of milk, took a few sips and then set it back on the coffee table on the coaster. "Do you believe what I tell you?" she asked.

"I try to. I try to give you the benefit of the doubt. But the truth is, Frannie, I half expect you'll take our child, move to Timbuktu and I'd never see you again."

He noticed she didn't say she wouldn't do that. The hell of it was, he understood why. If he turned out to be an SOB like her father or like this Darren character, she'd be off without a second thought.

When she turned toward him, her glossy hair fell over her shoulder. He thought about the times his hand had slid into it so easily. The whiff of a clean, spicy floral shampoo scent came with it, and he realized she got to him in a way Susan never could.

Her gaze was wide with doubts as she asked, "Do you really want me to come on Sunday?"

He loved playing Santa for his nieces and nephews. He wanted Francesca to be comfortable with him at the ranch so she'd bring their baby there often. He didn't want her to lock him out of her life. "Yes, I want you there."

She took a deep breath and let it out, as if this was a major decision for her. "All right. I'll make sure I'm not needed at the hospital on Sunday. I'll see if I can arrange it so I can stop in for a while."

"One of my family can pick you up."

He intended to make Sunday convenient for her. But those doubts were back in her eyes. She didn't know what his family would mean to their child. She didn't know if his family would be more than she could handle.

He was going to have to warn them all to back off. But that could be a hopeless cause.

"Ho, ho, ho!"

Francesca had been standing at the dining-room table at the ranch arranging food for the gathering. Patrick Fitzgerald had opened the front door to his son. All of the children ran toward him, including John's nine- and ten-year-olds. But little Seth, who came running through the dining room at full tilt, tripped and fell.

When he began crying, she realized his mom had gone to the guest-room closet for more napkins. Francesca rushed to him and hugged him. "It's okay. I don't think you're hurt, are you?"

The little boy shook his head. "I want to see Santa."

Francesca stood with Seth's hand in hers and guided him through the living room to the foyer where all the children were gathered with Grady. He was busy shaking hands with the older kids, patting the little ones on the head. But when he spotted Francesca with Seth, his gaze held hers. The intensity of his focus seared a path right down to her toes. She wondered if they could ever just be in the same room together without producing enough electricity to light up his tall Christmas tree.

She stepped forward a little. "Seth wanted to say hello to Santa. I think he was afraid he wouldn't get here in time."

Grady tried to smile under his Santa beard. "Not in time?" His voice was an octave lower than it usually was. "All the children are in time. Let's go into the living room and see what Santa has in his bag."

On the floor behind him sat a huge red bag with drawstrings. In it, he'd loaded candy canes, oranges, bags of gummy bears and puzzles. As Grady ho, ho, hoed his way to the living room with the bag, the adults laughed and followed, too.

Except for Maureen, who sidled up next to Francesca. "I think you're going to make a really good mom."

Surprised by the certainty in Maureen Fitzgerald's voice, Francesca asked, "Why do you think that?"

"Because you didn't hesitate to comfort Seth."

Francesca knew she was good with babies, and she loved kids. But would she make the right choices for her own child? Her mother had gotten trapped in a bad situation because of the decisions she'd made.

"You look troubled," Grady's mother noticed.

They were ten feet away from the fray, children gathered around Grady, parents keeping them corralled, excitement and laughter and Christmas spirit tumbling out of everyone. Francesca didn't have older women in her life to confide in, wise women who knew from experience about heartaches and difficult times. She wondered if Maureen did.

"I'm thinking about my own mother."

"You said she passed on a few years ago?"

"You remembered."

"You and Grady are having a child together, Francesca. I want to get to know you." She glanced at her husband, who was steadying the big red bag so Grady could pull out the treats. "I believe Grady will make a good father because Patrick was a good role model."

"That's my worry," Francesca confessed. "My mother was fearful of many things, my dad the main one. We left him when I was a child. She never learned to be her own person. She never learned to make forward-looking decisions or to take control of her own life."

"You have control of *your* life."

"I'm not so sure about that. My hours are erratic, so in a way I don't have control there, especially when emergencies crop up. And they often do with newborns in peril. Then there's the pregnancy, which I thought I had control over, but the diabetes put a wrench in that."

The older woman's eyes were kind. "You don't need control to make the right decisions. Maybe the best time of life is when fate is tumbling us around and we still manage to get up again."

"I can see why your children are so successful at whatever they do."

"And I can see why *you're* successful. It's the spirit within us that makes us who we are…and what we believe. You're a strong woman, Francesca. I was a little worried when I heard about your career. How would you shuffle responsibilities to deal with pregnancy and the time-demanding schedule of a newborn? But I think you'll figure it out."

"Grady told me about Susan."

Maureen looked surprised. "He did? Well, then, I guess you know it's hard for him to trust. She betrayed him on many levels and I don't know if he'll ever get over that."

That's exactly what Francesca had thought. "This baby is more important than my career."

"Have you told Grady that?"

"I haven't really had the chance. He thinks my career is all I can see ahead of me. It *is* important. It will give this baby a future. That's why I have to figure out a way to juggle it. So I don't lose it."

Maureen patted Francesca's arm. "I think you'll do fine."

Francesca realized the woman's support meant a lot. Because she was a calm wise voice or because she was Grady's mother?

The children were happily playing with their puzzles

when Santa gathered up his empty bag, tossed them a few more ho, ho, hoes and left the house. Francesca knew Grady would be changing back into his regular clothes in the barn. She slipped out a few minutes after he left and ran to the small side entrance. He'd dressed in the tack room.

When she opened the door and went inside, she saw he was still dressed. "Don't you want to stop being Santa yet?"

He turned to face her. "Actually, I was just imagining playing Santa with our son. Next year at this time, he'll probably be grabbing at my beard and yanking on my belt. The toys won't mean much, but the fantasy will start for him."

"I was thinking of next year, too. I guess…I guess we'll be sharing custody."

"Will we?" he asked soberly.

"Is that what you want?"

"I want what's best for all of us. I don't want you to feel cheated and I don't want to feel as if I'm missing out."

"How do we prevent either?"

"I'm not sure yet." Suddenly his mood changed from serious to jovial. He plopped into a wooden chair, grabbed her hand and pulled her onto his lap.

Laughing, she asked, "What are you doing?"

"I'm playing Santa Claus. What do you want for Christmas? And don't tell me a baby in perfect health. That's a given. I'm talking about your Christmas list. What's on it?"

A baby in perfect health. She hadn't told Grady their son could be premature or have other problems. But why alarm him? Why not just hope for the best outcome?

She could tell underneath Grady's laughter he was serious and she thought about his question for a few moments. "What I need most is a desk for my computer. I'll be working at home more after the baby's born and it would be nice to set up a little corner for myself. I can stay in touch with the hospital, receive updates on my patients and know exactly what's going on."

"You want a computer desk? Not a diamond necklace? Or a gold bracelet? Or a new designer purse?"

Leaning against Grady, she gazed into his eyes. Maybe he was unrecognizable in the Santa outfit, but she'd know those eyes anywhere. "Nope, just the desk."

"So you think you'll be working at home more?"

"I've been considering it…doing consultations more than hands-on practice. I don't know what I can arrange and how I'll handle it financially. I need to keep my foot in the water, professionally speaking, and yet I want to spend as much time as I can with my baby…our baby."

His arms around her held her a little tighter and she found she didn't feel trapped. She felt ready for Grady to kiss her again…with or without the fake beard.

Instead of kissing her, though, he said, "I have a solution to your problem."

"What?" she asked warily.

"Move in with me. If you're living with me, we'll both have access to our child and I could provide some of the child care you need, though we might want to have someone come in and help. You also wouldn't have to worry about a roof over your head."

"I'd have to pay my fair share."

"We could work it out."

Could they work it out? Was it what she wanted? Living with the father of her child? Did she dream of more?

No. She couldn't believe in dreams. Not when their child's welfare was at stake. She liked her independence. She liked living in the Victorian. She had been planning to share the big house with Gina.

Living with Grady. Should she even consider it?

"You can't keep this baby to yourself," he reminded her.

"No, I can't, but I do have to live my own life, Grady. I don't know if I can do that if I'm staying with you."

He didn't look as if he accepted that reasoning. The easy humor between them evaporated, and as gracefully as she could, she scrambled off his lap. "We've got to get back to the house or everyone will wonder where we've gone."

"I wonder that myself sometimes." His tone was acerbic and Francesca suspected he usually got his own way.

Not this time.

Chapter Nine

"Aren't you going in?" Tessa asked, a twinkle in her blue eyes.

With Christmas fast approaching in nine days, Tessa, Emily and Francesca had decided to go Christmas shopping Wednesday evening. Emily had met Francesca and Tessa at the Yellow Rose Diner for supper and then they'd proceeded to wander in and out of the specialty shops. Francesca had already found Grady a Christmas present online that she hoped would please him.

Now the three of them were standing in front of his saddle shop.

"He asked you to live with him," Emily reminded her. "The least you could do is stop in and say hello." Her voice wasn't as much scolding as it was teasing.

Francesca had told her friends what Grady had suggested. They'd both remained neutral on the subject. "What are you two going to do if I do stop in?"

Tessa pointed to a bookstore. "I need books for the kids and a biography Vince is interested in."

"If you finish first, come find us," Emily suggested. "If we finish, we'll come find you."

Francesca hadn't spoken to Grady since his family gathering on Sunday. The atmosphere between them had been strained as he'd driven her home. She knew why. He wanted access to his child and inviting her to live with him was the best way to get it.

"I won't be long," she assured them.

"I can spend hours in a bookstore," Tessa said. "So don't hurry on my account."

"Same here," Emily agreed.

After encouraging looks, they headed off across the street.

Francesca composed herself, attempting to appear placid, and opened the door to Grady's shop. Maybe he wouldn't be working tonight. If that was the case, seeing him was a moot point. Yet she realized she wanted to see him and that fact bothered her, too.

The bell over the door jangled as she stepped inside. She hadn't been in the front of the shop before. It was quaintly attractive with saddles on pedestals. Shelves displayed leather goods—from bridles to key chains braided with horsehair to a display of Navajo blankets. No one stood at the counter and cash register to the rear of the display area, but Francesca heard voices not far away—a man's and a woman's. She realized there was a small room off the front area of the shop and didn't know whether to venture into it or not.

Instead, she called, "Hello."

Grady emerged from the small room with what looked like a sample catalog in his hand. "Francesca! What are you doing here?"

A pretty, young woman with strawberry-blond hair, freckles on her nose and a Stetson with a chin tie followed him. She was holding a bridle.

Francesca didn't have a chance to answer his question before he added, "I'll be with you in a minute. I have to add a few things to Cassidy's order."

When Cassidy peered at Francesca inquiringly, Grady introduced them. "Francesca Talbot, Cassidy Dugas. Cassidy, Francesca."

"It's nice to meet you," Cassidy said, then turned back to Grady. "You'll have everything ready by the end of January?"

"At the latest," he assured her. "You want the saddle for your brother's birthday."

There was a note of familiarity in Grady's voice that told Francesca Cassidy Dugas was more than a customer. When Cassidy replied, she was sure of it.

"I want to surprise Jesse, so if he comes in, don't give anything away."

"I wouldn't do that."

Cassidy took some bills from her purse. "How much do you need for the down payment?"

"I usually require half."

The pretty woman's face fell. "I only have a third. I can give you the rest next week when I get paid."

"That's fine." He winked at her. "I know where you live. I can always confiscate that wagon I like so much."

She laughed, and in that laugh Francesca knew they'd been close at one time. She felt deep disappointment in her chest. Maybe it wasn't disappointment. Maybe it was something else she didn't even want to think about.

"I told you, if Jesse ever wants to sell that wagon I'll let you know." Cassidy gave him a smile that was feminine and teasing.

After Grady took her money, he rang up her down payment.

Cassidy waited for the receipt, glanced at Francesca, gave her a nod and then left the shop.

Off-balance at the interplay between Grady and Cassidy Dugas, Francesca stepped up to the counter. She said, "I could have come back later."

Grady didn't comment, but came around the counter. "Have you been doing some Christmas shopping?"

"With Tessa and Emily. They're over at the bookstore."

"And you stopped in to—"

"I stopped in to be…friendly, that's all. But I didn't know I was going to interrupt something."

"You didn't interrupt anything."

She knew what she'd seen hadn't simply been a shop owner and customer relationship. "Did you date her?"

"If I had, would you be jealous?" His eyes twinkled and he tried to keep from smiling.

When she didn't respond, just stood there, purse in hand, he shrugged. "I dated Cassidy a few years ago. Her brother and I were in school together. We went to the movies a few times and then to Lubbock for dinner.

But it didn't go anywhere. She's a wonderful woman, but I couldn't forget about Susan. And Cassidy wasn't…she doesn't sleep around." He crossed his arms over his chest. "I answered your question, now you answer mine."

"Of course I'm not jealous," she blurted out. "Why *would* I be?"

He took the purse from her arm and set it on the counter. Then he laid his hand on her belly, which was getting rounder by the day. "Because I'm the father of your baby. Because, whether you'll admit it or not, you like me just a little."

She finally had to admit to herself she liked Grady a whole lot. If she liked him any more…

She'd be falling in love with him.

No. She would *not* let that happen. She was not opening herself to getting hurt. Dreams like that were as wispy as the morning fog.

Coming closer to her, he clasped her shoulders. "Sometimes, Frannie, you can't hide everything you're feeling."

When he bent his head, she thought about pulling away. She knew she should. Every time he kissed her, their physical attraction blossomed. But the thought of being held in Grady's arms was too tempting to resist. Sometimes she hated being alone. Sometimes she longed for a bond that would last a lifetime. Was that a dream? She hoped not…because she didn't believe dreams came true.

His lips were warm on hers, mobile, coaxing. Everything about Grady was…coaxing. His "Aw, shucks, I'm just a cowboy, I didn't mean to tempt you" attitude was disarming. Somehow his smile, his gentleness and his innate sexiness curled around her defenses until she wondered what had happened to them! Even now, as she was aware of what occurred every time she was near him, that awareness didn't seem to matter. All that mattered was the grip of his large hand on her shoulders, the scent of him—cologne and man mixed with leather—the sensual provocativeness of his lips on hers. Thoughts galloped into that neverland of pleasure.

Pleasure increased when his tongue slipped inside her mouth. That pleasure was a tinderbox of desire. Her hands slid to his waist, tunneled under his leather vest to his flannel shirt. He was hard under that shirt, his muscles honed from ranch work and riding. She ached to really touch him again, to find out if the second union of their bodies could be as good as the first. Yet most men didn't find pregnant women attractive. Many men found pregnancy off-putting.

Pregnancy. Having Grady's baby. Figuring out what was best for their son.

She stilled and Grady slowly ended the kiss. Then he leaned back and studied her. "Now tell me if you weren't just a little bit jealous."

She couldn't hide the truth now. "Maybe I was. Just a little."

He laughed. "Well, I'm glad we got *that* settled. And actually I'm glad you stopped in. I was going to call you when I got home."

"What about?"

"My family always gets together on Christmas Eve. We go to evening Mass and then back to my parents' to exchange gifts. I'd like you to join us."

"I'm going to be on-call Christmas Eve. The hospital's always short-staffed over the holidays."

"If you get called in, so be it. But if not, I think you'd enjoy yourself. We sing Christmas carols and everything."

He added the last so tongue-in-cheek, she had to smile. "Tessa and Emily both asked me to join their families, but I don't think they'd mind if I spent Christmas Eve with you."

He studied her for a few long moments and then asked, "Do you really *want* to spend Christmas Eve with my family? Because I don't want you to do this out of some misguided duty to our unborn child. Sometimes I can't read you, Frannie, so be straight with me."

If she labeled this "duty" she'd be deluding herself. But she hated feeling vulnerable with anyone, and that included Grady. "Did you *invite* me out of duty?"

He shook his head with a wry smile. "You're good. Just when I think I'm making progress—"

"Progress goes two ways."

"I guess it does," he admitted. "No, I'm not asking you out of duty. I'd like you to be there. Laurie and my mother would like you to be there. The more the merrier."

"I want to come, Grady. Yes, I'd like to begin a tradition for our baby, but..." She hesitated, then plunged in. "But I like being with you."

"And that scares you, doesn't it?"

She nodded.

"We could just be parents with benefits," he joked. "Maybe you should think about that."

She had a lot to think about—Grady's sense of duty

and responsibility to his child, their attraction to each other. But she had the feeling Grady didn't let his mind go beyond that, and she shouldn't, either.

Parents with benefits? Sex should be the last thing on her mind right now. Yet when she looked into Grady's eyes her body quickened in response. He threw everything in her life into confusion.

"I'd better go," she murmured, knowing she was running away.

He knew it, too. But he thought she was only running from the chemistry. He was wrong. She lifted her purse from the counter.

"I'll pick you up at six-thirty."

"Six-thirty will be fine."

As she turned to leave, he called, "Frannie."

She glanced back at him.

"Don't think so much."

She couldn't respond, just pulled open the door and left his shop. Thinking was much safer than feeling, she reminded herself as she headed toward the bookstore and her friends.

On Christmas Eve, Francesca sat beside Grady on the sofa at his parents' condo after church services. It was as if they were a couple—yet weren't. Grady didn't touch her in front of his parents. She didn't know how she felt about that. Their relationship wasn't clear, that was true. But she also felt Grady was holding back. They weren't so very different after all.

As the children and adults finished their light buffet supper, Grady leaned closer to her. "I have your present at the ranch. I didn't bring it along. Do you want to stop there on the way home?"

She'd brought his present along. But she wouldn't mind privacy to give it to him. "Would you like to open yours here or do you want to save it for later?"

"Let's save it. I can put a couple of logs on the fire, we can put Christmas carols on, and I can give Shadow his new chew toy, too."

She laughed and it felt good. Her whole experience tonight with church and his family had been heart-catching. She saw how close this family was. Would her child be a part of this? How could she deny any child this type of togetherness?

"You've been quiet tonight," Grady murmured close to her ear. "What are you thinking?"

"I'm thinking your family doesn't realize how special they are. When I was a little girl, I would have done anything, said anything, been anything to have this kind of family—parents who hug their kids, grandparents who don't feel kids are a bother." She abruptly stopped. "Sorry. I shouldn't have let all of that spill out."

"You can let whatever you want spill out. We're friends now, aren't we?"

Was that what they were? She couldn't help but ask, "Like you and Cassidy are friends?"

"No," he admitted. "There are sparks between us that I never had with Cassidy."

As Francesca absorbed that, Patrick Fitzgerald stood and handed out the presents under the tree. She was surprised when she received gifts from Laurie, Jenna and

Maureen. After she'd left Grady that night in the saddle shop, she'd found gifts for his parents, brothers and sister. For Patrick she'd bought a book about old saddles, for Maureen a cookbook of favorite Irish recipes. She'd picked up lotions and bath products for Jenna and Laurie. John, Liam and Mark seemed to be prime candidates for treats from the candy shop. She'd had the most fun buying books for the children according to their age ranges.

When she opened Laurie's present, she discovered a delicate multicolored crocheted scarf. "It's beautiful," she told her.

"I make them in my spare time."

Francesca draped the scarf around her neck. It was perfect with her off-white sweater. "Thank you so much." Impulsively she gave Laurie a hug.

Grady's sister looked pleased and hugged her back.

Jenna's present was a small trinket box in the shape of a butterfly decorated with crystals. Francesca thanked her and gave her a hug, too.

Maureen stood by her side as Francesca unwrapped her gift. It was a mother's book, where she could record everything in her life she wanted her child to know. When she stood to give Maureen a hug, she was a little more hesitant, but Maureen wasn't.

Grady's mom gathered her in her arms and squeezed her tight. "We want you and your baby to feel at home with us. Will you remember that?"

Tears came to Francesca's eyes as she nodded. "Yes, I'll remember that."

The only one who had been standoffish all evening

was Liam. Now, as everyone disposed of wrapping paper and ribbons, as Grady went to the kitchen to refill their glasses, Liam sank down next to Francesca on the love seat. "Thanks for the candy."

"You're welcome. I hope you like cashew brittle."

"I didn't get you anything."

"Christmas isn't about that."

He gave her a quizzical look. "What do you mean? Everyone exchanged gifts."

"At Christmas you should give gifts because you want to, not because you have to."

He thought about that, then he asked, "Are you going to quit work after the baby's born and let Grady take care of you?"

She didn't know where Liam was coming from—if he was bitter because his wife had done that or if he was just trying to protect Grady. "I don't intend to quit working."

"How are you going to take care of the baby and be a doctor, too?"

"Women have families and careers these days," she pointed out to him.

He grunted. "That might work in theory."

"Grady asked me to move in with him. Did he tell you that?"

Liam's eyes narrowed. "Are you going to?"

"I don't know yet. My last relationship wasn't good for me, so I'm not rushing into anything now."

"Grady shouldn't rush into anything, either," Liam muttered.

"I know about Chicago," she said, wanting him to realize she knew how Grady had been hurt.

"Then you see we all just want to protect him. If you run off with his baby, it would tear him apart."

"I don't intend to go anywhere, not for a while anyway."

"What does that mean?" Liam asked suspiciously.

"It just means that I want my child to see more than Sagebrush. I want him to know there's a great big world out there that he can explore if he wants to."

"Mom said you were deeper than you looked."

"Excuse me?"

"Now, don't get all mad. That was a compliment. In my estimation, pretty women use their looks to get what they want. Sometimes that's all they've got, good looks. But you, you've got more than that. That's what Grady says, too."

"What else does Grady say?" Maybe she could figure out what he felt from what he'd told his brother.

"He says you're a challenge."

"He makes me sound like that wild mustang he adopted," she muttered.

Liam laughed. "I don't know about that, but Grady never has liked 'easy,' so a challenge could be a good thing."

The thing was, she *had* been easy the first night they'd met. For the first time in her life, she'd let her barriers down.

"Anyway," Liam added, "I'm sorry I didn't get you a present. So…how about if after the baby's born, I teach you how to ride? Grady says you don't know how."

"Are you patient?" she joked.

"I can be," he replied.

Whether Liam did take her riding or he didn't, she

appreciated his offer. "I'd like to learn how to ride. After the baby's born, we'll set it up."

Liam nodded, stood, turned away and then swung back to her again. "I just want you to know I think you're pretty brave taking on this family. That's not something just anyone could do." Then he went to the kitchen and picked up a fresh plate.

She wasn't brave. She was just hungering for a family of her own. But she wouldn't make the mistake of believing Grady could lead to that family if there was no trust between them. If all he was interested in was his child, how could *she* trust *him?*

After Grady lit a log in the fireplace at his ranch an hour later, he took Shadow out for a run. Francesca wandered around the living room, remembering when his house had felt like a home.

She set his present on the coffee table. The raffia ties and the green holly paper were masculine enough. She just hoped he liked it. Instead of worrying, she went to the kitchen and poured herself a glass of milk and a glass of apple cider for Grady.

Moments later, Shadow came bounding in, his master right behind him. Grady was still dressed from Christmas services in a blue cable-knit sweater with a gray turtleneck underneath, gray trousers and black boots.

He spotted the cider. "Thanks. You remembered."

She thought it was best not to reply. To her dismay, she remembered everything about Grady, everything about their time together, every conversation they'd exchanged.

"Do you want *your* present first?" he asked with a grin.

She looked under the tree and didn't see any wrapped packages.

"Oh, it's too big for under the tree," he explained, reading her thoughts. "It's in the spare room." Suddenly he crossed to her and took her hands. "Close your eyes."

"Grady…"

"Close your eyes and trust me."

Trust him—not to lead her into harm or danger or into something she couldn't handle. But at some point she had to take this leap of faith, even if they were just going to parent together.

"My eyes are closed. I promise I won't peek."

"And you're a woman who keeps your promises."

"As well as I can."

"That's the best any of us can do. Come on now, put your hand on my shoulder and follow me."

It was the oddest sensation walking down the dimly lit hall. Grady's sweater was soft, yet coarse under her hand. She could feel the straight strength of his back. If she bumped into him, their baby would touch his hip.

At the doorway to the room she didn't bump into him, but she came very close.

He turned, however, and took both of her hands in his, both the free one and the one in the cast. "Just come straight ahead," he ordered her. "There's nothing to trip over."

She could feel the floor beneath her feet and believed him. When he turned on the light, the shadows behind her eyes weren't as dense.

He said, "Okay, you can look now."

A beautiful, polished wood computer desk stood in

front of her. It was compact with a removable hutch. "Grady! Where did you—? How did you—? This is too much!"

He pulled her arms along his sides, careful not to hurt her casted one. "No, it's not too much. I wasn't going to get you something you didn't need. You said you needed a computer desk."

"But I didn't mean for you—"

"Would it make you feel better if I told you I got it on sale?"

She studied him, trying to gauge his truthfulness.

He shrugged. "It's one of those pieces of furniture that you'll be able to hand down someday."

When she looked up at Grady, she couldn't speak past the lump in her throat. He was a good man. Had she ever thought she'd meet one of those?

Finally, she managed to say, "I do appreciate your gift. I'll have a place to work now."

There was a glimmer in Grady's eyes that told her he was going to kiss her if they kept standing here. So she stepped back, grabbed his hand and said, "Now let's go see if you like *your* present."

A few moments later they'd settled on the sofa. She handed him the package and he balanced it on his lap. "Is it breakable?"

"Could be."

"Does it have moving parts?"

"Not exactly. Go on, open it."

"Anticipation is a wonderful thing," he teased.

"But anticipation isn't the real event. You've got to get past it to find that." When she glanced at Grady, she realized they weren't talking about his Christmas present any longer.

She felt her body warm in anticipation of feeling even closer to Grady. Tonight had been about family and acceptance and Christmas. Now they were left with just the two of them.

Grady untied the green raffia and slipped off the holly paper. When he lifted the lid off the box, he found two pieces of Styrofoam taped together. He separated them and discovered a handcrafted painted pony inside.

"It's beautiful," he said, noticing the artist's name on the horse. "How did you get one of hers? I heard this year's were all sold out. She only paints three hundred to sell every Christmas."

"I found it online. I noticed your collection by the fireplace the first day I was here."

"No one has ever given me one of these. The ones I've found, I've found on my own. Thank you. I like the horse painted on the horse's side. It's a freedom horse, right?"

"It's also known as a spirit horse, but yes, it represents freedom."

Carefully he set the horse on the coffee table. Then he leaned toward her. "I think a thank-you kiss is in order."

"How's that different from a regular kiss?" she joked, suddenly nervous.

"Let's try it and see." His voice was smoky with desire and she suspected he'd been waiting for this all night. To be honest with herself, she had been, too. What would Christmas Eve be without Grady's kiss?

Before tonight, Christmas hadn't seemed special. It had been a holiday that had reminded her of a longing for deep and abiding love, the respect and loyalty of someone who knew her and accepted her the way she was. Grady seemed to understand where she came from and where she wanted to go. More than that, he seemed to understand what she wanted for their child—two parents who would put that baby boy ahead of their own desires, wishes and aspirations. Would Grady be the perfect father? Could he be more?

The fire pop, pop, popped, and its hickory scent sailed on the draft. The odor of pine was strong, too. Grady's kiss brought to mind Christmas sleigh bells, favorite carols, smiles when gifts were given and received. Bows and shiny ornaments were only part of the story. Hearts ready to receive love were the other part. Could she love again? Could she accept love? Could Grady?

He was kissing her now, as if that was the only Christmas gift he wanted to give her. She touched his face, then laced her fingers in his hair.

He groaned, then pulled away, breathing hard. Recovering enough breath to speak, he said, "I want you to stay the night with me, Frannie. Will you?"

Chapter Ten

Francesca knew she shouldn't. If she did, one of two things would happen. Either she would get closer to Grady and she'd panic, wanting to run away, or tonight would show her they really had nothing but chemistry. Maybe that wouldn't be so bad. Maybe then she could just concentrate on her baby.

"Stop thinking," he commanded gently. "Do you want to stay or don't you?"

She wanted to stay. Oh, how she wanted to stay. "Grady, I don't know how pregnancy and hormones affect—"

He covered her lips with his finger. "Nod yes or no."

Gazing into his blue eyes, seeing the desire and hunger there, knowing hers matched it, she could only nod yes.

That seemed to be the signal he'd been waiting for. His hands delved into her hair, he searched her face and then his mouth devoured hers. This wasn't a slow stroll into desire. It was a diving plunge. Before Francesca knew it, she was swept away—by feelings and sensations that were heightened tonight. Because anticipation was the best fuel for passion?

All she knew was that she couldn't think very well when Grady kissed her like this. She reacted impulsively, matching his desire, stroking her tongue against his, trying to press as close to him as she could possibly get.

When the baby kicked, he felt it, chuckled and rubbed over his restless child. Then he drew her up from the sofa and swept her into his arms.

"Grady, I'm getting heavy."

"You may be ten pounds heavier. I lift bales of hay. Remember?"

She laughed. "You're comparing me to a bale of hay?"

He groaned. "I knew I wouldn't get that one by you. You know what I mean. I can carry double your weight."

Asleep on the rug by the fireplace, Shadow shook himself awake. But Grady said to him, "Stay."

That command seemed agreeable to Shadow because he settled again on the rug and closed his eyes.

Grady strode out of the living room down the hall to his bedroom.

Francesca had never been inside Grady's bedroom. Many times she'd been tempted to peek, but she hadn't.

Grady carried her through the doorway and she saw his room had a Western flavor. A four-poster, high-backed pine bed, king-size, took up its share of space. A suede throw with geometric shapes in brown and black lay over the deep brown dust ruffle. Chocolate-brown scatter rugs on the floor added soft, inviting appeal. He walked over those rugs now and carried her to stand beside the bed.

If she had any doubts at all, when he hugged her again, brought her close and said, "Frannie, don't be afraid," she realized he knew how momentous this was for her. Tonight wasn't just about the baby or their desire. It was about so much that had gone before and what could happen next if this was right.

"Do you want to undress me first or should I undress you?" he asked.

She didn't know if she was shaking because she wanted him so badly or because she was nervous, so she decided, "Let me undress you first."

"Go at it," he offered with a grin that was supposed to make her relax. Instead it just made her butterflies flutter more.

After she tunneled her fingers under his sweater and he lifted his arms, she raised it up and over his head. He tossed it and caught her for a kiss—a delicate, whimsical, let's-see-where-we-can-go kiss that curled her toes.

She reached for the turtleneck under his sweater and when it got caught on his chin, they both laughed. The moment was giving them the opportunity to be playful. And playful she was.

His kiss had been a surprise. Now she gave *him* one. She leaned into his chest, kissed above both nipples, ran her finger slowly down the center to where the hair arrowed under his belt buckle. He sucked in his stomach, and she knew she was arousing him. His body had gone taut, and he was hardly breathing. His stillness told her he was waiting for what came next, maybe trying to prepare himself for it. She didn't know what came next because she was playing this by ear.

"Do you want more?" she asked, letting her hand linger under his belt buckle.

"Of course I want more! But I won't let you have all the fun." With one quick motion he pulled her sweater up and over her head, quickly, yet careful of her casted arm. "Your breasts *are* bigger," he said huskily, appreciating them with his hands. His fingers spread over them, circled them, rounded the nipples with his thumbs.

"I know. It's hard for me to get used to. I was always small."

"No, just right."

His words warmed her the same way his hands were warming her, heating her, lighting a fire.

A few moments later the focus was elsewhere. Sliding his hands lower, oh so slowly, he let them lay on her rounding belly. "Is he moving?"

"A little. Not so much that you can notice. It's usually around midnight when he likes to kick the hardest."

Grady laughed. "So we're going to have a night owl?"

"Apparently."

Grady bent his head to her abdomen and kissed it. Then he kissed higher, over her breasts, up to her collarbone. Nuzzling her neck, he said, "I think it's time to get into that bed."

They had each other undressed in less than five minutes. After Grady threw back the covers, she slid in. The bed was humungous. Yet when he followed her and propped himself on his side, she wanted to be right there with him, at his pillow, her body touching his, her hand nestling in his chest hair.

They kissed, hard and wet and deep.

He broke away and rasped, "The past few weeks were like torture, foreplay without any satisfaction. I've wanted you again since that first night."

And she'd wanted him. But she found she wanted him in a different way now.

Oh, gosh! She had fallen in love with him!

The breath left her body. She felt dizzy with the idea of it. Then he was kissing her again and the startling flash of insight wound itself around their passion and hid itself in her desire. Grady awakened every womanly longing and some she didn't even know she had. His hands couldn't seem to get enough of touching her. His lips and tongue brought her to new heights of awareness about the desire they shared. She was breathless with anticipation until he touched her between her thighs. Her orgasm shook her as soon as his thumb made contact with the most sensitive spot on her body.

On her side, she held on to him, feeling as if a whirlpool were spiraling her away. He held on to her for a few moments, and then lifted her leg over his hip, thrust inside her, and the spiraling began all over again. His heat made her hotter, the length of him filling her surged through her to a new height of pleasure. His thumb on her nipple sent her spinning. Grady's kiss captured the sound of his name that echoed in her heart.

When the climax was over and the last ripple of pleasure had tingled away, when she lay wrapped in his arms, she was more terrified than she'd ever been. Her feelings for Grady rocked her and she didn't know what she was going to do about them. How could she pretend this had just been a physical encounter? She suspected that's what he wanted. He'd said he'd wanted her since the first night they'd met and the past few weeks had been like foreplay.

Could she handle simply being parents with benefits while loving him…knowing his feelings were only tied up with desire and his child?

"Stop thinking," he murmured to her, and his breathing became heavy and deep.

She couldn't. Not when she was truly in love for the first time in her life. Not when the man she loved might not love her.

Three days after Christmas, Grady threw clothes into a suitcase, unsettled more than he wanted to admit. Christmas Eve with Francesca had shaken him to his core. They'd experienced sex at its finest.

Afterward, he'd been rattled. Parents with benefits was a great idea, but what did it mean?

Francesca had seemed as rattled as he was. When they'd awakened the next morning, they'd eaten breakfast and he'd taken her home—her Christmas present in the back of the truck—without talking about the night before. She'd planned to have Christmas dinner with Vince and Tessa and Emily and Jared. He'd planned to have Christmas dinner with his family. Neither of them had known what to say or do next.

Now he was going out of town and that wasn't going

to help any of it. He wanted to talk to her about custody and that was going to be damn hard.

He picked up the phone on the nightstand, staring at the bed, remembering what had happened there. He had to call her and tell her he was leaving in the morning.

She answered her cell phone on the second ring. Had she been waiting for him to call? Why hadn't he phoned her before today?

Because he didn't know if he could trust another woman. Because he didn't know if he wanted to be more than a dad. Because Francesca had pulled away from him on Christmas morning, and he knew she had her own issues to deal with.

"Hi," he said, and waited.

"Hi," she said back, without taking the conversation any further.

"I called because I have to go out of town—to Dallas."

"This is sudden."

"Yes, it is. A friend of mine from college has a ranch there. There was a fire on his property. He's thinking about selling and doesn't know if he should or not. Anyway, he asked if I'd help him figure things out."

"You're good friends?"

"Yes, we are. We see each other a few times a year, whenever we can get away. Liam is going to stay here while I'm gone to watch over the place."

"He'll take care of the horses and Shadow?"

"Yes. He's great with horses, and he and Shadow are pals." He supposed he could have asked Francesca to watch Shadow, but that hadn't occurred to him.

When she seemed to have trouble finding something

to say almost as much as he did, he admitted, "Christmas was intense for both of us. Space might be good."

"It might," she agreed.

"When I get back, I have an appointment with a lawyer about a custody agreement."

After a moment's pause, she replied, "I guess I should see a lawyer, too."

Lawyers. Was that really the way he wanted this to play out? What other choice did he have? He had to protect his rights, didn't he? And his child's.

"We could probably do this without them, but I'd like something official, something in writing."

There was another long pause. "Because you don't trust me?"

"Frannie—"

"It's okay, Grady, I understand. You want to be a father and you don't want anything to interfere with that."

She made it sound so cut-and-dried.

"How long do you think you'll be gone?" she asked.

"Probably until after New Year's."

Was she thinking about New Year's Eve? A new year? The two of them raising a child?

"Have a safe trip, Grady."

"I will. I'll let you know when I get back."

They didn't have anything else to say so he added, "Take care of yourself."

"I will. Goodbye, Grady."

He didn't like the way that sounded, yet he had no choice but to say, "Goodbye, Francesca." He hung up the phone.

His world definitely felt as if it had shifted sideways.

Maybe this trip would give him the clarity he needed. If it didn't—

He'd keep his appointment with the lawyer when he got back and make becoming a dad official.

When Francesca wasn't at work, she could distract herself from thinking about Grady now that Gina had moved in. Grady had called a few times since he'd returned from Dallas two weeks ago after he'd spent a week helping his friend. But he hadn't come over to visit and he hadn't invited her out to the ranch again. Making love with him had ended the idea that they could be parents with benefits. They *were* more. At least there was more on her part. Apparently there wasn't on Grady's.

As Francesca went to the mailbox on the porch, she felt a wash of nausea. Lunch hadn't agreed with her. A cold wind tossed against her as she retrieved the mail and stepped inside the foyer once again.

It was Saturday and Gina was home with her. Her new friend was unpacking a box of books and loading them onto a bookshelf in the living room as Francesca entered.

Suddenly she felt sharp cramping in her abdomen. She took a deep breath.

Gina studied her intently. "Are you okay?"

"I'm not sure." Crossing to the sofa, she sat, letting the letters and magazines in her hand fall into her lap. The pressure in her tummy eased.

To distract herself, she flipped through legal-size envelopes until she froze at one that was just a little thicker than the rest. A lawyer's address was in the upper left-hand corner.

She tore it open. "The day of reckoning has arrived," she murmured when she could think again.

"What?" Gina asked.

"There's a letter here from Grady's lawyer. I'm pretty sure it's a custody agreement."

"You have a lawyer now, don't you?"

"I saw one last week for a consultation. He said if I received any documents I should bring them in to him."

Deserting the box of books, Gina came over to sit beside Francesca on the sofa. She pushed her black curls away from her brow. "What does the agreement say?"

Francesca skimmed the letter and gave a cursory glance to the other papers beneath, the tight feeling in her pelvis worrying her. She read them quickly. "It's a joint custody agreement giving me physical custody. It says until the child is a year old, visits are at my discretion. But then at age one and after, Grady has visitation at least two weekends a month until the child is five. Then we'll renegotiate. It's fair, but I just—" A stronger pain gripped her middle, twisted sharply inside her. She leaned forward, now knowing exactly what was happening and afraid to admit it.

"Francesca!" Gina cried, putting her arm around her, "What's wrong?"

"I'm having contractions. I shouldn't be. It's too early!" She automatically checked her watch to time the contractions. "Can you get me my phone? It's on the kitchen counter."

Gina ran to the kitchen and brought the phone to her. Francesca dialed Jared's number. She was so grateful when he answered. "Jared, I'm in labor."

"How long between contractions?"

"About five minutes."

"Is anyone with you?"

"Gina."

"Have her drive you to the hospital. I'll meet you there. Grab a bottle of water and drink that on the way."

The tight pain in her abdomen widened out this time until she had to grit her teeth.

"Francesca, are you having another contraction?"

"Yes," she finally managed to say.

"How close?"

"That one was about four minutes."

"Call 911. Now. I don't want to take any chances."

Gina must have been able to hear Jared because she went to the landline and dialed 911.

Francesca closed her phone and tried to remain calm. She told herself their neonatal unit was the best in West Texas. As Gina explained to the dispatcher why they needed an ambulance, Francesca opened her cell phone to call Grady. She felt something wet between her legs.

This could happen much more quickly than she ever imagined. They might not be able to stop her labor. She speed-dialed Grady, not sure if she wanted him to answer or not.

He did. "Francesca?" His question seemed wary, as if he suspected she'd received the custody agreement.

She couldn't discuss that now. She couldn't think about it now. "I'm in labor. I don't know if we can stop it. The baby's too early—" Her voice cracked.

"Where are you?" he asked in a clipped voice.

"Home. Gina called an ambulance."

"What can I do?"

Hold her in his arms. But she answered reasonably, "There's nothing you can do. If you want to come to the hospital, I'll make sure Jared keeps you updated."

"Updated, hell!"

She heard noises—horses whinnying…a door slamming. "Tell Madison I want to be in with you. Don't you need a coach?"

"Emily is going to coach me."

"Well, she can move over and give me a quick course."

There was more than one reason she didn't want Grady in that delivery room. "Grady, because the baby will be premature, there could be problems."

He went quiet and she heard the crunch of tires on gravel. "We'll deal with whatever happens."

She was grateful for his support. The distance between them didn't feel quite as cavernous.

But then he asked, "I *am* this baby's father, aren't I, Francesca? The baby is actually premature, isn't he? Because if—"

She hung up on him.

Grady rushed into the hospital, sick at heart. Why had he asked Francesca if he was the father? His doubts had surged again when she'd said the baby was going to be premature. But this was *Francesca,* not *Susan.* Francesca didn't lie.

Still, he didn't know what she was thinking now. His vulnerability unnerved him. He didn't know if the custody agreement was a good idea or a bad one. He didn't know anything where she and the baby were concerned. He just knew he wanted them both to be all right.

He had to stop for a pass to the maternity floor, then headed straight there. As he approached the nurses' desk he spotted Tessa pacing. She looked worried, a deep-down worried that made his gut turn over.

"Where is she?" He wanted to know.

Tessa gestured down the hall. "Emily's with her and Jared, of course. They thought it might be better if I waited out here. Jared might have to do a cesarean, depending on how it goes."

A cesarean. Jeez.

"I want to see her. I *have* to see her. I said something I shouldn't have when she called me." He started down the hall.

Tessa caught his arm, studied him for a good long moment and then said, "You can't go in there like that. You have to get suited up. Come on."

Five minutes later, Grady felt…weird. He was wearing a scrub gown, scrub shoes, a cap on his head and a mask. But he didn't care what he looked like.

Tessa escorted him to the birthing room. When she opened the door, her gaze met Emily's. She explained, "It's Grady."

Emily and Jared exchanged a look and they both nodded. However, Francesca, who was panting through a contraction, shook her head, her damp hair matted around her face.

Grady had to convince her to let him stay. He went over to the bed before anybody could say he shouldn't.

Emily moved aside and he took Francesca's hand.

Without preamble or explanations he said, "I shouldn't have asked you what I did. I know better. I *do,* Francesca."

She stopped panting, took a few normal breaths and focused on Jared. "Do a DNA test when the baby's born."

"No!" Grady protested. "I *believe* this baby's mine. Why do you think I want the custody agreement?"

"You want the custody agreement just in case. You don't trust me. You never will. I get that, Grady."

"We both need to work on trust," he determined. "But for the moment, believe me. I trust this baby is mine. Now tell me what's happening and don't leave anything out."

Francesca still seemed wary, but she nodded her assent. As Jared began to explain that they were monitoring the baby's heart rate carefully, as well as all of Francesca's vital signs and contractions, another contraction rippled through her.

She squeezed Grady's hand and pursed her lips together as her face turned red.

"Scream, for God's sake, Francesca. You're having a baby. Let it out." He couldn't imagine her trying to hide the pain, especially not from him. She'd tried to hide her pain all of her life and it was about time she let some of it go.

She gave a yelp, but it wasn't at all what Grady had advised.

Jared said to Francesca, "Look at me."

She did.

"With the next contraction, I want you to push harder than you've ever pushed. I want you to yell and scream and holler if you have to, but I want you to get this baby out."

"What's wrong?"

"Just do what I say, Francesca. Don't try to be a doctor now."

Emily, on the other side of the bed, rubbed her friend's arm. "Do what Jared says, Francesca. You know he's good."

Just then, Dr. Saxby came in the door with a team from the NIC unit.

"You're scaring me," Francesca said to all of them.

Emily pushed her friend's damp hair away from her cheek and Grady wished he could be the one to do that. But he'd messed up his chances with that for a while, maybe for a lifetime. He wasn't sure where they were headed. He just knew they all had to come out of this room in one piece.

Emily assured her, "We've assembled a team that's best for you and your baby."

Grady could see on Francesca's face when the contractions started again, and this time he moved close to her, bent down beside her and assured her, "You have the strength to do this for you and our baby. Come on, Frannie. Give the biggest yell you've ever given if you have to and push him out."

The next five minutes were hazy and traumatic. Francesca let out a yell like he never imagined she could. The baby slid into Jared's hands and at once he handed him off to the neonatologist and his team. They quickly inserted a tube down his throat, attached him to an IV and took him away in what looked like a plastic bubble.

Francesca had raised herself on her elbows, looking

after him. She seemed frantic to know what was going on. Grady heard the word *hypoglycemia.* He heard *IV glucose.* He heard *the lungs aren't fully developed.*

Then he saw Francesca's tears and he knew this had to be one of the hardest moments in a woman's life, when a baby she'd just brought into the world had to be taken away from her, and she didn't know if he'd live or die.

Grady put his arm around her, but she tensed and pulled away.

"He'll be fine," she said through her tears. "He'll be fine."

Emily crossed to Grady and clasped his elbow. "We have to deliver the placenta, Grady. Maybe you should wait outside now. I'll try to get Francesca calmed down and send her to her room. By then we might know better how the baby's doing."

"What exactly is wrong?"

"When a pregnant woman with gestational diabetes has a blood sugar spike, the baby responds to that blood sugar by producing high levels of insulin. As soon as he's born he's no longer receiving the extra glucose from the mother, so the levels of circulating insulin still in the baby can cause hypoglycemia. That's when blood sugar falls too low. Your baby requires treatment with an IV solution of glucose until the insulin and glucose levels have stabilized. He also has a breathing problem because his lungs aren't fully developed. But we're hoping over the next couple of weeks that will resolve itself, too. We have everything under control, Grady. Really. Now let us finish with Francesca, then maybe you can see her without that outfit on." Emily squeezed his arm.

When Grady's gaze met Francesca's, she looked away. Fear gripped his heart. Would their son live or die?

Chapter Eleven

Seated in a rocking chair two and a half weeks later, Francesca held her son in her arms in the Special Care Unit, so many emotions washing over her, she couldn't name them all. Those first days when a machine had breathed for Joshua Michael, she'd been filled with fear and panic. A few days ago, when he'd been upgraded from the NICU to this unit, she'd felt thankful and grateful and positively joy-filled.

Had Grady felt the same?

He'd been standing watch over Joshua since he'd been born. They'd decided on the name together. Still, she didn't know how Grady was feeling because they hadn't talked about anything other than Joshua's condition. Constant tension played between them. The question he'd asked when she'd gone into labor had created a rift she was afraid to mend.

If he kept doubting her, not only her word, but her decisions—

The doors to the Special Care Unit slid open. When she glanced up, she recognized the scrub-dressed doctor immediately.

Darren.

He passed by the other two sleeping infants in the unit along with the nurse who constantly monitored them. "How is he doing today?" Darren asked casually, as if he stopped in every day to check on the baby's progress.

"He's better, much better, and he's gaining weight. I'm hoping in another week I can take him home."

"I've checked his chart a couple of times. You and he are very lucky."

Her hormones were still all over the place and she felt her eyes growing moist. "I know we are. Thank you for the flowers you sent after Joshua was born. I haven't had time to write thank-you notes."

"You don't owe me a note."

Their eyes locked and she wondered what he thought she *did* owe him.

The doors to the unit slid open again and this time Grady strode in. He was wearing the paper protective apron as she was, and cap and mask, but his blue eyes searched hers. She knew the questions they held were a result of Darren being here.

Grady's shoulders were straight, his head held high and his stance was definitely defensive as he came to a stop beside her.

"Dr. Whitcomb?" he asked, reading the doctor's name tag.

Holding her baby in the crook of her arm, Francesca did the polite thing. "Grady Fitzgerald, this is Dr. Darren Whitcomb. He stopped in to see how Joshua was doing."

Darren held out his hand to Grady, and Grady quickly shook it.

"I'd better be going," Darren said. "If there's anything I can do, let me know."

That statement surprised Francesca and she just nodded.

After the doors slid shut again, Grady murmured to her, "Exactly what would he like to do for you?"

The look she gave Grady made him straighten. "What did he want?"

"He said he wanted to see if Joshua was okay. He said he checked his chart."

"He should stay away from you."

With her voice lowered, she responded, "He's a doctor in this hospital, Grady. I can't do anything about that."

When Joshua began to squirm in her arms, she rocked back and forth to calm him and to calm herself. "I've spoken with the chief of staff, Dr. Gutieras, and arranged for a two-month leave of absence. I also told him I'd be available for consultations. I'm hoping I can work part-time after that. That's a decision that has to go through the board."

"When will you know?"

"The next board meeting will be held in about ten days."

"Are you going to be happy working part-time?"

"I'll be happy taking care of this little guy." She rubbed her thumb over his tiny little hand, marveling at how perfect he was, marveling at how much she loved him already. He had her brown hair, but Grady's blue eyes.

She knew she had to bring up a subject she'd rather ignore. Her voice low, she ventured into territory they had to navigate. "Our lives have been in such an upheaval since the day I went into labor that we haven't talked about the custody agreement."

Matching her hushed tone, he said, "If you want to set that aside for now, I'll understand."

She kept her gaze on Joshua, afraid too much emotion would show. "I faxed it to my lawyer a few days ago. He feels the agreement was more than fair. I signed the papers, then had them notarized. They're in my locker and I can get them before I leave."

At Grady's silence, she finally met his gaze. They studied each other as machinery beeped, as an infant began to cry, as a nurse murmured to him and he quieted.

"Those papers are just a baseline," Grady assured her. "I simply wanted to make sure you would never cut me out of Joshua's life."

"You're his father, Grady. I wouldn't!"

He quickly came around the chair, crouched down and laid his hand on her arm. "Instead of worrying about those papers, I'd like to concentrate on something else right now."

Wary, she asked, "What?"

"I suggested this once before and I want to suggest it again. Instead of going back to the Victorian, bring the baby to the ranch with me. Let's really parent together."

Her indecision and doubts must have shown on her face.

He looked pained as he said in a low voice, "Frannie, in that one crazy, upside-down moment when your labor panicked me, I said something stupid. Don't let that keep us from doing what's best for Joshua."

Was she doing that? Keeping her distance? Hurting their son? Their attitudes, what they did and didn't do, how they interacted with each other from now on, would affect how Joshua saw life.

She pulled her arm a little tighter around their baby, felt Grady's clasp on her arm, gentle but firm. She thought about what visitation would mean—Grady coming to the Victorian, her dropping the baby off at his ranch. She didn't want Joshua *ever* to feel as if she deserted him. If he was shuttled back and forth, would he feel that way? Parents parenting apart was more complicated for the child than it was for the parents.

"I'll come home with you when Joshua leaves the hospital. We'll try it for a while. But if it doesn't work out—" She hoped she wouldn't regret her decision.

"If it doesn't work out, we'll fall back on the custody agreement or try something else. This is going to be a situation in progress, Frannie. We have to be flexible if we want to make it work."

Make it work. Make parenting work. Make their lives work. Make their relationship work.

Francesca knew with stunning, heartfelt sincerity that she loved Grady. There was no doubt in her mind. But learning to live with that love without making herself too vulnerable was going to be a very difficult task.

Still, she'd never stepped away from a challenge, and she wouldn't step away from this one.

Although she wanted to spend the whole day with Joshua, she knew Grady deserved his time with him, too. "Do you want to hold him now? I have to go down to my locker, pump milk and get lunch."

"I'd like to spend some time with him."

Carefully, Francesca rose to her feet, feeling Grady's hand slip from her arm. She wrapped the blanket more snuggly around her sleeping baby and handed him to his father.

After Grady took him into his arms, he bent his head to the little boy.

That's when Francesca left. Tears swam in her eyes again. She couldn't blame them on hormones this time. She had to blame them on longings and desires of the heart that might never be satisfied.

Francesca had just switched off the ignition to her car in the hospital parking lot a week later when her cell phone rang. Fishing it from her purse's outside pocket, she checked the caller ID and smiled. "Hi, Tessa."

"Hi, yourself. I hope I'm not calling too early."

"You're not. I just arrived at the hospital. Grady's meeting me here."

"Are you ready to take your baby home?"

"You mean to Grady's ranch."

"Any chance his home could be yours?"

Francesca tried to rub the tension away from between her brows. "I don't know what's going to happen. It seemed like a good idea when Grady suggested it, but now I'm not so sure. Maybe I should just tell him it was a bad idea—"

"Don't run, Francesca."

She remained silent.

"You might have gone to Grady's ranch after you delivered Joshua if Emily and Gina and I hadn't crowded around you."

"You didn't crowd around me. You helped me stay calm and deal with Joshua's condition. You helped me get my strength back so I could be at the hospital every day."

"Grady might have been able to do those things, too. Thinking back, we might have gotten in the way."

"No. You and Emily were just being the good friends you've always been. And Gina, she's helped a lot, too."

"I like her and so does Emily. You have good taste in friends."

Francesca laughed. "Thank you very much."

"You have all the baby clothes you need?"

"I do."

"We're still going to give you a shower."

"I don't need a shower. What I need is a crystal ball."

"I've heard they're hard to come by. Instead of using a crystal ball, just look into your heart. Keep it open, okay?"

"You've turned into a romantic."

"Or an optimist."

Francesca heard an interruption on the phone.

Tessa sounded a little breathless when she said, "Natalie was climbing across the coffee table. I had to rescue her before she fell."

"Is Sean practicing with the football Santa brought him for Christmas?" When Francesca had had dinner with Tessa and Vince on Christmas Day, Sean had proudly plopped the football in her lap. It was soft and just his size.

"Vince thinks it will encourage him to strengthen his arm, and he might be right. In the process, he gets to teach his son about the game he likes."

What would Grady teach Joshua? Horse care? Baseball? The importance of family?

"I don't want to keep you," Tessa said. "I know you're anxious about getting settled in at Grady's. After you do, and when you feel like talking, call me."

"I will. I have a feeling I'm going to be sleep deprived for a while, but it doesn't matter. I'm going to learn how to be a good mother, Tessa."

"You'll do just fine. Good luck and call me if you need me."

After Francesca said goodbye, she sat a moment in silence. A new life was about to begin....

The Fitzgerald clan had left!

Francesca felt mixed emotions as she sat in the nursery at the ranch at the end of her son's first day home, holding him. Laurie, Maureen and Jenna had been at the ranch house waiting when she and Grady had arrived with their baby. They'd helped with food and changing diapers and overall support. Francesca was so very grateful. Yet right now, with Joshua at her breast, she was relieved to have a peaceful moment with him.

Although she'd heard not a sound, suddenly she

knew she wasn't alone. Grady stood at the nursery door, watching her. She felt a little self-conscious, and goodness knows, she shouldn't be. She'd made love with the man. He'd seen her naked more than once. Yet breastfeeding Joshua, feeding Grady's baby, seemed even more intimate.

"Have you taken your blood sugar recently?"

It wasn't a question she'd expected. "Yes, I have. It's normal. I'm okay, Grady. It was gestational diabetes."

He nodded and stepped into the room. "You've been feeding him about every three hours."

"He seems satisfied. He's alert when he's awake. We just have to make sure he gains weight." She'd been pumping her breast milk since he was born and that's what he'd been fed at the hospital. There was no reason to believe he wouldn't continue to do well.

"Do you believe we finally have him home?"

She didn't know if Grady had deliberately used that word or not. *Was* this her home? Or would it just be her home temporarily? She loved Grady with all her heart. But what did he feel for her? She wasn't sure living with him for the sake of their baby was a good idea. When Joshua got older, Grady might want to have a separate life. Had he even thought about that?

The day had been exciting and stressful and tiring for both of them, and she didn't want to get into that conversation now. She didn't want to face conflict before they even knew peace. She didn't want to have to open herself up and ask a man if he loved her.

As Grady came closer, she felt her body respond to his presence—every nerve came alive, every muscle almost quivered with anticipation. There was still more physical attraction between them than she knew what to do with…even after everything that had happened.

"My mother says you're a natural, that you took to breast-feeding as if Joshua wasn't your first child."

"Don't forget, I've seen many mothers learn to breast-feed over the years. I think a lot of it had to do with Joshua. He took to me." She knew there was wonder in her voice, and that's what she still felt.

Her baby had stopped sucking now and was sleeping in her arms, making little noises every once in a while. She covered her breast with her bra, then her maternity top and buttoned it.

"You know I can give you a break from his feedings during the night." Grady chuckled when she showed surprise. "Don't look so dumbfounded. You pumped milk for the hospital. You can pump it for me. I can hold a bottle."

"But you get up at 5:00 a.m.!"

"So, I'll get up a little earlier if I have to and feed him first. See what kind of hours he sets. I can take at least one of the feedings, Francesca." He was leaning over her, tenderness in his eyes for their baby.

"You would really do that?"

"I really would. This is one of the reasons I wanted you to come to the ranch. We can help each other."

"Just how am I helping you?" she asked lightly.

"Aren't you going to cook me gourmet meals?"

He said it with such a straight face, she laughed. "Won't *you* be surprised!"

"I might be," he joked back. "The advantage to having

you here is being able to see my son whenever I want. In fact, can I hold him now? Do you think he'll wake up?"

The advantage to having you here is being able to see my son whenever I want. Grady's words saddened her. She wished there was more to their relationship than that.

When Grady stooped down to her, she caught the scent of day-end aftershave. She noticed the beard stubble beginning to show on his jawline. She remembered the heat of his body, the feel of his hair, the strength of his arms. She transferred Joshua to him, her heart hurting for everything she wanted and couldn't have. As she watched Grady cradle the baby, such love for both of them overcame her that she wanted to cry. She blinked rapidly while Grady's attention was on Joshua.

"Did Laurie and Jenna and my mother make you crazy being here today?" he asked without looking up.

When they'd gotten home and Francesca had seen all the baby supplies the women had brought, Grady had asked her if she wanted him to tell them to leave. She, of course, had said no.

"I appreciated their help. But it's nice to be alone with Joshua now. I haven't really had time alone with him. Do you know what I mean?"

"I do. First he was in NICU and then in the Special Care Unit with nurses around. Even when he was transferred to the regular baby unit, there were other babies and more nurses."

She laughed. "That's what a hospital is, Grady."

"I know. That's why I don't like them."

She couldn't help but ask, "And doctors?"

For a moment his attention was all on her. "I like one particular doctor who looks ready to drop over."

"No, really, I'm okay."

He took another studying look and then nodded. "Of course you are." There was something in his tone that bothered her. Something in his tone that added that little crosshair of tension.

She sighed as she took in the nursery he had created along with Liam. A cowboy on a bronc decorated one wall. On a second, a horse stood by a white fence. The crib Grady had purchased was heavy and masculine-looking. The dresser and changing table matched. Instead of a rocking chair, he'd purchased a wooden glider chair with cushions and an ottoman.

Now as he laid Joshua in the crib, she thought about the two nurseries, the two separate houses, the two separate lives. What was living here with Grady for a while going to prove?

She made sure the baby monitor was turned on, volume up, and stood beside Grady, looking down at their son. "He's a miracle," she whispered.

"A miracle the two of us helped create."

Their gazes met. "Sleep with me tonight," he suggested.

"Grady, I can't have sex—"

"I know you can't. I'm not suggesting that. If you sleep with me, we'll hear him. We can take turns. He might awaken often tonight being in a new place."

Grady was right. They could just nudge each other. Their sleep wouldn't be interrupted quite as much. "Aren't you going to work tomorrow?"

"Yes, unless you need me here."

"No, we'll be—"

"Fine," he completed. "I know. So will I. A little caffeine goes a long way."

Should she or shouldn't she? But then she realized this wasn't a life-altering decision. They were going to get some sleep and wake up to take care of their baby.

"I'll meet you in your room," she murmured.

Only Grady's quirk of a smile indicated he approved.

He headed to his room and she quickly headed to hers and did what she'd learned to do at the hospital when she'd been working around the clock. She took a three-minute shower. After she toweled off—only a few damp tendrils curling around her face because she'd swirled her hair on top of her head to keep it dry—she chose a pink silky nightgown she hadn't worn for months. Her tummy was getting flatter with her new exercise regimen.

She couldn't keep from looking in on Joshua before she went to Grady's room. Her feet were cold, her bare shoulders chilled. It was a blustery night. She knew the old Victorian would be creaking about now. She'd called there earlier to see if Gina felt deserted. But Gina had told her she was snuggled on the sofa with a down comforter, watching TV, sipping hot chocolate. After living with her family the past few months, she was actually enjoying the quiet. Francesca knew the Victorian's quaint charm. It had captivated Gina, too.

Chilled now, enough to make goose bumps rise on her arms, Francesca hurried to Grady's room.

The door stood open. He was sitting on his side of the bed in triangle-patterned gray-and-black boxer shorts. His broad back looked sturdy and strong.

He glanced over his shoulder at her. "I knew you couldn't resist taking another peek."

She smiled. "It's called new mother syndrome. I don't think I'll ever be cured from it."

When he slid under the sheet and plump comforter, she realized she would be crawling in with him. She stood immobilized for a moment.

"Get under the covers before you freeze," he advised her. "There's a cold wind tonight."

Practical. She had to view their relationship the same way. The king-size bed was so large, they wouldn't even be touching. She went to the side opposite from him, lifted the covers and crawled in, stretching out flat on her back, staring up at the ceiling.

"Ready for me to switch off the light?"

"Sure. If we don't fall asleep quickly, we might be up again before we get forty winks."

He turned off the light.

They lay there in the darkness, a thread of moonlight shining through the window.

"I didn't hang blinds because there's no one for a couple of miles. I like to see the stars and the moon when it's bright."

The bed was in a position that they could do just that.

He reached over and felt her arm. "You're still cold."

Yes, she was, but it was an inner coldness. She didn't realize she could feel so lonely, sleeping in the same bed with someone.

"*You're* warm," she returned. "And you showered." She could smell the scent of his soap.

"So did you."

She always used the same scented body wash and shampoo. Maybe its bouquet lingered longer than she imagined. "Grady, is this as awkward for you as it is for me?"

"It doesn't have to be awkward. Come here. Let me hold you and warm you up."

It was an invitation she could decline. She knew that about Grady. He was making an offer she could accept or refuse. He might not like what she did, but he didn't react in anger. So different from the other men who had been in her life. His kindness and patience were two of the reasons she'd fallen in love with him.

Because she was in love with him, she moved toward him.

He moved toward her.

They met in the middle.

"Turn on your side," he murmured. When she did, he wrapped his arm around her. The position was intimate, too intimate for her not to realize what was happening—he was becoming aroused.

When she started to move away, he said, "Don't. It's okay. I just want to hold you."

With his breath at her ear, his arm around her middle, his body as close as if they were making love, she fell asleep and dreamed of possibilities.

Chapter Twelve

When Grady walked into his house the following evening, a feeling overcame him he'd never experienced before. There was an aroma of something cooking in the oven. Joshua was sleeping in his car carrier, which was sitting on the counter, while Francesca made a salad.

"Hi," she said with a smile. "He just fell asleep again so I'm trying to put the rest of dinner together."

All too well he remembered the feel of Francesca in his arms last night. She'd slept. *He* hadn't during the first few hours. He'd been aroused and tried to distract himself from that with thoughts of the career Joshua might choose, the colleges he might attend. But he'd still been aware of Francesca's soft body against his, her silky hair escaping its topknot on the pillow, the satin of her gown against his legs. When Joshua had cried, he'd told her to go back to sleep, and he'd gotten up and fed him a bottle, appreciating every moment of holding him.

The next time *she'd* gotten up and told *him* to go back to sleep. That time he had…until his alarm had beeped. Then he'd wanted to pull her into his arms and kiss her, but something had held him back. She could go back to the Victorian at any time and take his son with her.

So now instead of kissing Francesca, he concentrated on Joshua. "Do you want me to lay him in his crib?"

"Would you? The chicken will be ready soon. Maybe we can eat before he wakes up again."

A few minutes later in Joshua's room, Grady adjusted the baby monitor. He was standing at the crib, smoothing his baby's wispy, dark brown hair, when he heard Francesca's cell phone ring.

Her leave of absence had started, but maybe the neonatal unit already needed her for a consultation.

He stood where he was, not wanting to eavesdrop, but unable to avoid it since her voice carried down the hall. Maybe because she was surprised by the caller.

"Darren?"

Grady's heart rate stepped up its pace.

"Thank you for the offer, but I'll have to pass."

Offer for what? Grady thought.

"But why should I need to go to dinner with you just to discuss my part-time position? Right now it's hard to get away. All of my time and attention are being taken up by the baby. Whatever you need to discuss, we can do it over the phone, can't we?... Yes, Chez Marie's would be very nice, but Darren—"

Grady heard the hesitation in her voice.

"I'm living with Grady now."

There was a long pause and Grady wondered if that was on Darren's side or hers.

"I know 'living with' isn't 'married to.' But as I said, my hands are full with a new baby. I know you're close to Dr. Gutieras and of course I'd appreciate a good word from you, but I can't go to dinner with you, Darren. Our personal relationship is over. You're a great doctor and I'll consult with you, but a professional relationship is all we're going to have."

Grady heard only silence now, not even a goodbye, and he wondered what had happened. After he exited Joshua's room, he heard the sound of Francesca chopping celery on the cutting board. She was chopping very fast and looked frazzled.

He wasn't going to pretend he hadn't overheard the conversation. "That was your old boyfriend?"

The look she gave him told him he shouldn't use that terminology, even in sarcasm. "What did Whitcomb want?"

"Basically, he wanted me to go out with him." She chopped some more.

"To discuss working part-time? What does *he* have to do with it?"

"He shouldn't have anything to do with it!" she said angrily. "It's up to the board. But he knows Dr. Gutieras very well. They play golf, they go out for drinks, they play cards together, and I think he wanted to barter. If

I went out to dinner with him, he'd put in a good word for me, say that keeping me on part-time would be beneficial for the hospital."

"And if you don't go to dinner with him?"

"We didn't get that far. I reminded him we weren't going to have a personal relationship."

"So now what do you think he's going to do?"

"I don't know. I hope nothing. But if he's angry about our splitting up, if he's angrier still now that he tried to resurrect our relationship and I rebuffed him, I don't know what will happen. The worst will be that I will either have to go back full-time or lose my job. I'll deal with whatever happens. I always have." Her voice had picked up firm determination.

"But you want to work part-time, right?"

She brushed her hair from her cheek, looking beautiful…but tired. "Yes, I do. Very much."

Following his instincts now, he went to her, took the knife from her hand and put his arms around her. "You'll get the part-time position. I know you will."

He would make sure that she did. She was not going to feel pressured by Darren Whitcomb about her job. His father was on the hospital board. Grady could ask him to call his cronies who were also on the board and pave the way for Francesca's request to work part-time. This problem was solved as easy as that. But he didn't want to tell Francesca what he had planned. He wanted to make it happen first.

Holding her, he stroked his hand through her hair and wished to hell he could take her to bed. That might eliminate all the tension between them. That might lead her to tell him what she was thinking and feeling about where they were going to go from here.

Yet if the board meeting was the day after tomorrow, he'd better get out to the barn and make the call. Pulling away from her, he rubbed his thumb across her chin. "I have to go out to the barn and do some chores. Do I have a few minutes before supper?"

"Sure. I still have to cook the rice."

He should tell her he liked having her here. He should tell her supper was the least of it. But he didn't…because he didn't have the courage to think about what the most of it might be.

Francesca had just laid Joshua down for his afternoon nap—the hospital board meeting on her mind—when her cell phone rang. Her heart sped up a little as she thought the caller might be Grady. However, when she checked the caller ID, she saw the call was coming from Dr. Gutieras's private number. Was the chief of staff calling her with good news or bad news?

After hellos, he said, "I'll get right to the point. I just wanted to let you know that your part-time position was approved. You'll be receiving an official letter in the mail, but I thought you'd like to know sooner rather than later."

"Thank you, Dr. Gutieras. This means a lot. I really was afraid the board might not go for the idea."

"Well," he drawled, "the calls from Patrick Fitzgerald didn't hurt. But you already had the votes you needed."

She was puzzled. "Calls?"

"Patrick has been a member of this board for three

years now and is well liked. He's also respected, so his vote of confidence goes a long way. And as I said, I could tell by the way the wind was blowing that you already had the votes you needed."

And just why would Grady's father make the calls unless Grady had asked him to? She felt first frustration and then anger rising up inside her. She didn't want Grady interfering in her career. Was this the way he'd handle their son? Try to smooth the way and not let him make his *own* way?

After another thank-you and goodbye to the chief of staff, Francesca wandered the house, restless and upset. Maybe this had nothing to do with Grady. Maybe his father had decided on his own to make the calls on her behalf.

She was still ruminating as she prepared a pot roast and set it in the oven at a low heat. Next she checked her laptop and found her recipe for chocolate pudding. Fifteen minutes later, she was pouring it into custard cups.

The door opened and she was surprised to see Grady. "You're home early." She tried to keep her tone neutral. Was he home because he already knew the verdict from the board?

"Word has it there's going to be a wind and snow storm this afternoon. I told everybody to go home. I didn't want them driving in that."

He took off his jacket and tossed it over a kitchen chair. "Something smells good."

"Is the weather the real reason you came home early today?"

"What other reason?"

"Tell me something. Did you ask your dad to make calls to board members on my behalf?"

His guilty look was the answer. "Francesca—" he began.

"Why did you believe you could exert control over my career?"

"Don't make it sound so dramatic!" he said. "If everyone wasn't on your side and you needed a couple of votes, what was the harm? Whitcomb might have been able to hurt you by voting it down."

"It sounds as if your father could influence enough board members that that would never happen."

"It was a long shot. When I told Dad about it, he wanted to help. I don't see what the harm is, Frannie. What's the problem?"

She couldn't believe he really didn't know her yet...that he hadn't realized her independence meant everything to her. "The problem is, I didn't know what Darren was going to do and it didn't really matter. I had talked to each of those board members. They knew my reasons for wanting a part-time position, as well as insurance benefits to go with it. It was no secret that lots of mothers might like similar positions. And what if Darren had pushed against it, simply for old times' sake? He could have pushed, but I still made my point with other members. They all have equal votes."

Grady harrumphed. "He's a cardiologist. The other members are teachers, business owners, a plumber. His influence could have swayed them."

"The board is set up to have balance from the hospital and the community," she reminded him impatiently.

Grady plopped his hat on the hat shelf. "Why are you so angry?"

"I shouldn't even have to tell you."

He took her by her arm and swung her around. "Explain it to me."

She stared him straight in the eye. "I want to live my own life, Grady. I want to run my own life. I want Joshua to learn to run his. I'll take care of him, I'll support him, but I won't go over his head to affect what's going to happen to him. That's control. When I learned your father had made those calls and you had probably asked him to do it, I felt as if you were trying to take control of my life…of our child's life."

"Getting that part-time slot might not have been so easy if Whitcomb had interfered," Grady still insisted.

"I would have fought my own battle if it had come to that. I think he finally realized from our conversation that what he did or didn't do wouldn't make any difference because he and I are finished. What were you trying to do, compete with him?" She didn't get a "don't be ridiculous," and that was an insight in itself.

Grady threw up his hands in frustration. "I was just trying to help."

"Well," she protested, "help is assuring me that no matter what happens, I'll find a way to work and take care of Joshua. What you did was take control. You want control over what happens to me, how I live my life and how I raise our child!"

"You bet I want control over how you raise our child. Just wait until he learns to drive and sneaks some beer. You're going to want control like hell then."

"My son won't drink and drive." Her voice was higher and louder than she intended.

"My son won't, either, because he'll have the right values. He'll be able to come to me and trust what I tell him."

"And you don't believe he'll be able to trust what *I* tell him?"

"What you and I tell him has to match, even if you're living on one side of town and I'm on the other."

"How can they match if we don't talk about the situation first?" He hadn't discussed with her bringing his father into the mix.

Now Grady looked angry, too. He grabbed his hat down from the rack, brushed it against his thigh, and then plopped it onto his head again.

"Why didn't you trust me, Grady, to let this play out the way it should? Why didn't you trust that I'd find another job if I had to? Why didn't you trust that I would do what was right for our baby?"

"And what about *me?* What if the right thing for you is moving back to Oklahoma?"

She gazed up at him with absolute sadness. "You still believe I might take your child from you. And I have to wonder, Grady, in the dead of night, do you still wish you would have had a DNA test taken?"

"No!" he erupted. "I have no doubt Joshua is my child. But I do have doubts that you'll stay."

How *could* she stay when he didn't love her?

He lowered the brim on his Stetson. "I think we'd better shut this down before it gets nasty. I'm going out for a while."

As he grabbed his jacket and left, she wanted to call out to him. But she couldn't. Not because she was afraid of his anger. Down deep inside, she knew Grady was a different man from her father...a different man from Darren. She didn't call out because she was afraid if she did, she'd find out she loved *him* with all her heart...but that love wasn't returned.

The wind roared as Grady drove to Liam's. His brother was surprised when Grady turned up on the steps of the row house he rented.

He beckoned him to come in with a warning over his shoulder. "You shouldn't be out. The wind's already over thirty-five miles per hour. It's supposed to go to fifty...with snow. What are you doing here?"

Grady didn't soft-pedal what was going on. "Francesca's upset. I had Dad make phone calls on her behalf to the board members."

"So she could get that part-time job?"

"Dad told you?"

"Yeah, he told me. He tells me everything. He tells you everything, too. *And* John. So why was she upset? Didn't she get the job?"

Grady opened the snaps on his jacket and lowered himself to the sofa. "She got the job. But the chief of staff told her she had the number of votes she needed before Dad made those phone calls."

"Oh, that was great of him. But I still don't get it. Why is she upset?"

"I *told* Dad to make the calls. She sees that as trying to control her life."

"You didn't ask her if she wanted Dad to make the calls?" Liam's voice sounded incredulous. He didn't even give his brother time to answer as he went on, "That's psychology 101 with women, Grady. You have to ask if it's what they want before you do it. Hell, that's why my marriage broke up. I never asked. I never really even knew what she needed. What does Francesca need?"

"She needs—" Grady stopped. "She had a rough childhood."

"Abuse?" Liam asked soberly.

Grady nodded.

His brother whistled low. "Then you can't put her in a position where she thinks you're making all the decisions and ordering her around."

"I don't do that."

"I asked around about her," Liam admitted. "I learned she lived with that cardiologist at the hospital before she moved in with Tessa Rossi. A friend of mine saw him for heart palpitations. He said he's a cold SOB. He smiles, but there's nothing behind it, unless another doctor is around. So if that's what she was dealing with before—can you imagine how hard it was for her to move in with *you?*"

Snow pinged against the windows. The howl of the cold front moving in told them its force was getting stronger.

Liam was right about Francesca. She was one gutsy lady. How much courage had it taken her to tell him about the pregnancy? How much courage had it taken her the day of her accident to call him again? He knew why she'd done it. She'd done it for the sake of their child. What had she said? She'd said she wanted their son to have another parent to rely on if need be. When she'd moved in with him, he'd insisted he was doing that for their child, too. But was he? Maybe his reasons had been more selfish than he wanted to admit.

The storm raged outside. Snow swirled and veiled whatever was on the other side of it. Francesca and Joshua should not be at the ranch alone in weather like this. She probably didn't even know he had a backup generator if the electricity went out. If the electricity went out—

Grady shot up from the sofa.

"Where are you going?" Liam demanded to know.

"Back to the ranch. Francesca shouldn't be there alone."

"Wait until this blows through."

"That's the point, Liam. I don't want it to blow through with her there and me here. I need to be with her and Joshua."

"Maybe you should admit what that means," Liam suggested.

"I'm older than you. You shouldn't be giving me advice."

"Isn't that why you came?"

"Hell, no. I just came to…to sort things out."

"Are they sorted?" Liam asked with a wry smile.

Grady thought about Francesca at that ranch with snow building up, the wind blowing against the shutters, cold drafts swirling through the house. Oh, yeah, he'd sorted it out. He'd been a damn fool not to have done it before now.

The sound of the wind moaned louder than Francesca had ever heard it. Snow cascaded down, frosting tree limbs, fence lines and ground cover. Where was Grady? That truck could handle almost anything, but still—

Joshua lay at her breast, nursing. As he did and she touched his little cheek, tears ran down hers.

What had she done?

Thinking about the past few months, Francesca knew she'd fallen irrevocably in love with Grady. Fear had kept her from telling him her feelings.

Suddenly she remembered what Vince had told her. He'd said, "Watch what Grady does, rather than thinking about what he doesn't say."

At the time she'd thought he'd given her a riddle. But now she realized what Vince had meant. Everything Grady had done since he'd arrived at her hospital room had shown her how much he cared. He'd made her breakfast and lunches and dinners. He'd driven her to the hospital because she needed to be there. She'd thought all of it had been about the baby. But had it?

Could *he* possibly have deep feelings for *her,* too? Could he possibly love her?

Joshua had fallen asleep now. She wanted just to hold him in her arms and never put him down. Yet she had to prepare herself for Grady's return.

A small, scared voice inside her head asked, What if he doesn't come back tonight? Wasn't that what she was most afraid of? Hadn't she given him plenty of reason not to want to come back?

As she laid Joshua in his crib, she realized her fear of loving Grady and expressing that love to him had muddled her thinking. He was a confident man, a man who was used to getting what he wanted most of the time. Yet he never used force, never used manipulation. He might be firm sometimes, but he was also tender and gentle and kind. She'd never had a man want to protect her before. Maybe that's why it had felt so strange. Maybe that's why she'd thought protectiveness was the same thing as control. But it wasn't. There was a difference. He wanted to protect her because he cared about her. At least she hoped that was true.

After she had adjusted the monitor in Joshua's room, she started his mobile. It played a soft tune and the moaning of the wind wasn't quite as invasive.

In the living room, she started a fire in the fireplace. When the logs caught, she closed the fire screen. If Grady was out in this storm, he'd be wet and cold when he returned. She could try to call him. But did she want to tell him her innermost feelings over a crackling phone? She doubted a cell phone signal would hold in this storm.

In the cupboard she found the thermos Grady sometimes used when he went to the barn. She heated milk on the stove, stirring in hot chocolate mix. While that was warming, she made a pot of coffee in case he'd prefer that. While the coffee brewed, she poured the hot chocolate into the thermos and capped it. Not knowing what else to do, she went to the front window and stared out into the storm, hoping the man she loved was safe…hoping he'd return soon.

Grady skidded around the last curve, warning himself to slow down. He wouldn't be any good to Francesca or Joshua if he rammed his truck into a tree. The white coating of snow seemed more than the windshield wipers could handle, or the defroster. But he didn't have far to go. Another right turn and down the lane. His hands gripped the wheel tightly and he realized he was more nervous now than he'd ever been. What if Francesca had her bags packed? What if she'd already left? That thought panicked him.

Until he saw the smoke puffing out of the chimney. Until he realized a light glowed in the living room. He didn't head for the garage, but parked at the front walk. After he switched off the ignition and lights, he jumped out of the truck. Then he ran up the walk and threw open the door.

Francesca was standing in the dining room at the window. When she turned to him, he could see she'd been crying. Damn, he was an idiot! An absolute idiot.

She started toward him. "Grady, I'm sorry."

"Don't," he said, tossing his hat onto the table. "Don't apologize. I was wrong to do what I did, especially without discussing the situation with you first. I *was* trying to control what happened. I didn't want Whitcomb doing any favors for you, or making your life any more difficult. I didn't want you to have to look for another job. I wanted you to depend on me to take care of Joshua while you worked part-time. What I did was all about what *I* wanted. That was wrong. I should have stopped to consider how you would see what I was doing."

She looked as if she wanted to touch him, but she didn't. She looked shy and vulnerable as she shook her head. "You weren't wrong. *I* was wrong for reacting so strongly when you and your dad were just trying to help. Grady, I've been holding something back for a while now."

His heart practically stopped. Was she going to tell him she was moving back to the Victorian?

"I love you, Grady. I've been afraid to think it, let alone say it."

It took a few moments for her words to register. But they did, and downright joy filled him.

He folded her into his arms and pulled her close. "You took the words right out of my mouth. I went to Liam for some sympathy. Instead, he told me things I needed to hear. And when he did, I realized I was jealous of Whitcomb. I didn't want him anywhere near you. Every time I'm in the same room with you, all I can think about is kissing you. I thought I was just fighting physical attraction, but I was fighting caring about you more. I love you, Francesca Talbot. I'm going to love you until my dying day."

"You love me? You really do?"

She sounded so surprised, so in awe of the idea. He knew he had to make her believe him. He dropped down on one knee in front of her, took her hand and brought her fingertips to his lips. She was crying again, but he could see this time they were happy tears.

He was feeling a little choked up himself, but somehow he had to get the words out. "I don't have a ring yet. I guess the two of us will just have to go shopping. But with or without the ring, I'm going to ask you the question. Frannie, will you marry me?"

Surprising him, she dropped down on the floor with him and wrapped her arms around his neck. Kneeling in front of him, she assured him quite solemnly, "I'll marry you, Grady Fitzgerald, whenever, wherever and however."

He laughed, covered her mouth with his and lit their passion with a never-ending fire he knew would last a lifetime.

Epilogue

April

"Where's Joshua?" Francesca asked, swinging away from the mirror, her satin-and-lace ivory gown twirling around her.

"Tell me when you're going to move!" Tessa scolded her.

Grady's mother adjusted the tulle and lace that spilled from the hat on Francesca's head. "Laurie has Joshua now. He's fine. You've got to let him out of your sight sometimes so he grows up big and strong," Maureen kidded.

Francesca laughed and relaxed. This was her wedding day and there was so much to think about. She was protective of her son, and Grady was, too. Grady. She'd be his wife soon. His wife. Reflexively, her eyes dropped to the ring on her finger, an antique setting in white gold with a princess-cut diamond. Soon there would be a wedding band below it.

"Don't get teary-eyed on us," Emily advised her, "or we'll all start crying."

Gina, dressed in teal chiffon like the other bridesmaids, handed Francesca her bouquet of pink and yellow roses. "Are you ready?"

She was more than ready. She'd never been this happy before. She could feel her love for Grady and his for her growing stronger every day. They understood where they'd both come from and where they were going. They both knew what a gift their son was and how their love for him, as well as each other, bound them together.

Francesca hugged Tessa, then Emily and Gina and Maureen. Grady's mom was fast becoming the mother she'd never had, Patrick Fitzgerald a surrogate father. Laurie and Jenna were like sisters now, and John and Liam brothers.

There was a knock on the door and Jenna poked her head inside. She was handling the guest book and making sure everything in the social hall went smoothly for the reception. "The music's about to begin. Mom, John's ready to escort you to your pew." Then Jenna disappeared and Maureen slipped out the door.

Francesca took a deep breath, looked at her bridesmaids and then said, "Let's do this."

The music began playing as Grady's mother was escorted by John to the front of the church.

Patrick was waiting for Francesca and offered her his arm. "I'm honored that you asked me to walk you down the aisle. You know that, don't you?"

She nodded and tucked her hand around his elbow.

Emily began the procession and Gina followed. Tessa, Francesca's matron of honor, went last.

And then it was Francesca's turn.

Patrick guided her with an easy stride that enabled her to see the smiles on their guests' faces. There was Vince, with Natalie and Sean, Jared with his and Emily's twin daughters, Amy and Courtney. Liam, who had been one of the groomsmen, gave her a quick salute with a grin. He visited her and Grady at the ranch often and they were becoming friends. He'd kept his promise and given her a few riding lessons. John and Jenna, along with Laurie and Mark, sat with their children.

For a moment Francesca panicked. Where was Joshua?

But then she heard her name and she looked straight ahead. Grady was standing at the altar, their baby in his arms.

"That's my boy," Patrick said proudly.

"That's my husband-to-be," Francesca murmured back.

When they reached the altar, Grady handed Joshua to his father. Patrick kissed Francesca on the cheek, and then went to the first pew to stand beside his wife.

Grady, in a black Western-cut tuxedo and without his Stetson, took her hand in his. "I love you."

"I love you, too," she whispered back. "I'm afraid if I blink, you'll disappear."

"Go ahead and blink. I'm not going anywhere."

* * * * *

DADDY BY SURPRISE

BY
DEBRA SALONEN

Debra Salonen comes from a long line of storytellers. At slumber parties, her mother would enthral Deb's girlfriends with stories of growing up on the prairie near Pierre, South Dakota. One goose-bump-inducing story involved unearthing a casket of a pioneer woman in an unmarked grave. Deb had no problem picturing her mother sitting in the dark, guarding the poor woman's remains while Grandpa Bagby rode back to town for the sheriff. It was a better story than the one involving rattlesnakes… Nobody got any sleep on the nights she told *that* story.

To Wanda Ottewell, for listening to my characters
with such an open mind and for providing a
safe environment for risk-taking.

CHAPTER ONE

KAT PETROSKI patted the bulge in her front jeans pocket. Not bad for a Wednesday, but nothing compared to what the regular servers would make that weekend when the town of Deadwood, South Dakota, filled with people celebrating the Days of '76—a yearly commemoration of the gold rush–era town's founding. For a week every July, thousands of people came to the Black Hills to see the rodeo, show off their Harleys and drink gallons of beer at Pop's, the popular Main Street saloon where she was filling in for a friend.

"Never count your tips before last call," Becky Jennings, her mentor in the bartending/waitress business, had once told her. A flat night of tips could make the time seem endless.

Bec, who decided she needed another day at home recovering from gallstone surgery, was a hard-drinking, chain-smoking, fortysomething gal who took no crap from anyone. Kat often wished she could be more like her, but she didn't have the height, weight or metabolism for it. A couple of beers was usually enough to put Kat under the table, which was why she didn't drink.

She'd made that mistake twice in the past and had two unplanned but gorgeous mistakes to show for it. Her sons, Tag and Jordie. The true loves of her life. At the time of their conceptions, she'd have given that title to their fathers, but neither Pete Linden nor Drew Petroski had lived up to their promises. They'd married her—once her father mentioned the word *shotgun*—but neither marriage had lasted. For reasons she was beginning to think might be linked partly to her parents' divorce when she was six.

Jordie's age, she thought with a sigh. Jorden Petroski. The sweetest, most eager-to-please kid on the planet—just like she'd always been. Eight-year-old Tag, on the other hand, was tough. Because he had to be. That was her fault, too.

"Hey, Kat, I need another beer," a voice boomed from a table in her section. "And give this guy a shot of Jäger. He's a virgin."

The man doing the ordering was Brian Whitlock. A regular. He drove a rig for Black Hills Moving and Trucking. About ten years older than her thirty-one, he lived near Nemo with his wife and three little kids. But he spent the better part of his life—and most of each paycheck—in one of the many bars and casinos along Deadwood's main street. The person he was ordering a shot for was a stranger. Clearly a R.U.B., an acronym that stood for rich, urban biker.

In this case, the man fit the name completely. His leather chaps were too pristine to be more than a week or two old. His expensive lace-up boots showed dust but no real scuffs. A hint of silver was evident in the sideburns showing beneath his do-rag, which was black with orange skulls on it.

When he'd first walked into the bar, she'd given him

a quick assessment—an acquired skill and necessary survival tactic in this business. Mid-thirties. No wedding band. She put his height at six feet, weight in the 180 range. Maybe less. The pecs and biceps displayed by his spanking-new black T-shirt told her he wasn't a weight-lifter. There was clear definition and form, but no look-at-me bulk. The logo on his shirt told her he knew how to use the Internet because she'd ordered one just like it for her stepbrother. Those shirts wouldn't be available locally for another week and a half, when the 2008 Sturgis Bike Rally started.

Like Deadwood's Days of '76, the rally drew all kinds of people from all over the world. The bikers brought their own brand of craziness, but their money was a boon for the Hills' economy. Quite a few came early and stayed for both events.

"Coming right up."

She slipped behind the made-to-look-antique bar, since Guy, the bartender, was playing dice with a couple of regulars while waiting for the night to pick up. Guy was a decent fellow, retired from some branch of the armed forces and big enough to keep order when things got rowdy. He acknowledged her with a nod as she filled the shot glass.

She inhaled a lungful of smoke-tainted air as she headed across the room. She wasn't surprised to see the R.U.B. watching her—she'd chosen to wear her Victoria's Secret push-up bra and low-cut tank top for a reason.

As Pete—ex-hubby number one—so eloquently put it when she'd unloaded Tag and his camping gear at his father's house in Rapid City, "I see you're wearing your Tits for Tips outfit. Ya should've gotten that boob job when I offered. Then you'd really haul in the cash."

Pete prided himself on being a breast man. Why he'd dated her was still a mystery—given the fact she was a modest B-cup. She'd turned down his offer of breast enhancement because she was still nursing his son at the time he offered. By the time Tag was done nursing, Pete had found himself a new, more generously endowed woman. Apparently a divorce was cheaper than surgery.

Pete was taking Tag and Tag's half brother, Aiden, camping at Deerfield Lake until Sunday, but he'd called that morning to say he was running late and needed Kat to deliver Tag, instead of his picking up their son on the way to the lake as planned. This meant Kat had had to dress for work earlier than she would have preferred, drive to Rapid, drop off her son, then take the I-90 to Sturgis to straighten out the mess regarding her vendor-booth application—which she'd just learned had somehow gotten lost—before heading to Deadwood. More driving, more gas.

Kat's other son, Jordie, had left earlier that morning to attend a Native-American powwow with Char, her good friend and fellow member of the Wine, Women and Words book club. Unlike Pete, Char had picked up Jordie. Right on schedule.

"Here you go, gentlemen," she said, carefully setting down the glasses within their line of vision but not so they could be knocked over too easily. Both patrons appeared to be about halfway down the road to drunk.

The R.U.B.'s gaze moved from her chest to her face. His eyes, which were an interesting shade of gray, seemed a bit out of focus, but he blinked twice and smiled. "Thangs."

The *K* didn't come out right, but his voice was pleasant—deep and cultured. And his smile was almost as sweet as Jordie's, only this guy's teeth were toothpaste-commercial white and beautifully aligned. It was a little early to tell, but she was afraid Jordie's were going to turn out as crowded and misaligned as Tag's. She and Pete argued about the inevitability and cost of orthodontia nearly every time they saw each other.

"I'm not really one, you know. A vershin," he said. "Eggcept where this stuff is concerned." He brought the glass to his nose and sniffed. "Urgh." He paused a moment as if debating whether or not to drink it, then he let out a sigh. *"Ifnotnowwhen?"* He ran the words together, then downed the drink in one gulp.

When he looked at her, his pretty gray eyes twinkled. She tried to convince herself it was the booze making them water, but then he winked. Maybe he wasn't as drunk—or as much of a R.U.B.—as she first thought.

That was when it struck her that he was actually rather handsome. A second later a cannon-fire warning sounded in her head. *Swoo alert. Duck, lady, duck.*

The last was an inside joke only her friend Libby would have gotten, but Lib understood better than anyone the power of *swoo*—a made-up word Kat's mother had used to explain why the women in Kat's family were drawn to downright awful choices in men.

"Some people might call it charisma, but that's a little fancy for the spell certain men can cast over us. Might be we're genetically susceptible to faulty pheromones," her mother had theorized—too late to do Kat any good.

By the time Kat understood the power swoo had on her, she was pregnant a second time and saying "I do" with Drew Petroski—the cutest, most immature outfielder she'd ever had the misfortune to play softball with.

She shifted sideways and leaned down to pick up the man's empty glass. She noticed his gaze followed the lace that peeked above the dip in her neckline. "That's nine seventy-five," she told them. "The beers are half price because of happy hour."

She braced herself for a ten and a "keep the change" from Brian, but to her surprise the stranger fished a twenty from the hip pocket of his new-looking jeans and dropped it on her tray. "The rest is yours," he said, his words overly correct, as though he was trying to act sober for her benefit. "For providing yet another rule-breaking, risk-taking, fantasy-living step toward reinventing myself. Y'know what I mean?"

Not even close. "Sure. Thanks." She had no idea what that speech was all about, but he wasn't the first drunk to think he'd found the road to enlightenment through an alcohol-induced haze. "Another round?" she murmured, backing away so fast she bumped into two people making their way toward the door.

"Oops," she said. "Sorry."

A man and a woman. Both in leathers—broken in in a way the R.U.B.'s weren't. The man—a big, burly guy with thick, fat fingers sticking out of black leather demigloves—steadied Kat with both hands, acknowledging her apology with a low grunt. The woman apparently thought her man's sweaty, unpleasant touch lingered a millisecond too long, because she shoved Kat back toward the table she'd been serving with a powerful straight-arm.

"Back off, bitch," she snarled, her bloodshot eyes squinting lethally.

Kat managed to keep her balance, but her hip grazed the back of the chair occupied by the big tipper. "Sorry," she told him.

"Don't apologize to that pretty-boy biker wannabe," the woman growled. Her voice held the same two-pack-a-day roughness Kat's mom's had held—before her diagnosis of throat cancer. She didn't smoke anymore, but she didn't talk much, either, thanks to the valve in her windpipe.

The woman, who was only a few inches taller than Kat, but a good hundred pounds heavier, took a breath, making her ponderous breasts strain against the American-flag tank top. "God, I'm sick of all these weekend warriors showing up thinking they're cool because they can afford to buy a Hog off the showroom floor," she said in disgust. "It's even worse at the rally. That's why Buster and me came early."

Buster, who was bald beneath the black scarf tied tight to his large, square head, looked slightly embarrassed. "Let's go, Mo."

As in one of the Three Stooges? Kat thought. No. Too fat for Moe.

"Mo? Are you sure? She looks more like Curly," someone said, voicing Kat's thought.

Kat covered her lips with her free hand to keep from laughing. Any response on her part would only add fuel to the fire. She just hoped the heavyset woman in question hadn't heard—

"Why you smart-ass, little shit. I was riding bikes when you were still sucking teat. What are you? A lawyer? Tax accountant? Some kind of desk jockey, I know that much."

The man turned sideways to the table so he could see the woman more clearly. He started to stand, but Kat put her hand on his shoulder and pressed downward. This tiff was on the verge of becoming a fight, and no one came out ahead when that happened.

"Oh, come on, folks," Kat said, keeping her voice light. "Let's not go there. Name calling doesn't make anyone feel better. Mo, right? Short for Maureen? I have an aunt Maureen."

"Who the f—"

"Hey. Watch your language. There's a lady present."

The words were so outdated, Kat had to laugh. "Listen, John Wayne, thanks for standing up for me, but I hear that word about nine thousand times a night."

"Are you sayin' I ain't a lady?" Mo asked. Her fists, each of which easily made two of Kat's, started bouncing around her sides. She gestured behind her for backup and nearly popped Kat by accident.

Kat dodged the blow, then had to scramble to keep from getting mowed over by the guy she'd been protecting from a pummeling. "Listen, you obnoxious cow, you can't just throw your considerable weight around and threaten hardworking barmaids who are trying to keep the peace. You're a disgrace to that flag, which, by the way, was never meant to be worn as bra. Half the stars are—"

Whatever slight he'd intended was stopped by a set of leather-encased knuckles that glanced off his elegant cheekbone. Kat had witnessed enough bar fights to know that if the giant biker had been sober, the punch would have broken the R.U.B.'s nose and maybe a couple of teeth. As it was, the impact sent the unsuspecting fellow straight into Kat's arms.

Her serving tray, which she'd tucked under her arm, hit the floor with a loud bang. Mo gave them all one last sneer, then grabbed Buster's meaty arm and split. Seconds later, the roar of a Harley outside shook the windows.

The sound made the man, who had Kat partially pinned against the table, lift his head. "Are they gone?"

In a heartbeat, she realized two things: his anatomy fit hers almost perfectly and his was the sneaky kind of swoo—you didn't know how powerful it was until you were leveled by it.

With a harrumph of disgust—at herself, not him—she pushed him back. "What kind of idiot picks a fight with drunken bozos three times his size?"

"Were they really that big?" he asked, gingerly rubbing his jaw. "I left my glasses in my motel room."

She looked at Brian, who let out a raucous hoot, then yelled something about the size of the stranger's *cojones.*

Kat shook her head in disgust. "Do you need an ice pack for that?"

"I don't think anything is broken."

"Well, the night is young. Sit down. I'll get you some ice, anyway."

She was gone before Jack could tell her not to bother. He was staying just up the street and was pretty sure he could walk back to his motel without help. Not that he didn't appreciate the concern he'd read in her pretty blue eyes, but this was his first bar fight.

One more thing to cross off the list, he thought, trying not to smirk. Smirking hurt. He might even wind up with a black eye. If he did, he'd use his digital camera and e-mail a shot of it to Jaydene, his ex-fiancée. Petty, sure, but a part of him wanted to show her proof that he, Jackson Boyd Treadwell III, wasn't a stuck-in-a-rut orthodontist with no sense of adventure. He could walk on the wild side when he wanted to. He'd simply been too busy going to school, then establishing his practice, to have time to experience any such recklessness.

Not that getting punched out actually had been on his list of things to do when he came to the Black Hills, but there'd been a moment when he stood up to that female bully that he'd felt heroic—invincible. Until her trained gorilla decked him. Luckily, the cute little barmaid whose honor he'd been defending was there to cushion his fall. In a really nice way.

He didn't usually find himself attracted to petite women. His mother was short, but he doubted if anyone had ever called her petite. Rosaline Treadwell was a five-foot-two-inch dynamo who had only recently traded in her stiletto heels for golf shoes when she retired from the bank where she was a vice president in charge of corporate loans. She'd been instrumental in helping Jack buy the building that housed Treadwell and Associates. "It's never too late for a perfect smile" was his marketing slogan, since his group of three dentists—two other orthodontists and one endodontist—catered to all ages. Jack specialized in adults. Kids were not his cup of Kool-Aid, as his sister liked to say.

"Hey, man," Brian, the guy who had offered to buy him a drink—which Jack had ended up paying for—said. "You got off lucky. I know that Buster dude. I seen him knock a guy unconscious once over in Sturgis. You could be missing some teeth."

Jack squeezed his jaw experimentally and bit down. Nothing loose. Thank God. He'd never hear the end of it from his mother if he returned to Denver needing emergency dental work. "Yeah, lucky me," he muttered.

"Here you go," the waitress said, returning with a glass of ice in one hand and a thick wad of paper towels in the other. She set both items in front of him. "The bar rags all smelled funky and I couldn't find a zipper kind of baggie. That's what I use when my kids get hurt. I put a couple of cubes in the bag, then cover it with a towel and let them whack the ice with a hammer. Distracts them from the pain and gets rid of some of their frustration."

He could picture the image perfectly. He would have smiled, but his face was beginning to ache. "You have kids? Plural?"

Maybe he was drunker than he thought because he could see his harmless question had caused some offense. Her pretty blue eyes narrowed. "Yes, I do. Two boys."

"I…um…meant that as a compliment. You look too young to have one kid, let alone two."

Some of the fight went out of her posture. "Oh. Thanks. Let me buy you another shot," she said, turning on the heel of her thick-soled running shoes. She paused to pick up the tray she'd dropped, then hurried across the room.

Her trim build reminded him of a long-distance runner—compact and lean. He swam laps every morning, but he'd been thinking about diversifying his workout routine to see more than two walls at opposite ends of his pool.

When she returned, he asked, "Do you run?"

She looked at Brian as if the question required an interpreter.

"10 Ks? Marathons?" Jack tried.

"Me?" Her eyes sparkled with humor, but there was something sad in her expression, too. As if the word triggered a case of might-have-beens. "I run after my kids. That's about it."

"Weren't you in track in high school, Kat?" Brian asked. "I swear, that's what somebody told me. Because you were always the fastest on our softball team."

She shrugged. "Another lifetime, Brian. Or maybe a dream. I can't remember which." She leaned closer to Brian and added something Jack couldn't quite catch.

Jack hated being the odd man out. People whispering behind his back. He'd experienced enough of that when rumors about his father had pretty much ruined his chance to fit in and have a normal life.

He dumped the glass of ice upside down on the towels. A couple of cubes rolled off the edge of the scarred tabletop.

She squatted to retrieve them, which gave Jack a fine view of her bosom—fleshy tan mounds squashed together by a black lace bra that peeked ever so provocatively above the edge of her low-cut top.

He forced himself to look away. Why? He asked himself as he slapped one corner of the paper towel over the other. She'd dressed provocatively to draw attention. Only an uptight prude—as Jaydene had labeled him—would be too self-conscious to stare.

Before he could change his mind and take another look, she bounced to her feet, dropping the dirty cubes into Brian's empty beer glass. She picked it up, then said, "I didn't mean to be rude, but anybody who knows me knows I don't have time to work out. I love sports, but I haven't even played softball since the year Brian and I were on the same team."

"That's 'cause she got knocked up a second time," Brian said gauchely, causing twin spots of red to appear on her cheeks.

Jack palmed the already soggy handful of ice and paper towel like a wad of dog poop from one of Jaydene's whippets and pressed it against his cheek. His whole face was starting to hurt.

"Do you have any aspirin or acetaminophen on you?" she asked, her brow knit in concern.

He shook his head.

She glanced over her shoulder toward the bar. "I'll bring you something. I'm a mom. I don't leave home without a full pharmacy in my purse. But you have to be discreet, okay? My boss thinks he could get sued if you had a bad reaction."

"I'm not allergic to anything," Jack said, trying not to move his jaw too much. His words probably sounded garbled, but she smiled as if she understood him completely.

Like that was possible. No woman he'd ever met really got him—including his fiancée and his mother. Everyone saw the outward signs of success—nice home, luxury car, booming practice—and assumed he was someone he wasn't. Happy, secure, confident. All things he pretended to be.

It had taken a surprise and rather shocking confrontation with the woman he'd intended to marry to make him question his everyday reality. Like him, Jaydene pretended to be someone she wasn't. Serious—she worked in a bank and volunteered at an adult school. Responsible—four years older than Jack, she seemed wise, witty and slightly irreverent. And in the three-plus years they'd been dating she'd never once expressed an interest in kinky, multiple-partner sex until the afternoon he showed up unexpectedly at her home and found her involved in a ménàge a trois—via the Internet.

Just picturing the lurid image of her legs spread on either side of her laptop with the little eyeball camera trained on her most private parts as her two partners—both men—did the same was almost enough to make him toss his last shot of anis-flavored booze.

After the initial shock had worn off, they'd talked. She'd called him repressed. Unadventurous. Boring. She'd implied that her participation in online sexual encounters was because she knew he would have shot down any suggestion that, as a couple, they try swinging.

And she was right.

He'd swung in a different direction. He took a long overdue vacation from work. Kissed his mom and sister goodbye, then jumped on his shiny new Harley and headed to the Black Hills. Close enough to Denver to get back quickly if he was needed, yet far enough away that it wasn't home.

He'd picked the Black Hills of western South Dakota for two reasons. First, he was a closet fanatic of all things Old West. He didn't decorate his house in antiques or anything, but he watched every television series and miniseries that came along. Every incarnation of *Lonesome Dove.* He had the entire *Deadwood* series on DVD. He also owned an extensive collection of western movies, from *Dances with Wolves* to the John Wayne classics. Recently he'd turned to romance novels to get his western fix, since his two favorite novelists, Zane Grey and Louis L'Amour, were long dead.

Second, the Hills had a reputation that almost rivaled Las Vegas's infamous "What happens in Vegas stays in Vegas" slogan. He was ready to cut loose and experience what Jaydene claimed he'd been missing. This was his time and he planned to live it to the fullest.

She just hadn't warned that the experience would hurt.

CHAPTER TWO

KAT WAITED PATIENTLY for the R.U.B. to leave. She'd brought him a glass of water about an hour ago without his asking, but he'd failed to take the hint. Or stop drinking. Now he claimed to be killing the pain, but she had a feeling he wasn't talking about the ache in his bruised jaw. Her gut told her this guy had woman problems.

"Kat!" Brian hollered, motioning her over. "Jack here says he wants to get a tattoo. I told him that was Master Jäger talking, but he says he don't know anybody by that name."

Laughing at his own joke, Brian would have toppled off his chair if Kat hadn't been close enough to steady him. "Can I call your wife to come pick you up, Brian? You're in no condition to drive."

"Huh? No. Me'n my friend need another round."

"Not unless your friend plans on letting you sleep it off in his hotel room." Brian wasn't a bad guy; he just didn't know his limit.

"Aw, Kat, you're no fun. What happened to you? You used to be fun. 'Member when we played on the same softball team? You 'n me 'n…um, what was your second husband's name? I forgot."

She rolled her eyes. "Me, too. About as often as he

forgets to send his child support." She didn't care if that was more information than the stranger who was staring at her needed to know. She looked at him and said, "What about it, mister? Are you claiming responsibility for this inebriated galoot?"

His left eyebrow rose in a perfect arch that gave his face a sort of Daniel Craig look. She'd seen that particular James Bond movie three times. Now, there was a man with big-screen swoo. "How 'bout if I buy him dinner?"

"Good idea. Make sure he orders coffee, not wine."

He nodded but made no effort to get up. She assumed he was waiting for a menu, so she explained, "We're just a bar, but there are a bunch of restaurants around. The one next door has a pretty decent chicken-fried steak."

He blanched, which made the faint bruise on his cheek more noticeable.

"Are you feeling sick?"

He shook his head. "No. It's just…well, my dad took drugs for his high cholesterol since his mid-forties, had quadruple bypass surgery and suffered a fatal heart attack when he was fifty-eight. A chicken-fried steak sounds lethal." He paused a moment, then shrugged. "That's what I'm going to order."

"You have a death wish?"

"Me? Heck, no. Ask anybody who knows me. I'm boringly predictable. Especially where food is concerned. I wash my prewashed spinach," he said, tellingly.

She didn't see what was so bad about that. She might, too, if she could afford the bagged stuff.

"This trip is about doing things I would never normally do," he added.

"Like get a tattoo," Brian repeated. "That's why he

came in here. To get drunk enough not to feel the needles, but I told him how bad it was when I got this baby done." He yanked up his shirtsleeve to show them the large, colorful parrot on his upper arm. "Hurt like freakin' hell. Worth it, though. I call her Linda, after my wife. That's Spanish for beautiful."

"Leen-da," Kat said softly, using the accent she'd picked up while satisfying her foreign-language minor.

The stranger must have heard because he looked at her sharply…until Brian slapped his hand on the table. "Hey. I know. You can hire Kat to do your tat, man. She don't use needles. She does that other stuff. What's it called, Kat?"

"Henna," she supplied, wishing the bar was busier so she'd have an excuse to get out of this conversation. She'd operated a booth for years at summer street fairs, giving artful, semipermanent tattoos. Henna was a stain that bonded to the skin and didn't wash off, but faded slowly enough to create the illusion of a tattoo—without the regret that often came later.

Brian's newfound friend looked interested. "That's brownish red, isn't it? But you can do black, right? A friend of mine got a really elaborate armband design that looked like the real thing from a distance. And in photos," he added, as though that was important to him.

She assumed he was one of those people who put a lot of stock in what others thought. The kind who'd judged her all her life.

"I only do henna."

He scrutinized her a moment. "You don't have any black henna?"

"Actually, there's no such thing. Black dye contains

PPD. I can't remember what that stands for, exactly, but it's outlawed by the FDA."

He exchanged a look with Brian. A guy look. She knew it well. *Law? Law? We don't need no stinkin' laws.* It was the same with marriage vows. "But it's still used," the man insisted. "Like I said, my friend was on a beach in Florida over spring break when he had it done. No side effects. No problems whatsoever."

"Yeah. Same with my wife," Brian said. "Linda had one done on her leg when we were in Mexico. Liked it so much she bought a kit. She was going to give Kat some competition at the street fair but never got around to it. Like usual. It's collecting dust with all the other crap in my garage."

"Could I buy it?" the R.U.B. asked.

"Hell, you can have it, man. No problem."

Kat had an opinion about Brian's wife's lack of successful endeavors, but she kept it to herself. "How long ago did you buy it?" she asked. "An out-of-date product could be even more dangerous."

Brian frowned in thought, but before he could come up with a date, her prospective customer said, "I'm healthy as a horse, and like I said earlier, not allergic to anything. Will you do a design in black if I supply my own ink?"

"Don't you want to know how much I charge?"

"Not really," he said, confirming her first impression. He must have money. And she'd be a fool not to let a hundred bucks or so float into her pocket—even if she wasn't crazy about using a product she'd never tried.

He had several plusses in his favor. He wasn't a sweaty, stinky behemoth, like several of her former clients. And a part of her was really curious about what was under that do-rag. A receding hairline, no doubt.

"You don't have to worry about the price, Jack," Brian said, slapping the man on the back. "Kat'll treat you fair. She's gonna be a schoolteacher pretty soon and then she won't have to work here no more."

Kat grasped the convoluted logic. She'd been working at a bar too long. She was beginning to talk drunk.

"None of my teachers were ever that pretty," Jack complained.

"Mine, neither," Brian agreed.

The two men toasted their mutual deprivation.

Kat sighed as she pulled her pen from her hip pocket. "Here's my number," she said, neatly printing the seven digits on the grainy white surface of a napkin. "Call me tomorrow. I want to research the black dye on the Internet. If it's too risky—"

He cut her off. "It's my risk, and I'll sign a paper abslo…absov…absolving—tough word—you of any responsibility."

She was curious about why this was so important to him, but she knew better than to ask in front of another guy. Not if she wanted a truthful answer.

"If you want to buy Brian's so-called black henna, that's up to you. I'll let you know my answer in the morning. But I don't have a cell, so you'll have to call before ten if you want to set something up."

"What happens at ten?"

"I take my son to his summer arts program. I normally get back around eleven, though, so I could probably fit you in then."

"Can you do more than one tattoo?"

"I have a folder full of designs. The price depends on the complexity and how long it takes."

"No problem. Do I come to you?"

She gripped her pen a little tighter. Normally she did her work in a booth surrounded by other vendors. She'd done tats at her house for friends and family members, but she'd never invited a stranger to her home before. Nor had she gone to a man's motel room. The second image felt a bit too sleazy. "I guess that'll work. We can do it on the deck. I'll give you directions when you call."

That seemed to work for him. He carefully folded the napkin and put it in the pocket of his jeans. She turned to leave, but a hand on her wrist stopped her. "I don't know your last name, Kat."

"Petroski."

He repeated it slowly, as if committing it to memory. She happened to look at his lips as he murmured the syllables and a tingle coursed through her body from the top of her scalp to the tips of her toes.

A direct hit of swoo.

"I'm Jack Treadwell," he said, offering his hand.

She swallowed a gulp of courage. *He wants to shake your hand, not kiss you, you idiot.*

She squared her shoulders and held her breath as she gave him her hand. She tried not to notice how smooth and warm his skin felt. Not sweaty as Drew's had been the first time he touched her—pulling her to her feet after accidentally bowling her over on the softball field. Or rough from working on engines the way Pete's were to this day from his hobby of building hot rods. One quick, firm shake, then she yanked back. "Gotta go. If you don't call, I'll assume this yearning to get tattooed was the Jäger talking."

"Oh, I'll be there. One more thing to cross off my list."

She knew all about lists—goals. She was one semester away from realizing a dream she'd set for herself when she was ten. She wanted to be a teacher and change people's lives. The way Mrs. Findham—her fifth-grade teacher—had changed hers. Lois Findham. The first person to see Kat's potential and praise her efforts. To a child caught in an emotionally brutal custody tug-of-war, the positive attention had given Kat a smidgen of hope.

Not that Kat's path had been quick or easy—thanks to the reckless choices she'd made—but she was so close to the end of the tunnel she could almost shout with joy.

And shout she would this coming December after she completed her student teaching. In the meantime, the extra cash this R.U.B. was offering would come in handy. And despite the fact that she felt a dangerous level of swoo emanating from him, she wasn't worried. She'd learned her lesson—twice.

This was a business transaction, not a date. Besides, he really wasn't her type. In fact, she didn't even like motorcycles.

JACK WATCHED Kat for a few moments longer as she made her rounds. A bright spot in an otherwise stereotypical bar decorated in an Old West style that was probably far, far from the real thing. He considered himself fairly well versed in Old West history and legend—enough to know that the facts behind the legend often got blurred in the retelling for the sake of the story. He didn't expect to see much of the *real* Old West here—at least not during this hectic celebration, but he could buy a forest-service map and head into the Hills. Do some exploring. *Wind up lost.*

He wasn't sure whether the voice in his head was his mother's or Jaydene's. Frowning, he took a drink from the glass of water the waitress—Kat—had brought without him asking. It was cold and delicious. He hadn't realized how parched he was. Maybe he was also drunker than he'd thought. Kat had seemed to think so when she'd urged him to get some supper.

"So, how 'bout a fricken…shicken…fried chicken steak?"

Brian chortled. "Okay." He dug in his pocket for what Jack hoped was money, not car keys.

"Lesgo," he said, tossing a ten on the table.

Jack added another twenty just to be safe. He'd lost track of their bill several rounds ago. He looked for Kat to thank her and confirm their meeting the next day, but she was nowhere to be seen.

The disappointment he felt surprised him. She was pretty. And nice. But that didn't mean he'd ever give in to the attraction he felt for her. He'd made it a rule never to date women with children. He didn't like kids. It didn't take a psychiatrist to figure out why. His father's career as a dentist—and his life—had been ruined by a lying, conniving child who had been coached by his greedy, low-life parents to say Jack's father had touched him inappropriately. And since Jack's dad had been performing the dental procedure on a weekend—free of charge—to an underprivileged child, there hadn't been any staff or dental assistant to say otherwise.

Jack had been fifteen. Even in a city the size of Denver, the rumors had gotten around. His once respected, beloved, community-minded father found himself defending his honor, his veracity and his livelihood. The team of lawyers that represented his father's insurance company had pushed for a settlement to avoid the cost of a jury trial. They'd argued that the scandal would blow over faster—and his family would be saved the humiliation of appearing in court and hearing the allegation voiced against him—if he agreed to settle.

Money changed hands. The charges were dropped. His father was never the same. Nobody was.

All because of a lying little brat.

Jack paused in the doorway of the bar for one last glance over his shoulder. With any luck, she wouldn't look as cute and appealing tomorrow when he went to her house to get yet one more thing crossed off his list. Dull and unadventurous Jack was going to get a tattoo. Sort of.

He told himself if he liked the looks of it—and the way it made him feel—he might get the real thing done later on. Changing his image might be the first step in changing his life. Maybe Jack would no longer be a dull boy.

Maybe.

CHAPTER THREE

"HI, MOM."

Kat looked up from the washing machine, where she was fishing for a gray sock plastered like a leach to the enamel basket. The voice wasn't the one she'd been expecting. She'd heard a car pull into her gravel drive and the sound of the neighbor's dogs barking—an early-warning system she didn't have to feed—and had assumed it was Char bringing Jordie home from his first overnight powwow.

Char had already called twice that morning to explain why they were running late and apologize for missing Jordie's art class. Kat had been quick to assure her that the activity was on a drop-in basis, so Char could take her time. "Keep him," she'd teased. "I had the house to myself last night. You wouldn't believe how well I slept."

A lie. She always returned from work keyed up, so she'd spent several hours online researching PPD, contact dermatitis and other side effects of so-called black henna.

"Tag!" she exclaimed now. "What are you doing here? Are you okay? Did something happen?"

Her son heaved his disappointed-old-man sigh—that was what she called it—and dumped his backpack on the peeling vinyl flooring. "Aiden got poison ivy. Him and Dad are meeting Michelle at urgent care. Dad said I could come home, instead of hanging around the waiting room for who knows how long. I'm gonna see if there's anything on TV."

He didn't ask for permission, nor did he offer her a hug. He used to. Until last year. She really hated the distance that came with growing up.

"Not so fast, young man." She ripped a dryer sheet in two and tossed one half into the dryer. "Give your mom a hug or she'll hide the remote."

He rolled his eyes but complied.

He smelled awful—sweat, campfire, musty sleeping bag and fish—and wonderful. She squeezed him tighter than she knew he liked and as expected he protested with a groan. "Mo-om."

"Sorry," she said, plucking a twig from his white-blond hair. He was growing it long—to get his dad's attention, she figured. His father hated long hair, of course.

A horn beeped.

"Dad wants to talk to you."

To apologize for inconveniencing her by bringing Tag home early? *Yeah, right.*

She exited the door Tag had just entered and crossed the five-foot-by-four-foot porch her landlord euphemistically called a patio-slash-deck. It had been tacked to the double-wide modular home before Kat moved in, and in his opinion warranted an extra seventy-five dollars worth of rent. Kat didn't agree, but she paid it, anyway because the location provided easy access to both Sentinel Pass, the town she called home, and the northern Black Hills communities of

Lead, Deadwood and Spearfish where she worked and went to school.

She took a deep breath of fairly cool morning air as she trotted down the slight incline to the driveway. "Hey, what's up?" she asked, rising on her toes to look inside the older Ford Explorer. "Not feeling so hot, Aiden?"

The boy in question, slim and dark-haired, was strapped in a booster chair in the backseat. Although the same age as Jordie, Aiden had his mother's slight build. Michelle was half-Korean, and Aiden had thick black hair and dark brown eyes. Nobody who saw Tag and Aiden together believed they were half brothers.

The child shook his head and squirmed uncomfortably, although Kat couldn't see any visible evidence of red patches on his skinny arms or legs.

"It's around his butt," Pete said, as if reading her thoughts. He looked more irked than sympathetic, but it was hard to tell, thanks to the two-day growth of stubble on his jaw and neck. A neck that had thickened considerably in the years since their divorce.

"He had to take a crap when he and Tag were hiking and he used leaves to wipe."

"Ooh." Kat cringed, remembering when something like that had happened to Tag. His genitals had become so inflamed he'd had to sit in a special soak for several days. "That's too bad, Aiden. But it'll go away with the right medicine."

Twin tears welled up in the boy's eyes and his bottom lip started to quiver. Kat knew her ex-husband well enough to know he wasn't cutting Aiden a lot of slack.

Pete made a face when he looked in the rearview mirror, but he didn't say anything. The scolding would come, Kat knew. Pete was as emotionally distant as Kat's father, which was one reason she'd divorced him.

"I'll be back for Tag in a couple of hours," he said. "I figured he'd be better off here than hanging around a waiting room."

She agreed, but she didn't appreciate Pete's treating her like a drop-in child-care center. "You should have called first, Pete. What if I wasn't here?"

He shrugged. "You know what reception is like around Deerfield Lake. It was faster to swing by. If you weren't here, I'd have just taken him with me."

"I might have had plans."

He put the car in gear and eased back a few inches. "Do you want me to take him or not? I really don't have time for this, Kat."

Well, neither do I, she wanted to shout. But she didn't. Shouting was what her parents had done. Every time one had dropped her off at the other's house there'd been shouting. She'd promised herself she wasn't going to do that to her children—even if it made her look like a doormat.

"He can stay, but keep your cell phone on. If I have to meet Char to pick up Jordie, I'll drop Tag off in town." She didn't mention her potential tattoo client.

"Whatever."

She waved at the sad little tyke in the backseat. Pete was always hardest on those he loved most, but how do you explain that to a six-year-old?

She watched the car drive off, wondering as usual if she could have done things differently where both her ex-husbands were concerned.

"Mom," Tag called from the porch. "Jordie's on the

phone. He wants to stay longer with Char. He said he's learning how to make arrowheads. How come I can't do that? I never get to do anything fun."

Kat had to work to keep a straight face. "You were fishing and camping, remember?" she asked, dashing back to the house. She took the phone from his outstretched hand. "Char took Jordie to the powwow because I worked last night. You know that."

His bottom lip stuck out belligerently, but she sensed that his disappointment stemmed more from not being with his father than from not attending a Lakota festival. He shrugged and walked back into the living room, where he had a video game set up.

Kat hopped up on the washer and put the phone to her ear. "Hello, son. Are you having a good time?"

"Yeah. It's cool. We ate Indian tacos last night."

Jordie loved food. "Mmm. Sounds yummy. What else have you been doing?"

"Swimmin'. And dancin', 'n playin'." He bubbled on about his various activities in a way that made her smile. Her younger son was most like her, and the tenderness she felt toward him had the ability to bring her to tears at the strangest times.

"I'm glad you're having fun, honey. Can you put Char on? I don't see any reason you can't—"

"Okay. I haffa go. We're gonna make arrowheads. Bye, Mommy."

"Bye, honey boy. I love you."

There was a loud clunk followed by a laughing voice. "Wow, Kat, that kid is hell on wheels. How do you keep up with him?"

"I don't. That's why I sent him with you," Kat said,

smiling. She slipped off her perch and tucked the phone under her ear so she could stuff another load into the washer. How two boys who had to be bribed to bathe could go through so much laundry was beyond her. "I fully expected you to be sick of him by now. Are you a glutton for punishment or what?" She and Char were close-enough friends to know when the other was kidding.

"He's having a lot of fun and everything is fine at the shop so I thought we'd stay another day, if you don't care…."

"That's fine, Char. As long as you're not sick of him, I'm fine with you keeping him another night. I'm a little surprised," she said. Major understatement. "But…"

"I know," Char said. "I expected to be exhausted at the very least, but he's a great kid, Kat. Really easy to be around, and the other children have sort of adopted him. Like a junior mascot or something."

Kat could picture it. Jordie was very good at blending in. Something he got from her, she figured.

"Hey," Char said. "I forgot to ask you earlier. How'd you do on tips?"

Thanks to a certain tipsy R.U.B. she'd made double what she usually took home. "Pretty good. Enough to get my radiator flushed."

Char chortled. "Keep talking dirty like that and I'll kick your kid out of my tent in favor of some young stud."

Kat smiled. Big talk from someone who practically qualified as a nun. Their mutual friend Libby theorized that something in Char's past had caused her to protect her heart with a fierceness that scared away most men.

"Jordie loves money. Maybe you could hire him to sell raffle tickets for the chance to woo you."

"Woo. Sounds closely related to your swoo. No thanks. So, what are you going to do with a night off by yourself?"

"That depends on whether or not Pete comes back for Tag."

"Huh? What happened to the fishing trip? I thought that was supposed to last all weekend."

Kat explained about Aiden's medical emergency.

"Oh, man, that sucks. Sounds like a trick a big brother who knows what poison ivy looks like might have pulled on a littler kid he isn't crazy about."

Kat hadn't considered that. "You're right. If I'd been more outdoorsy as a child, one or more of my half siblings probably could have sucked me into falling for that. I'll ask, but I hope for Tag's sake he didn't. Aiden's mother would make his life more miserable than usual if she found out."

Pete's second wife, Michelle, tended to be very protective of her two children, Aiden and baby Cassidy, to the exclusion of her stepson. Kat gave Pete credit for including Tag in family outings as much as he did, because she was sure Michelle didn't make it easy for him. Or Tag.

She and Char talked a few minutes longer. Char had spoken to Libby the night before and had the latest scoop on another mutual friend and book-club member, Jenna Murphy. Jenna and Libby were in California at the moment but were due back soon.

"So it looks like we're still on schedule for our regular meeting," Char said. "You're hosting, right? Tell me the title of the book again. I'll stop by the mall on the way home tomorrow."

"*Water for Elephants.* You'll love it. I promise."

They hung up a few minutes later without Kat disclosing the fact that she'd scheduled a tattoo at her home. Maybe because she didn't do impulsive things that involved strange men she met in a bar and her friend would assume Kat was desperate for money—which she usually was. But she preferred to think she didn't mention the tattoo because more than likely the handsome R.U.B. would be a no-show. He hadn't called, after all.

A good thing, she told herself. She didn't have time for men with potentially lethal swoo. Not when she was so close to finally getting her life on track. And as her mother had proved more than once, nothing could derail a great plan faster than the wrong man.

Kat had just set down the phone when it rang. Her hand shook slightly as she snatched it up before Tag could get the extension. If this was the biker named Jack, she preferred not to have to explain the call to her son.

"Hello?"

"Um…good morning. Is this Kat?"

"Yes."

"I'm Jack. We met at the bar last night. By the way, thanks for trying to keep me from making a complete ass of myself. I'm sorry about that incident with the Three Stooges woman."

She snickered. "Mo. How's your jaw?"

"A little sore, but I think I have you to thank that I'm still talking this morning. Was that guy she was with as big as I remember or is that the booze talking?"

His humility and embarrassment seemed in direct contrast to Pete's attitude. "He was rather large."

"That's what I thought." He paused. "So, um…are we still on for that tattoo?"

She swallowed the lump that suddenly thickened in her throat. *He's a client. Free money. You can do this.* "I printed out the information about the black dye. This is nasty stuff and it can cause some really bad reactions. I'd like to go on record as one hundred percent against the idea of using it, but if you're supplying the ink, I'll give it a try. No promises."

"Great. Brian dropped the stuff at the front desk this morning. Apparently he handles his liquor better than I do, because I could barely open my eyes until about an hour ago."

She liked it that he was honest about his hangover. Most men of her acquaintance would have pretended they could handle anything.

"I'll do it, but I have a small change of plans. My son came home early from his camping trip and his father could show up at any time to pick him up. Since I'd planned on doing it outside…well, if having an audience makes you uncomfortable, we might have to reschedule."

He didn't answer right away. "How old is your son?"

"Eight. He'll be nine in September."

There were a few seconds of dead air, then he said, "You'll be there the whole time, right? I guess it's okay."

She didn't understand what he meant by the comment but assumed he'd asked about Tag's age fearing she might need to juggle a toddler on her hip while applying the tattoo. "Do you have a pen handy? I'll give you directions to my place. Say at two?"

"Perfect."

He listened without interruption until she mentioned the turnoff for Sentinel Pass. "If you see a big white tepee, you've gone too far."

"Sentinel Pass? Is that the town where some film crew is supposed to be making a movie? Brian was talking about it last night."

Rumors had been flying ever since Libby's new husband, Cooper Lindstrom—a popular TV personality—had arrived in the area in response to Lib's online ad. And once Jenna's boyfriend, producer/director Shane Reynard, showed up a few weeks later, the truth had gotten splashed all over the newspapers.

"It's a television show, not a movie," she told him. "A half-hour sitcom. And the actual onsite filming isn't starting for another week or two. My friend's fiancé is the director."

"Cool. Never watched a TV show being made, but I'll be back in Denver by then."

A good thing to remember, Kat told herself. In case his swoo started to get to her. A very good thing.

JACK WONDERED why nobody warned him that the roar of a motorcycle engine magnified the pain of a hangover. The noise and vibration traveled up his spine making his brain feel as if it might explode inside his helmet. He'd meant to take another handful of painkillers before he left his hotel room, but a call from his mother had thrown him offtrack. Now he had to hurry or he'd be late for his appointment.

"Stop acting like a petulant little boy," his mother had scolded. "Jaydene will come around eventually."

Come around. The irony of her word choice would have amused him if he hadn't been slightly nauseous from the greasy meal he'd consumed the night before.

"Mother, as I told you before I left Denver, Jaydene

and I are history. She wants a different kind of life than I do." One that involved multiple sex partners.

"Oh, for heaven's sake. She's a senior loan analyst on the fast track for my old job. You're an orthodontist with a flourishing practice. I introduced you to Jaydene for a reason."

Until that moment Jack had forgotten that his mother had set him up with Jaydene. He'd arrived for dinner one night at his family home and had found a stranger at the door. A striking, thin brunette in very high heels.

In his gut, Jack had known for some time that something wasn't quite right between him and Jaydene. For one thing, he didn't share her fascination with provocative, sexually themed paintings and sculpture. For another, she talked constantly—especially when they were making love. Giving directions or being verbal about one's pleasure was one thing. Carrying on a thrust-for-thrust play-by-play got old, in his opinion.

But his mother had claimed the two were perfect for each other, and Jack tended to humor his mother. Partly out of habit and partly because his father had demanded it. "Your mother's word is law around here, son. She's smarter than both of us put together. What Rosaline says goes."

Well, Jack was sick to death of bossy, manipulative women. He was on a motorcycle in the middle of nowhere to prove to himself that he could make decisions without benefit of a committee. This meant taking risks his mother would abhor and his ex would admire.

If he survived the bike ride to Kat Petroski's house.

When he'd finally opened his eyes that morning, he'd told himself he was going to call her to cancel. Only a total schmuck would consider getting a fake tattoo. But the thought of numerous needles pricking his skin made him queasy. He hated needles so much he wouldn't undergo even the most benign dental procedure without complete sedation.

Was there some kind of subconscious link between his fear and his feelings for his dentist father? His sister seemed to think so, but Jack didn't like to dwell on the past. His father was dead, so any anger or disappointment he harbored toward the man was a waste of energy.

Still, one thing Jack had learned from hanging out in the bar so long last night was that no amount of alcohol could numb his anxiety enough to make him get a real tattoo.

A fake one was going to have to do.

And if he were being honest, he wanted to see Kat again. If for no other reason than to assuage his curiosity. She'd appeared in his dream early that morning. A winsome spirit with a lute that she claimed she couldn't play. "I'm looking for a man who can make my lute sing," she'd said.

"Is that a clever way of asking for sex? Did my ex-fiancée send you? What is it with you women? Is sex all you ever think about?" he'd railed at her from the fence he'd been sitting on.

She'd cocked her pretty head and grinned. "I bought this lute for my son and I need to find a teacher. If I wanted to have sex with you, I'd say so." Then she'd licked her bottom lip and given him a suggestive look that made him wake up with a woody.

Juvenile. Silly. He attributed his distressed libido to the fact he hadn't had sex in four months. At least he hoped that's all it was. She really wasn't his type. And he planned to remember that even if her kids weren't around when he got there.

He passed one garishly colored billboard hawking some kind of tourist trap called the Mystery Spot, then half a mile later he saw the sign Kat had mentioned. It featured a giant white tepee set against a bright blue sky. Native arts and crafts for sale. Four miles ahead at the Sentinel Pass turnoff.

He eased off the gas and looked around. He didn't want to have to backtrack.

Nice area, he thought, starting to take stock of the scenery. The highway wound through the middle of a wide valley bracketed by pine-covered hills to the right and a red-capped bluff of some sort to the left. The homes spread out along the road seemed hedged in by the escarpment.

Jack didn't think he'd enjoy living someplace that could be mowed down by an avalanche come winter.

"You worry about the most improbable things, Jackson," Jaydene once told him. She'd always used his given name, instead of his nickname. She claimed it was more dignified.

As soon as he spotted a split-rail fence leading to a steep driveway, he put on his blinker and checked over his shoulder to make sure it was safe to turn. He was still getting used to the feel of his bike, which was both fast and vulnerable.

A cacophony of barking dogs greeted him as he veered to the right toward a small, but neatly maintained manufactured home. No animals came out to nip at his tires, but the noise didn't let up until he turned off the engine. He put down the kickstand and got off. His butt felt tingly and a little sweaty. Something else they didn't tell you when you were bike shopping.

The sound of a door slamming made him turn toward the house. A young boy flew down the steps and raced to where Jack was parked.

"Sweet ride, man," the kid said. "Are you lost?"

"I'm looking for K—"

"He's in the right place, Tag," a woman's voice said from the porch. "But he's half an hour early."

Jack looked toward the house. Kat. Barmaid. Woman of his dreams.

"This guy's here to see you, Mom? Why?"

"He's a customer from the bar last night. I'm giving him a tattoo. Like I do at the street fair," she added, obviously trying to make his presence no big deal. "I just talked to your dad, Tag. He's on his way here."

"With Aiden, too?"

Kat shook her head. "No. His mom's keeping him home. You're sure you didn't have anything to do with what happened?"

"Mom!" the boy exploded. "I told you. Aiden went into the bushes to take a dump. He didn't ask me for help."

She stared a moment, lips pursed. "I believe you. I just hope he doesn't decide he needs someone to blame."

Jack watched the exchange with interest. If he'd ever raised his voice to his mother like that, she'd have had a bar of soap in his mouth so fast he wouldn't have had time to blink. She also wouldn't have trusted him so easily.

"Children lie," she'd told him years later when his father's accuser recanted his testimony. Too late to help his father regain even a small bit of what he'd lost.

"Your father learned that the hard way, son. I hope you're not as gullible."

Being accused of molesting young boys was bad enough, but being known as the son of a pedophile who beat the rap had its own sort of horror. And add to that the fact Jack's wisdom teeth came in early, making his canine teeth shift forward.

Kids lied. They could also be very, very cruel.

"Hey, Fang Boy, how do you suck cock with vampire teeth?"

"If your daddy did it, you must diddle little boys, too, right?"

Jack had grown up fast. The first thing he did when he went to college was get braces, using the money his late grandmother had left him. He was so happy with the end result and how it made him feel about himself, he opted to specialize in adult orthodontics, instead of family dentistry.

"Fixing a patient's bite is one thing," his father had argued. "Messing with what God and genetics saw fit to produce is not our place."

Jack knew his father secretly had hoped Jack would revive the Treadwell family practice after he graduated, but Jack had other plans. He didn't like kids, and he would never willingly put himself in the position of being alone with one.

"Don't touch the bike," he told the boy, who was squatting a foot or so away, studying the bike's engine.

"I ain't gonna hurt it."

"I know. Because you're not going to touch it, right?"

The kid—Tag, his mother had called him—looked ready to make a smart-ass comeback, but he didn't get a chance because his mother shouted from the porch, "Taggart John Linden, get up here this second. You are *not* going anywhere until you clean up this mess."

The boy's upper lip curled back and he muttered something Jack couldn't hear, but he sprang to his feet and dashed away like a young gazelle.

Jack was tempted to get back on his bike and leave, but as he reached for the key in his pocket, he heard Kat say, "I'm ready for you."

Her sweet tone was so far from provocative only an absolute, hard-up idiot would be turned on by it, but suddenly he didn't want to be anywhere else.

CHAPTER FOUR

IT TOOK KAT a few minutes to get things set up to her liking. She needed space to move around and visualize her canvas. Not that she considered herself an artist. But she had great respect for the history of henna art and she always tried to do her best for the customer.

"This is the first time I've had a client come to my house," she said, studying the placement of the straight-back kitchen chair she'd brought outside.

"Really? Does that mean you're a virgin, too?"

His voice was kind of scratchy—the ways hers was in the morning after she worked at the bar. But she had no trouble discerning the humor he'd intended.

"Yep. That's me," she teased back. "Both boys were the product of immaculate conception. Or so their fathers would like to believe," she added softly.

"Divorce is never easy. My sister went through a tough one last year. No kids, fortunately."

She pointed to the chair for him to sit down. "Yeah. Emotionally you already feel like a failure, but with kids in the picture you have to deal with their fear and guilt and hurt. It's tough."

He started to say something else, but she unfurled the drop cloth she would use to protect the deck with a crisp crack. Divorce wasn't the best topic to discuss before starting a tattoo. Just thinking about her failures made her tense and unhappy.

"So, you're from Denver. Nice city."

He gazed at her a moment before shrugging his surprisingly broad shoulders. Had they gotten wider and more masculine overnight?

"It's home."

"You have family there?" Not too obvious, right? She assumed he was single, but assumptions had gotten her in trouble in the past.

"My mother lives about a mile from me in one direction and my sister's half a mile or so in the opposite direction. No wife or kids. I was engaged until a couple of months ago."

Aha. "You traded your fiancée for a Hog."

His smile looked pained at first, then it brightened. "And I got the better end of the deal, too."

She chuckled softly as she opened her kit—a modified, plastic fishing-tackle box. "No bitterness, I see."

"The breakup was a good thing." His slight hesitation made her think this might be the first time he realized that. She could still recall the exact moment when the truth about her choice to divorce her exes hit home.

"Well, good," she said. "You have a fresh start, a road trip and, soon, a temporary tattoo to take home with you."

She stepped back and looked around, satisfied that everything was the way she wanted it, then handed him a plastic binder filled with laminated sheets of designs. Some pages included photos of the work she'd done on other clients. "Pick out which designs you'd like me to do and I'll quote you a price. Take your time. I'm going to check on my son."

Kat hurried inside, not liking the lack of noise she heard coming from Tag's direction. Her son wasn't above pouting until the last minute, then racing through whatever chores needed to be done—especially if he knew she was in a hurry. "Tag?"

He wasn't in the living room, but she was relieved to see that the video game was off and the snack plate he'd used earlier was no longer on the floor. She hurried down the narrow corridor to his bedroom. "Tag? Are you ready? Your dad should be here any minute."

She knocked once, then opened the door. The image of Tag standing at the window watching for his father was so sad and familiar she had to clap her hand over her mouth to keep from crying out. She couldn't count the number of times she'd stood just like that. Waiting and wondering. *Will Mom remember? Or will she be so busy with the other kids she forgets about me?*

Kat was the only child her mother shared with Kat's father. Kat's half siblings included two older children from her mother's first marriage and two younger kids from the guy she married after she divorced Kat's dad. And the web of extended family—some blood relations, some not—on her dad's side was just as complicated.

There had been times in her life when Kat felt like a jackalope—the mythical animal that was half jackrabbit, half antelope. She not only looked different from all of her half siblings, she always felt strange and unwelcome.

"Something wrong, kiddo?"

"I don't like him."

"Your dad?"

"That guy. The one on the motorcycle. He's a fake, Mom."

She vacillated between wanting to praise his insight—Jack wasn't an authentic biker—and feeling compelled to correct his manners. "He's a client, Tag. A stranger. And we have no right to judge him."

Tag turned to face her. "Dad won't like him, either. He might make us stay here until you're done giving him the tattoo."

"Your father doesn't have any say in what I do, Tag, and I'm not a fool when it comes to taking risks. This guy isn't dangerous."

After hearing the story of Jenna's rape in college, Kat wasn't about to take chances. Plus, she'd worked in bars long enough to sense the dark side of people. Jack Treadwell might be a little down on women at the moment, given his recent breakup, but he didn't seem the type to turn violent.

"Maybe not, but Dad isn't going to like him."

Kat didn't really care what her ex-husband thought, but she didn't want Tag to stay awake all night worrying. She picked up his bag and motioned him to follow. "Come on. You can wait on the porch with us until your dad gets here. Maybe if you talk to Jack, you'll like him better."

"He's a—"

"Don't say it. Whatever *it* is. You know the rule."

Tag rolled his eyes and muttered under his breath, "If you can't say something nice, don't say nothin' at all."

"Anything," she corrected. "Come on."

He followed behind her with enough distance to make it appear he was leaving the house on his own, not because his mother made him. She dropped his bag on the top step, then picked up her duplicate order form and pen and turned to face her client. "So, what's it going be?"

Jack looked up, apparently so engrossed in his choices he hadn't heard her return. His eyes were an unusual shade of gray, which made her want to study them. He glanced down and pointed to a design on the page. "You've done some really nice stuff here, Kat. What a pity they wear off eventually. Have you ever considered doing the real thing?"

She kept one ear on her son's faltering footsteps. "Not really. This is a hobby. To do it professionally I'd have to get more training, and I already have a career in mind."

"Teaching?"

She blinked in surprise until she remembered Brian mentioning her major the night before. "That's right."

"Body art might pay more," he said, his tone wry.

"That could be true in a state like South Dakota. Next door in Wyoming, starting salary for a teacher is almost 10K more."

"So you're planning on moving after you graduate?"

The screen door opened.

"No. I'll be happy just to have summers off to be with my boys. I'm not going anywhere. Tag and Jordie love it here." She motioned Tag to come closer. "I don't think you two were formally introduced. Jack, this is my son, Taggart. Tag for short. His brother is at a powwow with friends."

Jack leaned forward to shake Tag's hand. "Good to meet you. Your mom said you're going camping. Cool. Not something my father ever did with me."

Tag's hand looked small and grubby next to Jack's. And something about the image made Kat's eyes well up. She tried to hide her embarrassment by hurrying Tag off. "Wait on the step, honey. That way your dad won't have to honk and get the neighbor dogs all riled up." *Or get out to give me grief about my client.*

To her surprise, Tag didn't argue.

Once he was seated, she looked at Jack and said, "So, which did you choose? I think you said you wanted a couple, right?"

"This strand of barbed wire around my upper arm, for sure," he said, flipping back a couple of pages in the binder. "And what about this one for my neck?"

She'd had an idea which she thought would look best and was pleased when his choice matched hers. "Good," she said.

She was close enough to see his cheeks color a bit at her praise. She found his blush terribly sweet. And took a step back.

Sweet and swoo were a dangerous mix. "Anything else?" She tried to keep her tone stiff and professional.

He gave her an odd look but quickly skimmed ahead to one of the upper-torso shots. "This one caught my eye right off the bat."

She felt her eyebrows shoot upward. "Really?"

"What's wrong with it?"

"Nothing. It's one of my favorites, but I don't do it a lot because it costs quite a bit. And takes me nearly an hour."

"Is time an issue?"

She glanced at her wrist. No watch. She'd forgotten to put it on. "Um…I guess not. Henna takes longer to dry, so that adds to the overall time, but if you're sure about using the black…"

"Yep. Positive." He reached down and picked up a brown paper sack. "I read the printout you clipped to the binder, but nothing in the report has changed my mind."

Again, she wanted to ask why, but didn't feel comfortable probing into personal matters in front of Tag. "I'll give the ink a try, but no promises. We'll start with your arm. If it comes out okay, then I'll try another."

"Excellent," he said with a smile. "If it works out, I'd like this one right here." He poked a spot to the right of his heart.

She stepped closer and leaned over to see which image he was pointing at. A rose with a thorny stem and tears dropping from the points. The image cried, "Back off and leave my broken heart alone." At least that was what she'd been thinking when she'd drawn it.

Bloody thorns. A surefire swoo stopper.

"You got it," she said, suddenly feeling much better about her decision to do this at home.

A second later, the neighbor dogs started barking.

"Dad's here," Tag called.

"Uncharacteristically good timing," she murmured before dashing to the steps to give her son one last hug. He indulged her—probably to make up for earlier—then he hurried away, clomping down the steps in a noisy descent.

She stood for a moment, then waved when she saw father and son look her way. She didn't hang around to see if Pete wanted to talk to her. Instead, she walked straight to her supply box and picked up her bottle of mehlabiya oil. She'd already decided to follow her usual procedures even if she agreed to try a different dye.

"I need you to take off your shirt, then scoot the chair

closer to the railing. You'll lean forward and rest your right arm like so," she said, demonstrating.

"No problem." His words were muffled and when she looked at him, she saw that he was in the process of yanking off his T-shirt. Arms lifted, he struggled a moment, his bare chest and torso displayed with heart-stopping clarity.

He was a perfect blend of Pete's leanness and Drew's roundness. And most women would have killed for that skin tone. No visible tan lines. "Do you go to a tanning salon?" she asked, without meaning to say the words aloud.

Once his head was free, he looked at her. "Pardon? Tanning? God, no. Too busy. But I swim laps. Heated pool, so I can do it year-round."

A swimmer's shoulders. Of course. She should have known. Pete had been on the water-polo team in high school when they first started dating.

She cleared her throat. "Can I get you a glass of water or a pop before we start?"

"Water would be good. My body is definitely dehydrated after all that booze last night. I hope I didn't make too big a fool of myself."

She shook her head. "I was afraid I might have to tattoo over bruises today, but luckily Mo and Curly left pretty quickly."

His chuckle was low and intimate. Kat was sure he hadn't intended it as sexy, but her body reacted as if it was. Damn. He wasn't making this easy. But she was determined to stay detached and professional. Even if she had to hang out in the kitchen a few minutes and practice yoga breathing.

"Get settled. I'll be right back."

Jack watched Kat walk away. Well, walk wasn't the right word. She seemed to bound with natural grace. She was a petite ball of energy, and he liked her. Her kid he could live without. Sullen. Even with his back to the adults, Jack had sensed the boy's animosity.

My fault, he thought. *I could have handled things better where the bike was concerned.*

But what he didn't know about kids could fill more pages than Kat's tattoo portfolio. And he was okay with that. There were plenty of women around who didn't have children. Maybe not quite as many who didn't *want* children, but if he kept looking he'd find one.

Someday.

In the meantime, he could appreciate Kat as a woman and an artist. He didn't know why she didn't regard herself as an artist, but the sketch he'd picked for his back was gorgeous. A Celtic cross with ivy and some kind of lily entwined around it. He'd been drawn to it immediately, and expected to pay dearly, although she hadn't named her price yet.

"Hey, Kat, you were going to tell me how much. I want to be sure I have enough cash. I'm assuming you don't take credit cards."

She returned a moment later with two large acrylic tumblers filled with ice and water. The one she handed him had a straw. "This way you can drink without moving your neck," she told him. "When I start on your back."

After she sat her glass on her worktable, she passed him an invoice with his total bill circled at the bottom. "How's that look?"

Cheap. He'd add a healthy tip to bring it up to what

it should be. "No complaints." He handed it back. "I have the cash in my pocket. Do you want it up front?"

She shook her head. "Let's make sure they turn out the way you hoped. Now, for the last time, are you sure I can't talk you into real henna? It's a centuries-old tradition and the color is really beautiful as it fades." She frowned. "Technically, the dye is permanent. The reason it disappears is your body grows new epidermis and sloughs the dyed cells off."

He shook his head. "If the chlorine in the racket club's pool doesn't affect me, nothing will. I swear on my life I won't sue you if Brian's stuff leaves a scar. Do you want me to sign some kind of consent form?"

"I would if I had one," she said, releasing a deep breath. Her sigh had the unintentional result of reminding him of his dream. He took a drink through the straw to ease the lump in his throat. He needed to keep his focus on something other than her charming little body, her smell, her touch. It wasn't going to be easy, but small talk might help.

"So, tell me more about this Hollywood thing. Are they hiring locals to be extras?"

She put her hands on the outside of his shoulders to get him squared up the way she wanted. He felt tilted slightly to one side, but his view of the hillside was less provocative than watching her move. The reddish dirt reminded him of home. He'd done his share of hiking around Red Rocks.

She used a piece of fabric to wipe the area where the tattoo would go. Her touch was firm and practiced.

"Extras?" he prompted.

"Oh, yes. Sorry. I was visualizing this design and got

distracted. The TV show. Right. They are hiring people. My friend Libby put my name at the top of the list."

"I've never been around a movie or television set. They're not doing this for a couple of weeks, you said?"

"Uh-huh. I don't know the exact date."

"But you signed up?"

"Well…um…sure. I can always use the money. As long as the filming doesn't fall during the Sturgis Bike Rally."

The guy he'd bought his bike from had urged Jack to attend the event. "Motorcyles like you have never seen in your life, man," the guy had raved. "And the partying. Totally crazy."

Jack had purposely planned this trip to avoid the mayhem. A fact that would have made Jaydene laugh since his attitude seemed to support her contention that he was antisocial and unadventurous.

"You attend the bike rally?"

"Have for years. I can do a couple of grand's worth of tattoos when the bikers are in town. A lot of their lady friends want the look, but not the permanence. I do body piercing, too."

He tried to look over his shoulder to where she was squatting. "Really? Maybe I—"

She used the heel of her hand to push his head back down. "Piercing involves needles. No way around it. Now, sit still. I'm sketching in the gap from my stencil. Your biceps are pretty well developed for a dentist."

For a dentist. A general assumption he'd come to expect. His wasn't the most glamorous of occupations, but as a little boy he could still recall how proud he'd been when his father came to the school to inspect his classmates' teeth. Free. "Just doing my civic duty," his dad would say humbly.

Years later—after the accusation and brouhaha—people had speculated about his father's motive for volunteering to do the school exams.

Jack closed his eyes and concentrated on the strange feeling of a pen lightly dancing across his skin. The heat from her hand was there, too. The sensation was utterly sensuous and hypnotizing.

He wasn't sure how or when, but the next thing he knew Kat was shaking his opposite shoulder. "The first one is done, but I think we're going to have to move inside before I do the one on your back and your chest. The wind's come up. Feels like rain."

Rain? Not a good thing for a biker.

He blinked and sat upright, a little groggy from his nap. "I fell asleep."

"I know. Happens all the time. The applicator works like a micro massage or something."

His embarrassment eased. He picked up his shirt, but she grabbed it from him. "This ink is drying fast, but not that fast. Why don't you go inside and check out the design in the mirror? See if the black ink is living up to your expectations."

He stood, covering his yawn with his left hand. She held the door open for him. "The bathroom is straight ahead, first door on the left."

The vanity was spotless, but also jam-packed with juvenile toiletries—boy kind. A comic-book hero toothbrush. Some other action-figure soap dispenser. Two hairbrushes. Two tubes of toothpaste. Neither was the kind his father would have approved of.

He turned sideways. The image on his bicep was larger, and much darker, than it had looked in the picture. The black seemed to shine like newly spilled tar. He assumed the brilliance would fade pretty quickly. What surprised him was how vibrant and dynamic the design looked when he flexed.

"What do you think?" she asked from the doorway.

"I'm beginning to understand why people get tattoos. This is great. I love it."

"Phew," she said, wiping an imaginary bead of sweat from her smooth brow. "I'm glad. The gothic barbed wire has a lot of detail."

He looked at her in the mirror, standing close enough for him to see but not close enough to actually make contact with him. He found it funny that she remained so aloof after she'd just spent twenty minutes touching him. He wondered if her edginess was because of the small space he'd inadvertently invaded.

When her gaze met his, he saw for the first time just how blue her eyes really were. Like a Rocky Mountain lake reflecting the sky on a sunny day. Gorgeous.

She quickly retreated and motioned for him to proceed ahead of her. "We should probably get to the others right away. I want the ink to have time to dry before you take off. It could be a problem if you got caught in a storm."

He looked around as he returned to the kitchen. The living room was small—about the size of his office waiting room—but every bit as neat as the other parts of the house he'd seen. Probably a tough accomplishment with two young children. He could see stacks of board games under the coffee table and what looked like an Xbox or some video-game apparatus. Although his office manager stocked several of the latest games for their younger clients, Jack had never owned one. His father hadn't approved. He thought video games created fat, lazy kids.

Kat's son wasn't fat. Jack couldn't speak to the kid's ambition.

"How do you feel?"

"Fine. Although I'm a little embarrassed. I can't tell you the last time I took a nap."

"It was after eleven when you left the bar."

"And then I stuffed myself with chicken-fried steak. It was delicious, by the way." He even took a photo of the monster-size plate covered in white gravy. Rib-sticking, a heart attack on a plate, as he'd heard people say.

He lowered himself onto the straight-back chair that Kat had carried inside. "Let me put this pillow on the table. Rest your forehead on it and put your hands in your lap. Do you think you can hold this position for half an hour?"

"I'll try."

She cocked her head as if surprised by his answer. His sister often accused him of being too honest. "Girls like a little mystery, Jackson. You don't always have to spell everything out in black and white."

Maybe, but hyperbole wasn't his style. Which was why he felt compelled to set the record straight where Kat Petroski was concerned. "You know I'm not an experienced biker, right?"

She looked up from the binder she'd brought into the kitchen and set on the counter beside the sink. "Pardon? Oh, right. I already guessed that."

"Because the bike looks new?"

She danced a fingertip across the fabric of his jeans. "Your leathers aren't broken in. But, hey, you have to start somewhere. It's not a comment on your ability to handle the bike or anything."

She picked up her stencil and leaned forward. The smell of ink and something delicious, like oatmeal cookies, filled his nostrils.

Damn. Between her touch and her scent he was going to be lucky if he managed to keep from making a fool of himself. He turned his chin so he could see the door of the refrigerator. A small collection of school photos were grouped in one corner, with the rest of the space devoted to art projects and papers. A spelling test with a big red A-plus on it. A kid's pencil sketch of trees and a very large bird, probably an eagle.

He couldn't remember his mother ever hanging a single thing he or his sister produced anywhere in the house. She wasn't the sentimental type, his father once told him. "Mom lives in the moment. It's a good place to be."

But at the moment, soft hands were touching his back and a faint breath tinged with wintergreen drifted across the hair on the nape of his neck. Gooseflesh formed across his arms.

"Are you chilled? I can close the window. Probably should, anyway. Sometimes the rain doesn't give you any warning."

"I'm fine. Maybe you should skip the one on my chest. Would you believe I left my rain gear in my hotel room? Talk about unprepared."

She shrugged. "Worst case, you can put your bike in

my shed and I'll give you a ride to Deadwood. I need to pick up my check from the bar."

"You're not on duty tonight?"

She leaned down to his level and shook her head. The saucy curls bounced. Up close he could tell the sun-streaked colors varied from very light cream to burnt gold. He'd never been drawn to blondes, but that bias didn't seem to apply to her.

"I was filling in for a friend last night. I'd work there more often—the money's good—but finding a sitter is always a challenge."

"What about your sons' father?"

"Fathers. Plural. Two boys. Two ex-husbands. And as much as I'd like to say Pete and Drew are totally committed to making sure their sons' mother gets an occasional break, I'd be lying."

He couldn't help but smile. She didn't sound as if she expected things to be any other way. He wondered why.

"Can't you write that kind of arrangement into your custody papers?"

"Oh, that's how things started out, but life intrudes. Younger siblings develop rashes. Stepmoms have second and third babies. Schedules change, and since I remember what it's like when divorced parents bicker, I try to keep things on an even keel for my boys. Even if it inconveniences me."

He found that commendable. Heroic, even.

He'd been thinking a lot about what constituted a hero. Even before he knew for sure he was coming to the Black Hills, he'd read about some of the local characters, like Wild Bill Hickok. Was his enduring fame due to the circumstances surrounding his untimely death? Or did his legacy stem from a code of honor he'd held to dearly until that fateful night in the Number Ten saloon?

Jack wasn't sure, but the idea of exploring off the beaten path came back to him. "How long have you lived in the Black Hills?"

"All my life. I was born in Spearfish, but between my parents' divorce and my own marriages, I've lived all around. Custer. Sturgis. Belle Fourche. Rapid. You name it, I probably lived there."

"So, if I wanted a tour guide who could show me the *real* Black Hills, you'd be the one to hire, right?"

She bent down to his level again. "I've never done that before."

"Would you be interested?"

"Do you mean I'd drive you around in my car?"

He shook his head. "On my bike. It came with an extra helmet. You could give me a running history of the area and tell me where to go."

She frowned slightly as if thinking over the proposition. "When?"

"Tomorrow? If it doesn't rain."

"Well…Jordie is supposed to go to his dad's tomorrow for a week, and Tag has another two days of camping scheduled, so I suppose I could. But I couldn't do it for free."

"Of course not." He did some quick math. Eight hours. Forty dollars an hour seemed fair. He quoted her the price.

"Seriously? Deal."

She flashed a bright smile, then quickly ducked her head and went back to work. "No more talking. You're making my ink dry too fast."

He was careful not to chuckle. Didn't want to move and ruin her artistry.

He wasn't an impulsive kind of guy, but in two days he'd made two big, impulsive gestures. So far, he was very satisfied with the first. He only hoped the second would prove equally smart.

After all, there had to be worse things than riding around the mountains with a beautiful blonde on the back of his bike.

CHAPTER FIVE

"READY?"

Jack couldn't hear her voice over the roar of his engine, but he read the word on her lips. Her pretty pinkish coral lips that glistened in the morning sunshine. The storm had blown itself out during the night and the day looked very promising, Jack thought, turning off the deafening rumble of his engine.

He removed his helmet and got off the bike. In the background, her neighbor's dogs barked with a furor that surely would have meant dismemberment if they were loose.

"Enough," Kat shouted in the dogs' general direction.

The barking stopped.

"Nicely done," Jack said. "You're going to make a great teacher."

She seemed pleased by his remark, but she didn't acknowledge it. Instead, she repeated, "Are you ready for this?" She patted her purse, which had enough straps to qualify as a backpack, too. "I picked up a bunch of promotional fliers in case you change your mind about doing the tourist thing. And I have a really detailed forest-service map, too."

Something he'd been thinking about buying. Jack

liked that she seemed to be taking her role as his guide seriously. That made the arrangement seem less like a date. Which it definitely wasn't. He couldn't afford to date her, not after last night's dream. Another sizzler.

He bent to retrieve the spare helmet he carried. "Sure am. Everything square with your sons?"

She nodded but didn't elaborate. Maybe she sensed that he wasn't really into kids.

"I listened to the weather report and it looks like you caught a break. Hot and sunny all day."

The storm he'd ridden home in the day before had produced a mere sputter of precipitation, but the strong headwind had left him chilled to the bone, despite his leather jacket.

He'd spent the rest of the evening under the covers, his nose in a book he'd picked up at the convenience store. The more he read about Seth Bullock, local lawman-turned-entrepreneur, the more intrigued he became about the man behind the myth. According to the book, he'd founded a town in 1890. Maybe they'd have time to visit Belle Fourche, too.

"I'm ready for a little heat so I can show off my cool tattoos," he said, running a finger along the neckline of his T-shirt. He was careful not to touch the actual tattoo, even though he felt the urge to scratch it. Kat had been adamant about keeping his hands off it. "Shower with warm water, no soap. And pat dry," she'd said.

"I thought you might be thinking that, so I brought along some sunscreen," she said, holding up her bag.

He opened one of the side compartments. "Great. Drop it in. I'll put some on later. I've been cooped up indoors way too long and need a little color."

She hesitated—the mother in her probably wanted to slather him down, anyway—but after a moment tucked her bag into the space. She shook her head lightly before donning the helmet. The sun made her hair sparkle with white-gold highlights he had a feeling were completely natural.

As she tightened the chin strap, he studied her. For a small woman, she was nicely proportioned with a little extra padding where it counted. Her bright yellow tank top appeared to have a built-in bra because he couldn't see another set of straps. Her faded denim jeans fit her like a second skin. On her feet were well-worn hiking boots, and tied around her waist was a long-sleeved white shirt.

A man's shirt, he could see by the label when she turned to walk to the bike. Probably belonged to one of her husbands, he thought, frowning at the unsettling sensation in his belly. Why should he care if she still wore a former husband's shirt?

"So where are we going first?" he asked, throwing his right leg over the seat and scooting forward to give her room to get settled.

"You have two choices—north or south. I suggest south. Sylvan Lake. The Needles Highway. Harney Peak. If you're up for a hike, you'll get a fabulous view of the entire Hills."

"How long does it take to get to the top?"

Even though she wasn't snuggled against his back, he felt her shrug. The sensation made him all too aware of her. This could be a long day, he thought.

"I can't remember. I haven't done it in a while," she said.

Me, neither.

As if realizing her comment could be misconstrued, she added too quickly, "Four hours, I think. Up and back. Depending on how fast you are. I mean, how fast you walk." Her groan made him smile. "Can we go now?"

"Good idea. I think I'd rather ride than walk, but I'll let you know when we get there, okay?"

She nodded so vigorously their helmets clicked.

He looked down to make sure her feet were on the pegs, then he started the bike. When her hands settled lightly on his waist, he felt their warmth permeate his whole body the same way her touch had yesterday. It was a reward in and of itself. He didn't understand it and told himself any woman's touch would do the same thing to a guy who hadn't had sex in months. But a part of him knew that wasn't true.

Shifting sideways enough to make eye contact, he asked, "Can you hear me?" He tapped the side of his helmet near his ear.

Her smile showed pure delight. "Wow. That's perfect. I was expecting some crackling walkie-talkie thing. And I can hear music in the background. Daughtry. One of my favorites. How'd you know?"

He didn't want to admit that he'd seen the name on a list on her table yesterday. He'd downloaded it to his MP3 player last night. Probably a dumb gesture, given he'd never see this woman again after today, but he'd done it, anyway.

"Are you an *American Idol* fan? It's one of the few shows the boys and I agree on. Although that's not something they'd tell their fathers."

Jack didn't ask why. He knew why. There'd been hundreds of things he didn't tell his dad. And vice versa. Especially the big stuff.

"Turn left when you leave my driveway," she said, leaning into him, even though she didn't need to in order to be heard. "I hate crossing traffic, but it's fairly light this time of day."

"For the height of summer, I've found the traffic pretty tolerable. Especially compared to Rocky Mountain National Park."

"You won't say that when we reach Hill City," she said with a low chuckle that wormed its way into his very core. "And there's always a crowd around Mount Rushmore."

He checked both ways, then gunned it. The bike shot across the road smoothly. Kat resumed talking once they were up to speed.

"If we're not hiking Harney Peak, we can afford to take our time. I can show you some of the back roads, since you said you were interested in history. If this were a four-wheeler, there are all kinds of places I could take you."

He didn't doubt that for a minute. He could think of a few that weren't on the map. But the thought disappeared when the semi they were passing suddenly pulled out to pass the car ahead of it.

Jack swerved to the shoulder and cranked on the gas. The bike shot ahead and easily cleared both vehicles, but the sensation of flying, along with a rush of adrenaline, made his entire body tingle. "Holy crap," he muttered. "That semi driver must not have seen me. I flashed him, too."

Kat's heart felt squeezed to the size of a peanut and

she could barely find the breath to say, "Thank God you have sharp reflexes. That could have been ugly."

"I agree. But you helped by leaning the right way with me. You've done this before, I think."

"My first husband had a bike in high school. He sold it after Tag was born. Broke his heart, he claimed, but I notice he hasn't bought one to replace it."

She sat back and relaxed her death grip around his waist. "For being new to riding, you did that well."

His chuckle was low and masculine. "Thanks. It comes from driving with an inherently high adrenaline level."

Again, he downplayed her praise. His modesty was refreshing, but sometimes it rang false. She was about to test her theory when she reminded herself that she was a paid employee, not a prospective girlfriend. This wasn't a date.

She cleared her throat and looked around, wondering what to point out. A familiar sign made her cry, "Oh!"

She lifted her arm and pointed. "There's the turnoff to Sentinel Pass. We can start your tour there. Hang a right at the big white tepee."

Once they were off the main highway, she inched back. "You better slow down. The potholes are bad enough in a car. On a bike, they'll probably loosen old fillings. Everybody is hoping the new money coming to town will encourage the county to fix the road."

He didn't say anything, but the bike bobbed and weaved until they reached the outskirts of town. Since there was no traffic behind them, he pulled to the shoulder and stopped to look around.

Pointing toward the large purple-and-yellow billboard a few feet away, he asked, "What's the Mystery Spot?"

"Sentinel Pass's one and only tourist trap. My friend Jenna owns it with her mother. Her father was the mastermind behind it. He was also a scientist who taught at the School of Mines during the school year. He died a few years ago. The Spot is sort of hokey, but in a good-spirited way. My sons love it. In fact, Tag—the one you met—was going to work for Jenna this summer, but it didn't work out."

"How come?"

"Too much driving on my part." And considering the price of gas… "He's still mad at me."

"My mother wouldn't let me work when I was a kid, either. Because of my asthma. I don't remember how old I was, but it seemed like everybody I knew had a summer job—even the girls. I felt left out."

That had been one of Tag's arguments, too. "When he has a car of his own, he can work wherever he wants."

"But he won't have as many choices and he won't have had this experience to put on a résumé."

She sat back with a snort. "Why do people who don't have kids always have the strongest opinions about how to raise them?" she asked. "He won't be nine for another couple of months. This so-called job was really my friend's attempt to help me out with child care this summer while giving Tag a chance to earn a little spending money."

"Oh. I see." His chuckle sounded conciliatory. "Sorry. You're right. Not my business. But I do remember giving my mother a hard time for depriving me." He said the word mockingly. "Fortunately, I discovered swimming that summer and my asthma got better. Plus, I was living in a city where I had access to public transportation. So, I'll keep my mouth shut from now on, okay?"

She nodded, embarrassed by her outburst. She wasn't usually so quick to take offense. Ever the peacemaker, her mother used to say.

"Let's cruise through town," she suggested. "I'll point out all the historic spots. Like Seymour, our dinosaur. And the post office where Libby worked as postmaster."

"She's married to what's-his-name…the talent-show guy?"

"Cooper Lindstrom. He and Lib are so much in love it almost hurts to see them."

He put the bike in gear and slowly made the turn. Kat sat up a little straighter, hoping to see someone she knew. How often did a mother of two get to ride behind a handsome guy on an awesome new Harley?

"Why?"

"Why what?"

"Why does it hurt to see them together?"

She hated the way he not only listened, but actually heard what she said. She wasn't used to that. "Um…well—" how honest did she want to be? "—because seeing Libby and Cooper together makes you wonder if that all-encompassing, only-in-romance-novels kind of love is ever going to come your way or if you're going to be a freakish statistic that throws off the bell curve your whole life."

He didn't say anything for a moment, but stopped the bike in the visitors' parking just the other side of the fire station. He turned off the engine and removed his helmet. Kat did, too, even though her cheeks were on fire.

"I want to meet these people," he told her when they were both standing.

"Are you making fun of me?"

He shook his head, but he was smiling, so she wasn't certain he meant it. "I've never seen that kind of love and I want to."

She was still trying to make up her mind whether or not he was kidding when a voice called, "Kat? What are you doing here?"

Kat spun around so fast she almost dropped her helmet. "Char. Why aren't you at the tepee?" They hadn't talked since Char brought a happy, exhausted Jordie home the day before.

"I had to mail a bunch of stuff. Thank God for Internet sales, that's all I can say." She looked from the bike to Kat to Jack and back to Kat. "I told you I've forgiven eBay for screwing up Libby's original ad, right? I mean, why not? It all worked out. And it was partly Lib's fault for thinking she could post an ad without naming an exact dollar figure."

Kat hadn't really paid much attention to Libby's original ad, which had been responsible for bringing her plight to Cooper's attention, but she did know that Char listed a great many items on the online auction site. "I guess… Um, Char, this is Jack…" Her mind went blank.

"Treadwell," Jack supplied. "Nice to meet you."

They shook hands. "He's from Denver. I'm showing him around the Hills."

One of Char's dramatically arched eyebrows lifted. "Starting in Sentinel Pass?"

"Yeah," Kat said, standing her ground. "That's the point, isn't it? All the hype about the TV show is supposed to bring tourists in. Jack's a tourist. He wanted to see the place. Right?"

Jack's enigmatic gray eyes were glinting with humor, but he nodded gamely. "I especially want to see the famous lovers."

Char's explosion of laughter nearly made her drop her fistful of mail. "Which pair? We've got two, you know. This love thing seems to be catching. Might be something in the water. Which is why I drink wine."

Kat rolled her eyes. They'd had this discussion before. Char had made it clear she didn't believe in love, despite her addiction to romance novels. "Libby and Jenna aren't back yet, are they?"

Char shook her head. "I'm picking Jenna up at the airport on Sunday. She said she tried to call you last night and didn't get an answer. Libby and Coop are flying home later. He didn't want her traveling without him. I don't know why. She's pregnant, not an invalid."

Kat knew why. Neither of her exes—or anyone else in her family—had ever worried about her like that, but then, nobody had ever loved her the way Cooper loved Libby. Which probably wasn't surprising. To be loved, first you had to be seen for who you really were.

"Kat?"

Kat blinked, glancing from Jack to Char. "Huh? Sorry. Zoned out for a minute. I was…um…trying to map out our next stop." *Liar.*

"I told Jack if he's still here on the tenth, Cooper is throwing a big party for the town. Everyone is invited."

Libby had mentioned something about a whole-town celebration since their wedding had been so small and rushed to dodge media intrusion. "I didn't know they set a date. Lib said they wanted to coordinate it around the Sentinel Pass filming."

Char shrugged as if that part of the deal didn't interest her in the least. "How's Jordie?"

"Good. I think he's in love with you."

Char kicked her beautifully beaded moccasin against the base of Seymour's pedestal. "He's the sweetest kid I've ever known. If I had a kid, I'd want him to be just like Jordan."

Kat heard a funny catch in her friend's voice, but before she could give it more thought, a horn honked behind them. Char pivoted like a dancer and gracefully loped to the large, dusty four-wheel-drive truck that sat double-parked on Main Street.

"Don't you people work for a living?" the driver hollered good-naturedly through the open passenger window.

Char hopped up on the running board. Kat couldn't make out their conversation, so she turned to Jack. "That's Mac. Libby's brother. He and Lib own the Little Poke gold mine, which is going to be one of the spots the film crew plans to use locally."

Jack looked puzzled. "That truck looks like it's on its last leg. I thought gold was worth a lot of money right now."

"I think you're right, but it also costs a fortune to get it out of the ground. Are you interested in mines? I could ask Mac to give you a tour."

He shook his head. "Naw. That's okay. Dark tunnels don't really appeal to me."

Her, neither. But she couldn't help thinking that his list of phobias was growing. Kids. Needles. Tight spaces. But he knew how to drive a bike. That had to count for something.

Not that she had a mental scorecard going or anything. Nope. She wasn't going to rejoin the dating game till her boys were in high school. Maybe college.

Jack studied Mac's truck a moment, then scanned the street. His expression said he didn't see what the whole fuss was about, but that was probably to be expected since he didn't know Libby and Cooper.

He nodded toward the bike. "We should probably be going, huh?"

"Right." She waved to her friends. "See you later, Mac. Say hi to Megan for me. I'll call you tonight, Char."

"Bye. Nice meeting you, Jack. Hope to see you around."

She felt funny hopping behind Jack with her friends watching, but once she'd made it clear that her interest in the man was purely mercenary, she was sure they wouldn't try to play matchmaker.

Powerful swoo not withstanding, the guy wasn't her type. Even if she was in the market. Which she wasn't.

CHAPTER SIX

ACCORDING TO HIS ODOMETER, they'd traveled just under a hundred miles when the first sense that something wasn't right sank into his consciousness. They'd twined along the Needles Highway—a most impressive and at times confounding landscape. He'd been tempted to change his mind about walking to the top of Harney Peak when they stopped at Sylvan Lake, but by then the morning was almost gone, so he'd chosen to head to Custer State Park, instead.

And he was glad he had. The views were amazing, the road just challenging enough to be able to drive and talk. And the conversation had been heady. Kat was not only sweet and accommodating, she was smart. And she knew her Black Hills lore. He liked it that she didn't buy history's attempt to whitewash reputations.

"Seth Bullock is a perfect example," she was saying, leaning closer as she had every time she had a point to make. Normally, he'd have enjoyed the contact, but at the moment, his skin was tingling—in a not-so-pleasant way—around the areas where she'd put his tattoos. "He was strong enough to hold on to what he grabbed in Deadwood and smart enough to make friends with powerful people, like Teddy Roosevelt. Did that make him a good man? The people who lived in the little town near present-day Belle Fourche—I can't remember the name at the moment—might not have liked him much when he made a deal with the railroad that changed the line from their town to a spot through his land. Sure, he offered citizens of the town free lots if they wanted to move, but what about the ones who'd invested their life savings on a dream that he crushed?"

"I guess the HBO show got canceled before that happened," Jack said, trying to keep from wiggling.

She sighed and leaned into him a bit more. "Yes, well, just because a person is portrayed one way on television doesn't make it the truth. I mean, the actor who played Seth Bullock was excellent. Great eyes. Did you know that one of Seth Bullock's grandsons said his granddad never needed a gun because he had a stare that could stop a bull elephant?"

Jack didn't know that. Nor did he care, particularly. Something was wrong, but he didn't know what to do about it. He'd have to tell her soon if it didn't get better. Luckily, she hadn't seemed to notice anything was amiss.

"And one thing I've learned from Libby's experience is that TV and reality are quite often very far apart. If something isn't entertaining, it isn't relevan—" She paused. "Is something wrong? You seem really tense."

He swallowed. "I think I may need some of the sunscreen you brought. My neck feels a little hot." At least, he hoped it was the sun and not something else making his skin burn.

She pulled back and a second later he felt her fingertip prod his shoulder. Then the nape of his neck where the tattoo started.

He heard her swallow. "I can't see the color exactly because of my sunglasses, but the skin looks a little puffy. Let's stop somewhere for a cold drink and I'll check it out."

A nice ice bath—or jumping into one of the lakes they'd passed—sounded better, but he followed Kat's directions into the town of Custer. A few minutes later, they were seated across from each other at a pizza joint.

"Char claims this is the best pizza in the Hills," she said after taking a long drink from the glass of water the waitress had left with the menus. "How does your back feel?"

He stuck his fingers in his glass and fished out a couple cubes of ice. "It's starting to sting a little. Is that normal?"

He ran the instant relief around the back of his neck, locating the source of the anguish. The tattoo.

He looked at Kat, who was frowning. "If you're having an allergic reaction to the dye, it sure came on fast. From what I read, most reactions happen ten to fourteen days after application. Maybe we should find a clinic to check it out."

He made a scoffing sound. "I told you, I'm not allergic. But even if I were, I don't need a doctor."

She shook her head. "Men. That's exactly the reaction I'd expect from both of my exes. What is it with your gender? Haven't you heard of anaphylactic shock? This could be serious."

"The tattoo itches a little. Maybe that's the way the ink dries. No big deal. Can we order? I like pepperoni-and-mushroom."

"Me, too." Her smile looked conciliatory. "Actually," she admitted shyly, "I like pepperoni and anything."

She pulled out her forest-service map and showed him where they'd been and the road she planned to take back home. He pretended to pay attention, but the truth was growing more apparent by the minute that she was right and he was wrong. Very wrong. The fire was spreading from the tattoo on his back to the others. He wrapped both hands around the tall, red-plastic water glass to keep from scratching the spots that now felt as though an army of ants was setting up camp under his skin.

He shifted his shoulders without meaning to.

Kat's eyes narrowed. "It's getting worse, isn't it."

He slumped back in the booth, sighing as the air-conditioning-chilled vinyl made contact with the burning cross on his back. "My arms and chest are starting to tingle, too."

He waited for an "I told you so," but instead, she got up and walked away. Jack watched her cross the room to the pay phone hanging on the wall. She thumbed through the phone book suspended on a chain beside the phone. Her back was to him when she tucked the receiver under one ear.

She returned to the table at the same time as the pizza arrived. Jack's appetite had waned. Nerves, he figured. He hated doctors almost as much as he hated needles. "Thank you," he and Kat both said when the waitress slid the steaming hot pie in front of them.

"There's an urgent-care facility a few blocks away. We can walk there, if you want. The receptionist said it was quiet at the moment and they could see you right away."

He could tell she was serious about having him looked at—probably to protect her own interests, since her tattoo had created the problem. "Nobody ever died of itching."

"One of my half-brother's uncles died of an allergic reaction to shellfish. He didn't even know he had a sensitivity until it was too late."

Jack scowled. "I'm not going to die in the next ten minutes. Can we eat first?"

She didn't say anything. Maybe she was used to men acting like stubborn fools. She sat and slid a piece of pizza onto her paper plate. After a brief pause—to pray or see if he'd changed his mind, Jack wasn't sure which—she started eating.

She ate with gusto. Jack would have, too, if he could have kept his mind on chewing. He tried, but it was no use. The problem was a problem.

When the waitress returned to check on them, Jack had no choice but to ask for their bill and a take-out box. Kat pulled some extra napkins from the dispenser and offered to leave the tip.

He had to give her credit. He didn't know a single person who wouldn't have said, "I told you so."

Forty minutes later, a young doctor with an English accent gave Jack the news. "Beautiful work. Too bad you're allergic."

"How is that possible? I've never had a reaction to anything."

"You've probably always been allergic to whatever was in that ink. You just never got exposed to it before now. I can give you a shot to keep your symptoms from getting worse, and I'll prescribe a cream to help with the itching."

"Am I safe to drive my motorcycle back to Deadwood?"

The man's face scrunched up. He consulted his watch,

then sighed. "Generally it's best not to drive or operate heavy machinery after taking this shot. You will probably feel drowsy within the next half hour or so. Your wife is in the waiting room, correct? Can she drive?"

Jack didn't want to explain who Kat was, so he merely shook his head and said, "We're both on the bike. She doesn't have a motorcycle license."

"Well, then, I suggest you get a motel room in Custer, have your wife fill the prescription I'm going to give you and tuck in for the night."

Jack swallowed and let out a sigh of frustration. The cost of guide services was definitely going up.

"I'M AN ADULT, Char. The man is sick. The drugs knocked him flat. He's not a threat and there are two separate beds in the room. I'm perfectly safe."

Kat had called her friend after a great deal of soul-searching. She'd weighed her other options—catching a bus, calling one of her half siblings for a ride or hitting the street to find another room—this motel had only the one left when they'd registered. In the end she'd decided to take the path of least resistance. She'd sleep in the spare bed in Jack's room and beat him into submission if he tried anything fresh. Not that he could. He was out cold from the shot he'd been given.

"I only have one thing to say to you, Kat," her friend replied. "What would Libby do?"

Kat smiled for the first time in hours. She felt miserable. Responsible. And pissed off. She should have listened to her intuition and refused to use that crummy old ink. She planned to throw it in the toxic chemical recycling as soon as she got home.

"Well, Libby got knocked up by a man she barely knew. Are you sure we want to go there?"

Char's laugh eased a bit more of Kat's tension. "Good point. Hey, you're a responsible adult and the guy's swoo is completely nonfunctioning, right? Along with certain important body parts, I gather. So why exactly did you call me? Permission? Or confession?"

"Neither, you goose. I wanted to let someone know where I was in case Jack wakes up in the middle of the night and murders me."

"Hmm…maybe I should come after you. Custer's not that far away. I could be there in an hour after I close up."

Kat sighed into the small phone. Jack had insisted she use his cell to make her arrangements. "If you can find someone to pick you up, I'll pay for their gas," he'd said. "This is completely my fault and I feel like a total schmuck." Not something either Pete or Drew would have admitted.

"No," Kat said to Char. "Don't change your plans. He's already sound asleep. I bought a book in a gift shop down the street. I'll read until I can't keep my eyes open, then sleep in the chair."

"I thought you said there were two beds."

"There are, but it just struck me that I barely know the guy, Char. I'm not that comfortable around him."

"You looked pretty comfy behind him on that bike."

Kat wandered to the railing and looked at the motorcycle parked below the second-floor room. She had felt at ease with Jack until he started to show signs of an allergic reaction. She blamed herself, even though she'd tried her best to talk him into using henna.

"He's a nice guy. Smart. Funny. But still a guy. When I tried to talk him out of using that damn black ink, would he listen? Heck, no. He's as bullheaded and single-minded as either of my exes." She let out a sigh. "I'm starting a new chapter in my life, Char. One that doesn't depend on a man to make me happy, fulfilled or even to pay the bills."

"I know, Kat. And I'm pulling for you, but the guy is pretty cute. So unless you tattooed his pecker, he might be able to get it up. If you're there, anyway, what would a little safe sex hurt?"

Kat's bark of laughter made two strangers strolling along the sidewalk look her way. She ducked her head, blushing. "You're almost as bad as Jenna. She says the most outrageous things."

"And look how things worked out for her. She wound up with a great guy *and* a dog. I'm just saying, think about it and keep your options open. A lot of places have complimentary condoms at the front desk. You could ask. In case he makes a sudden, perky improvement."

Kat rolled her eyes. She was a mother. She hadn't had sex in...well, a very long time. She might consider some friendly, noncommittal sex once she completed her degree and had a job. Movies and sex every other Saturday night with a single coworker or something. But she sure as heck wasn't going to jump the bones of a perfect stranger who was nearly comatose from an allergic reaction she'd caused.

Shaking her head, she said good-night and tucked the phone in her pocket. She'd left the door slightly ajar so she could quietly slip inside.

"Is your friend coming? Did you tell her I'd buy the gas?"

Kat licked her lips and walked to the bed closest to the bathroom. Jack was stretched out like a man staked to die in the sun. Before going outside, she'd applied the thick white cream to his tattoos, which now resembled shiny black etchings outlined by a raised foundation of brilliant-red flesh. He'd stripped down to his navy blue shorts but had modestly pulled the top sheet up to the middle of his chest.

"She can't come. I told her not to break her plans because you weren't in any shape to attack me if I stayed here."

He opened his eyes and turned his head slightly. "My mother likes to believe she raised a gentleman. Her number's on my phone under 'Mom' if you need reassuring."

That made Kat smile. He really was a nice guy. Normal. Decent. She'd be fine. "How do you feel?"

"The itching is better, but my brain feels groggy. Definitely a good thing we're not on the bike. But I feel bad about screwing up your night. You didn't have a date, did you?"

Her hackles went up. That was the kind of question Pete would have asked. Before she could set him straight, he added, "I mean, as a single mom, if you have a night off without kids, you have every right to do something fun. And watching a dumb-ass guy who didn't listen to your very sound advice squirm in itchy agony probably doesn't qualify."

Her temper disappeared. "Oh, don't be so sure. I don't get the chance to gloat all that often."

His snicker sounded sleepy and she expected him to start snoring, but instead, he mumbled softly, "Beautiful, smart *and* a sense of humor. Perfect combination."

He thinks I'm smart?

She shook off the small shiver of pleasure his words gave her. "I bought a book to read. The light won't bother you, will it?"

She waited for an answer, but the only sound that came from his perfectly shaped, utterly masculine lips was a light snore.

Smiling, she unlaced her boots, kicked them off and tucked her stocking feet under her as she settled into the surprisingly comfortable wing chair. With a nice fat pillow from the bed under her arm, she got comfortable and prepared to read about the early pioneers' attempts to bring social structure to the raw, turbulent towns of the pre-annexed Black Hills.

She loved the subject matter, and the author's writing was intriguing, if not gifted.

But the sun and wind and fretting over Jack's condition quickly caught up with her. Her eyelids fluttered closed and her breathing evened out. Just a quick nap, then she'd watch *Letterman,* she told herself.

CHAPTER SEVEN

THE PEN FELT heavy and awkward in her hand. She couldn't explain why. As a teacher, she'd done her sums in ink ever since leaving school. Miss Marshall, her teacher, had proclaimed Katherine the smartest student and had awarded her a good-conduct ribbon, as well as a brand-new pen-and-ink set she'd gotten from back East.

The pen remained one of Katherine's most prized possessions. Perhaps because, from that point on, she'd felt as if her life had controlled her and not the other way around. Her parents had convinced her to move with them to the frontier where teachers were in short supply.

But so were doctors. And when the influenza came, it took them both. And her younger siblings.

Thank the good Lord above that she had a job, or else her life could have been much, much worse. She'd managed to save enough money from the tiny stipends she earned to keep the land her father had claimed—until the railroad came.

Of course, they'd paid her pennies on the dollar for the claim her father had given his life to procure. And her strident voice—a lone, strident voice, it seemed—against the bullying tactics of the railroad had cost her her teaching position. The board of citizens voted to find someone less confrontational. But they gave her a good recommendation to assuage their lily-livered consciences.

And so she'd answered an advertisement for a teacher in the Dakota Territory town of Deadwood. Room and board provided.

"And did it ever once occur to me to ask if the room included walls that kept out the snow in the winter and grasshoppers in the summer?" she murmured under her breath.

She'd sat down beside the small hearth of her dilapidated home to compose a list of complaints. Money abounded in this mud hole they called a town. She'd seen the gold for herself, spilling from a cloth bag gripped in the stiff fingers of a corpse that very morning. The man's body hadn't been discovered by the vermin some called men, or he surely would have been naked, as well.

She'd done her civic and humane duty and gone to the sheriff—a brooding hulk of a man who terrified her just a hair less than his gun-toting friend. The man they called Mad Jack. Not to be confused with Jack McCall, the infamous idiot who killed the town's most talked-about resident, Wild Bill Hickok.

Sheriff Seth Bullock and Mad Jack—she had no idea if the man had a surname or not—disposed of the body, but not before sharing a smoke and nudging it with the toes of their filthy boots. She'd gone home in disgust, planning to begin the search for a new position in another town. Even Kansas City would be better than here. Possibly Denver.

She had nothing holding her here—even though she'd grown to care for her students. But how could she possibly expect to make a difference in a place where life was so cheap and decency so far from anyone's mind?

She began to write. As was often the case when she was composing, she became so absorbed in the process that she lost her connection with the world around her. She didn't realize the door behind her had come open until she felt a cold shiver trace down her back. She twirled and saw him standing in her doorway.

Her heart climbed into her throat, making speech impossible. She gripped the pen as if to use it as a weapon. A study in futility. The man was known to have survived numerous gunshots and knifings. Death by pen? The thought made a nervous giggle bubble up and slip past her lips.

He cocked his head slightly in a way that most women probably would have found attractive. In fact, Katherine did find him attractive. In a self-destructive way that she was too smart to let sway her.

"I knocked," he said, his deep, smoke-roughened voice filling the tiny space.

"I didn't answer, but still you entered."

"I told Seth I'd check on you."

"Does that make you a dutiful friend or a curious interloper?"

"I lope pretty well. Or rather my horse does." He closed the door and took a step closer.

Close enough for her to see the hint of humor in his eyes, which she noticed were the color of smoke. What an odd thing to notice when she was about to be violated.

At least she assumed her time had come. Men who dealt with death so cavalierly surely would have no qualms about committing rape.

But his attempt at humor confused her.

"What is it you want, Mr.…?"

"Jack will do." He looked around. "Small place. Cold, too. You should have better. Maybe if you had a husband. A family."

"I had a family. They died. If I had a husband, he'd have probably caught gold fever by now and be up some gulch with a pan and a rocker."

His gaze returned to her and he studied her as intently as he had her accommodations. She employed all her resources to keep from squirming like a bug being tormented by a bully. No, she thought, that was the wrong analogy. His gaze wasn't harsh or dissecting. It took her apart but not cruelly.

"Rocks—even the kind with gold in them—aren't something that holds my attention. Learned that a long time ago. If I'm gonna gamble my time away, I prefer to do it with cards. The odds seem a little more even."

"Why?"

"There are a lot more rocks than there are cards in a deck."

She couldn't help but smile. But she wished she hadn't when he seemed to take her expression as an invitation to move closer. He was only a step away from where she was sitting. The room, which served as bath and kitchen, as well as sleeping area, was totally inappropriate for entertaining. Especially for a single woman and a man who was not a family member.

"You shouldn't be here," she said as teacherly as possible.

"I know. But I find I'm powerless to make myself leave. Until today I hadn't realized how beautiful you are. And strong-minded. You didn't approve of how Seth and I handled the situation with that body, did you?"

"I did not. You treated the deceased with less respect than most people would have given a dead dog. Your attitude has made me reconsider my place here. If the town's elected officials—"

"Nobody elected me to nothin'," he said, his voice rising. "We saw to the body as best we could. Did we wring our hands and mutter a prayer for his soul? No. Because, frankly, that body is the fifteenth I've helped Seth deal with since I got here. Old. Young. Sick. Gunshot. Murdered. Hung. Run down by a wagon. Every death—friend or stranger—adds another layer between you and fear. It's the only way to keep the blackness at bay."

Strangely, she understood. She'd cried when her mother passed. After giving birth five times, Mama's body had been the most worn down and susceptible to the fever. But as the others succumbed, Katherine had slipped a sort of fine kid glove over her heart. Layer by layer until she didn't feel any pain. Or anything at all.

She couldn't say how it happened, but wordlessly, she rose and went into his arms. Strong, sinewy arms barely cloaked by the coarse material of his coat. He smelled of snow and smoke. He smelled like a man. It had been so long since she'd inhaled those scents up close. They carried with them powerful memories. Her father washing up after a day of working the earth. Her brother sneaking in after courting his beloved Isabeth. Her mother handing her the baby to dry off after he tumbled in the creek behind their home.

She'd missed the touch of these strange male creatures. Her father's hand of support on her shoulder. Her brothers' hugs. Men had courted her, at times. She'd held hands with one or two and danced her share of reels. She'd even kissed Jeremiah Conroy before he headed west to seek his fortune. But she'd never felt drawn like this—a horse to the proverbial water. And she knew, deep down, that she would drink as much as she could take in.

"You are soft in all the right places," Mad Jack told her, his hands taking liberties no man had taken before.

"And you are not. But I sense a softness in your heart that I expect very few people see."

His low chuckle made a shiver course through her body, opening wells of feeling she'd never known existed. Her mind, thankfully, had stopped thinking about all the bad things that could—and probably would—come of this encounter. Propriety and honor were words that lived outside this moment, outside this room.

What mattered now was the roughness of his beard against her palms as she framed his face with her hands. He'd shaved that morning. She could tell. But the outline of stubble told her he was the kind of man who could grow a beard in a week, if he were so inclined.

"How is it that you don't favor a beard in winter?" she asked, bringing her cheek to his. She rubbed back and forth, enjoying the sharp but soft bristles.

"I do when I'm away from camp, but barberin' seems right when you're seeking the company of a lady." He reached behind her, his fingers skimming lightly over the pins that held her tightly twisted bun. "May I?"

She nodded. The only answer possible and one that seemed silly, given how many rules she'd already broken. But the moment his fingers scraped upward, loosening the heavy mane from its braid, her fate was sealed. The pleasure was instant and overwhelming. She put her lips to his. Primly. Puckered. The way she'd learned that one other time.

His answering touch was so different, so powerful and invasive, her heart stopped as his tongue parted her lips and entered her mouth. Was this normal? But the question barely had time to cross her mind before she answered back, her tongue seeking, tasting, exploring.

She was so preoccupied with the sensations she was experiencing in this new and strange arena, she didn't notice at first that he'd managed to remove her outer jacket and was working on undoing the buttons of her shirtwaist. "Oh," she said with a small gasp. "Of course."

He looked at her with a dangerously handsome slant to his mouth. Did he expect her to push him away? That would be the smart choice, but it was not her intention.

"My mother explained that when a man and woman have physical relations, men often prefer the woman to disrobe."

He threw back his head and let out a roar of laughter that both pleased and mortified her. She felt the heat that had been in other places flood her cheeks. She turned away, but he caught her shoulders and made her face him. "You are the most honest, forthright woman I have ever met, Miss Katherine. You don't belong with a man like me, and I've spent every day since you arrived in this godforsaken place trying to stay away from you. But we're here now, and I want you to know that you can trust me.

"I might not have much in the way of land or goods,

but I have my honor. My reputation. I don't cheat at cards. I don't shoot men in the back. And I don't lie to women."

"You didn't laugh because I'm naive and unworldly?"

"No, ma'am. I laughed because you are real and good—two things I never expected to *find* in this godless land, much less touch."

She finished unbuttoning her shirtwaist and went on to remove her skirt and the extra layers of petticoat she'd added for warmth. Her small stove was almost out of coal, but the instant his hands touched her, the heat within her body more than made up for the room's chilly temperature.

He shed his clothes just as fast and pulled back the quilts on her bed. The mattress was lumpy but the sheets fresh from her Sunday washing. He climbed in first and pulled her down so her body was stretched out atop him. She felt exposed and awkward. Her buttocks bare for the world to see—if the world had been looking. But then his large, rough hands covered her nakedness, squeezing her flesh in a way that sent liquid desire to a very specific crux between her legs. She wriggled in response.

"Not too much movement too fast, my pretty kitten. I haven't been with a woman in a long time. We don't want this to be over before we start."

"I don't know what to expect exactly or what's expected from me," she admitted, sharing a confession she'd never said aloud before, even though there had been so many times she'd doubted her abilities, her intelligence, her right to call herself a teacher.

"That's how we learn, my dear, and I would be honored to be your teacher."

So, she became the student. He slowly explored her

body and taught her to trace the same map across the hollows and valleys, plains and hills of muscle and bone of his. He touched her in the most intimate way possible and showed her how to experience pleasure she'd never expected.

"Oh!" she cried when he touched the pulsing, engorged spot in the mound of her feminine seat. That was what Mother had called it, but Mother hadn't said anything about the intoxicating—almost painful—release that came from a steady manipulation of the tiny button. "No more. I don't think I can stand to go there again. Beautiful though it was."

He smiled and gave her a look that nearly stopped her heart. "Honey Kat, that was the outer door. Beyond lies another world you'll want to visit time and again."

She didn't believe him. If that were true, her female friends would have talked about it. Her mother would have said something. Unless she'd never visited such a place. Maybe you only reached that world with someone like Mad Jack. A rogue. A scalawag. A—

Whatever other name she'd been about to call him was lost the moment he flipped her on her back and pressed himself against her. His male part was touching her female part at almost the exact placement of her lovely little button. She tested the fit by wiggling her hips.

The corners of Jack's mouth curled upward. "Now you can wiggle all you want, love."

"Except you're heavy."

He raised up slightly, but that lessened the pressure on her new favorite place. She reached behind him and put her hands on his buttocks. The muscular mass flexed and he shifted forward slightly. "Good," she said, closing her eyes.

She focused on the feelings, not the mechanics, and the voice in her mind that seemed to know what came next told her to open her legs. She did, even though that meant Jack's manhood fell between them. But opening wider solved the problem. He pumped his thighs slightly and the obstacle in question found an opening made for it.

"This might hurt for a minute."

He sounded so apologetic she started to say, "It's okay." But before the words could form on her lips, he gave a quick, solid push and was inside her. There might have been pain, but she was too startled to think about it. The sensation of a foreign body sharing space with hers was too unnatural, too frightening.

"Easy, there, love. It's okay. Trust me. Everything starts to get better now. Rock against me. Move a little and you'll feel it."

She did trust him. Enough to shift her hips.

"Uh. Oh. Yes."

He nodded in agreement but his eyes were closed and he appeared to be concentrating very hard. So she closed her eyes, too, and focused on what she was feeling. Color. Heat. Need.

The latter urged her on, searching for something she couldn't name. She moved with an urgency that didn't seem natural until suddenly it was as natural as breathing. And her breath was gone. Lost in an explosion of sensation that left her panting.

He'd told the truth. A door had opened to a new world of wonder and hope. The kind of place you prayed you'd go to when you died.

Maybe that was why he'd been so cavalier earlier about the dead man. Because Mad Jack knew there were alternatives to living. Some were just more permanent than others.

CHAPTER EIGHT

JACK AWOKE incrementally, and not without some regret. Damn, he'd had a great dream. He couldn't remember all of it, but certain images were crystal clear. The sex. He couldn't name another time he'd come that hard. And the woman in his arms had enjoyed it, too. No faking of that orgasm, he thought with a satisfied sigh.

"Umm-um..."

He opened his eyes at the unexpected sound, which hadn't come from his lips. His heart rate sped up as he looked around, trying not to make any movement.

Strange ceiling. Room-darkening curtains that cried cheap motel room. Extra-firm mattress that didn't feel familiar. And a warm, naked body curled up beside him.

He turned his chin to the left, halfway expecting to see long blond curls. But no. The head resting on his outstretched arm belonged to a real woman. Not the schoolmarm in his dream. This bed-head coif stuck up in every direction. She looked so adorable he couldn't help but smile.

Kat.

Even though he wasn't sure how she'd gotten from the other bed to his. Or wait. Had he been the one to switch?

He looked to his right. "Oh, crap," he muttered softly.

A second messy bed—the one he'd started the night in—was just beyond his fingertips. A cold shiver passed through his body. There was going to be hell to pay any minute.

As if picking up his disquiet, his bedmate stretched and wriggled in a way that made him horny as hell. For half a second. Then, she opened her eyes and blinked.

He felt the instant she realized where she was and that another person was right beside her.

"Oh, my God!" she exclaimed, scrambling sideways, dragging the covers with her.

Her look of abject horror was so obvious Jack felt naked and exposed as the sheets slipped off his body. Rather than fight her for control of the covers, he vaulted into the second bed and yanked the comforter to his waist.

His reaction pissed him off. That was exactly what Jack Treadwell would do. Mad Jack, the person he'd been in his dream, probably would have stood up and proudly walked to Kat's side to calm her down and maybe make love to her again.

He looked across the distance between them to where she sat, pulled into a tight ball of knees and eyes that had the proverbial deer-in-headlights look—right after making contact with a bumper. Too wide and not quite believing what happened really happened.

"Kat, I'm sorry." He wasn't. Not really. But it seemed like the right thing to say. "I don't know what happened. Or how. Exactly. I mean…I don't remember crawling into your bed. Maybe the meds…"

"I… We… Oh, shit. We did more than sleep together, didn't we?"

He nodded, praying the sense of jubilation he still felt

didn't show on his face. "Yeah, we did. Although…" He shut his mouth. Telling her that he'd actually made love to another woman in his dream probably wasn't a good idea. "I… Um… We… I'm sorry?"

She didn't appear to be listening to his pathetic apology. She pulled the sheets away from her chest and looked down, as if checking to see that her body was in one piece.

Jack couldn't help feeling a little offended. "It was straight sex. Nothing kinky. Just ask my ex. I'm as white-bread boring as it comes. No pun intended. I didn't hurt you. Did I?"

She looked at him, her face screwed up in either pain or horror. He wasn't sure which. "I can't believe I did this."

"We," he corrected. "We did this. There were two of us—at the very least," he added under his breath.

Her eyes narrowed. "Oh, that is so typical. Sex is just sex to guys, but I am not in the habit of jumping into bed with strange men. Or—" she whipped her index finger back and forth between his bed and hers "—letting strange men climb into bed with me. How did this happen?"

He could mention his dream, but he didn't think she'd buy his excuse that he wasn't himself. That he'd become an Old West gunslinger named Mad Jack. "Like I said. Maybe the drugs. I could have been sleepwalking." *With a six-gun on my hip.*

A laugh percolated upward, but he tried to cover it with a cough.

"Do you think this is funny?"

"Um…no? No. I don't."

She put her head in her hands and groaned. "Oh, God, not again. Please. Not this time. Not this man. No, no, no. It can't be."

"Hey, Katherine, I mean, Kat. Is your real name…? Never mind. Um, look, I know you're upset, but would you please not act like there's a dead body on the floor?"

She looked up sharply, her hands falling to her lap. The sheet dipped slightly, making it hard for him to remember what he was supposed to be saying.

He cleared his throat and made himself look into her eyes. Her clear, blue, gorgeous eyes that were swimming with tears. He wished he could hold her and comfort her, but he knew she didn't want that. "Kat, what happened was a mistake. Unplanned. Unpremeditated, I promise. But it's not a huge deal, right? I mean, we're both single, and I can fax you my clean health record when I get home. I had a full workup a couple of months ago and haven't been with anyone since. Until last night."

She used the corner of the sheet to wipe her eyes. "Why?"

"Why what?"

"Why did you get a full checkup?"

"I wasn't sure I could trust my ex-fiancée."

"Because you thought she might sleep with a stranger? Like I just did?" Her voice cracked, and he acted on his impulse to comfort her. Mad Jack would have.

Leaning between the beds, he spotted his navy blue shorts and quickly pulled them on. Advancing one knee at a time, he approached her. "Kat," he said softly, lightly touching her arm. "I don't remember exactly what happened. How we got together. How I came to be in your bed. In fact, the last thing I remember clearly is watching you read. Your lips make this kind of fishy look. It's cute." He tried to demonstrate.

Her upper lip quivered in a near snarl and he stopped.

"But the parts I do remember are really good. Hot and passionate. Like an X-rated movie, only with a plot."

She pushed his hand away. "In your dreams maybe."

Maybe. Had he imagined everything? "We didn't have sex?"

She shook her head. "Of course, we had sex. That part was real. I meant your X-rated movie scenario. I don't do X-rated. Ask either of my ex-husbands. I'm too uptight."

"Like a proverbial schoolmarm?"

She let out a little cry. "You're making me crazy. I don't know what happened or why, but it shouldn't have and I know there's going to be hell to pay for it."

He sat back on his haunches. "Why?"

"Because that's the way things happen in my life. Do you want to know my track record? O-for-two. Men were put on the planet to disappoint me. And vice versa, if you ask them. The swoo giveth and it taketh away."

He blinked. "You lost me."

"Better now than later," she said cryptically. Pulling in a deep breath, she gathered her sheet and blanket like a regal cape and scooted off the bed, showing obvious care not to touch him. She paused to pick up her clothes, then hurried to the bathroom. Once inside, she tossed the blankets to the floor and closed the door.

He heard the lock click emphatically.

He blew out a sigh of his own and pivoted to rest his back against the headboard. What a hell of a way to ruin a perfectly wonderful dream, he thought grouchily. If he closed his eyes, he could still picture his dream self. Cool and confident. A cross between Adam Cartwright and Clint Eastwood's character in those spaghetti westerns that made him famous. All charisma and untamed dark energy. A helluva lover. *Better than I ever was with—*

"Stop gloating."

He opened his eyes. He'd been so caught up in the memory he hadn't even heard her open the door. His face went hot, but he denied the charge. "I'm not. I'm…remembering."

"Well, don't," she snapped. "What happened didn't happen. Not really. That wasn't me."

"You were hot."

"Shut up."

"*We* were hot."

"I don't want to talk about it. What happened was a mistake. I've made plenty in my life. All involving the wrong men. I don't even know you well enough to say just how wrong you are, but…never mind. I need to go now. Can you drive? Or should I call my friend to pick me up?"

He looked down. The swollen mass on his chest looked almost normal. A slight puffiness still outlined the black tattoo that encircled his bicep, but the itching had subsided. He shifted around so she could see his back. "I feel okay. How's my neck look? Maybe great sex is a better cure than antihistamines."

Her low growl filled the room, as if from one of her namesake's larger relatives. Puma. Cougar. Angry lioness. "Then get dressed, because we're leaving."

She marched toward the door, chin high, but he could tell she was blinking back tears. "I'll wait outside. And I need to use your phone again," she said, snatching the cell from the table where she'd set it the night before.

"But I'm starving," he said, getting up. The bulk of his clothes were right where he'd left them, neatly draped over the chair in the corner. He pulled on his pants. Strange how his clothing had felt different when he'd been Mad Jack. "Can we at least eat breakfast, first, then I take you home?"

She fumbled with the safety lock.

"I'll meet you at the bike," she said, opening the door. She glanced at her watch. "Tag's dad is going to have my head if he tries to drop off Tag early and I'm not there."

She was out the door before he could ask her why the guy thought he had the right to drop off their kid outside the set times. Jack finished dressing and used the bathroom. He would have liked a shower, but that was going to have to wait. Besides, he wasn't in any hurry for his tattoos to wear off. They were a reminder of the best night of his life. If not for them, he probably never would have been in the same room with Kat, let alone the same bed.

KAT FOUND a shady spot within eyeshot of the motorcycle that reminded her all too vividly of the coal-black horse that Mad Jack had ridden in her dream. She groaned softly and fought back tears. Not only was she a loose woman of questionable morals, she was losing her mind. She needed help. And there was only one person she dared call. Libby.

After a deep breath to steady her hand, she flipped open the phone and punched in the number, remembering too late that there was a time difference between the Hills and the West Coast.

"Hello?"

"Lib? Did I wake you?"

"Kat? No, I'm up. Jenna and I have started taking early-morning walks along the beach. She spent the night with Shane, though, so I'm alone. Coop insists I carry my phone when I go out. I figured this was him checking up on me. He worries like an old woman."

Kat smiled for the first time in what seemed like several centuries. "He loves you, Lib. It's good to worry when you love someone."

"I know. I tease him about it, but actually he's so sweet I can hardly believe this life of mine is real."

Kat was envious. It was natural to kindle a little flame of hope when you witnessed love of this kind in someone else's life. For a while there, Kat had even dared hope that that kind of love would happen to her. But, no. Instead, she'd spent the night with a client and wound up making love to a figment of her dream—only for real, too.

"Is something wrong, Kat?"

Kat wasn't sure where to begin…or if she should mention the dream part. Would everyone think she was crazy? Maybe she was. "I gave a guy a couple of tattoos and he wound up having an allergic reaction."

"To henna? Is he suing you?"

"No. Not exactly. He provided the ink… That's not why I'm calling. Before his body started swelling like a puffer fish, he'd asked me to show him around the Hills. A paid guide. I said sure. I never turn down a chance to make money, right? But when we got to Custer, he started to go into anaphylactic shock and had to see a doctor. Because of the shot the doctor gave him, he couldn't drive. We had to get a motel room." She paused. "The town is packed. There was only one room left."

Libby giggled. "This story is starting to sound familiar. Was it in a stable?"

Kat let out a small wail. "Not exactly. And there weren't any angels or drummer boys, but…I suppose there could be a baby," she said very, very softly.

Libby was quiet so long Kat wasn't sure she'd heard her strange confession. Then, her voice filled with gravity, she said, "You must have had a good reason to sleep with him. I'm going to assume he's a really great guy and you've fallen in love with him."

"Nice try, Lib, but I don't even know him. He seems okay. Safe. Nice. But I didn't mean to sleep with him. And I didn't. Not exactly. Not *him* him."

"I'm not sure I understand."

"It's complicated."

"Try me. I'm sitting down now."

Kat looked around to be certain nobody was close enough to overhear her confession. "The guy I slept with was in my dream. He was a gunslinger back in 1876 or something. I was a schoolteacher. I remember seeing a dead body on the street and I told him he was callous and unfeeling, then the next thing I knew we were ripping each other's clothes off."

"In your dream."

"I thought so. And I can understand why I dreamed this. I was reading a history book about Seth Bullock and I sorta remember dosing off. But I have no idea where this Mad Jack guy came from. I mean, he's nothing like the Jack I tattooed. Nothing."

"Hmm," Libby said in a tone Kat knew well. Her friend wasn't the type to jump to conclusions. "So, in your dream, you made love with Mad Jack."

"Big-time. It was incredible."

Libby coughed. "But when you woke up, the real-life Jack was in bed with you?"

"Exactly."

"Awkward."

"Tell me about it." Kat knew her body. She had no doubt whatsoever that the sex she'd enjoyed in her dream actually took place.

Neither said anything for a minute or so, then Libby groaned. "They didn't have AIDs in the eighteen hundreds, Kat. You have to go get checked right away. And you're the most fertile person I know. At least, tell me you're on the pill."

Kat closed her eyes and looked skyward. "Why would I be on the pill, Lib? I have no social life. I have no time for a social life."

Libby cleared her throat. Kat knew what was coming next. "When you go to the doctor to get checked, ask him for a morning-after pill. There's a small window of opportunity. I can't remember how long. Are you home?"

"Not yet. I'm waiting for… Oh, there he is."

"Mad Jack?"

Kat snorted. "No. The allergic dentist from Denver."

"Well, whatever you do, don't panic and marry the guy. I'll go online and see what I can find out about your options. We'll figure this out, Kat."

"Thanks, Lib. I'm feeling a lot less homicidal—and/or suicidal—than I was earlier. I'll call you when I get home."

She closed the phone and stood. Jack waited beside the bike, helmets in hand. She took hers from him, but didn't put it on. "Maybe we should have breakfast. And talk."

CHAPTER NINE

THE COFFEE SHOP was packed. Jack's bike was just one of a dozen or more parked in a glittery array of chrome and leather on the street. Kat watched him exchange a few polite nods with the other newcomers. He didn't stick out as a R.U.B. quite as much as she'd imagined he would.

Had something changed? Or was it her? Making love with a person probably had that effect. She'd only been with two other men in her life. And she'd only gone to bed with them after the usual rites of courtship, which had involved wine and beer, respectively. Plus, she'd been distracted by their swoo.

She'd been so sure that Jack's swoo was manageable. And he'd been dead to the world last night when she'd checked to see if he was still breathing. But something had gone wrong. And she honestly didn't know what to say to him.

"Got a booth in the corner, hon," the waitress who was seating people told her. "Good timing."

"The food must be great here," Jack said, taking a plastic menu from a rack on the counter. "Judging by all the business."

"Our cook believes in serving big portions. Soaks up a lot of the mornin' after," she replied wryly as Kat and

Jack trailed behind her. "You both look like you could use a splash of this." She filled two thick white mugs from the steaming carafe in her hand without waiting for a confirmation, then turned to leave. "I'll be back in a few."

Kat slid into the side of the booth facing the back of the restaurant. She'd worked the Days of '76 and the bike rally for enough years that people tended to recognize her. Not that she was a celebrity, like Cooper, but she didn't feel like putting on a fake smile if someone greeted her. Jack took the opposite side, although it wasn't as easy for him to slide in, thanks to the straps on his leather chaps.

He pulled one of the cups closer and ripped open two packets of sugar. He glanced at the menu as he stirred his coffee. "I'm going for the number four, I think. How 'bout you?"

I'll take a morning-after pill, please.

Yes. That was definitely the smart thing to do. Just to be safe.

"English muffin. Extra crisp."

He looked at her. "That's it? I'm buying."

"It's not about money." Although it was *always* about money. Most months she barely scraped by. Student loans, grants, a couple of small scholarships, an occasional check from her father when he sold a buffalo or two. The child-support payments her ex-husbands made barely covered food and clothing for her two growing boys. Any sacrifices that were required to make ends meet came on her end. "I'm not hungry."

"Oh. I understand. You're upset. My sister lost thirty pounds during her divorce. She said she just couldn't eat."

Kat smiled. "I was the opposite. I gained weight both times. Food was comfort."

"Then you must have been a toothpick before you got married, because you're perfect now."

She would have corrected him—she was anything but perfect—or explained about the stress of being a single mom with two rambunctious boys. But their waitress returned to take their order.

Kat was reluctantly impressed that Jack got her request right and added two large orange juices. A luxury at her house.

"So, do you want to talk about what happened now or after breakfast?"

Never. "Now, I guess," she said, taking a sip of coffee.

He reached around to his back pocket and produced a handsome leather billfold. Kat could see several credit-card logos that she recognized. The cards were either gold or platinum. There was cash, too. A lot more than she ever carried. But she knew he wasn't trying to impress her because he quickly tucked it away after he found what he was looking for. "Here's my business card," he said, sliding it across the table. "I have a service that knows how to reach me twenty-four/seven."

She studied the high-end, professional design. Treadwell and Associates. "How many associates?" she asked.

"Eight. Wait. Seven. I'm the eighth. We provide a full gamut of dental options for the whole family, from children's dentistry and orthodontia to an oral surgeon and adult cosmetic dentistry. That's my area."

"You don't work on kids."

"No."

He said the word with such finality she had to ask, "Why?"

"My father was a family dentist. Worked alone for

thirty years. Had a thriving practice. Loved helping people so much that he often opened the office on weekends to work on kids who couldn't afford to pay for dental services."

Something in his tone reminded her of the dead look in Mad Jack's eyes when he told her why he gave up on people. "One day, one of his charity kids accused my dad of touching him inappropriately. The politically correct way of saying my dad was a pedophile."

"Oh, my God. What happened?"

"Nothing good. Dad's insurance company talked him into settling on the condition the complaint was dropped. That's not the same as being vindicated in court. Rumors spread. Dad's business fell off. He retired early. And died too young."

Kat could hear his pain. She didn't blame him for not wanting to work on kids. "I'm sorry."

"Me, too. Dad was a great guy. He loved kids. He didn't do what that child said he did. The boy later recanted. Claimed his stepfather coached him and his mother—a drug addict at the time—made him say what he did."

"How horrible for your family."

Jack shrugged. "I still followed in his footsteps. I simply specialized in an area that doesn't require me to deal with children. I'm not good with them. Ask your son."

Kat already knew Tag's opinion of Jack, but she kept it to herself. "I think I heard you say your mother lived near you. Did she remarry after your father passed?"

She pictured her own mother. Now on husband number five. Or was it six?

He fiddled with the empty sugar wrapper. "No. She

had her career to occupy her. Banking. She was a vice president of one of our local banks. She just retired."

Kat slipped his card into her hip pocket. She already had his cell-phone number programmed on her phone at home. Not that there would be any reason to contact him. Not if she did the smart thing.

She realized he'd asked something that she'd missed. "Sorry. What?"

"Since we're strolling down memory lane, I wondered about your childhood. Happy? Messed up? Normal?"

"Normal?"

His eyebrow arched in a way that told her she'd revealed more with one word than she'd intended. "I have no idea what that is. But I'm pretty sure it doesn't involve fighting for custody of a kid you then ignore because of all the other drama in your life."

"Your parents are divorced, I take it."

She took a deep breath and let it out. "Okay. Here's the short version. My mom is a needy person who grasped at any hint of security. My dad is a rancher who likes people to think he's more successful than he is. Mom saw the outward trappings and thought she had it made. Only, by the time I was born she realized she'd made a terrible mistake. Dad abuses alcohol and when you're in the middle of nowhere with two kids from a previous marriage and a tiny baby and a crazy man who tells you you're dirt, your options are limited. She took his pride and joy—a ridiculous boat of a car that my half brother called the pimpmobile—when she left. Dad couldn't very well sic his attorneys on her for custody of the car, so he went after me. They battled for years."

"He must have wanted you in his life."

"He wanted to win. He has this Old West thing about never giving up a square inch of land or a single concession when negotiating with the enemy. He tells everyone my mother made him spend my college fund on lawyer fees."

He cocked his head. "Do you have a relationship with him now?"

"Sorta. I lived with him when I was in high school. Mom was married to a psycho preacher at the time and I didn't have anywhere else to go. Dad pretty much ignored me the whole time, but that was okay because I had my buffalo to keep me occupied."

His cup wobbled as he set it down. "Buffalo?"

"I talked Dad into buying a few head of bison when I was a sophomore. He kept them even after I moved out and got married. The boys and I visit the ranch to check on them every couple of weeks."

"Where's this?"

"Near Belle Fourche. Northern Hills. Lately, Dad's gotten involved in marketing the meat for sale. His half of the herd, not mine. But he keeps my freezer filled, and that's come in pretty handy at times."

She was saved from spilling any more of her guts by the arrival of their food. As promised, Jack's platter-size plate was heaped with three eggs, hash-brown potatoes and a slab of ham half an inch thick.

Her muffin looked silly by comparison.

Their waitress slapped down a bottle of ketchup, a little container of hot sauce and a plastic tub filled with various flavors of jelly without being asked. "Enjoy," she said. "Holler if you need more juice."

They ate in silence for a few minutes. Jack had very nice manners, she noticed. He chewed with his mouth closed. Something she was constantly harping on with Tag. Of course, part of his problem was that eye tooth, which was coming in sideways.

"So, is it safe to say you and your dad aren't close?" Jack asked after washing down a bite with a gulp of juice.

She nibbled on her muffin but couldn't work up an appetite. "I wanted us to be when I was a little girl. Now we mostly talk about the herd when we see each other. I tried living with him another time, too. When Tag was a baby and Pete and I first broke up. It didn't last long. Dad wanted a live-in maid, and I wanted a father who gave a damn."

"What happened?"

She sighed. "I convinced Pete that my milk was going to dry up and he'd have to pay for formula if he didn't help me rent an apartment in town. I was just getting back on my feet when I met ex number two." She snickered softly. "They say mistakes aren't mistakes if you learn from them, right? I learned that nursing is not a surefire form of contraception."

He laughed. "That's wisdom for you—arriving too late to be of any help when you need it most. So where's your mom live?"

"Spearfish. Her last husband moved out a week after she was diagnosed with throat cancer. Poor Mom. She always believed she was getting a guy to take care of her, but it never worked out that way. Fortunately her sister, my aunt Roberta, was available to move in. Her doctors claim to have the cancer in remission, but now

Mom's dealing with depression. I think she's worried that no man is ever going to love her again."

She shook her head. "This is really unpleasant conversation for breakfast. I'm sorry."

He shrugged. "Don't apologize. I asked."

"So what about you? Are you close to your mom?"

"More so when I was engaged to a woman she thought was perfect for me. Actually, I think Mom took our breakup harder than either Jaydene or I did."

His eyes glinted with a roguish look that reminded her of the man in her dream. Her heartbeat sped up, despite her attempt to ignore the little thrill that shot through her body.

Okay. So she wished Jack was her dream lover in real life. But he wasn't. And she wasn't a virginal schoolmarm, either. *Forget about Mad Jack.*

"What was that?" he asked.

Had she muttered that out loud? Oh, dear. She really was losing it. "Nothing. I guess I should be grateful my parents are utterly self-absorbed. I don't take advice that well. My mother used to call me 'sweetly stubborn.'"

Jack refilled both their cups from the insulated carafe their waitress had left behind, then he eased back in the booth. His tattoos were still a little tender, but thankfully the itching had subsided.

He watched her nibble on a piece of muffin she'd topped with grape jelly. He found the gesture childlike. And a fist—solid and unfamiliar—wrapped around his heart and squeezed. He might have feared that the chicken-fried steak from a few nights earlier had already clogged his arteries, but his subconscious mind told him that wasn't the case. He liked this woman. A lot. Even if she wasn't her dream alter ego. Katherine. Who was much better suited to him. After all, the schoolmarm's children went home to their own families each night. Kat's didn't.

"Are you done?" she asked, consulting her watch. "I should be going."

"In case your ex-husband brings your son home early."

"Partly. And by the way, I don't go out of my way to accommodate Pete. I do it for Tag. Because he has enough drama in his life from his stepmom and half siblings without watching his parents' power struggles."

That made sense. In a way. And normally he would let the statement go unchallenged. But instead, he asked, "Aren't you afraid that you might be sending the wrong message?"

"Pardon?"

"Well, you're a strong woman, and catering to your ex-husband's whims might make your son think that's what women do."

Her eyes narrowed. "Armchair parenting again."

"Huh?"

"Call me when you're a father and we'll ta—" She stopped abruptly and didn't finish the sentence.

He wanted to ask why, but suddenly he understood. They'd had unprotected sex. She could be pregnant. With his child. The food he'd devoured shifted uncomfortably in his belly.

"You're not... You don't think..."

Her cheeks turned rosy pink and she wouldn't meet his eyes. "I don't know," she said, making a show of folding her paper napkin. "But my friend reminded me that there's a pill I can take that wasn't readily available when I got pregnant with my sons."

He'd heard of it. "I thought it was only prescribed in Europe."

She shook her head. "Apparently not."

Jack picked up the bill their waitress had deposited on the table a few minutes earlier and stood. His mind was jumping all over the place and he really couldn't think.

Did he approve of her plan? Sure. Of course. He must. Because the alternative was so not in the realm of possibility it didn't even bear scrutiny. Right?

Once they were outside and preparing to get aboard his bike, he asked, "Just out of curiosity, would you have used that pill if it had been available when you became pregnant with your sons?"

Her frown intensified. "That's not a fair question. At the time I might have welcomed the option, but I can't imagine my life without my boys. Tag and Jordie are the best thing that ever happened to me."

He believed her. She was a natural-born mother. His mother was not. "But considering the circumstances—getting pregnant out of wedlock—surely the thought of having an abor—"

She cut him off. "Not my thing. And I was married to both their father's before either of my sons were born."

The flinty look in her eye reminded him of Katherine. She stood her ground, too, when it mattered. "Got it. Like I said, I was just curious. Shall we go?"

She nodded, then pulled on her helmet.

Seconds later, they were on the road headed back toward the heart of the Black Hills. Jack looked around with a funny sense of disorientation. Nothing looked familiar. Probably because he'd been suffering from an allergic reaction when they first pulled into town. Either that, or he still had one foot in another time.

CHAPTER TEN

"SO WHAT DID HE DO? Just drop you off at your door and drive away? That doesn't sound very heroic," Jenna complained.

Jenna had been so busy since her return dealing with the Mystery Spot and trying to prepare for the filming that was scheduled to begin next week that Kat hadn't had much chance to talk to her. This was the first Jenna had heard about Kat's close encounter with the dentist from Denver.

Thanks to blabbermouth Char.

"Well, she couldn't very well ask him in when Pete and Tag were sitting in the driveway when Kat and the R.U.B. pulled in, could she?" Char asked.

"What were they doing there? I thought Pete had planned to keep Tag all weekend."

So had Kat. But thanks to her damnable luck—and Pete's demanding new wife—he'd been forced to cut short his camping trip. "Michelle didn't think it was fair to Aiden to miss out on all the fun, so she planned a family day on Sunday. Naturally that didn't include Tag," Kat said, frowning.

"Could have been worse. Jordie's dad could have brought him back early, too," Char said.

Kat looked at Libby for help.

Char was a dear friend, but men were immediately suspect in her book until they proved themselves worthy. And since Libby—mother confessor of them all—had been in California at the time of this fiasco, Kat had turned to Char for help in deciding what to do about Jack.

To Kat's chagrin, Char insisted on calling Jack "The R.U.B.," even though she knew his name.

"The fact that Jack played along and didn't blow her cover makes him somewhat heroic, doesn't it?" Libby asked. "He could have pulled out an imaginary six-gun and started a real showdown."

Jenna and Char looked at each other as though completely lost. "He carries a gun?"

"Isn't that against the law?"

Kat knew it was time to get the Wine, Women and Words book club back on track. She reached for the talking stick—a gnarled, venerable limb that had been with them since the beginning—and rapped it on the floor. The talking stick secured the speaker's right to be heard without interruption. Unfortunately the sound was muffled by old shag carpeting, but the motion caught everyone's attention.

"About the book—didn't you all love it?"

Libby nodded with enthusiasm. "I was particularly impressed by how the author was able to pass back and forth between two times—the past and the present—with such fluidity."

Kat shot her a warning look. There were elements about that night with Jack that she hadn't told anyone else. Her dream. Mad Jack. The only reason she'd told Libby on the phone that morning was because it had seemed so surreal and she'd been desperate to make sense of what happened. But that didn't mean she planned to share news of her mental instability with the other members of their group.

During the ten days that had passed since that fateful night, Kat had given a lot of thought to what transpired—and why. She'd finally decided someone must have slipped a couple of hallucinatory mushrooms on her pizza. That was the only reasonable explanation.

Libby didn't agree. She believed in things like fate and destiny, soul mates and love that could transcend time. The stuff of fiction, in other words, Kat thought with justifiable bitterness, taking a sip of the sparkling grape juice Char had brought, instead of wine.

Libby was the only pregnant one among them, but the other three had agreed to forgo alcohol at tonight's meeting.

At least, Kat hoped Libby was the only pregnant one among them. She couldn't swear to the fact because when it had come time to make that monumental decision regarding the morning-after pill, her decision-making ability stalled. Thanks to Tag and Jordie.

She'd peeked into Tag's bedroom one night and discovered Jordie curled up beside his brother. He'd been sneaking into Tag's room in the middle of the night ever since they moved into this three-bedroom house. Kat was waiting for Tag to throw a fit and demand his privacy, but he never did.

The thought had occurred to her for the first time that maybe the two brothers traveled together in their dreams.

For a good hour images of their childhood had flashed before her eyes and she'd known without a doubt that being their mother had been her destiny—even if a happily-ever-after with the love of her life was not so preordained.

If fate or the swoo or a bad mushroom had tricked her into screwing up again, so be it, she'd decided the next morning. She'd deal with the consequences when the time came. Just like she had the times before.

"You know, Kat's R.U.B. is still around," Char said out of the blue, and so far from the subject of the book that Kat squawked and pointed the talking stick at her. "Well, it's true," Char said, defending her point.

"But not relevant."

"Interesting, though," Jenna said, her pretty red ponytail whipping back and forth as she looked from Char to Kat. "I thought you said the biker-dude dentist was headed back to Denver, Kat."

According to the last of the dozen or so messages Jack had left on her phone two days ago, she could reach him by cell "...if the need arose." She hadn't returned any of his calls because...well, she knew how this game ended, so why bother with the middle innings?

He hadn't specifically said he was leaving town, but his tone had held a certain resignation, which she'd assumed meant he'd given up on her neurotic behavior and had returned home. "Um...I've been running every which way this week getting things organized for the rally. I still can't believe I forgot to turn in my vendor application," she said wearily, softly knocking the talking stick against her brow. "Now, I'm going to have to find a way to farm out the boys, because there isn't any room for me on Main Street and they're much too young to see what goes on in Thunder Alley."

Thunder Alley was the name of a popular campground a few miles from downtown Sturgis. For a week every August, the flat, mostly treeless field became a bustling city filled with thousands of people doing pretty much exactly what they wanted.

"Are you sure you want to do that, Kat?" Jenna asked. "You'll make twice as much as an extra once filming starts."

"I know. I talked to Shane this morning. He told me he's not going to need the extras until the middle of next week, so I should be able to do both." Shane Reynard was both the director/producer of the television show and Jenna's unofficial fiancé. "Unlike Libby and Coop, we're not in a huge rush to tie the knot," she'd explained when she first arrived at Kat's house. "We're quite content to live in exquisite sin."

Kat was happy—really happy—for her friend, and Jenna's determined effort to see that Kat was hired as an extra couldn't have come at a better time—except where child care was concerned.

"Normally I could switch weeks with Pete, but he and Michelle are flying back East to visit Michelle's parents."

"And let me guess," Char said. "They're not taking Tag."

Kat shook her head. "Pete claims it's because he has to return early for work. Can you imagine how miserable Tag would be? Alone with Michelle and the kids?" She could.

"And Drew's on the road this week. I know because he was late with his check and his wife gave me this big sob story about cutbacks and the price of gas— Never mind. You've heard this story before." She held up the dog-eared copy of the trade paperback she'd gotten at the library. "Speaking of stories, didn't the author do a marvelous job of making you feel what it would be like to be old? I felt a lot more sympathy for the things my mother has been going through. I know she's not that old, but cancer can really age a person."

Libby took the talking stick from Kat. "I cried every time we were in the old man's point of view. I felt so sorry for him—locked in a body that wouldn't cooperate. Reduced to a person no one listened to or respected. I thought he and my grandmother would have been good friends if they'd known each other."

Mention of Mary—Libby's grandmother who had practically raised Libby and her brother, Mac—caused a temporary sidetrack of conversation. Kat was sorry to learn that the lovely old woman seemed to be declining faster than anyone could handle—especially Lib.

"At least she lived her life with style and grace for nearly every one of her ninety-plus years," Jenna insisted. "My mother will be the first to tell you she wasted way too much time worrying about what my father thought, instead of following her dreams. I can honestly say I've never seen Mom happier or more alive than she is now. Have you seen her yet? The transformation is amazing. And she truly owns the part she plays on the show. It's exciting."

Kat listened to this new topic for a few minutes before taking back the talking stick. "I can't wait to see your mom in action, Jenna, but I have a couple more study questions about the book to bring up. The person who hosts is supposed to think up six, right?"

Char groaned. "You take everything so literally."

Kat ignored her. "Did anyone else think the ending was unrealistic?"

"Me," Char said with feeling. "Nobody would saddle himself with that kind of responsibility on a whim."

"I thought the circus owner was kind and compassionate," Jenna said. "He respected the past. Think of the stories the old man could tell."

"Until he broke a hip or dementia set in and he couldn't remember his name," Libby put in.

The defeat in Lib's voice told Kat that Grandma Mary was worse off than any of them knew.

"Taking care of an old person can be as draining as caring for an infant," she went on. "In some ways, it's worse because you don't expect any help from a baby, but a part of you can't let go of how that person used to be."

Kat's grip on the talking stick slipped. Any mention of the word *baby* made her nervous. She felt fine. No early-warning nipple tenderness like when she was first pregnant with her boys, but she wouldn't feel completely out of the woods until her period started—in another day or two.

Char caught the stick with one hand, but the look she gave Kat seemed particularly intense. "You're kinda spacey tonight, Kat," Char said. "Are you okay?"

"Sure. Fine. Like I said, it was a crazy week. And that whole thing with the R.U.B.…I mean, Jack…well…" She cleared her throat. "Who's ready for dessert? Since the story was about a circus, I bought Cracker Jacks, ice cream and all the toppings for sundaes, and two flavors of cotton candy—turquoise and hot pink." She made a face. "Those are the colors. I have no idea what flavor either is supposed to represent. Can you believe they sell it pre-spun in a bag? That's just wrong, isn't it?"

She'd stood up and was halfway to the kitchen when she realized nobody else had moved. She pivoted on one heel and followed the group's collective gaze toward the door—where a man was standing at the closed screen. His hand lifted to knock.

"Um, hello," he said. "Sorry to interrupt. I saw the extra cars in the driveway, but your son said they belonged to the neighbor and it was okay to come up."

Kat had sent the boys out front to play catch. Apparently they'd decided to play a trick probably meant to embarrass both Kat and Jack.

Char jumped to her feet. "Hey, I remember you. We met on the street, and someone matching your description bought a couple of nice pieces of jewelry from my shop yesterday while I was in town at the bank."

Jack stepped closer to the screen but didn't open it. "Right. Kat pointed out your very unique store when we passed it. I didn't see you. Was there a video camera?"

She laughed in a very un-Char-like way. "Better. Pia, my clerk, is into men. Believe me, if you'd been wearing a skirt, she wouldn't have been able to tell me squat. But in your case I got a full description. Right down to your boots and the color of your motorcycle."

Kat looked for support from Libby, who smiled benignly. Either pregnancy had robbed her of any desire to meddle in her friends' lives or she was still thinking about her grandmother. Jenna's gaze seemed to take in every detail of the moment—the writer in her obviously intrigued.

All three women looked at Kat expectantly. She

could tell they felt she should invite him in. Stifling a sigh, she changed directions. Opening the door, she motioned him inside. "I figured from your phone message you were back in Denver."

"Really? Which one of the dozen or so led you to think that?" he asked just loud enough for her to hear.

Kat's cheeks turned uncomfortably hot.

He let her off the hook before she could come up with a plausible lie…excuse. "I lucked out. My hotel had a cancelation, so I was able to extend my stay until today. I planned to be on the road this morning. But after talking to Brian last night, I decided it was kind of silly to buy a bike and come all this way without sticking around for at least a few days of the Sturgis Rally. He said I couldn't get a true sense of the wild and woolly Old West until I hung out in Thunder Alley." He shook his head and said to the other women, "I'm a total sucker for history."

"Thunder Alley!" Kat exclaimed, forgetting about their audience. "I thought you didn't like crowds."

His gray eyes were inscrutable. Dressed all in black, he resembled his dream counterpart more than he could possibly know. "All part of the experience," he said with a shrug of the shoulder she'd tattooed. She couldn't see it because he was wearing a lightweight button-up shirt. "I have more vacation time saved up than I know what to do with, so since I'm here, I figured I might as well give it a try."

"Were you able to get a room?" Char asked, drawing Jack's gaze away from Kat's. "Hotels are usually booked solid months in advance."

"So I found out. Brian offered to rent me a room at his place for a grand, but his wife wasn't exactly thrilled.

He tracked me down today to tell me she kicked him out. Filed for divorce. And changed the locks on the door."

Kat winced. She looked over her shoulder and told the others, "He's talking about Brian Whitlock. Lives in Nemo. I can't remember his wife's name. They have three little kids. The youngest is Jordie's age. They were in T-ball together." But a part of her mind hadn't let go of the words *a grand.* He was seriously considering spending a thousand dollars for a place to sleep for a week?

With an extra grand in the bank, she wouldn't have to work at the bar part-time while she was student-teaching.

As if reading her thoughts, Jack said, "I stopped by to see if you know anybody who might have a spare room to rent."

She made a split-second decision. Not unlike the circus owner in the book they were just talking about. Jack needed a place to stay. She needed money. Her boys could bunk together, and it wasn't as if she was going to sleep with Jack again. That was a one-night aberration. *Maybe if he were Mad Jack...* She shook her head. "No. I mean, yes. I mean, you could stay here. In Jordie's room. He and Tag can share a room."

He didn't jump at the offer, and for a few stomach-sickening seconds Kat felt the same way she had when the parent who was supposed to pick her up on exchange day didn't show. She felt unwanted.

"Um...I appreciate the offer," he said hesitantly. "But I think you better run that by your sons first. The older one and I got off on the wrong foot. The little guy seemed pretty friendly until...Tag, right?...elbowed him. I don't think they'd be too happy to have me bunking here all week."

Kat could picture what he described. Tag called the shots and Jordie went along with whatever his big brother wanted.

"Tough. They're not paying the rent. I'm the grown-up. I get to make this call."

Libby cleared her throat and sat forward, her hands pressed together in her lap. "Um…Kat, this is none of my business, but I can't picture Pete being okay with you letting a stranger sleep across the hall from his son." To Jack, she said apologetically, "That's not to imply anything about you, but Pete's as suspicious as they come."

Damn. Leave it to Lib to state the obvious. Kat didn't have the slightest doubt about Jack and she knew with every ounce of conviction in her soul that he would never be a threat to her boys. If anything, they intimidated him. He even believed them when they said she was home alone.

But Pete was another story. When he found out, there would be hell to pay. Maybe another trip to the custody mediator. She couldn't put Tag through that again. Nor could she afford it.

With a sigh, she looked at Jack and said, "Unfortunately Libby's right. I was seeing a positive balance in my checkbook when I start student-teaching, but Tag's dad would definitely throw a hissy." She tossed up her hands. "But I'd be happy to ask around. In fact, Lib, maybe he could rent Gran's old cabin."

Libby shook her head. "The film crew has nailed down every spare bed in Sentinel Pass. And most couches, too. I told Coop the timing sucked, but they didn't have any choice."

Kat shrugged. "I guess you could look in Rapid. I doubt if Spearfish would have anything. Maybe Custer."

The name Custer made Jack look at her.

"I have an idea," Char said, springing to her feet. "Let me ponder this while I help Kat serve dessert. Jack, have a chair while Libby and Jenna grill you… I mean, entertain you. Come on, pal," she said, taking Kat's elbow. "I'll help make the sundaes."

Char hustled her into the kitchen with barely a backward glance. Jack had dropped into her chair and kicked out his feet as if he were home. The weird part was he didn't look out of place. She didn't know how that was possible.

Char snapped her fingers in front of Kat's face. "Girl, this is not like you. Goddamn. The swoo has taken your brain and replaced it with a sea sponge."

Kat made a face. "Shh. He'll hear you. This is a small house," she said in a low whisper. "Get the ice-cream bowls out of the freezer and put them on that tray. Everything is all ready to go."

She reached into the overhead cupboard for the ridiculously overpriced parcels of gossamer sugar. She'd had to hide them behind the tinned vegetables to keep the boys from pilfering.

"What are you thinking?" she asked, stretching to locate the last bag.

"That you have it bad for that guy."

Her hand brushed against a can of peas and she had to do a quick impersonation of a juggler to keep everything from falling out. Once the last can was back in place, she turned and faced Char. Hands on hips, she barked, "I do not."

The volume of her protest seemed to echo in the small room. The room where she'd sat with her nose mere inches from Jack Treadwell's perfectly shaped pectoral muscles.

She scowled at Char and returned to the very important job of setting out the cotton candy in an artful manner. "I need the money, Char. Next semester is going to be tough because I won't have as much time at night and after classes to work. That's the only reason I agreed to set up my tent in the campground. You know how crappy that area can be for a woman alone. The last time I worked there Pete was with me. Nobody gave me any grief because…well, Pete is Pete. But this year…"

"That's part of my plan, swoo girl," Char said, setting down the tray she'd carried from the freezer. She rubbed her hands together. Whether from the cold or in expectation, Kat couldn't say.

"Huh?" She picked up the two extra packages of spun sugar and debated what to do with them. She'd planned to give them to her boys as a reward for behaving while her friends were here. But after that stunt with Jack…

Char's voice cut into her brooding. "…I take Jordie for the week? He and I got along great while we were at the powwow. I have to be on the road a couple of days, but I always stay with friends who have kids, so he'd be more than welcome. And I could use the extra help on the weekend at the tepee."

"Really?" The offer was unexpected, and generous. "He'd love that. What an adventure. But honestly, Char, I didn't think you were…well, that into kids."

Char's lips pursed in a kind of introspective way. "They're a fact of life, and I like yours just fine."

"I'm glad. But Jordie's dad isn't the problem. He doesn't really care what I do as long as it doesn't cost him more child support." She hated to say the words out loud because she never wanted Jordie to think his father didn't love him. Drew did love his son; he simply loved whatever was going on in his life at the moment more.

"I know. And believe me, Jordie does, too. And he's okay with his dad's shortcomings. You've more than made up for them by being a super-cool mom."

"Really?" The warm feeling in her midsection was cut short by Jenna's voice calling from the other room.

"Are you churning that ice cream by hand or did you have to milk the cow first?"

Char growled. "We're coming. How do you stay so slim when you eat like a horse?"

Jenna whinnied in response.

Char added spoons to the tray and started to leave, but Kat stopped her. "I really appreciate you offering to keep Jordie, but what will I do with Tag? I suppose I could call my dad, but…"

Char motioned with her head, which as usual sported unusual highlights. Tonight's were maroon. "I have a plan for him, too. I just wanted to see if you were cool with me taking Jordie."

"Why wouldn't I be? He hasn't stopped talking about the powwow since he got back. He says you rock."

Char beamed, but she kept walking. "Okay, you voracious dessert eaters. Did you explain to the R.U.B. about the book and why we're eating enough sugar in one sitting to induce a diabetic coma in a person who doesn't have the disease?"

Everybody chuckled, but that didn't prevent them

from digging in. Jack, too, since Kat gave him her portion. Her stomach was too upset to digest anything.

"Actually, Char," Jack said, using his spoon for emphasis, "I read *Water for Elephants* when it first hit the *New York Times'* list. My then girlfriend was on a reading kick and insisted that we read the same books so we could discuss them."

The women all exchanged a look that even Jack could interpret. He tossed his head and laughed. "Yeah, I know. That makes me a real wuss, doesn't it? But to be fair, I got to pick every other title. And we wound up reading some good books. Personally I loved this one, although I had issues with the ending."

Libby looked at Kat and gave a little nod Kat hoped nobody else saw. She picked up a box with a familiar logo and carefully opened it to withdraw a kernel of caramel popcorn. She drew it closer and poked around with her finger. *Do they still put prizes inside?* She didn't know.

"Kat?"

She looked up. Oh, God. Somehow she'd tuned out the conversation that had been going on around her. "Um…yes?"

Jenna checked with the others first, then said, "Char suggested that I take Tag home with me. Mom and her friend, Rollie, won't be coming for a few days. Tag could have her bed until they get here, then there's always the couch."

"But you're busy at the Mystery Spot. Didn't you say you're shorthanded at the moment?"

"Yes. That's the point. Remember when we talked about him *working* for me this summer?" She said the word in a way that reminded Kat that the previously discussed job—the same one she and Jack had argued about—was more about keeping Tag busy and feeling useful than actually earning a living.

"But without your more experienced people there, Tag might be a nuisance."

Jenna shook her head. "I don't think so. I was about his age when I started helping out. There are plenty of things for him to do—even just picking up trash. I promise I won't overwork him. He'll have fun, too."

Kat wasn't sure what to say.

"Um…wasn't your reason for Tag not working at the Mystery Spot the cost of gas it would take to drive him there?" Jack asked.

Kat sensed her friends' surprise that she'd discussed her son's job—or lack of one—with Jack. "Yes," she said shortly.

"Well, I have to cover for my manager all week," Jenna said, her tone triumphant. "If he's staying with me, then it wouldn't cost you anything. We'll bike there and back together. So?" She eyed Kat. "Can he come home with me?"

Kat wanted to say yes. Knowing the boys were safe and having fun with people who wanted to spend time with them would free her to work as long and as hard as she could stand it. And no child-care bill would mean more money in the bank this fall. "Are you two sure you know what you're getting into? We're talking boisterous little boys. They're not sweet and docile like Megan."

"My four-and-a-half-year-old niece," Libby explained to Jack. "She's an angel. For everyone, except her father, who she has wrapped around her finger."

"Oh," Jack said.

His tone was polite, but uninterested. Kat could tell he wanted to hear her decision.

"Just promise me," she said, "you're not doing this because you feel sorry for me."

Libby shook her head. "We're trying to help out, you goof. That's what friends do. With both kids out of the house, you could rent Jordie's room *and* Tag's, if you were so inclined."

"Maybe Brian needs a place," Char said with a loud raspberry tacked on for good measure.

Everyone laughed, but Jack set the record straight. "Brian moved in with his mother. I suggested he give AA a try, but that didn't go over so great."

Kat could imagine. Her dad had blown up at any insinuation that he had a problem with alcohol. She'd heard from several sources—including Buck himself—that he'd stopped drinking, but Kat wasn't holding her breath. Besides, even if Dad was reformed now, the damage his drinking had inflicted on others continued to haunt all of his children, including Kat.

"Brian's a nice guy. This might be the wake-up call he needs to get his life back on track. I'll try to bring up the subject with him the next time I'm working at Pop's. Which won't be until *after* the rally," Kat said pointedly. "So it looks like I have a room to rent, Jack. Do we have a deal? A thousand dollars for a bed and private bath. Tonight through, say, Sunday morning? We have Coop's big party in Sentinel Pass on Sunday afternoon, right, Lib? I could pick up the boys there."

Jack set his dish aside and put out his hand to shake.

Kat braced herself for his touch. She'd been thinking

about his hands and the yummy sensations they'd created in her body far too often since that night. To her surprise, he kept the contact short and sweet, businesslike. She stepped back just the same. Even a little residual swoo would not go unnoticed by her observant friends.

She glanced at Jenna first, then Char. "If you're sure about this, I'll go talk to the boys."

Jenna and Char looked at each other a moment before scrambling to their feet. "Let us," Jenna said.

Char nodded. "If they don't want to come, I don't want you to pressure them into it. Not that you would, exactly, but you know how you try to make everybody happy and well…never mind. Give us five minutes."

"Ten," Jenna corrected. "Tag and I have to negotiate his *salary*," she added with a wink.

They disappeared out the door before Kat could decide if she'd been insulted or not. She glanced at Libby, who was staring with an amused, proud-mother look on her face—even though her body was barely showing the baby bump the gossip magazines had been speculating about.

"I can understand why Jenna's so enthused about spending time with Tag," she said conversationally. "From the moment she saw those Burnese mountain dog puppies, she's had motherhood on the brain. But what's up with Char? I didn't think she had a maternal bone in her body."

Kat couldn't say. In fact, Char had resisted Kat's initial plea to babysit Jordie that fateful Wednesday when she'd subbed for Becky at Pop's. Something must have happened that made the boy less of a previously assumed pain in the butt.

Kat wasn't too worried about how her sons would behave. They were well mannered and polite and they ate with their mouths closed—most of the time. She was proud of them and confident they could be trusted to play in grown-up sandboxes when required. They'd be fine.

She only hoped she could say the same for herself. She'd agreed to spend six nights under the same roof with a man who'd somehow managed to nail her without a single drop of booze passing between her lips. Whatever kind of swoo Jack possessed, it was unlike any she'd known before. *And* it seemed to bridge two worlds—the present and the past.

That fact alone should have scared the hell out of her, but it was too late to back out now. The boys would regard this opportunity to stay with Char and Jenna as a mini-vacation. The only kind Kat could afford. Especially if her period failed to show up on time.

She could handle Jack and his time-traveling swoo, she told herself firmly. He was here. And now. And that was how they both were going to stay.

CHAPTER ELEVEN

"ARE YOU SURE about this? I could probably buy camping gear and set up a tent."

He was helping her change the sheets on her son's bed half an hour or so after the ball that he'd inadvertently set in motion took off like a rocket. Those book-club women really got things done, he silently acknowledged.

"It's fine," Kat mumbled, giving the top sheet a crisp snap. Jack inhaled fresh air and sunshine, not the artificial perfume of a dryer sheet. "I fold and tuck the corners," she told him.

He knew how to make a bed, but he didn't argue. Instead, he did as asked, and continued to look around the room. It felt on the small side and was definitely decorated in the eclectic clutter of a young boy, but he couldn't spot a speck of dust on the shelves above the desk, and there was no lingering odor of sweat socks that he remembered from being in an all-male dorm in college.

"Didn't I hear you tell Tag that you never went camping?" She was already done with her side and waited with the lightweight cotton blanket balled against her chest. Her eyes had that challenging twinkle he'd noticed the night they met.

"That's true, but there's a first time for everything, right? And I'd give it a try if this was too uncomfortable for you."

Something in her expression changed. Softened. She gave him the same indulgent smile she'd used with her son that afternoon of the tattoo. He got the impression she'd forgive his shortcomings as long as he was honest about them. Why? Because the men in her life were never truthful? Or were they just never up-front about their flaws?

"I appreciate the gesture, but this probably isn't the best venue to try out a new skill. I can tell you from experience that the campgrounds are wall-to-wall tents and bodies. And if you don't have the right equipment, the mosquitoes will eat you alive."

She plumped a pillow, then picked up a matching blue-and-white-stripe pillowcase. Wedging one end under her chin, she added, "By the way, how are your tattoos?"

He yanked the collar of his recently laundered T-shirt down and to the left, exposing the slightly withered-looking outline of his favorite tattoo. "Almost gone. Truthfully, I'm really sorry I didn't listen to you in the first place. I remember those pictures you showed me of how henna slowly fades. I would have preferred that. Plus, we might have skipped a trip to the emergency room."

The pillow plunked to the bed. The pillowcase hung limply in her hand. Her mouth was open wide enough for him to see four fillings in her molars. Other than those, her teeth were perfect. "Wait a minute. Did you just admit that you were wrong and I was right?"

He nodded slowly. Was that a trick question? "Yes. I should have listened to you. You're the expert. I was paying for your expertise. I tell people that all the time in my business. But some patients—people like me, apparently—come into the office with one thing in mind and can't be dissuaded. You did your best to talk me into a better choice, and we both know I was wrong."

Her cheeks flashed with color and she quickly resumed her task. With a tender pat, she smoothed the striped bedspread and stepped back. "There you go. I hope you'll be comfortable. The mattress isn't extra long, you can stretch out at an angle."

He'd noticed the clever conformation of the bunk bed the first time he'd visited the house. Instead of the double-decker model he remembered from his first year in the dorm, this unit sported a double bed on the bottom and perpendicular to it, creating an L-shape, was the upper twin, with a ladder built in to the end support.

"I'll be fine," he said. "With the pillow on that end, you get a sort of cavelike effect. I like that. Butch Cassidy and the Sundance Kid holed up in a cave with their gang. I always thought that sounded kind of adventurous."

She bent over to gather up the dirty sheets. As she did, she explained the rationale behind the bed purchase. "Before we moved in here, we lived in a two-bedroom apartment. I gave the boys the bigger room and I slept on a futon beside my desk so I could study at night. But when my mom got sick, it looked as though I might wind up taking care of her, so I went hunting for a bigger place. Since this bed can accommodate three, I figured I could give her my bed, move Jordie in here—

he sneaks in most nights, anyway, then if we had company, I could take the top bunk."

"You're awfully quick to give up your bed," he said casually.

Her shoulders stiffened. "What's that supposed to mean? Listen, I thought we established that I'm not easy and I don't usually jump in bed with—"

He held up both hands. "Whoa. Not what I meant. You're generous. You put other people's needs ahead of your own. I wasn't putting you down."

"Oh."

"But since you brought up the subject, is it okay to ask what you decided? I thought you might call and let me know. About the morning-after pill, I mean."

She hugged the bundle in her arms tighter and rested her chin on the fabric with a sigh. She worked the corner of her mouth—the mouth he'd been fantasizing about for days—with her bottom teeth for a few seconds before answering. "I should have called. I'm sorry. But I figured if you didn't hear from me, you'd assume no news was good news."

Her blasé tone didn't gibe with the serious look in her eyes. But she changed the subject before he could pin down her answer to something more concrete.

"I better toss these in the laundry basket and go over my checklist for tomorrow. A new venue means new challenges," she said with an air of resignation. She glanced around once, then left the room.

There would be time, he told himself. As he'd gathered from her very friendly friends, Kat was setting up a tattoo booth in the wild and woolly campgrounds he'd heard so much about. In fact, Libby, the auburn-hair beauty to whom the others seemed to differ, had pulled him aside while Kat was helping her sons pack.

"Kat won't ask for help, Jack, but we're all worried about her working the tattoo booth inside the campground. I've always heard anything goes in Thunder Alley. Normally I wouldn't have pushed the idea of a relative stranger moving in, but you seem pretty decent. I'll sleep better knowing you have her back."

He could have sworn he detected a slight emphasis on the word *sleep*. Had Kat shared with her friends the fact that she'd spent the night in his bed?

He followed her through the spotless kitchen. Jack had offered to help Libby clean up once Kat had joined Jenna and Char in the driveway with the boys, but she'd shooed him outside to "keep an eye on things."

He'd watched from the deck, curious as to how Kat's sons would react to the news of the coming week's arrangements. Both appeared to react favorably. The younger one actually jumped up and down with joy and wrapped his arms around Char's thighs in a quick hug.

The elder, Tag, glanced Jack's way—his look pensive. Jack figured he was trying to work out all the angles. Jack had been a little older when his father's troubles started, but he'd found that kids sensed what was happening no matter how diligently their parents tried to keep the truth from them.

But whatever Jenna was saying seemed to work like a balm on the boy's suspicions, because within minutes Tag was grinning with obvious excitement. He looked more like his mother when he smiled. Except for his teeth. Even from a distance, Jack could tell the kid was a candidate for braces.

As he watched the fivesome turn and head back to the house, Jack felt very much the outsider. He knew why. He not only lacked the desire to connect with Kat's children, he didn't have the slightest idea how to go about it if he were so inclined. He'd painted himself into a proverbial corner and he didn't possess a key to the door behind him. Not that he'd use it if he had one, but...

"Are you sure your sons are okay with this?" he asked Kat as she returned from the adjoining laundry room. She stopped abruptly, as if surprised to see him.

And why wouldn't she be? All he seemed capable of was following her around like a puppy dog.

She picked up a small yellow sponge and rubbed at an invisible spot on the countertop. "They're kids. And male. Both get to do something unexpected and fun—without their mother. What's not to like?"

"Well, they can't be too happy about me being here."

"Tag's the only one who caught that part of the deal."

She squeezed the water from the sponge with more force than seemed necessary, then turned to look at him. "He did ask if I was going to marry you."

Jack nearly swallowed his tongue. "Why?"

She shrugged. "I don't date. He's seen you here twice. I guess that qualifies as a serious relationship in his book." Her tone was light, but he sensed something broken and sad behind the sardonic chuckle. "Wanna finish off the cotton candy on the deck?"

Not really. He'd already eaten a chocolate sundae he didn't want. "Okay."

She opened a cupboard, rising on the toes of her cheap rubber thongs to reach a fluorescent-blue bag. "Grab a couple of waters from the fridge," she ordered.

He did as asked. When he turned to face her, a bottle in each hand, she told him, "We wash and reuse bottles. That's tap water. Hope you don't mind."

"I recycle under threat of never hearing the end of my boorish waste from my sister. I say, 'Bring it on.'"

Her laugh seemed genuine. "I'm really lucky to be living in a time when being cheap can pass as environmentally conscious."

Her admission was so Kat. Honest and unpretentious. Slightly apologetic when, in fact, the world should have been apologizing to her. He realized with sudden clarity that he would have fallen head over heels in love with her at that moment. If he weren't in love with someone else. Katherine. The schoolteacher. The woman of his dreams.

Ever since that night in Custer, he'd found himself thinking about Katherine—a victim of fate, yet so brave and resilient—at all the wrong times. On his bike in traffic. Placing a bet at the blackjack table. While taking a walking tour of Lead.

Had Katherine visited the nearby mining town when she lived in Deadwood? he asked himself. Right before he remembered that she wasn't real and he was losing his mind.

Kat was real. She wasn't Katherine, but she certainly was desirable. Sexy.

Kat regretted inviting Jack outside the moment he joined her at the railing of the small deck. She wished she didn't feel like jumping out of her skin every time he accidentally touched her. But she did.

"Wanna grab a chair?" she asked, pulling one of the four molded-plastic deck chairs from the stack in the corner. She dropped it in her usual spot and sat, kicking off her flip-flops to rest her heels on the top railing. The white-painted wood looked about as chipped and peeling as Jack's tattoo.

The sight had made her faintly queasy when he'd shown it to her earlier. Now more than ever she was glad she'd thrown the black ink in with the hazardous waste. Jack's were the last black tattoos she planned to give.

He sat beside her. A little too close, but she refrained from saying so.

"Are your tats still itchy?" she asked, wiggling her toes in the slight breeze. The night was warm but not muggy.

"Not bad. The antihistamine helped. No lasting ill effects."

We hope.

Kat didn't want to talk about her decision, but he deserved to know. Just in case.

"You asked me a question earlier and I sort of avoided answering."

"I noticed," he said, his tone amused. A refreshing change that she didn't expect to last.

She let her feet drop to the deck, then she turned to face him. "Listen. I don't expect you to understand something I don't entirely get myself, but…um…I was all set to go into the clinic. I told myself it was the smart thing to do, given the circumstances, but then…I didn't go."

"May I ask why?"

He sounded serious. Maybe even concerned, but at least he wasn't shouting or looking for something to punch the way her father did when he was upset. He'd never struck her, but she'd lost track of the times a beer bottle went flying across the room when he and her mother were arguing.

She looked at Jack a minute longer. His brow was gathered in a questioning look, but he didn't appear coiled and ready to explode. Kat actually felt safe enough to try to explain her rationale. "My mother has always said things happen for a reason. I used to think that was Mom's excuse for all the wrong turns she made in life. I promised myself I was going to plan better and not let my life be subject to the whims of fate. But—" she took a deep breath and let it out "—apparently I *am* my mother's daughter."

His head tilted slightly as if trying to figure out her meaning.

"I slept with you that night, Jack. I didn't plan to. If I had, I would have brought along birth control. I'm a savvy woman of today. I know about STDs. I'm not embarrassed to walk into a store and buy condoms. But sex was so far from my mind—" She stopped when she noticed his frown. She'd hurt his feelings.

Reaching out, she touched his arm. The way she might comfort Jordie. "I don't mean that you're not a sexy, desirable guy, Jack. You are." Her fingers were tingling in a very un-motherlike way. Swoo alert. She pulled back her hand. "But that night you were puffy and itchy and practically comatose. I still can't believe you managed to… Never mind."

He snickered softly, adding to her surprise. What was with this guy? Didn't he ever get mad?

"Maybe I wasn't myself," he said cryptically. "But given that we made love without benefit of birth control, certain repercussions might follow. And you led me to believe that you were going to eliminate that possibility."

"I know," she said, looking down. "I planned to. But there was a voice in my head that said you wound up in my bed for a reason. I don't know why, but I didn't feel right about trying to undo that, regardless of what happens."

Neither spoke for several minutes, then Jack asked, "So…if you wound up pregnant, did you plan on calling me?" His tone was faintly accusatory.

At last. A reaction she could understand. "Of course," she said defensively. "As complicated as it would probably be having a long-distance father in the picture, you and the baby still deserve to know each other."

He turned his chair to face her, then leaned forward, elbows on his knees. In that angle, she could only see his silhouette clearly. And his profile was so clearly Mad Jack's her heart started pounding like a long-distance runner's. The pulse in her head made it hard to make out what he was saying.

"…get one thing straight, Kat. I never planned to have children. Your sons will attest to the fact I'm not a daddy kind of guy. But if our being together that night created a baby, I *will* be a serious part of that child's life. I firmly believe in taking responsibility for one's actions—even if that means one of us has to move."

She swallowed harshly and tried to regain her composure. So many thoughts were racing through her brain she could barely pick which one to focus on. The word *move* lingered long enough for her to grab it.

"Move?" she cried, her voice a full octave higher than normal. "Are you serious? I can't move. Tag's dad would come unglued. Drew is a little more laid-back where

Jordie is concerned, but even *he* would take me to court if I tried to leave the area before his son turns eighteen."

His gunslinger—no, swimmer—shoulders lifted and fell. "Still, moving a family would be simpler than moving my entire business."

"Ha," she snorted. "You don't know my family. Not only do I have two sons and two spoiled ex-husbands, my mother's sick. Throat cancer. And my father's totally unpredictable. My older stepsiblings think he's crazy—too many years of hitting the bottle. I'm more inclined to blame it on cussed orneriness, but if I left, who would make sure he didn't sell off all the bison? Half the herd is mine. I can't leave them."

His mouth dropped open once or twice, but instead of a reply, he started to laugh. His reaction was so contrary to the fight she'd been expecting, all she could do was stare. For a moment. Then it struck her that he was laughing at her. People had been poking fun at her expense for years. Silly little Kat. Foolish girl most likely to screw up. Her bottom lip started to quiver and she had to blink fast to keep the tears back.

Jack's laughter stopped as quickly as it started. "What's wrong? Are you crying?"

Damn. Her neighbor's burglar-proof exterior spotlight was probably shining right on her face. "N-no. But it's not nice to laugh at—"

He cut her off by reaching out and taking her hand. "I'm sorry, Kat. I didn't mean to hurt your feelings, but you have to admit, worrying about the bison is a pretty unusual excuse for not leaving an area. Why do you think your father would get rid of them?"

She sniffled and pulled her hand free to brush away

the stupid tear that had formed in the corner of her eye. "I got sucked into the story of the bison when I studied history in high school. I spent months finding out everything I could about the animals, and then I located a small herd that was for sale. I begged Dad to buy them. To my profound surprise he did. But he's never let me forget that *my* animals are eating *his* grass and feed—even though Tag and Jordie and I are the primary ones who check on the herd and make sure they're okay."

She smiled, picturing the herd that had more than tripled in size over the years. "They're amazing animals. Healthy. Well adapted to the land. Just give them water and room to graze and they take care of the rest."

Jack was watching her with the same look she'd seen on her father's face when she started talking bison. "I'm hoping that when Tag and Jordie are old enough, we'll be able to sell part of our share and buy some land. Dad isn't going to live forever and you never know from one day to next whether you're in his will or on his buffalo chip list."

"*Buffalo chip list,*" he repeated, his tone still decidedly amused. "Okay, I concede. Relocating a herd of bison might be more difficult than moving half-a-dozen dentists. But just barely."

She edged out of the direct light and stood to lean her lower back against the railing. What did a person say to that kind of agreeableness? Why wasn't he arguing? Where was the bluster and name-calling that always came in a fight?

He took a leisurely drink from his reused plastic bottle. She just didn't get him. Which was a surprise in and of itself. Mostly the men in her life followed a recognizable pattern of behavior. They wanted something from her, took it, then left. Period.

Jack was different.

He joined her at the railing, their shoulders a respectable distance apart. "I have a favor to ask, Kat."

Finally. Here it comes. Can you help me out with a load of laundry in the morning, honey? Could you spot me a few bucks till I get home? Do we really have to sleep in separate rooms, sweetie pie? It's not like we haven't already done the evil deed.

"I know you're busy, but do you think you could show me the bison before I leave?"

"Huh? You don't believe there's a herd."

"No. Of course, I believe you. I just want to see one. A real live North American bison. On the hoof, not packaged in my grocery store."

"Why?"

"Because they're bison, and..." His tone was so wistful he reminded her of Jordie, who shared Kat's passion for the animals. She understood completely, but she held her breath as she waited for him to finish.

"...I don't know. Latent guilt, I think."

"Pardon?"

He took another drink from his water bottle. His throat moved in a masculine, sexy way that had been her undoing more than once in the past. "I told you how much I love history, but one of the things I've never really been able to get my mind around is the massacre of the buffalo. I've forgotten the exact numbers, but there were millions of head roaming these lands before the white hunters came." His head shook slowly from side to side. "I feel like I need to apologize, but I've never seen a bison."

She took a drink, too. The cold liquid helped take her mind off her sudden, all-too-urgent desire to reach out and kiss him. He was a nice guy, but he wasn't the *right* guy. He might give lip service about honoring the big woolly beasts she'd come to love, but a few minutes with her dad would change that. Hell, two hours with her father had been all it took to put a rifle in peace-loving Drew's hand. Before the day was out, her new husband had his first kill. An innocent jackrabbit with nothing on its mind but dinner and a little procreation.

She knew what would happen if she took Jack to her father's ranch. She had nothing to lose, so she told him, "Sure. One day this week. I'll let you know." She turned to leave. "I gave you the extra key, right? I like to lock up at night. The neighbor's dogs would probably tell me if someone drove up, but why take chances?"

And she was all about playing it safe. Which was exactly why she was going to bed. Alone.

CHAPTER TWELVE

KAT HAD VACILLATED about taking Jack to see the bison for four days. Not because of the forty-five-minute drive and her current state of exhaustion—she was used to running on very little sleep—but because it might mean bumping into her father. She hadn't seen Buck in a month, although she usually called him once a week. Kat used the herd as an excuse to check up on him.

Buck, whose real name was Buford Earl Garrity, rarely initiated a call. In the past the only time he phoned anyone was when he was drunk. She'd thought about giving him a heads-up before they left the house but decided against it. As far as she knew, he was still alive. And sober. And if they bumped into him today, so be it, but she wasn't going out of her way to introduce him to Jack. Why hasten the inevitable?

"Stay in the car. I'll get the gate," she said, opening her door. "We can't hang around long and I'm not sure where the herd is. I hope this wasn't a waste of time."

Time. Precious time. So much to do, and yet here she was, trying to please Jack because she felt she owed him for being so nice to her and helpful at Thunder Alley. His presence alone seemed enough to keep the really persistent drunks away. And more than a few of the lady bikers seemed attracted to him. They drifted past her booth to flirt with Jack and wound up getting a henna tattoo.

Her profits were mounting. Which was a good thing because not only had her usually like-clockwork period not arrived, she woke up this morning to discover her nipples felt overly sensitive. She told herself the latter was a result of the dream she'd had. Her and Mad Jack on the prairie. Making love. Nothing but bare skin and blue sky. The sensuality of the breeze on her skin had been enough to— "I'm sorry. What did you say?"

She had her hand on the gate but hadn't opened the complicated contraption when she realized Jack had gotten out of the car and was approaching.

"Over there. Is that the herd?"

She stood on tiptoe to see where he was pointing. A slight hillock between her and the pasture that interested him blocked her view. She put her booted foot on the bottom strand of barbed wire beside the weathered wood post and hoisted herself up. Squinting against the early-morning brightness, she followed his outstretched arm.

He stepped close. Their bodies were almost touching, and for a split second she remembered her dream. Jack's body was a lot like his dream counterpart, even if they were miles apart in every other way.

"I thought at first they were cows, but then I spotted that big one. Is that the alpha male?"

"That's them, but they're a few head short. I wonder where…" She stretched upward and the wire she was standing on pulled loose from the post. She slipped.

It was just a few inches, but the rusty barbed wire could have meant a bad scratch at the very least. Fortunately Jack caught her. His arm went around her middle in a graceful swoop and he stepped away to keep both of them from getting hurt.

Her back was tight against his front. Their hearts were nearly level, and even through their clothing she could feel his speed up from the adrenaline. Her heart was beating fast, too. Probably from a different cause. She didn't want to think about it because if she did, she'd have to admit that Jack was growing on her. She thought about him more than she thought about Mad Jack. And in this morning's dream, for the first time, the two seemed to blur. One second she was kissing her wild and dangerous gunslinger, the next her sweet, charming orthodontist.

She was very confused. But one thing Kat knew for sure was that she wasn't making the same mistake she'd made with her ex-husbands. No matter what.

She wriggled free of his hold. "Thanks. Dad needs to do some fence work."

Jack appeared ready to say something, but a loud *put-put-put* sound made them both turn to locate the source.

"Oh, nuts. Here comes my dad. I was hoping we could sneak in and out without running into him."

"Why?"

"You'll see," she muttered softly. Or maybe he wouldn't. Both her ex-husbands were still friends with Buck. They hunted his land every fall and usually wound up staying overnight after partying a little too hard. Buck could drink anybody under the table.

"Hey, Daughter. I thought that was your car. Who's that with you?"

Buck Garrity looked every bit the larger-than-life

western rancher he portrayed himself as. Six-four in his youth. Three hundred pounds at his heaviest. His first family—a complex mix in its own right—was practically raised and his wife dead when he met and married Kat's mother. Despite the toll alcohol had taken on his liver, an ongoing battle with gout and some concerns about his heart, he exuded a rugged, healthful vibrancy that her mother still called the most powerful swoo on the planet.

"Jack, this is my father, Buck Garrity. Jack is from Denver. He's renting Tag's room from me this week because he was too late to find a place for the rally. I told you this in the phone message I left a few days ago. Do you ever check your messages?"

Her dad didn't answer. Nor had she expected him to. He opened the gate and walked out to shake Jack's hand. To Kat's surprise, Jack didn't appear the least bit intimidated or cowed.

"Nice to meet you. I was curious about the bison and Kat was nice enough to show me your herd."

"*Her* herd," Buck corrected. "I gotta admit I never would have bought 'em if she hadn't pestered me to do it. Now I can't picture the place without them. They're funny beasts. Smart and curious in a way cows aren't. Did she tell you about 'em?" he asked, motioning for Jack to follow.

Kat stifled her groan. This was so like her father. If he was in the mood, he could be as charming as any politician. And no one had ever accused him of being dumb. He knew more about bison than Kat could ever hope to know. For that reason alone, she hung back.

Her father noticed. He stopped midsentence and

looked at her. "I almost forgot. Your aunt called here looking for you. Needs you to call her back."

Kat frowned. There'd been a message on her machine when she got home last night, but it had been after midnight when she listened to it. Something about her mother's breathing.

Aunt Roberta had moved in with her mom about a year ago after her husband passed away. The two sisters hadn't talked in years—some hurt feelings or family blow-up—but when mom was diagnosed with throat cancer and needed help, Roberta sold her home in Iowa and moved to Spearfish, where Kat's mother lived.

Roberta was a nice woman, but she lacked her older sister's energy or imagination. Kat was afraid her mother might die of boredom, but she didn't say so, since Kat herself wasn't in a position to nurse her mom back to health.

"Can I use your phone, Dad?"

Buck unclipped the cell phone he wore at his waist and handed it to her. Then he turned back to his guest. "Bison are like elephants," he started. "They're a matriarchal herd with an alpha female, and they have a pecking order like chickens."

Elephant chickens. That was what Tag used to call them when Jordie was little.

Smiling to herself, Kat glanced at the two men one more time before heading to the car to call her long-winded aunt. Her gaze met Jack's. There was something deep and unreadable in his look. Pure swoo. Her knees buckled, but fortunately she was close enough to the fender to reach out for support.

Her heart sped up and suddenly she felt too warm.

She quickly punched in her aunt's number. "Hi, Roberta. It's me. Sorry I didn't call last night. I'm working my booth at the Alley and got in real late. Is Mom okay? Can I talk to her?"

"Oh, good. It's you, Kat. I was afraid I'd miss you today. Your mother is resting at the moment. We had a little scare last night. She was having trouble breathing. I called 9-1-1."

"Really? It was that bad?"

Her aunt sighed. "Probably not, but your mother couldn't tell me not to. She could barely whisper."

Roberta wasn't a decision-maker. "I'm so sorry I wasn't there to help. What happened?"

"The EMTs gave her some oxygen. That helped a lot. They wanted to take her to the hospital, but you know your mother. Once she could talk, she said no. But I'm taking her to the doctor today. At the very least, we need to have one of those bottles of oxygen around."

Kat breathed a silent sigh of relief. Her mother had fought back from the horrible diagnosis and surgery for throat cancer. She'd made it through chemo and radiation. But her will to live had suffered greatly these past nine months.

In a way, Kat understood. Her mother believed she needed a man in her life. And now she felt unattractive, unworthy of love. Kat's heart broke for her, but she didn't know how to change Mom's core belief.

"Thanks for calling, Roberta. I'm really sorry I'm not there to help, but tell Mom I love her. I'm at the ranch at the moment and I could maybe swing by on my way back to town but—"

"We won't be here, honey Kat. We'll be at the

doctor's office. Just try to check in from time to time. You can call me late, if you need to. I know how busy you are. Your mom knows, too. Don't worry. Things happen the way they're supposed to."

That truism again, Kat thought, closing the phone after saying goodbye. Her entire family had turned into fatalists. They'd never been very religious, although they'd attended church sporadically, depending on her mother's needs at the time. One of Kat's stepfathers had been a minister. Her mother used to say she'd fallen in love with his message, then learned too late that he didn't believe it.

Holding the phone firmly, she jogged after the two much smaller figures that were approaching the sixty or so head of bison scattered about a small bowl-shaped valley. The matriarch watched them intently. Younger bulls snorted nervously. Babies scampered awkwardly to their feet and huddled close to their mothers.

The men had stopped moving, so Kat was able to catch up rather quickly. "How come they're so close to the ranch, Dad?"

"Don't know. We cut and tagged half the cattle last week so I could supply some stock for the Deadwood rodeo. Maybe they were wondering what was happening."

"You didn't take out any of the bison, did you?" She and her father had had this argument many times over the years. She was never positive he respected her wishes.

"Naw. The only one they wanted was Leon. And he's too much trouble to move."

He pointed to a massive bull nibbling on a tuft of grass. The beast's shaggy mane gave him that definable look most people associated with bison. No one knew his exact age, since they bought him from a petting zoo with dubious records, but he was a majestic-looking beast. Most of the other animals were younger.

Now that she had a better view of the herd she could tell the numbers looked right. It wasn't that she didn't trust her father to care for the animals—and some losses happened no matter what—but she'd always felt that because she was who she was, the herd ran some risk of being ignored to death. Or casually sold at market. Not because Buck needed the money or was tired of the work. Simply because he could. She'd seen her father do all sorts of petty acts to hurt her mother—and her by association. Kat didn't want her beloved bison to become a pawn in a power game.

"It's getting late, Jack."

"Don't tell me you're doing that silly brown stuff again. What a racket!" Buck exclaimed, shaking his head so hard his straw cowboy hat nearly fell off. "Anybody dumb enough to get a tattoo in the first place is smart enough to only pay for it once."

Instead of looking embarrassed as she'd expected, Jack laughed. "Not all of us." He pushed up his sleeve and showed the faint shadow of what had been barbed wire. "Your daughter is an artist and she does a real steady business."

"What the hell? She got you to try one of those henna things?" He spat for good measure.

Jack snickered. "I wish. She tried to talk me into the henna, but I had to do it my way. Brought my own ink. It must have been old and mixed with gasoline or something because I wound up sicker than a dog."

Her father obviously couldn't believe a real man

would do such a thing. His mouth still hung partly open. "Why didn't you just go to a legitimate tattoo parlor?"

Jack shrugged. "Needles. Can't stand needles."

"Oh," her father said, like a true kindred spirit. "Me, neither. But that brown stuff is just too girly for my taste."

Kat laughed for the first time in her father's presence in she didn't know how long. Even hearing him say the word *girly* sounded funny to her. For a man who claimed not to care what people thought of him to worry about being emasculated by a temporary tattoo struck her as ridiculous. But in a way, it made sense.

Suddenly something clicked in her head and she understood that no matter how she lived her life or what she accomplished, her father would still make judgment calls based on his own sense of what mattered.

Both men were staring at her, she realized. She didn't care. "See you later, Dad. Oh, and by the way, Mom's not doing too hot. Just FYI."

"You know I hate abbreviations," her dad said with a growl.

"TDB," she said with a small wave.

Jack hurried to catch up. "TDB?" he repeated softly. "I don't know that one."

"Too damn bad."

His laugh made the matriarch of the herd give a loud snort, and a second later the entire herd was on the move. Kat could hear her father muttering as she locked the gate behind them, but for once in her life, she honestly didn't care what her father thought. Period.

TDB, Jack thought, looking out the side window at the rolling landscape as Kat drove them back to her home. The green pastures dissected by cultivated farmland and small ranches reminded him of northeastern Colorado. He'd thought about moving to Fort Collins out of college, but his mother had convinced him Denver had more opportunities. He liked Denver, but he was sorry now that he hadn't at least tried somewhere new so he could say he had.

"Your father's a real character," he said.

"That's a polite way to put it. Although both my exes get along great with him. He's what you might call a man's man. Like John Wayne."

Jack nodded. "Yeah. I can see the comparison. I've never been a big John Wayne movie buff. Although my mom gave me a complete set of his Westerns for Christmas, and I have to admit, some of them aren't bad."

He turned to look at her. The way she was working that bottom lip told him she was deep in thought. Planning. Juggling. Trying to fill everyone's needs except her own. He'd never met anyone like her. Always ready to help, even when she was exhausted. And she had to be. He was pooped just from trying to keep up with her.

"We're stopping at the house before heading to Blood Alley, right?"

That made her smile. He'd seen enough fistfights, fender benders and drunks with blood running down their faces the past couple of days to make him rename Thunder Alley.

"Yes. So you can get your bike. I'm not opening the booth until later this afternoon. One of Char's friends is holding down the fort for me. He does Lakota painting."

"Where are you going, if you don't mind my asking?"

She hesitated long enough to make him think she might, but she answered, "Sentinel Pass. To see Libby.

You heard about Coop's big party on Sunday, right? The whole town is invited."

"Yeah. You mentioned it the other day, but I never heard what kind of party it is. Birthday?"

"No. A belated wedding party. He feels guilty about how fast he and Lib got married. Everyone in Sentinel Pass knows Lib and would have been invited if it wasn't for the paparazzi, so now he's going to do a big bash for all the locals."

"This coming Sunday?"

She nodded.

"Libby asked you to help?"

She nodded.

"And you told her, 'No. Sorry. I can't take on anything else because I'm already running myself ragged.'"

He could tell by the way her eyes widened behind her sunglasses that he hadn't done a good job of disguising his sense of outrage on her behalf. Even Kat's father seemed to think nothing of making demands on his daughter's time, despite the fact that she was juggling any number of jobs, raising two kids alone and going to school. And the guy was rich. While Kat had been on the phone, Buck had described in detail his recent safari adventure. Trips like that didn't come cheap.

Jack's father, for all his faults, had been one of the most generous men Jack had ever known. His mother might attach a few strings to her gifts, but not his dad. He just gave and gave. The fact that the boy who'd accused Dad of inappropriate behavior had been a pro bono case had seemed to irk Jack's mother more than anything. Why, he wasn't sure.

"By help," Kat said, drawing his attention back to the

present, "I plan to show up and do some creative mingling. Quite a few of the crew members will have arrived in town by then, and Libby's afraid the two factions will wind up sitting on opposite sides of the street and never interact."

"What about your booth?"

"I never work on Sundays unless the boys can be with me. We usually go to church, then do something that can't be misconstrued as work. Hiking the Michelson Trail or swimming at Sheridan Lake. Or renting a bunch of movies. I don't work *all* the time."

"Hmm. Sorry I got all defensive on your behalf."

She smiled. "No problem. It was kinda sweet. Sounds like something Mad— Never mind. What do you think of the rally so far?"

Mad. She'd been about to say a name. Madeleine? Madonna? She didn't know about his dream, so it couldn't have been Mad Jack.

He put the thought out of his head and answered her question as diplomatically as possible. He couldn't tell her the truth. That he liked watching her work. That he hated the men who leered at her and the women who acted better than her. That he was falling in love with her and wasn't sure what to do about it.

She'd made it abundantly clear that he was not her type—whatever that meant. Some women were their own worst enemies. Even smart women, like Kat. And his sister, Rachel. They made choices based on superficial reasons and later were shocked by the depth of their regret.

Fine, he told himself. Kat's decisions were none of his business. This was his time to find himself and expand the boundaries that nearly caused him to make a choice based on the wrong reasons.

He'd learned from that near miss. He was his own man now. He hadn't talked to his sister or mother in three days, although he had texted them both to let them know he was okay. In his travels around Blood Alley, he'd observed unpleasantly naked people doing the kinds of things his ex participated in. So far this trip, he'd imbibed more than was wise, eaten ridiculously unhealthy food and, let's not forget, made love to a stranger. Hell, at this rate, he'd be Mad Jack before he left the Hills.

CHAPTER THIRTEEN

I'M PREGNANT.

Impossible though it seemed—the odds were so in her favor for once. They'd only made love the one time.

I mean, come on, she thought, scowling at her reflection in the mirror. The chances seemed infinitesimal.

But she'd awoken that morning with the truth in her head. Still no period and her nipples definitely felt chafed. And the thought of the smell of coffee left a bad taste in her mouth. And she was horny as hell.

All signs she couldn't ignore. The last had been her ex-husbands' favorite pregnancy side effect. Raging hormones blocked her normal inhibition and turned her into a much less repressed version of herself.

She looked around the door of the bathroom to check her bedside clock. Too early to make a trip to the pharmacy for a home pregnancy test. Not that she needed a little blue stick to confirm what she already knew. But Jack probably would.

Today was Sunday. Cooper's big party was scheduled for this afternoon, and Jack planned to take off after putting in an appearance—at Libby's request. He'd made reservations at a motel in Edgemont, the state-line town where he'd stayed on the way here from Denver.

She couldn't wait to pick up her sons. She missed Tag and Jordie so much she got a little weepy thinking about them. She'd talked to each boy every day and felt the experience of being away had been good for them, but she was so ready to have them back. If her friends would let them go.

Jenna couldn't say enough about Tag's work ethic and rapport with the tourists who came to the Mystery Spot. "He seems so much older than eight. Well, almost nine, as he tells all his coworkers. I think he has a crush on Robyn." Robyn Craine was Jenna's manager at the Mystery Spot. She was due to return to college in a couple of weeks, and Jenna was already sweating the loss.

Char seemed equally pleased with how her time with Jordie had turned out. "He's an awesome kid, Kat. If I had a kid, I'd hope he'd be just as cool."

There had been a funny catch in her friend's usually unflappable voice when they'd talked last night, but Kat had been too exhausted to question it.

This year's rally had nearly done her in. She'd worked through the heat, the wind and the quick summer squalls, in addition to the great horde of humanity that passed just beyond the flaps of her tent.

She'd seen everything from a woman who crashed her bike in front of Kat's tent and nearly decked the paramedic who came to her aid to several naked people doing things they'd never have done in public if they were at home. The only thing that really surprised her, though, was Jack. He rarely left her immediate vicinity. He was like a self-appointed watchdog. And his presence had felt surprisingly comforting.

Thank God for Jack, she'd thought more than once.

Now, she didn't know what to think. They hadn't really talked about what might happen if the inconceivable happened—she conceived. Although it was tempting to postpone the inevitable, she knew it would be easier to talk this out face-to-face rather than over the phone.

From previous experience—both of her exes would have jumped at the plan she was going to offer Jack—and given Jack's admitted aversion to children, she wasn't expecting him to want to be too involved. So if he'd kick in a reasonable amount of child support, she'd let him off the hook parenting-wise.

She swallowed the bad taste in her mouth and leaned over the sink to give her teeth another go with the toothbrush. The mint flavor helped, but not much. She got a little queasy thinking about what was in store for all of them, but they'd adjust. They'd get by. Just like always.

In the meantime, she had Plan A. She quickly fluffed her hair with wet fingertips and faked a smile. What she planned to do was wrong on so many levels she'd lost count, but darn it, the worst that could happen already had, so why the heck not give in to temptation and tell him goodbye in a way he'd never forget?

She looked down at the skimpy tank top she'd pulled on, braless. Her nipples, which truly had a mind of their own even when she wasn't pregnant, made two distinct dots against the stretchy white fabric. Two pregnancies notwithstanding, her breasts weren't bad. Mad Jack had called them perfect.

She sighed and shook her head. She wasn't going to think about him. She was going to seduce Jack. Jackson Boyd Treadwell. He'd given her his wallet to hold while he participated in some group tug-of-war the other day.

She'd peeked inside on the excuse she might need to know his blood type. A slightly dated group photo of Jack, his mother—Kat could tell by the eyes—and his sister was the only personal item he carried.

Despite their spending the better part of the past five days together, she didn't really know him. He was a pleasant, generous, nicely mannered enigma. With a great body, gorgeous masculine lips and a butt that really did look sexy in chaps.

He might not be the steely eyed gunslinger of her dreams, but he turned her on, and that seemed as good a reason as any for what she was planning to do.

With a final glance in the mirror, she left the bathroom. Her heart was pounding more than she would have liked. Through the open windows in the living room, she could hear birds singing. The sky still held that pinkish glow she loved best.

The cool breeze tickled her bare legs as she dashed down the hall. With the most minimum of knocks, she opened the door and leaned in far enough to make out Jack's outline on the bed. He slept on his side. Just like Tag. Pillow bunched under his head. Arm stretched out. The covers were pushed down to his waist. His chest was bare.

Her mouth went dry and her courage almost left her. But that indefinable something that got her into this mess in the first place felt more powerful than ever. Swoo. Desire. Hormones. She didn't know its name. And at the moment she didn't care. She just knew this would be her last chance to create a memory, not a dream.

Jack heard the door open, but he kept his eyes closed. Kat's house was so small and poorly built he'd actually heard her get out of bed and pace around a bit before brushing her teeth. He hadn't expected her to stop at his door, but she had. Now she was advancing slowly toward the bed.

He assumed that since he was leaving in a few hours, it was time for the I'm-not-pregnant-and-there's-really-no-reason-for-us-to-see-each-other-again talk. She'd adroitly managed to avoid the subject of their night together any time he tried to bring it up. He might have pressed harder if he hadn't observed that most people in Kat's life demanded things of her without any regard for her own agenda.

There was another reason he hadn't pushed her for an answer. He liked her. More than liked. He was ridiculously attracted to her. There was a distinct chance he was falling in love with her. Kat. Not Katherine, the woman in his dream. It had taken this week for him to see that Kat was everything Katherine was—and more. While both women were smart, witty and brave, Katherine projected a sort of self-contained perfection. Kat was far from perfect, but she put herself on the line in ways Mad Jack's schoolmarm would never dare.

Kat would take on any bully—even her father—to protect a friend…or her beloved bison. Unfaltering in her loyalty. Maddeningly single-minded when it came to her friends and family. The kind of person he wished his mother had been when his father had been in trouble.

Maybe somewhere along the way, he'd concluded that familial integrity only existed in yesteryear. His subconscious even provided the woman of his dreams. But then he met Kat. And reality was so much better.

Unfortunately she'd kept him at arm's length in a neat little box of her own design. He would have been hurt if he didn't understand exactly what she was doing—and why. He'd done the same thing with relationships all his life.

A board under her heel made a creaking sound and he used the cue to move. Trying not to overplay his role, he let out a muffled moan and rolled to his back.

"You're awake, aren't you?"

He kept his eyes closed, but he couldn't prevent a grin. "Maybe, but if you're naked, I'm pretty sure I'm dreaming."

She hopped onto the bed beside him. Her weight made the mattress sag just a little and he rolled toward her. "I'm not naked...but I could be...if you wanted me to be."

His eyes flew open. "Really?"

She wasn't nude, but the few scraps of cloth she was wearing were more provocative than she could possibly know. White tank top that dipped low across the tops of her breasts. Their fullness outlined in shadow, her nipples clearly erect. The shirt's hemline barely skimmed the elastic waistband of her French-cut panties. He could see a few golden-blond curls peaking out beneath the lavender silk.

He swallowed hard and shifted slightly so he didn't embarrass himself. "Tell me you're not here to—"

She leaned down and kissed him. "I'm here because I want to be. No hidden agenda. No strings. We're unattached people who like each other, I think. I'm not wrong, am I?"

Like truly didn't cover the depth of his feelings, but it was enough for now. He reached out and gently ran his hand along her cheek and jaw. "You're not wrong." Then he pulled back the sheet to welcome her closer.

The room was light enough for her to see his body's reaction to her offer. She didn't lie down beside him as he expected. Instead, she curled her feet under her and lifted up slightly to pull her tank top over her head. The sight of her beautiful bare breasts and lean, tanned torso made every ounce of testosterone in him surge through his blood.

"You are incredibly sexy," he said. "Gorgeous. Absolutely gorgeous."

Her cheeks were too pink. That didn't surprise him. He knew she didn't handle compliments well, but he couldn't help lavishing praise as he touched her. "Your skin is the prettiest color I've ever seen. Last time, I thought it was candlelight that gave it this warm, sunny glow, but no. This is you. Beautiful Kat."

She cocked her head in question. *Last time.* He didn't want to mention his fantasy woman, Katherine. Now was not the time to bring up another woman's name—even if she was a figment of his imagination and probably some subconscious incarnation of Kat.

To distract her, he took her hand and brought it to his lips. He kissed each fingertip, stained with henna. There wasn't a part of his body he wouldn't trust to her capable hands. He wanted to tell her that, but he didn't think she'd believe him.

She wriggled close enough for him to smell her warmth and raw sexual perfume. Need hit him at a gut level. It took all his self-control not to pin her below him and take what she appeared to be offering.

"I woke up horny," she said. "Foreplay is nice and all, but I'm...um...ready for whatever."

Not what he was expecting to hear. Not his shy, strait-laced Kat. He'd never even heard her swear. But when he looked in her shining blue eyes, he understood. This was about mutual need. The sexual tension that had been building all week wasn't one-sided.

"Then by all means, my dear, hop aboard," he said, flopping backward—exposed. Vulnerable.

She looked her fill and actually licked her lips. "Nice package," she said, her blush intensifying. "I understand that's the correct lingo these days. I don't remember looking that closely last time."

"Thanks. I aim to please."

"I can see that, but if you don't mind…I…um… Oh, heck, I'm just going to say this. You mentioned something about fantasies when I first met you. And that got me thinking about something I've wanted to try but didn't exactly know how—or who—to ask. Would you be up—no pun intended—for a little…um…bondage? Nothing kinky, just…"

The word threw him for a second. It reminded him of Jaydene. But only for a second. This was Kat. Sweet, shy, adorable Kat, who was offering him yet another chance to prove something to himself. If he dared.

He held out his hands, wrists together. "Anything you want. I'm your man."

Her grin lit up the room for a second before she vaulted from the bed. "I'll be right back."

She returned with two men's ties. One a sober blue. The other a gaudy paisley print. "I promise this won't hurt," she said, taking his left hand and stretching it out toward the knobby bedpost.

"I probably shouldn't admit this," she went on, "but

when I bought this bed for Tag, I actually thought the headboard had all sorts of possibilities." Her blush was so adorable he almost blurted out his love for her.

Not yet. Too soon. She wouldn't believe me.

"I promise not to tell him," Jack said. Like that kind of conversation would ever come up. He'd never talked sex with his dad, and couldn't imagine discussing the subject with someone else's kid.

She climbed over him to secure the other wrist. He watched as she made a quick, efficient flip of the wrist and pulled a loop through the knot. "Where'd you learn to tie so well?"

"The ranch. My dad didn't think I was smart enough to go to college, so he wanted me to have some marketable skills."

"Like tying up men?"

She laughed. "Like tying up horses."

She sat back and looked him over. "Cool. Now I pretty much have you at my mercy, don't I?"

He flexed first one arm, then the other. He definitely wasn't going anywhere. "I believe you do, Miss Katherine."

He winced. The name had slipped. He saw her eyebrows knit for a moment, then she shrugged lightly and straddled his waist. She wiggled provocatively. He wanted to touch those perfect breasts. But when he reached out, his arm stopped well short of her.

"Whoa. I don't think I like this. I can't touch you."

"Sure you can. But only the parts I let you touch." To prove her point, she leaned over and put his left hand on her breast. His right fingers came in contact with her leg.

He closed his eyes and stretched to get the most for

his reach. Then she moved again. She put her hands on either side of his face and leaned down to kiss him.

"I didn't expect this, you know," she told him, running her tongue across his bottom lip.

"Expect what?"

"Everything. You surprised me. On so many levels." She trailed tiny kisses down his neck and across the top of his collarbone. Her fingers played with his flat nipples until they stood rigid. Every sensation wreaked havoc on his self-control, but the ties around his wrists kept him from trying to take over the seduction.

This was happening on Kat's terms.

She tickled him lightly under the arms. He bucked as if she'd pinched him. "No fair. I'm ticklish. I admit it. Oh, crap, you're not going to use that against me, are you?"

She didn't answer. Instead, she slid downward until she was kneeling between his legs. She very gently dragged her fingernails across the sole of his foot. He practically levitated off the bed.

"This is so illuminating. Big, strong, motorcycle bad boy who picks fights in bars is ticklish. I could so use this against you if you were going…"

She didn't finish the thought. Instead, she looked in his eyes for a heartbeat or two, then slowly came forward, her gaze dropping to his waist. As she neared his middle, she licked her lips in a slow, provocative way that made his heart start to race. She lowered her mouth to his body, teasing the tip of his penis with her tongue before closing her lips around him.

Handicapped as he was, he had to acknowledge that he was at her mercy, but what sweet mercy it was. She used her teeth, her tongue, and…oh, yes, her mouth. "Kat!" he cried. "You're killing me."

He twisted and pulled against his constraints, which he realized did add an element of adventure he'd never imagined. He was all hers, in every way possible.

Panting with the strain of not coming, he begged her to let him go. "I need…hands…please…you…Kat. Kat." She pushed him to the edge of his restraint, then suddenly she pulled back and looked at him, a smoldering half-hooded look of satisfaction and lust on her face. She moved toward him again and a second later settled her body over his.

They'd done this before, and yet they hadn't. That first time had been in the dark, in a dream. This was real, undeniably real.

She put her hands flat against his chest and started to move in a primal circle of life, her hips lifting and falling, her vaginal walls tightening and releasing. Since he couldn't do anything else, he closed his eyes and lived each second, each sensation.

He'd never felt a buildup like this before. His release seemed to start in the far corners of his extremities and implode to his very core, making him buck his hips into her as fast and hard as he could. He had no idea if she was on the same plain as him. He wanted to please her and feel her mutual pleasure, but his orgasm was too mind-blowing. All he could do was shout her name as he gave in to the all-consuming sensations that he knew he'd never forget.

Kat collapsed against Jack's heaving chest. *Holy garbanzo beans!* she silently cried. Who knew that a couple of ties could add a whole other dimension to sex?

She had no idea where the nerve to suggest bondage came from—maybe his earlier hints that his ex-girlfriend had called their sex life boring. *Maybe I'm a closet control freak,* she thought, tucking her chin to keep him from seeing her smile.

Whatever the reason, the result was the best sex she could ever remember having. Talk about going out with a bang, she thought with satisfaction.

But there was no denying a bittersweet quality, too. The best sex ever was never going to happen again because Jack was leaving. The thought made her breath catch.

She lifted her head and looked at him. His eyes were open as if he was watching her, maybe trying to read her mind. She smiled. This had been her idea, her tiptoe over to the wild side. "You okay?"

He didn't answer, but when he gave the ties a little tug, she knew it was time to undo her handiwork. The knots were the quick-release kind and all she had to do was pull the free end and the fabric slithered to the sheets.

He blinked in surprise. "Wow. You're amazing. In ways I never imagined."

"Never?" She couldn't help feeling a little hurt. After all, they had had sex once before and it had been pretty good, too. She thought. Not quite as phenomenal as this time, but—

He pulled her to him and rolled to his side. "What I meant by that is I've never met anyone who could tie that particular kind of knot."

"Oh."

"And as for the way you made love to me…well, there simply aren't enough words. Unbelievable. In a good way. A great way. Am I making you mad?"

He must have felt her start to tense up. "No. Not really. I just think people have been underestimating me all my life. And I let them. You're less likely to be a disappointment that way."

The furrows in his brow told her he was pondering her statement but before he could say anything, a loud *beep-beep-beep* made them both startle. Tag's clock radio was set for Sunday-morning church.

She scrambled off the bed and hit the off button. The fact that she'd tied Jack up and had her way with him on her son's bed without even thinking about going to church on the morning she realized she was pregnant and unwed… She swallowed a small cry and looked around for her clothes.

"Are you running away again?"

A reference to her horrified reaction the last time they made love, no doubt. "We have a busy day ahead." She yanked on her panties and top. "I'll make coffee."

He caught her hand. "Kat, can you at least wait long enough for me to tell you I think you're amazing and that was the best sex I've ever had?"

Her, too, but she didn't turn around. "You promised to help me refold the tent and put it away."

He made a sound of pure exasperation and sat up. "Oh, no," he said, smacking his forehead with the heel of his hand. "We forgot birth control again."

Now. This was it. *If you can tie up a guy and have your way with him, you can tell him about the illegitimate baby you're going to have.* "I didn't forget. I just didn't bother. After all, you can only get pregnant once."

He frowned. "What's that me— Holy sh— You're not serious. You can be sure this soon?"

"I haven't taken the test, but I know my body."

She left him then. To think. To get his excuses in order.

She showered, got dressed and made coffee. A whole damn pot, which she realized too late she shouldn't drink and had to heat up water for caffeine-free tea. She was on her second cup when Jack entered the kitchen, familiar tote bag in hand.

He poured himself a cup. Black. Took a couple of quick sips, then set his mug on the counter and walked to the table where she was sitting. He pulled her chair out as if she wasn't on it and turned it so he could go down on one knee in front of her. "Kat, I know we don't know each other well, but—"

"If carnal knowledge counts, I know you better than I ever knew my second husband."

He gave her a serious look.

"Sorry."

"We know each other pretty well in several ways, but I'm asking you to marry me."

There hadn't been any mention of a shotgun. She gave him credit for that. But neither was there mention of love.

"Thank you, Jack. You're the closest thing to a hero I've ever known, but my answer is no, thank you."

He looked shocked. "Why not? I can provide for you…and the boys. I know there are logistics to work out, but—"

"I know all those things, Jack. And this week you've proved to me what a great guy you are. I hope we'll become good friends as our child grows up. But I can't marry you."

"Can't or won't?"

"Both."

"Why?"

"Because I'm holding out for the fantasy," she admitted, then wished she hadn't said the word out loud. A woman like her couldn't afford fantasies. "I know. That sounds silly and juvenile and I should probably put our unborn child's welfare first, but frankly, I tried that. Twice. And it didn't work. I wound up in the middle of a legal battlefield, the same way I was raised. I won't do that again. The next time I get married it's going to be for love."

He put out his hands. "But I love you."

She looked at the ceiling. "No, you don't. You're telling me that out of a sense of duty. You're a dutiful son, a responsible doctor and a good person, Jack. But I need to know that the man doing the asking wants me for the right reasons, not because he feels an obligation to a baby we accidentally made one night."

"Kat, I didn't expect any of this when I came here and I'm probably making a complete mess of my proposal, but I really have developed strong feelings for you. I think it's love."

He sounded so earnest she had to smile. "I appreciate that, Jack. Let me know when you're sure."

"You're being facetious."

She shrugged. "I've had good reason to be where the men in my life are concerned. I know you're not Pete Linden or Drew Petroski, but some of the mistakes I made in the past were because I didn't understand who I was and what I wanted out of life.

"I do now. I know that being a good mother to my children and becoming a teacher are important parts of who I am. I'm also a woman who deserves to be loved for who she is—mistakes and all. And until I find the right man, I'm not saying 'I do' again. Baby or no baby."

CHAPTER FOURTEEN

JACK PICKED a can of soda from a huge plastic barrel filled with ice and soft drinks. There was a full bar with a margarita machine set up on the grass behind the Sentinel Pass fire station, but since he was headed back on the road today, he decided to stay sober. Not to mention that his mind was still reeling from the morning. Amazing sex *and* being told he was going to be a father? *Yeah, not your normal morning,* he thought, looking for Kat.

They'd driven separately to the party. She was meeting her kids here and she'd been positively giddy at the prospect.

He spotted her near the silly concrete dinosaur. She was holding Jordie, the littlest boy, on her hip while listening with rapt attention as the older boy told her something. She really was a wonderful mother. He didn't have to worry about her caring for their child with equal love and devotion. But was that enough?

He popped the tab on his drink and tasted the sweet, cool liquid. His hand shook slightly and he felt the strangest urge to cry. His dad had been gone so long, but Jack could almost feel his presence. If he were here today, Jack knew what he'd say to him.

"I'm sorry, Dad. You were the best pop a kid could ask for, and I'm sorry I even once doubted that you were innocent. I wanted to believe you. I told myself I believed, but then a tiny bit of doubt would creep in and I'd ask myself, 'Why didn't he have an assistant working with him that day? Why'd he go to the office alone? Was he trying to hide something?'"

Jack lifted the can to his lips and forced himself to swallow past the lump in his throat. His guilt had been there at the back of his mind for years. His father passed away without either of them talking about Jack's doubts. Now, of course, it was too late.

But Jack never once questioned that he and his sister, Rachel, had been the most important people in their father's life. Yes, Dad had adored—*worshiped* might even have been the right word—their mother, but that relationship was complex and beyond young Jack's ken. His father's steadfast love, though, had carried Jack through some really rough times. If he and Kat were going to have a child, then Jack owed it to his father—and himself—to be the best father he could be. As scary and life-changing as that sounded.

"Hey," a voice said. "You're Kat's friend, aren't you?"

Jack turned to look at the man addressing him. It took him a second to place the guy. He'd been behind the wheel of the truck the day Jack and Kat visited Sentinel Pass. "Yeah. Jack Treadwell. You're Libby's brother, right? The miner."

The guy gave a snorting sound that probably qualified as a laugh. "Mac McGannon." They shook hands. Mac's were rough and huge. They never would have fit inside a patient's mouth. "Mining has turned into a hobby now that I have a rich brother-in-law. Coop thinks we'll make more money off it by building a B and B on the property and giving mine tours."

"That sounds like easier work."

"Not if you're not crazy about people," he said wryly. "Just look at all these strangers. And the real tourists won't start coming until after the television show airs." He shook his head with a certain degree of resignation. "Times are changing. 'Course, it's been that way for a while. The old ones die and their families sell out, instead of coming back here to live. Maybe this boost to the economy will bring new families in." He frowned. "Doesn't look good to have houses sitting empty. Fire risk, for one thing."

Jack noticed for the first time the volunteer fire-department logo on the man's black T-shirt. They talked a bit longer about what kinds of challenges small communities like Sentinel Pass were experiencing. "We had a doctor here years ago when I was a kid," Mac said, his dark eyes checking from time to time on the whereabouts of a little girl who seldom left her aunt's side.

Kat had told him the tragic tale of Mac's wife, who, on the verge of leaving him for another man, crashed her car into a ravine and died. Fortunately Mac had refused to let his wife take their daughter with her when she left. A four-year-old beauty. Jack couldn't remember her name.

"Just out of curiosity, are there a lot of houses for sale around here?" Jack asked.

An idea had started to take shape in his mind as Mac spoke of the community and its possible rebirth. Sentinel Pass wasn't Denver, but Jack had been ready for a change at so many levels for so long it wasn't surprising that he was starting to look at the place with new eyes.

Mac thought a moment. "Mrs. Smith's place is going on the market tomorrow, I heard. She passed away a couple of months ago. Her son and daughter have been trying to decide what to do with the place. They've been renting it to Shane and Coop." He pointed to a very recognizable blond guy across the plaza and a dark-haired fellow Jack had never seen before. "Shane's the writer, producer, director…hell, I don't know what he does. He and Jenna are together."

Jack could see that. Not only were they holding hands and talking with an intimacy that belonged to people in love, they had a dog. An enormous, gorgeous beast with black, white and rust-colored markings. The animal seemed perfectly trained, because it watched the children filing in and out of the bounce house that had been erected in the parking lot, but never made any effort to chase them.

"Anyway, I was just talking to Jill and Peter. They had a real-estate agent from Rapid give them a market appraisal. Makes sense to sell, since neither of their families wants to live here."

Jack nodded. A flutter of excitement coursed through his body. He didn't make crazy, impulsive leaps of faith. But he knew someone who did. Mad Jack. And he didn't even have to ask what Mad Jack would do. He knew the answer. "Are they still here? Mrs. Smith's kids?"

Mac looked around. "Right over there, talking to Elana Grace. She owns the Tidbiscuit. Our local answer to Starbucks," he added dryly. He squinted slightly as he looked a moment longer. "I don't know who the gal in the hat is. She didn't come with Jill and Peter. Maybe she's one of the TV people, although she looks kind of familiar…"

Jack checked her out. Beauty-queen posture. Same Ann Taylor-kind of skirt and blouse his ex-fiancée might have worn. The straw sunhat looked chic and expensive. Jaydene definitely would have been able to identify the brand of purse she was carrying.

"No one I know, which I guess isn't surprising since this is only my second time in town," he said.

He wiped his hand on his pants and held it out. Mac didn't notice at first, his attention still trained on the stranger. "Oh. Sorry," he said, quickly shaking Jack's hand.

"No problem. I appreciate the tip about the house. I've been thinking about relocating to the Hills. This might work out."

Mac's coal-black eyebrows rose in unison. He glanced in the general direction of where Kat had been standing, then returned his gaze to Jack. Jack half expected him to ask something he wasn't prepared to talk about, but instead, Mac said, "Libby called you a stand-up guy. That's good enough for me."

Mac started to leave, but Jack stopped him. "Um…I know I'm getting ahead of myself, but do you know who I'd call about putting in a pool?"

Mac looked only slightly abashed, but he recovered quickly. "Me. I got a backhoe just sitting at the mine collecting dust now that my brother-in-law is my partner. Number's in the book. Give me a call when you're ready."

His low chuckle stayed with Jack, but it wasn't the sound that had tormented him as a kid. It was okay. Inclusive, even. He had a feeling he and Mac McGannon might be friends one day.

But first, he had a house to buy.

KAT WATCHED Jack conversing with Mac as covertly as she could manage, but apparently she wasn't subtle enough to avoid Char's acute observation skills. "You've been nailed by some serious dentist swoo, haven't you?"

Before Kat could deny the charge, Tag, who had been counting some of the tips he'd earned from working for Jenna, looked at them and said, "That guy's a dentist?"

"Orthodontist," Kat corrected. "He straightens teeth."

Tag gave her a look. "I know what an orthodontist is. You and Dad have been fighting about sending me to one long enough."

Kat felt a blush coming on. She hadn't realized Tag was aware of her ongoing argument with Pete, who believed that their son's crooked baby teeth weren't worth the hassle and expense of getting straightened. She'd agreed to wait until his permanent teeth started coming in, but now it was obvious Tag had inherited her family's crooked teeth. Kat didn't know how she'd managed to avoid braces, but she thanked her lucky stars since neither of her parents probably would have noticed—even if her teeth looked like Tag's.

"We both agree you'll need braces, Tag. We just can't agree on the timing," she told him.

"Or who will pay," Char added.

Kat gave her a dirty look. She'd overheard way too many shouting matches about who owed what when she was a kid. Tag deserved better. And once she was a teacher with a decent salary and possibly even dental benefits, she'd take him in—even if his father claimed he couldn't afford to pay half.

"Did I hear someone say *braces?*" a familiar voice asked. "Hi, Char. Tag."

Tag nodded, but didn't greet Jack until he spotted Kat's severe stare. Manners counted. Period. Tag knew that. "Hey. Where's your bike?"

"Next to the fire station. Mac said it was okay to leave it there. I…uh…have a couple of Rally T-shirts in the side pouch for you and your brother. If you want 'em. No big deal. Just thought…"

Kat was surprised. And touched. She hadn't seen him buy the gifts and hadn't expected him to, but she could tell by Tag's smile he was intrigued. Maybe even willing to forget that he didn't like this R.U.B. who'd been renting his room.

"Cool. When I can I see it?"

Kat looked at Jack, who appeared to be studying Tag with an intent frown on his face. His gaze never left her son's mouth.

Uh-oh. Orthodontist alert.

"Right now," Jack said, his tone casual. But Kat was attuned enough to him to know he was thinking about something else. "It's the only bike there. The saddlebag is snapped shut. Help yourself… Uh, sorry. If that's okay with your mother, I mean."

Kat looked at Char trying to convey a leave-us-for-a-second message. "This is Sentinel Pass. Nobody's gonna steal him or any… Oh, okay. Come on, Taggart. Let's go find your brother. He'll want his present, too."

"Thanks. And, Tag, come right back to thank Jack. Jordie, too."

"I know, Mom."

Kat watched her eldest son walk away. He was getting so grown up. A week with Jenna had changed him. He seemed more confident and aware of the world around him. He wasn't her little boy anymore.

"He needs to see an orthodontist," Jack said without preamble. "Bring him to Denver and I'll do X rays and an initial evaluation for free."

For free. He knew her well.

Instead of being offended, as some people might have been, she was thrilled by the offer. But she had to turn him down. Again. Just as she had his proposal.

"I'm all set to play an extra in the filming this week. It's good money. With the you-know-what coming and my student-teaching this fall, I need to sock away every penny."

He didn't comment right away, then he said, "He could ride back with me, and you and Jordie could come pick him up on the weekend."

Kat blinked at the outrageous suggestion, momentarily forgetting that Jack didn't even like kids. What kind of mother would send her child off with a stranger? Well, he wasn't a stranger to her, but he was to Tag. She could picture Pete's reaction. "We have orthodontists here, Jack. There's a very reputable group that worked on all my halfsiblings. I'm the only kid in the family who missed out. My dad takes all the credit, of course."

Her flippant response apparently fell on deaf ears. "I'll do everything pro bono. Start to finish. By the time he's in high school, he'll have a smile as perfect as Cooper Lindstrom's."

"Why would you offer to do that? Is it because—"

He cut her off. "I was that kid once, Kat. My dad wasn't an advocate of orthodontia unless there were bite issues, and my mother controlled the purse strings. I didn't get my teeth fixed until I was in college. Kids can be brutal. It messes with your head in a way parents don't understand. Let me do this for Tag."

"But you don't even like him."

His scowl was so pissed off—so Mad Jack—she let out a little yip. "If that's what you think, then this morning was an unforgivable indulgence on your part."

She was immediately ashamed. He was right. He might have gotten off on the wrong foot with the boys, but he was a good man. She'd trust him with her life. And Tag's teeth. But the decision didn't rest with her alone.

"Tag's dad would never go for this. He probably wouldn't even let me take Tag to Denver for an initial consultation. You should have heard the unflattering things he had to say about you after you dropped me off that morning. You're an outsider."

"And I'm obviously interested in you."

She nodded. "That's part of it. Pete's like my dad in that way. He doesn't want me, but he can't stand the idea of someone else in my life, either."

Jack shrugged his broad, solidly made shoulders. "Tough. He doesn't have a say in that. I am involved and I'm not going to disappear." He started to say something else, but instead, pulled out his phone. "What's his number?"

Kat's jaw dropped. "You've got to be kidding."

He waited.

She put her hand flat to her belly. This time was bound to come eventually, she thought. She rattled off Pete's cell number and waited to hear what was said, but Jack stepped away to conduct his conversation in private.

Peeved, she started after him, but was stopped when a small body barreled into her. "Mommy, Mommy, look what Tag stole from that man's motorcycle."

Jordie pointed at Jack, who was looking their way with a grim expression on his face.

Kat sank down and pulled her younger son into her arms. "It was a gift from Jack. Your brother doesn't steal."

"Told ya," Tag said, sticking out his tongue. He and Char walked up. Tag was already wearing his new shirt, although Kat could see the purple neckline of his other shirt under it.

She helped Jordie try on his new shirt, too. The size was right, age-wise, but it was still a little big. He ran his fingers across the logo, which showed a skull where the headlamp should have been on a stylized motorcycle emerging from a blazing inferno. "Wow," he uttered, looking at Char to get her reaction.

"Cool," she said, giving him a high five.

Jack joined them a few seconds later and both boys thanked him for the gifts without Kat's prompting. He seemed pleased by their reactions, but he looked at Kat and said, "He's going to meet me in half an hour at the bar where you were working when I first got to town."

Kat was too stunned to respond until Tag nudged her, a questioning look in his eyes. Kat smiled and ruffled his hair in a way he hated. "I need to go with Jack for an hour or so. It's business. Do you think you could hang out with Char and keep an eye on Jordie? They're going to be serving lunch pretty soon."

Tag looked from Kat to Jack and back. "I guess so."

Kat cleared things with Char, then waited while Jack gave her his cell number. "We'll be back ASAP," he said, flashing a small insider smile Kat's way. "I still have a long drive ahead today."

Kat knew that. She wasn't going to forget it. Men made big promises—to love, honor, forsaking all others as long as you both shall live—then they left women like her and her mother.

She and Jack didn't talk the whole way to Deadwood. Kat was oddly content to lean against his broad back and hold on. She didn't want to think about all of the pressing personal issues on her slate, so she focused on her mother, instead. She'd talked to her aunt earlier. Mom was doing better. Medication was lifting her spirits. Kat was relieved, but she still felt guilty for not getting to Spearfish to see her. She hadn't even introduced her to Jack. And now, it was too late.

She looked up and let the wind steal her sigh. Next week. Hopefully she'd have time after the filming to take the boys for a visit. She had no idea what the job involved, but she was sure she could handle playing an extra.

She was a natural. She'd been an extra all her life.

PETE WAS SITTING at the bar when they arrived. Guy was behind the bar, as usual. He acknowledged her with an understated nod. "Hey, Kat, thought you'd be at the movie-star party. Did you hear they're going to do some filming out front?"

From what the publicist who'd cornered her first thing that morning had said, the film crew was going to be all over the Black Hills taking footage that could be edited into a final cut. "Great for business, huh?"

"Hope so. What can I get you?"

"Water would be good. Guy, have you met Jack?"

"You're Brian's friend, right?"

The two shook hands. "I'm Kat's friend."

Guy glanced at Pete, then back. "O-kay. Beer?"

Jack shook his head. "Another time. Thanks." He looked at Pete and said, "I'll get us a table."

Pete scowled. Kat knew her ex hated to be bossed around. She took her glass of water and followed Jack. After some mostly indistinguishable grumbling, Pete joined them. He set his half-finished draft on the table, then flipped the chair around backward and straddled it. "So, what's this about you being a dentist and wanting to help my kid? Seems pretty obvious you already helped yourself to my ex."

Kat couldn't prevent the blush, but a swift kick to his shin helped alleviate some of her embarrassment.

Pete ignored her. "You're the same guy who was getting a tat the day I picked up Tag, aren't you? Tag said you weren't too friendly."

"Would you let some kid you never met before climb on your twenty-thousand-dollar bike?"

The answer sounded more like Mad Jack than her Jack, but it apparently made sense to Pete. "He should know better. His mom lets him get away with too much."

Kat closed her eyes and sighed. She'd known Pete would get around to assigning blame sooner or later.

"He's a kid," Jack said firmly. "I could have handled things better, but I haven't been around kids much." He shrugged. "Anyway, here's the thing. I asked Kat to marry me."

She jolted upright, completely not expecting that revelation. "And I said no," she quickly inserted.

"I hope to change her mind in the near future. But

the point is I plan to be around your son and Jordie for a long time to come. If the tables were reversed, I'd want to know who was hanging out with my kid."

Pete looked at Kat and said, "You're knocked up."

She tried to bluff. "Didn't you hear what I said? When he asked me to marry him, I said no."

She could see that confused Pete. And Pete hated to be confused. He liked things nice and simple, black and white.

Her brief sense of dodging a bullet—at least temporarily—ended when Jack's eyes narrowed and his gaze locked with hers, but instead of outing her, he said, "About your son's teeth. I'll tell you straight out I specialize in adult orthodontia, but even *I* can tell he's going to need braces. And the sooner you get started, the easier it's going to be on him."

"And you're volunteering to fix his teeth out of the goodness of your heart," Pete said snidely.

Jack's jaw muscle tightened. "I'm volunteering to absorb the cost—whether I do the work or you take him to someone else—because his mother can't afford to have her son's teeth fixed on the paltry amount of child support you pay her."

"Are you saying I'm cheap?"

"Yeah, I am."

Both men jumped to their feet and sort of scratched the ground like a couple of young bull bison trying to impress the dominant female. The thought made her laugh out loud.

They turned to look at her. "I just realized that I'm the matriarch of this tribe," she said, "And I've been doing a pretty damn good job despite the lack of support from my ex-husbands."

She pointed her finger at Pete. "We're changing the amount of child support you pay. Tag couldn't do Little League because I couldn't afford all the driving. That's plain wrong." His scowl looked so much like her father's she almost lost her nerve, but she made herself go on. "Which reminds me. Why am I providing round-trip taxi service to your house? From now on, we pick a half-way point to meet."

"What are you talking about? I was at your place twice last week."

"Oooh. You swung what? Five, six miles out of your way to take your son camping? That was really big of you, Pete."

He had the grace to blush.

"And another thing. No more just dropping him off when you run into some problem with your wife and other kids. That hurts Tag. He may not show it, but it does. It hurt *me* when my parents treated me like a bag of produce."

Pete looked ready to argue, but Jack stepped to her side and put a very large, solid hand on her shoulder. He didn't say anything. He didn't need to. Pete got the message.

"Fine. I'll tell Michelle that as long as we don't have to pay for his teeth out of pocket, the money can go to child support. Within reason," he added, giving Kat a meaningful squint.

She was too riled up to be reasonable. She'd been reasonable all her life, and frankly, unreasonable was a lot more empowering. But before she could unload any of the thousand or so long-held complaints she had, Jack said, "You can start by taking Tag while Kat's working as an extra for the TV show. She shouldn't have to scramble to pay for child care when your wife is a stay-at-home mom and you have a pool in your backyard."

Pete gave Kat another black look, but he muttered, "Fine."

Kat wasn't sure exactly what got settled, but neither man seemed inclined toward chitchat, so she and Jack promptly left. As they approached his bike, he said, "I'm sorry if I came on too strong in there. You're more than capable of speaking for yourself, but I noticed with my sister that divorce seems to bring out the worst in people. My ex-brother-in-law got incredibly petty over the dumbest things."

"It's okay. Pete has control issues where women are concerned. It was the main reason behind our divorce. His current wife takes a lot more than I was willing to put up with."

Jack handed her the extra helmet, but she didn't put it on right away. "Just for the record, what are your plans?"

"I'm going back to Denver to start the process of moving."

"What? You're moving here? Seriously?"

"Would you find that easier to believe if I told you I put a down payment on a three-bedroom house in Sentinel Pass today? Well…a small one. I didn't have my checkbook. And it's contingent on a walk-through. I've only seen the place from the outside."

Her jaw dropped. "There aren't any hou— Oh, my God. Mrs. Smith's place? That's where Cooper and Shane are staying."

"Past tense. Coop and Libby are keeping her house, and Shane is at Jenna's. Some crew members are renting it this week. That's why we didn't go inside. But Mrs. Smith's son and daughter were in town to put it on the market, and I made them an offer. They took it."

She shook her head, trying to process this twist. "Jack, we don't even know for sure if I'm pregnant. I haven't taken the test yet. You can't turn your life upside down over this. What if I'm wrong?"

His smile made her heart do a double flip. "Then we have to keep trying till we get it right."

"Jack," she said in her most fervent mother-knows-best tone, "that doesn't make any sense. You barely know me. You're not in love with me. You can't be."

His arm snaked out and he raked her flush against his body. "I know everything I need to know, Kat. I just need to convince you of that. And I can't do that from Denver." He kissed her lightly. "Maybe we could start with a date. You know—the thing two people who are interested in each other do to get to know each other better?"

His grin packed about a thousand watts of swoo, and Kat had trouble remembering what she was going to say. "But…but what about your business?"

"My dad used to preach about the importance of building up a practice and developing strong client relationships, but I watched those valued clients flee like rats from a sinking ship at the first hint of rumors that were patently untrue. Dentistry is my career, not my calling. And certainly not my life. I don't think I realized that until…"

He didn't finish. If he'd said, "until I met you," she wouldn't have believed him, so she didn't press for details. Her head was spinning, and at the moment all she wanted was to get back to her sons. "We should go."

He nodded in agreement and stepped away, reaching into his pocket for the key. "If you don't mind, I think I'll drop you off in Sentinel Pass and keep driving. I want to make Edgemont before dark and I have a bunch of calls to make. But tell Tag I'll be back as soon as I can. If you want to get the ball rolling with a local orthodontist, no problem. Just tell him I plan to consult on the case and send the bill to me."

She yanked on her chin strap. She couldn't think. Her mother liked to say, "The proof was in the pudding." If this talk of moving panned out, fine. She'd deal with him the same way she did Pete and Drew. If he never came back…well, she'd do what she always did. Get by.

CHAPTER FIFTEEN

"YOU MEAN YOU DON'T even know if there *is* a baby?"

Jack was already tired of this discussion and he'd just started it. He'd waited all week to invite his mother and sister to dinner so he could break the news. Rachel, who'd phoned every evening to check on him, had heard bits and pieces of what had transpired on his journey, but he'd asked her not to tell their mother until he had the majority of his plans finalized.

Fortunately their mother had been playing golf in Grand Junction with a group of retired friends, so he'd been able to conduct most of his business in private. She'd only returned that morning and hadn't questioned his invitation to a Friday-evening barbecue.

"Why doesn't anyone believe me?" he asked, more to himself than either of the women sitting at the table across from him. He'd overcooked the salmon. No one seemed to notice. "I don't care if Kat is pregnant or not. And for the record, she called me on Monday and said she took a home pregnancy test and it was negative. But she still feels pregnant. She's going to give it another week before she sees a doctor."

"Why would this Kat woman say she was pregnant if she didn't know for sure? That sounds terribly irresponsible, Jackson."

"Mom, I think you're missing the point. What Jack is saying is he loves Kat, which is short for Katherine, I believe, and wants to marry her no matter what."

Jack smiled his appreciation. He could tell by the haunted look in his sister's eyes that any talk of love was a painful reminder of her broken heart. Her whirlwind affair and tumultuous marriage had ended so badly she'd barely been able to get out of bed for a month.

"Don't be ridiculous, Rachel. This is Jackson we're talking about. He isn't some flighty character in a romance novel. He's deliberate and intelligent. He makes thoughtful, balanced decisions based on facts and realistic projections."

Jack and his sister exchanged a look. "No, Mom, that's you," Jack said as gently as possible. "I'm more like Dad. I've been trying really hard most of my life not to be because we all know how badly he got burned. But I can't fake it anymore. What happened to Dad was unfortunate. It nearly killed him and left you so jaded about people you forgot Dad's purpose for being a dentist—to help people. Especially children.

"And whether you meant to or not, your fears affected me and my choices. But not anymore. I'm going to work on kids and at least half my practice will be offered free or at reduced prices for people who normally wouldn't be able to afford to take their kids to an orthodontist."

All the color drained from his mother's still-youthful-looking face. Her reddish brown hair lacked even a hint of silver, thanks to her well-paid stylist. "Please tell me you're joking. That's exactly the kind of people who try to take advantage of the system. The boy who accused your father had been coached by his drug-addict parents.

By the time he recanted his statement, it was too late. Both your father—and his practice—were devastated. Neither was ever the same again."

"I know, Mom. But Dad took shortcuts when he was doing pro bono work. He didn't keep a nurse in the room with him. I assume that was because her wages would have been out-of-pocket."

He watched her face change. She didn't deny the fact, which Jack had only guessed. He'd spent most of his drive home from the Hills trying to remember what little he knew about his father's case. There had been a lot of whispers and closed-door conferences with lawyers and investigators. He'd felt his father's shame, and even though Jack never wanted to admit it, he'd had moments of doubt. What if the reason his father didn't have a nurse present was because he'd planned to do something unsavory all along?

But somewhere around Cheyenne another thought had hit him. His trusting father would have tried to honor his own need to help children while conceding to his banker wife's penny-pinching thriftiness.

"Paying staff to fix the teeth of a child who would probably wind up doing drugs or rotting in jail like his father seemed a waste of good money," his mother admitted. "I didn't know how low some people would sink to take advantage of a kind soul. I just didn't know."

Jack wondered how much his mother's sense of guilt had shaped his later decisions, like specializing in adult orthodontics and never dating women with children.

"Mom," Jack said, touching her arm. "Nobody's blaming you. Those were bad people. Dad didn't deserve what happened, but there's no changing the past and I'm tired of letting fear rule my life."

"Jackson, please don't—"

"I'm moving to an area that can't support my tiny window of specialization, Mom. I need to get back into mainstream dentistry, and that means working with children."

"How'd you do it?" Rachel asked. "How'd you overcome your fear?"

Jack looked at her. He heard something deeply personal in her question. He answered honestly, knowing full well neither Rachel nor Mom would understand. "I simply asked myself, 'What would Mad Jack do?'"

Rachel smiled as though she did get it.

His mother let out a low moan. "But what about your beautiful house? The market is soft right now, Jackson. You'll never get what it's worth."

"I'll make money on it no matter what, Mom. And I'm keeping the office building. My colleagues are delighted to continue with our present arrangement. Actually they were thrilled because my not being there means one more piece of the client pie."

He got up and walked around the table. "Mom, Sentinel Pass isn't that far from Denver. I was talking to Kat's friend Libby the other day. Her brother, Mac, makes the drive here about once a month for parts for his mining operation."

Rachel perked up. "Sentinel Pass? Isn't that where the new television show is being filmed? Wow. That's cool. Could you introduce me to a movie star?"

He rolled his eyes. "The only one I met is married to Kat's best friend, but who knows? You can visit me anytime. I'm thinking about building a guest cottage on the property once I finish remodeling the main house and put in a pool."

His mother moaned again. He knew she was thinking about the cost, but what she didn't understand was he'd spend every cent he had to win the heart of the woman he loved.

KAT HELD ON to the counter of Libby's bathroom vanity with her free hand. Her knees felt as if they might give out. Probably because her heart was barely beating and she was breathing too fast and shallowly.

How could this be? she asked herself for the hundredth time, staring at the little plastic wand of the home pregnancy test.

A knock sounded on the door. "Well?" Libby hollered. "What's the verdict? Yea or nay?"

She'd used her mother as an excuse to leave Cooper's big party early on Sunday to drive to Spearfish. A quick stop at the grocery store for *ice cream* had allowed her to pick up a testing kit. And later that night after visiting Mom, who brightened considerably seeing her grandsons, Kat had followed the directions to the letter.

The result had left her baffled. Was there such a thing as a false negative? Could her kit have been old or defective? Maybe she'd tried too soon.

She'd fretted about whether to call Jack, since she still felt pregnant, regardless of what the test said. When she'd finally called him, his reaction had only added to her confusion. How could anybody be that calm and understanding about something so life-altering? He had to be faking all that sweet concern for her state of mind.

But why would he? She didn't get it. Nothing about Jack made sense. Mad Jack she got. He was like all the other men in her life—take what you want and move on. But her Jack? He might be gone, but he rarely left her mind.

And that had scared her more than she wanted to admit. If she wasn't pregnant, then any connection she had with Jack would be lost.

So what? A voice in her head had cried. But the answer wasn't simple. It had grown in strength all week. And by the time Libby had shown up on the set an hour earlier, Kat had been sitting on the curb like a mindless zombie.

Libby had managed to pry out the truth in a matter of seconds. Then, in a bossy but loving way, had insisted on purchasing a second test for Kat to take while the crew was on break. "You have to find out, Kat. It's not fair to you or Jack to drag this out."

Kat opened the bathroom door. "It's negative, too," she said simply.

Libby checked the plastic wand for herself, then nodded. "You're right. It is. I guess that means you're not pregnant. These things are pretty accurate, you know."

"But what about my symptoms? I never miss a period. Never. And my breasts are tender. And I'm queasy all the time—not just in the morning. How do you explain that?"

Libby put her hand on Kat's arm and gently pulled her into the hall. "Let's have a glass of iced tea and talk."

Kat shook her head. "Shane wanted all the extras back on the set in half an hour."

"I'll give you a written excuse," Libby said dryly.

"Besides, half an hour in Shane time could mean three hours on the clock."

They'd already discussed at length the crazy way a television production operated. Despite Shane's passion for schedules, the actual filming seemed dependent on any one of a dozen variables—lighting, wind, the right electrical cords, hair and makeup. Kat wasn't entirely convinced anything got done.

Not that the result mattered to her. Getting paid to do nothing wasn't such a bad thing. She'd managed to find an out-of-the-way corner to work on the last paper she had to turn in for her independent-study class. She'd chosen to write about frontier women in support roles that truly helped to settle the West. Women like Mad Jack's schoolmarm in her dream.

"Kat?"

Kat startled, realizing she'd missed whatever Libby had been saying. "See? Look how ditzy I am. This is me pregnant, Lib. Seriously. Pete used to get so mad at me when he was talking to me and I'd space out."

Libby sat on the rocking chair she always chose when they had book club at her house. Kat perched on the edge of the sofa, restless and a little dazed. She wasn't sure what this meant or what she should do next. Carry on with her life, she supposed. But what about Jack, who was supposedly moving to Sentinel Pass because he thought she was pregnant? She'd messed everything up. Worse than usual.

"Pete has control issues. Forget Pete. Thanks to Jack, he's finally living up to some of his parenting obligations, instead of blaming you every time Tag does something remotely wrong."

In the five days that Jack had been gone, Tag had spent the majority of the time at Pete's house. There was a certain amount of complaining on both parties' part, but Kat was beginning to think Jack—who claimed to know nothing about kids—was more intuitive than she.

"So? Do you want to talk about this false pregnancy?"

"Not really. I feel stupid. And a little betrayed. I mean, I know my body. I can't understand how I got this wrong. Maybe I should see a doctor. There might be something really wrong with me. My mom has cancer, you know."

Libby made a face. "Whoa. No quantum leaps allowed. You're young and healthy. Your mother's throat cancer was the result of a lifetime of bad habits. I think if you'd step back and take stock of your life at the moment, you'd see that any change in your body could be attributed to stress."

"When is my life not stressful, Lib?"

"Good point. But it got more so when Jack showed up."

"Because of his swoo?"

"Because you care for him. Actually I think you love him, but you won't let yourself admit how you feel."

Kat shook her head. She fought the impulse to spring to her feet and start pacing. "I can't love him, Libby. It wouldn't be good for him. I've screwed up every romantic relationship I've ever been in. Jack just had his heart broken. He deserves someone more stable." Like the schoolmarm in her dream.

"Oh, I see. You're not the person he could or should love, so at a deeply subconscious level your body convinces you you're pregnant so he'll marry you?"

Kat stopped fidgeting. In a way, that made sense. But then she remembered. "I turned him down when he asked."

"But maybe a part of you is hoping he won't take no for an answer. Maybe the part that still feels pregnant. Because you don't believe anybody could love you and want to marry you without an ulterior motive."

"Like the threat of my dad's shotgun." Kat's stomach turned over.

Libby sat forward and pounded her fist on her knee. "We all have to deal with baggage from our past, Kat, but I'd wring your father's neck if I had the chance. You've got to start believing that you're not your mother. Or your father. You're you, Kat. One of the nicest, most loving decent people in the world, and I'm sick of you being less than kind to yourself."

Kat couldn't help but smile at her friend's passionate outburst.

Libby sighed heavily but smiled, too. "Kat. Why wouldn't Jack love you? He's smart, and he knows you're exactly what he needs. Why can't you see that?"

Kat pictured herself huddled in the backseat of her mother's car—fingers pushed deep in her ears to block the hurtful words of her parents' shouting matches. How could two people who claimed to be so much in love they didn't even stop to think about birth control wind up hating each other—and the child they made—so much?

She stood. "I need to talk to my dad."

She would have preferred to pose her question to her mother, but her last visit had confirmed Kat's suspicion that her sweet but nosy aunt didn't take a hint well. There was no such thing as privacy with Roberta around.

"What about the boys?"

Kat slapped her brow with the heel of her hand.

"Another brain fart, as Jordie would say. Michelle was supposed to drop Tag off at the Y today to hang out with Jordie after his summer art program. I'll pick them both up on my way to the ranch."

"I could watch them if you want to talk to your dad alone." Libby smiled that loving, happy smile she always got on her face when thinking about her husband. "Cooper loves playing daddy. He won't admit it, but I think he really, really wants a boy." She put her hand on her rounded belly.

"Thanks, Lib. I appreciate the offer—and everything else, too. But the boys have been bugging me about seeing the bison. They can take the four-wheeler out and do a head count while Dad and I talk."

Not that she was expecting any huge breakthroughs. Her father wasn't all that self-aware, although he was good at assigning blame. Talking to him might be a mistake, but she needed to find out why her body had tricked her into believing something that wasn't true.

Then she had to call Jack. She felt terrible about inadvertently creating this stupid firestorm. He'd probably lose a whole bunch of money by backing out of his purchase of the Smith house. And who knew what else he'd done to start the ball rolling?

She didn't know how he would take the news. Would he be angry? Or relieved? The two prime emotions Pete and Drew would have displayed—most vocally. But Jack was an enigma.

Tomorrow. She'd call him in the morning and that would be that.

CHAPTER SIXTEEN

An empty Jack Daniel's bottle in the trash wasn't a good omen, Kat thought as she passed through the kitchen of the log home she'd always loved. The place seemed pretty tidy, though. Not the way it had when her father was on a bender and she was expected to keep it clean.

She called out his name but didn't get an answer, so she headed toward his bedroom at the back of the house. It wasn't unusual for him to take a late-afternoon "nap" on days that began with a cocktail for breakfast.

After a quick stop at home to change into her jeans and boots and grab a few things for the boys, she'd driven into Rapid to pick them up. Shane had thoughtfully cut every one of the extras a check after they'd wrapped up filming. Hers included a nice little bonus for providing henna tattoos to the wives and girlfriends of the staff who'd traveled from California for the week.

Jenna had suggested the idea when Kat had complained about being bored the first day of filming. The tattooing had been a nice diversion on Monday and Tuesday. After that, Kat had used the downtime to study. Two fewer worries that might have added to her stress—her paper was done *and* her car had a full tank.

She paused to glance out the window. Even through the thick log walls she could hear the tinny rattle of the old quad her father let the boys drive. "Find the herd and take an accurate head count," she'd told them. "But don't hop the fence. This is rutting season and the young bulls are very unpredictable. Got it?"

Tag had heaved his old-man sigh while Jordie had jumped up and down with excitement. She wasn't sure her younger son understood what rutting meant, but no doubt his world-weary older brother would explain if the opportunity to point out the act arose.

She shuddered with resignation and walked the rest of the way down the hall. "Dad?" She knocked lightly on his bedroom door.

She didn't enter until he answered, "Huh? Kat? Is that you?"

She opened the door, her heart climbing into her throat. To her surprise, he wasn't stretched out in bed, rumpled and bleary-eyed. He was seated at his desk. His computer was on and a stack of bills rested beside the keyboard. "Am I interrupting?"

He pushed himself back and stood. "A welcome break. Is that the quad I hear? You musta brought my grandsons along."

She came a little closer, still not trusting the clear look in his eyes. Maybe he only had a little nip before the bottle ran out, she thought. "They're going to find the bison. Is that okay? They haven't been here for a while and I—"

"Of course, it's fine. I figured Jordie was probably going through bison withdrawals about now. He does love the big woollies."

Her heart twisted oddly. She hadn't realized her father was so observant. "I know. He's a softie. Like me."

Buck's bushy left eyebrow rose. "I wouldn't say that. You can be as prickly as any one of those rosebushes in the garden. And you're as tough as nails when it comes to keeping your boys in line."

She blinked. Was that a compliment? It almost sounded like one. "What's going on, Dad? Are you loaded? You don't look drunk, but free compliments? That's not like you."

She waited for an explosion, but instead of blowing up at her remarks, he laughed. "You got that right. I ain't saying otherwise. But fact is, that bottle you probably spotted in the trash is the last of my hidden stash. I'd forgotten I planted it in the tack room. Emptied the whole thing down the sink."

He seemed sincere, but she wasn't buying it. "I've been after you for years to stop drinking. Why now?"

He shook his head. "I don't know. It's not like I found God or learned I have cancer or anything. I just woke up one morning with a bad hangover and told myself this is a stupid way to waste what's left of my life. I called a friend of mine who goes to AA and he picked me up for a meeting."

"You're going to AA?"

He made a wobbly motion with his hand. "Joining things isn't my way, but I know they're there if I need a little help. And Ray, my buddy, says I can always call him."

She didn't know what to say, but the fact that he was lucid and in a fairly good mood might actually work in her favor. "Want a cup of coffee?" he asked.

She started to say no. She avoided caffeine when she

was pregnant. But then she remembered the test she'd taken at Libby's. "Okay."

She followed him to the kitchen and hopped up on a stool at the counter. "Dad, I wanted to talk to you about you and Mom. Your marriage."

He groaned. "What for? That's old news."

"But I've made the same mistake. Twice. And now Jack's asked me to marry him. I don't want to blow it again."

"Are you knocked up?"

She stuck her tongue out at his back. "No, I'm not." She couldn't believe how much satisfaction it gave her to say that—even though she still felt most of the symptoms that had convinced her she was pregnant. And she still hadn't gotten her period, either.

"Then why the hell do you want to get married?"

She let him finish filling the carafe before answering. "I didn't say I did. But he's buying a house in Sentinel Pass and moving his practice up here from Denver. He doesn't seem to want to take no for an answer. Why? I really have no idea."

Buck chuckled softly. "No. I don't suppose you do."

"What's that mean?" she bristled. "That I'm so unlovable only a man who got me pregnant first would want to marry me?"

His eyes narrowed in a way that used to scare her to death. She crossed her arms and didn't look away. He took a step closer. Her heart sped up. The little kid in her was ready to pee her pants, but she clenched her jaw and waited.

"If your mother and I made you feel unlovable, Katherine, I'm sorry."

Katherine. The name sounded funny coming from his lips. Formal, yet tender. Respectful, even. Her jaw dropped. "Really?"

He nodded. "That's what you want to know, isn't it? Why we fought so much? Why you got caught in the crossfire? I'm not stupid. I know you felt like you were to blame most of the time, but it wasn't you, honey girl. I'm an ornery old cuss who doesn't like to admit when he's wrong. I was wrong a lot when I was married to your mother. I loved her more than any woman ever, but we couldn't be alone in a room without either making love or trying to kill each other. It might be some weird chemistry. I don't know."

Kat truly hadn't expected his honesty. Or frankness. "You guys fought about me all the time, but then when I came here to stay with you, you ignored me."

His face screwed up in a sheepish look she couldn't ever remember seeing. "I didn't know squat about raising a little girl, but I was afraid if I let your mother have you all the time, she'd convince you I didn't want you."

"You did? Want me?"

"Hell, yes. Why do you think I helped you buy those damn bison? You know we've never made a dime on them, and I could have fattened a couple thousand head of cattle on the grass they eat. But I kept 'em. Because they were yours and you love them and I...well, you know."

Even now he couldn't say the words, but she understood. He loved her. He'd always loved her. He just didn't know how to show it. Except where her herd was concerned.

The revelation left her a little dizzy. Maybe coffee

wasn't such a good idea. She might spin right off into the sky like a dust devil.

And what any of this meant to her relationship with Jack, she didn't have a clue.

She thought about asking her father for advice—maybe this new touchy-feely Buck could offer her some insights into how to handle a crazy man who was poised to turn his life upside down for nothing. But just as she opened her mouth to speak, the high-pitched pinging sound of a quad engine revved at full bore came in through the window.

Buck turned and looked outside. "Uh-oh."

She was out the door and down the steps before the four-wheeler entered the yard. Tag was driving, his thin body hunched forward as if willing the quad to go faster. Jordie's arms were clenched around his brother's middle, but she couldn't see any more than the crown of his helmet.

Something was wrong. Her maternal instinct told her that. She just didn't know what. Had the bike hit a bump and Jordie got tossed off? Their helmets were hand-me-downs and probably not as good as they should be. She'd never forgive herself if—

"Mom, it wasn't my fault," Tag said, turning off the ignition as the quad rolled to a stop. He hopped to the ground, gesturing excitedly. "I told him to stay on this side of the fence, but he saw a baby by itself. No mother bison around. Jordie thought it might be hurt or caught in wire or something. He wasn't even halfway between me and the bison when this young bull came out of nowhere and charged him. Jordie's fast, Mom. He would have made it fine if he hadn't tripped."

By now Kat was at the vehicle. Her fingers lightly skimmed over her son's back and chest, but he continued to keep his hands locked across the lower half of his face.

"Did the bull stomp him?" Buck asked. "You point out which one it was and I'll shoot the mo—it…dead on the spot."

Jordie's eyes went wide and he let out a muffled cry.

"The bull never touched him, Grandpa. You know they don't see that good, and once Jordie was on the ground the bull veered off in the other direction."

"What happened to your mouth, honey? Can I see?"

He shook his head.

"I think he broke some teeth, Mom."

Kat looked at her youngest son's eyes. Tear tracks had left grayish streaks in the dust on his pudgy cheeks. His muffled sniffling and constant blinking told her he was ready to burst into tears again.

"It's okay, sweetie. Accidents happen. Don't cry." She scooped him off the seat and into her arms. He looped his arms around her neck and buried his face in her neck as she carried him to the porch. His tears came in earnest and within seconds he was wailing.

"Don't worry, Jordie boy. Let Mommy see." She sat on the top step and settled him on her knee. She gently pried his hands away, trying not to let the sight of blood and dirt around his mouth influence her already queasy stomach. "There's so much dirt I can't really see. Dad, could you get us a glass of water?"

Buck was already charging into the house as she continued to comfort her son. "Don't make yourself sick crying, Jordie. It'll be okay. I promise."

How? a little voice asked. Every penny she'd earned this summer was spoken for once she started student-teaching.

She carefully loosened the chin strap of the helmet and eased it over his ears. His hair was damp with sweat and stuck up in spiky clumps.

"I brought some ice, in case there's swelling," her father said, joining her on the step. He laid a towel across her knee and set a plastic bag of ice beside her foot. Pulling Jordie a little closer, he bent down to take a look. "Open up, kiddo," he coaxed in the gentlest voice Kat had ever heard.

Eyes squeezed tight, Jordie clenched his fists and slowly opened his mouth. His tongue looked gritty. "Yuck!" Tag cried. "You really did eat dirt."

Jordie's tears started again. Kat gave her older son a severe look. She was just reaching for the glass of water Buck had set beside the ice when her dad jumped to his feet. "Here. Wait. This will work better," he said.

He grabbed a nearby hose and turned the water on low. Jordie tried to bolt, but Kat said firmly, "We have to see, honey. You can do this. Lean over the step and rinse and spit. Good idea, Dad."

It took three tries to get his mouth clear enough for a good look at the damage. His front two teeth had been bent all the way back, exposing their little roots. The tooth just left of the middle stuck sideways like a piece of jagged glass. It was broken and seemed to have punctured the inside of his cheek. A couple of other teeth looked loose, but Jordie wouldn't let her touch them.

"What a mess," her father declared, which made Jordie start to cry again.

"Dad," Kat complained. "It's not that bad, honey. We'll call a dentist and see if we can get you in right away."

"On a Friday night? In August?" the Buck of old said in disgust.

Her father was right, but she couldn't just sit there and wait until Monday. "There must be someone we can call in an emergency."

"How 'bout Jack?" Tag asked.

Kat looked at Jordie, who nodded. "J'k," he said, the word whistling through the gap in his teeth.

"Too bad Jack's in Denver,' she muttered.

Denver. A drive she could make in seven or eight hours if she left now.

Her father straightened and reached into his pocket. He held out a key ring. "Take mine. It's got a full tank of gas and there's room for the boys to stretch out in the back. Plus, I won't have to worry about you breaking down. It's got a built-in phone and you can let me know when you get there."

Her car was a compact. It got better mileage. But it was also old. And needed the radiator flushed. Buck's SUV was brand-new. Kat had never even been in it. Her hand was shaking as she reached for the keys. "Are you sure?"

When she looked at her father, she was almost certain she saw a hint of tears in his eyes. But he turned away before she could be sure. "Load up the boys. I'll pack you a lunch so you don't have to stop."

She closed her fingers around the fancy key ring. She could do this. For Jordie.

"STOP PACING."

"I can't. If you don't like it, go home."

"No. I want to meet her. And you might need me."

Jack looked at his sister. "You're not a dental assistant."

"I know. But when I was, like, fifteen or sixteen, Dad used to pay me to come in on Saturdays to do some filing and help out. He wasn't very busy by then, but I learned a little bit. At the very least, I could be a witness."

He swirled to face her. "Don't tell me Mom got to you during dinner. Kat is not an opportunist. She hasn't been coaching her son to screw me over. She isn't like that, Rachel."

"If you say so, but why risk it? I'll be your assistant and everybody's happy."

He was sorry he'd checked his answering machine from her house. He'd walked her home after their mother left so they could talk about her life, which she felt was going nowhere since her divorce. She'd been standing close enough to overhear Kat's frantic voice message. And she'd listened just as attentively when Jack called back.

Jordie was hurt. A couple of broken teeth. She needed Jack to look at him and tell her what to do.

Jack was touched that she trusted him enough to call. And here was a chance to put his new plan into effect. If he couldn't handle sweet little Jordie, he couldn't be a regular dentist.

He'd given Kat directions to his house. If Jordie's teeth needed immediate attention, they'd go to the office. Apparently with his sister at his side.

The flash of headlights in his driveway set them both into motion. Rachel opened the door and let Jack lead the way to the unfamiliar SUV that was idling a few feet away. The inside dome light was on, so Jack could see Kat behind the wheel. She'd turned to face the backseat. The rear windows were tinted, so Jack couldn't see any movement.

He rapped lightly on the passenger window. It disappeared quietly into the door. "Hi," he said. "You made great time."

"Luck and lack of traffic," she said. Her gaze shifted to the person behind him.

"This is my pesky sister, Rachel. I was at her house when you called and she thinks she can be of some help, although I doubt it."

Rachel bumped him from behind to reach out to Kat. "Hi. Sorry to meet you under these circumstances. How's your little boy?"

Kat shook Rachel's hand, but Jack could tell she was frazzled and the only thing on her mind was Jordie. "He's asleep," she said in a low whisper. "I took your advice and stopped at home for his pillow and favorite blanket and I gave him some children's painkiller."

Jack poked his head inside the car and looked in the backseat. His heart twisted. Beneath the jumble of pillows and blankets, Jordie was curled up beside his older brother, whose arm was around the younger boy protectively. If he'd ever worried that he couldn't love these children, his fear vanished in an instant, and he felt a powerful need to protect them and care for them.

"Instead of waking him here, then moving to the office, why don't we just head over there now? If Tag doesn't wake up when we move Jordie, Rachel can wait in the car with him."

"I'm awake, Mom," Tag said softly. "Jordie's breath stinks, but I didn't want to move him."

Kat smiled for the first time, and Jack had no trouble reading the depth of love she felt for her older son.

Jack opened the passenger door and got in. To his sister, he said, "Follow us."

Her Porsche Boxter was parked behind the third door of his three-stall garage.

"I really appreciate this, Jack," Kat said as she backed out. "You have no idea."

"I think I do. I'm only sorry you had to drive so far. If this had happened a few weeks from now, I would have been closer." He shrugged. "Although then, I might not have had a state-of-the-art dental facility at my disposal. I haven't gotten that far in my relocation plans."

"You know, we really have to talk about that," she started. "I took—"

"We will. Later. Or tomorrow. You're staying at my house tonight, of course. Turn right at the corner."

She made a soft sound of exasperation. "When did you get so bossy?"

"Dr. Treadwell, Mr. Hyde," he said, wishing they had time for a private moment. She looked like a woman who needed a hug and he was just the man to give her one. But this wasn't about them. "Turn left at the next light and move into the far-right lane."

He could see the tiniest glimmer of a smile on her lips, but she didn't say another word until they reached the office. "Pull up to the front door. If the security people come by to check on us, Rachel can deal with them."

Jack hopped out the moment the car came to a stop. He motioned for his sister to park beside the SUV, then he tossed her his key ring. "Go ahead and open up. The code is Mother's birth date. If you tell her that, I'll never whiten your teeth again." He hurried around the car to where Kat was holding the rear passenger door open. She had a confused look on her face, so he explained, "Mom's kind of vain about her age, and everyone who works here has the code. If she thought they knew what it stood for, she'd be royally ticked off."

He could tell Kat was trying to be polite, but her main focus was Jordie. He heard her suck in a breath when Jack bent over and scooped the half-asleep child up in his arms. He turned and kept walking even as Jordie started to fuss. "No, Mommy. I'm fine now. I don't want to see no denith."

His lisp broke Jack's heart.

In his kindest, gentlest tone, he tried to soothe the boy. "This is an old-fashioned dentist office, Jordie. We have balloons and candy for our patients. My dad was a dentist, and he believed that every child who was brave enough to open his mouth to have his teeth checked deserved a reward."

"Candy?" Tag said, his tone skeptical. "I thought candy was bad for your teeth."

"It's sugar-free," Rachel said. She was waiting with the door open. "I turned on the lights in the first exam room, Jack," she said, pointing down a hallway he rarely visited. Cosmetic dentistry was on the second floor.

She locked the door and hurried to catch up. "Do you like Xbox?" she asked Tag.

Jack glanced over his shoulder and saw the look Tag gave her. Half curious, half get-out-of-my-face, crazy lady. God, he loved that kid.

"I played Grand Theft Auto at my friend David's house once. It was pretty cool. You got to run over girls. And the helicopter cut people's heads off."

"Taggart John Linden!" Kat exclaimed. "Tell me you're kidding."

He blanched, obviously forgetting about his mother's presence in his effort to sound cool. "Oh, Mom, it was just the one time. Now his mom keeps the R-rated games locked in her desk."

"Interesting. I've heard of that one, but never tried it," Rachel said. "But I know for a fact that Jack's got Madden. Do you like football?"

Jack could tell Tag was dying to follow Rachel wherever she might lead, but he hesitated, looking to his mother for his cue. "Go ahead, hon. You don't have to be in the exam room with us. But don't play with anything else. And tell Mrs.…um…Rachel thank you."

"Just Rachel. I'm nobody's missus."

Jack hated the fatalistic tone he heard in his sister's voice. Rachel was one of the coolest people he knew. She deserved better where love was concerned. So did Kat.

"We'll be in here, Tag," he said, turning to enter the exam room. He carried his patient to the perfectly proportioned chair that was covered in a jungle print. On the ceiling was a mural of monkeys, colorful birds and snakes that looked right out of a Disney movie. Regulars to this office knew that if they pointed out a very tiny Tarzan figure hiding behind one of the trees, they'd get an extra prize at the end of the exam.

Jack handed the blanket that had come with Jordie to Kat. "Are you warm enough?" he asked his patient.

Jordie nodded. As Jack had hoped, his attention was drawn to the colorful display and away from the tray of sterilized tools on the counter behind them. "Have you ever had an X ray of your mouth, Jordie?"

"No," Kat answered, "but he had a checkup last fall in school. He brought home a certificate that said everything looked good and he had no cavities."

Jack pulled on a pair of latex gloves and used his foot to position his stool. He sat so he was eye level with Jordie. "That's great. That means your teeth are strong. But I won't know for sure until I look inside. Can you open up for me?"

Tears glistened in the boy's eyes, but he bravely inched his jaws apart. Jack angled the overhead light to give him a crisp view. He did his best not to let anything show on his face. "Wow. You are one tough kid, Jordie. Did you leave a dent on the rock you hit?"

Jordie grunted mutely.

Jack looked at Kat. In his peripheral vision, he noticed that Rachel had returned. He told them both, "For tonight, I'd like to get some X rays and affix a little sealant to the two broken teeth. They'll probably need to be pulled, but I'd like to save them if possible."

"You mean like a crown? On a baby tooth? Won't that be expensive?" Kat asked.

Before Jack could figure out how to put his answer in a way that wouldn't sound like charity, Rachel said, "Our father had one strict rule. Family was always free. Remember those crazy cousins of Mother's who planned their entire vacation around coming to Denver to get free dental work? Drove Mom nuts," she added.

Jack had no idea what she was talking about, but he nodded gamely and played along. "And how many times did he have to redo Aunt Peggy's bridge? A dozen, at least."

Kat looked from Jack to Rachel and back. He

couldn't tell if she bought the lie or not, but she finally sighed. "I'm not family."

"You will be," Rachel said, patting her back. "I have no doubt about that."

Jack would have hugged her, but he had too many things to do before he lost his patient to boredom, fear or fatigue. Any one of the regular children's dentists in the building could have done things faster and more efficiently, but Jack didn't want to make any mistakes, and he was determined to do his best for Jordie.

Kat watched for as long as she could, but when the stress of the day and the long drive finally caught up with her, she curled up in the chair Rachel had dragged in from the waiting room. She let her head nod into the soft blanket that carried her son's scent and closed her eyes.

She knew in her heart of hearts that Jack was treating her son as if he were his own. Rachel was at Jack's side performing every command her brother made with surprisingly few mistakes, given this wasn't her job. Kat thought she heard Jack say something about counting beans for a living, but mostly she'd tuned out their banter.

Her son was either too scared or too tired to complain about anything Jack did. And Kat was too groggy to follow beyond the basics. They'd all agreed that Jack would fix what he could tonight to make sure there would be no infection and pain. In the morning he'd call one of his colleagues to confirm that Jordie was on the right treatment path. Everything was going to be free.

Kat would have felt like a charity case, but she didn't. She felt…cherished. And special. Jack stepped up and did what needed to be done. The way Mad Jack would have. He was a hero in every sense of the word.

And she loved him. The real Jack. Not her imaginary dream man. But she still couldn't agree to marry him. All her bluster about deserving something better than a man who only wanted to do the right thing by their child was bull. She was a good mother. She was determined to be a dedicated teacher. But she was so lousy at relationships she wouldn't dream of ruining this wonderful man's life by agreeing to marry him.

She simply had to make him wake up and see the reality of their situation before he ruined his perfect life.

CHAPTER SEVENTEEN

"YOU'RE GONNA marry me and that's that."

"I'm not one of those women from the bar, Jack. You can't tell me what to do."

"Hellfire and damnation, woman," he said, throwing his hat on the dusty ground between them. "Has anyone ever told you you're the most pigheaded person this side of the Missouri?"

Katherine continued to rock, the knitting needles in her hands keeping time to the *click* of the chair against the uneven planks of the porch. "I am not. That distinction is reserved for the man who insists on marriage despite the fact he could be shot and leave me a widow on any given day that he puts on that holster."

His steely gray eyes narrowed to that squint so many feared. "People die, Katherine. Not just people who use guns. Your family took sick and left you all alone, but you can't stop living because you don't want to feel that pain again. Pain is what reminds us we're alive. Pain and love."

"Maybe I don't deserve to be alive."

He cleared the distance between them in two long strides and yanked her to her feet. The grip on her wrist stung, but she didn't pull away. She met his angry gaze chin high. "Don't you see? You're alive for a reason. I've had more close calls than you ever want to know about, but I'm here now—with you—because we have a purpose beyond just living out our days. We have a chance to make a family. To bring normal to this wild place."

He let her go, undid his gun belt and let it drop. It landed with a thudding sound nearly as loud as her heartbeat.

"Without you, I will die. It's only a matter of time. My reflexes will slow. A young pup looking to make a name for himself will beat me to the draw. You're my last hope, Katherine. Can't you see that?"

KAT SAT UP in bed, heart racing. She looked around and recognized nothing. She had no idea where she was. Or when. The dream had been so real. She could still taste Jack's kiss. A hint of mint from the leaf he'd picked near her porch. He'd called her his last hope.

"No," she said, shaking her head. She wasn't anybody's hope. She was a lodestone. A burden. No matter how hard she tried to tread lightly in other people's lives, she always managed to screw up. Just ask her two exes.

The Jack in her dreams was poised to give up his way of life for her. The Jack in real life was in the process of throwing away his established business to move closer to her. Talk about utter madness. She didn't get it.

Why me? she wanted to shout at the top of her lungs.

She closed her eyes and took a deep breath. When she opened them, she felt calmer. But she wasn't going anywhere today until she got an answer.

She hopped out of the guest-room bed. She'd been too exhausted to notice much last night. By the time they got back to Jack's house and she'd put the boys to bed, she'd barely had enough energy left to brush her teeth and crawl under the covers.

The room was lovely. The gold- and rust-colored silk spread contained strands of teal that picked up accents in the wall hangings and dried flower arrangement on the Craftsman-style dresser. Everything was so perfect she suspected a designer had had a say in the decor.

After peeking in on the boys, who were crashed on an air bed in the room beside hers, she took a shower and dressed in record speed. The light murmur of a television coming from the first floor let her know that Jack was awake and moving around downstairs.

At least, she hoped the woman's voice she heard was Diane Sawyer and not Jack's sister. While Kat liked Rachel and hoped to see her before she left town—and thank her for her help last night—at the moment she needed some alone time with Jack before the boys woke up.

She followed the sound toward the back of the house. She couldn't help but admire the home's tasteful design, although there were too many breakable art objects on low tables to give the place a kid-friendly feel.

Her flip-flops made a *shush-shush* sound on the terrazzo tile. Jack must have heard her coming because he met her at the doorway. "Kat. You're up. I was hoping you'd be able to sleep in. How are you feeling?"

"Pretty good, thanks."

"I have the water on if you'd like tea."

He didn't move when she stepped closer. Even

though she had every intention of ending things with him today, she was tempted, so very tempted, to throw herself into his arms for a good cry.

Damn hormones. Even if she wasn't pregnant, something was whacked out inside her body. Maybe what she was feeling was swoo whiplash.

"Do you have any juice? Something cold sounds good."

"Pineapple orange?" he asked, ushering her into the kitchen/dining nook, which with its twelve-foot ceilings, arched windows and faux-suede paint job the color of the juice he'd just offered to give her could have appeared on the pages of a decorating magazine.

She froze the second she caught sight of two women seated on the opposite side of the large, U-shaped counter. Their reflections were visible in the shiny perfection of the gold-flecked onyx marble countertop. Rachel and an auburn-hair woman who simply had to be Jack's mother. She looked exactly the same as the photo Kat had found in his wallet.

"Kat, this is my mother, Rosaline. And you remember Rachel, of course."

Kat screwed up her courage. She'd never had a great relationship with either of her mothers-in-law, despite the fact that they were very nice women. She'd always wondered if the circumstances behind the weddings to their sons had put a strain on their relationships from the get-go.

"Good morning," she said, taking a step closer. She wasn't sure if she should offer to shake hands. "Did Rachel tell you what a hero your son is?"

Rosaline's perfectly sculpted eyebrow arched with an air of disdain. "I'm absolutely certain she didn't leave out a single detail. That's all she's talked about all morning."

Kat looked at Rachel, who shrugged good-naturedly. Her mother's waspish tone seemed to drift right past her. Kat was envious. "Oh, Mother, get off your high horse. Jack and I have both told you that Kat is the one. You'd better be nice to her, or you'll never see your future grandchildren. And believe me, Kat's kids are great and you're going to want to know them, too."

Kat was too shocked by Rachel's assumption to respond. Until Jack took her hand and put a cold juice glass in it. She immediately set it down and faced Rachel. "You're jumping to conclusions that aren't based on fact. I came here because Jack is the only dentist I know who might possibly have helped us on a Friday night. Maybe if I'd been thinking straight, I could have called around, but when your child is in pain, all you can think of is how to fix things the fastest."

"So you drove eight hours to Denver," Rachel said, a knowing smile on her lips.

Kat felt her face heat. "I trust him."

Rachel crowed triumphantly. "You love him, Kat. It's okay to admit that."

Kat looked at Jack, who took a deep breath and let it out. His sigh was filled with a frustration that probably went back to the day his parents brought his baby sister home from the hospital. "For someone who has—as recently as yesterday—declared love to be an emotional black hole that sucks all joy and hope from one's soul, you sure seem eager for me and Kat to get together. What's that about?"

"Your sister needs therapy," Jack's mother said.

"She won't admit how unbalanced the divorce left her. She's probably projecting her unfulfilled dreams on the both of you."

Rachel laughed. "Whatever. The point is, Mother, that you and I are in the wrong place at the wrong time, and we're leaving right this instant so Jack and Kat can talk."

When Rosaline started to protest, Rachel shushed her. "That was our deal, remember? You had until Kat woke up to try to convince Jack that he was making a huge mistake." To Kat, she said, "*I* don't think that, but Mother hasn't had a chance to get to know you. Once she does, she'll come around. I was thinking I might lock her in a room with Tag and an Xbox and see what happens. What do you think?"

Kat kept her opinion to herself.

Rachel, who obviously was used to getting her way, hustled her mother out the door with barely a chance for the older woman to voice her protest. Rosaline's last words were, "Call me when your company is gone, Jackson. We need to talk."

Kat echoed the sentiment once the sound of Rachel's sports car's engine faded. "Jack, we need to talk."

"I know, Kat. But first I want to show you something."

His tone reminded her of Jordie when he brought home an art project that spelled MOM in macaroni. "What?" she asked suspiciously.

He stepped closer and turned sideways before carefully rolling back the edge of his loose, short-sleeved Hawaiian shirt.

Her involuntary gasp made her sip of juice lodge sideways in her throat. Tears burned in her eyes as she coughed and sputtered. "You have a tattoo. A real one."

He nodded, stretching his neck to look at it. "I know. See what it says?"

She brushed the tears from her eyes—coughing tears, not real tears—and looked again. Her name in a heart. How cheesy. But knowing how much he feared needles and everything he'd endured with the black ink made her eyes fill with moisture again. Real tears this time.

"It says 'Kat.'"

"Yeah, it does. Thank God you don't go by Katherine."

His tone was light, but she knew he wasn't kidding.

"Were you drugged?"

He shook his head. "I had one of my colleagues give me a prescription for a mild tranquilizer, but I didn't fill it. I decided that since I'm asking you to be brave enough to risk marriage again, I needed to get over my old phobias, as well."

She shook her head. "Jack, they're not the same thing. Marriage is a lifetime commitment."

"I know. So is a tattoo."

She smiled. She couldn't help it. "Jack…"

"Kat…"

"You're crazy."

He nodded. "Some might call me mad."

A flutter started in her belly and quickly passed through all her limbs. "What did you say?"

He ran a hand through his hair—longer now than when she'd first met him and speculated about his receding hairline beneath his skull-and-crossbones do-rag. Had he grown into his looks these past weeks or had her perception of him changed?

"I know this is going to sound bizarre, but the first night we were together at the motel, I had this dream where I was a gunslinger named Mad Jack and I swept this beautiful schoolmarm named Katherine off her feet. I was prepared to love her, then get the hell out of Dodge, as they say, but instead, I fell in love with her."

"You? Or Mad Jack?"

He made a face as he pondered the question. "A week ago I would have said Mad Jack. I honestly didn't think I was capable of being someone like that. In charge of my life. Fearless. Independent. Afraid of nothing—not even needles."

"What changed?"

"You made me realize that I could do anything I wanted. Even when I failed—like with the black ink—you didn't judge me. That was really empowering, Kat. And I've seen you do the same with your children. It's what's going to make you a fabulous teacher."

"Really?"

He nodded. "Funny how other people can see things about us that we seem to miss. It took a figment of my subconscious to get over a lifetime of fears. Needles. Kids. Love."

"You were afraid of love?" She was afraid her knees were going to give out.

He led her to the stool his mother had been sitting on. "Afraid to love completely, honestly. Afraid to be vulnerable. I think that's one thing we have in common."

She sat, but her focus was fixed on what he was saying. "I've been vulnerable all my life, Jack. I never take precautions to protect myself. Obviously. I have two children to prove it."

He put his hands on the armrests of the stool and leaned in to kiss her forehead. "Neither of your sons was an accident. They came into your life to fill a void. Just like you came into mine to fill an empty spot where my heart should have been.

"Kat, you have to marry me. I told you about my dream. I've risked your laughing at me—or worse, calling me crazy. I can't bare any more of my soul than that."

Did she dare tell him the truth?

Before she could make up her mind, the sound of voices—her children's voices—filtered through the doorway. She expected Jack to pout about the interruption. Both Pete and Drew would have. Instead, he threw back his head and laughed. "In here, boys," he called in a booming voice. "Who wants pancakes?"

To Kat, he added, "Soft food for Jordie."

That was when she knew the truth. Jack was not a mistake. He was a gift. And only a fool would turn her back on someone fate went to such great lengths to put in her life.

Unfortunately Kat had yet to tell him the truth. She wasn't pregnant. She still hadn't seen a doctor, but two over-the-counter tests seemed to trump her symptoms, which probably were the result of stress, as Libby suggested.

Once he found out about the baby—or rather the lack of a baby—he'd probably rethink his proposal. What man wouldn't? What man in his right mind would marry someone like her? Someone with all her baggage—two ex-husbands, two kids with bad teeth, a crazy, convoluted, completely dysfunctional family and a herd of bison?

Not a single man she could name. Not even Mad Jack.

JACK WAS SHOCKED by how fast the morning shot by. Jordie seemed to rebound from his ordeal with inordinate healing ability. Just a casual check of his mouth showed excellent improvement. Jack had made an appointment for two o'clock with the colleague he'd most trust with his own child. Kat had made calls to her parents, her girlfriends and both boys' fathers to keep them abreast of what was happening. She planned to leave right after the checkup, unless there was some pressing need for action that Jack had missed.

He was sorry their heart-to-heart had been interrupted, but he couldn't blame the boys for wanting to be near their mother. A video game kept Tag occupied, but Jordie had refused to leave Kat's side even for a minute—until Rachel showed up with ice cream and watermelon.

"Outside on the patio, boys," she said, marching through the kitchen like the Pied Piper. "My brother likes a neat house. He'd never condone a seed-spitting contest indoors."

Jack had never seen this side of his sister before and wasn't sure why she was taking such an active interest in two children who may or may not wind up being part of the family. The answer to that question rested with Kat, who had turned him down so often he wasn't sure what to expect.

"We'll be right out," he called after her. "I need to draw Kat a map to get her safely out of town. You know what traffic is like around here."

Rachel rolled her eyes, but the boys seemed to buy the excuse. Even Jordie.

Once the glass door closed behind them, he turned to Kat and said bluntly, "Yes or no? Are you pregnant?"

She winced in a way that made him regret his lack of tack. "The simple answer is no."

"There's a not-so-simple answer?"

"My mind says I'm pregnant. My body acts like I'm pregnant. The home pregnancy tests I've taken say I'm not. I plan to see a doctor next week. Libby thinks it's stress. My aunt said it could be a tumor on the ovary. She used to be a nurse. I called to ask her advice *for a friend.*"

The suggestion made his knees weak, but he pulled her into his arms and hugged her tight. "Do you have health insurance?"

She shook her head. "The boys do through their dads, but not me."

He eased back slightly. "All the more reason to get married right away." He kept his tone light, but he was serious and he wanted her to know that.

"I'm not your schoolmarm, Jack. I don't need rescuing."

"Did I say that Mad Jack rescued her?" He shook his head. "He swept her off her feet, but she's the one who saved him. His life—like mine—was going nowhere. She made him look beyond what he knew and take a leap of faith toward a life he wanted but didn't think he deserved. Sound familiar?"

Her teeth caught her bottom lip and she nodded ever so slightly. "You've got that part right. I don't deserve you, Jack."

"Because I'm such a fabulous catch?" he asked incredulously. "You were right about me from the start, Kat. I'm a R.U.B. That's one letter short of a rube. In many circles, I'm a joke. But I'm not as much of a joke as I was before I met you." He pointed to his arm. "I have the tattoo to prove it."

She shook her head. "You're not a joke to me, Jack. I got hit with a serious shot of swoo the moment I saw you."

"I have swoo?"

"Big-time."

"Really? Enough to, say, sweep you off your feet?"

"Yeah."

"And make you agree to marry me?"

She didn't answer right away. "Don't you want to find out what the doctor says first?"

He shook his head. "I don't care what the doctor says, Kat. If there's something wrong, I want to be at your side every step of the way. If the negative sign should have been a plus, then I want to experience every part of our pregnancy."

"Our?"

"Yours, mine, Mad Jack's…"

She laughed, then. A real laugh. The kind that made him believe in all possibilities—even those in dreams.

She didn't answer right away, but he could tell she was tempted to say yes. "I still don't know why you want to marry *me*."

He kissed her with all the passion she'd unleashed in his formerly barren soul, and when they were both breathless and laughing, he said, "Because with you, I'll be living my dream, Kat. Instead of just reading about the Old West, I get to move to the Black Hills, make mad, passionate love to the prettiest gal in the county—who also happens to be my wife—and raise bison in my spare time."

"What about being a stepdad to Jordie and Tag?"

"I'm looking forward to the challenge of convincing them I'm not a complete nerd."

"Good luck with that," she said, imitating her eldest son's disdain to a T.

Jack put both hands over his heart as if wounded and staggered backward. "As soon as I get to the Hills, we'll sit down and I'll tell you about my dad. He was a great guy who had got taken advantage of. I spent a lot of time thinking he was a chump, and I think I was so worried the same thing could happen to me that I missed out on a lot of life. He never would have wanted that for me, and I'm pretty sure he was behind my decision to walk into that bar in Deadwood that night."

"Why?"

"When I was a little kid, I called him Pop. I'd actually forgotten that. But when I looked at the name of the bar—Pop's—I remember thinking how ironic it was that my first stop on my walk on the wild side was a place that shared the name with a man who ruined his life by taking a foolish risk."

"What kind of risk?"

He shook his head. "Not an unreasonable one. He was just trying to please everybody while still honoring his own passion for helping people. I'd forgotten that, too. But now I know that somewhere in heaven my dad is smiling with all his might."

She looked thoughtful a moment, then asked, "What about your mom? I don't think she's going to be quite as pleased with all these changes you're proposing."

"One major hurdle at a time, okay? You have people in your life who will probably try to hold tight to the status quo, too, but we'll deal with them in time. Together. If you say yes."

In time.

The phrase struck Kat as appropriate. She'd fallen in love with him in another era. They'd had a crash course of courting in two weeks. But the fact that she'd turned to him without hesitation in her son's time of need seemed a clear sign. He was the one.

But was she the right woman for him?

He stroked his thumb across her brow. "Listen, Kat, I won't push you into my agenda. We have all the time in the world—baby or no baby. But you need to know one thing. I'm the most goal-oriented, single-minded person you've ever met. That's the part I got from my mother. I'm moving to Sentinel Pass. I've already talked to a couple of builders in the area. I'm looking into what I need to get licensed in the state and move my business."

He paused to make his point. "But I don't intend to be the workaholic my father was. I want to explore the Hills with you and the boys every summer when you're not teaching. I want us to be a family—just as soon as you're ready."

Ready? She'd been ready her whole life for what he was offering. If she was brave enough to take a giant leap. Maybe she wasn't the best woman for him, but she was the one he wanted…and she wanted him. She was tired of doing this alone, being the matriarch of her herd. She was ready to share the dream.

She glanced into the backyard. The boys looked relaxed and happy. Even serious Tag. They needed Jack, too, she realized.

"Before I give you my answer to your proposal, I think you should know that I fell in love with Mad Jack first."

"Beg your pardon?"

"He was in my dream, too. That first night in Custer. I loved how he knew his own mind and didn't give a damn what other people thought of him. That didn't seem to fit the image I had of you back then. I'd just given you a temporary tattoo to impress your ex-fiancée, remember?"

His head bobbed. "Okay. I'll give you that. But what do you mean you fell in love with Mad Jack. He was in my dream."

"He was in mine, too. And I was Katherine. Strong, confident, a woman on a mission. I didn't think she was needy, like me."

He gave a soft snort. "You're the matriarch of your herd, Kat. Everything you've accomplished in your life, you've done alone. Just like Katherine."

"But she was loved—until her family died."

He pulled her close. "Oh, sweetheart, you were loved. Your family just had a lousy way of showing you. But your sons adore you. And I plan to spend the rest of my life proving just how much I love you." He kissed her tenderly, then asked one more time, "Will you marry me?"

She answered with all her heart, on behalf of the woman she was and the woman she knew she could be. "Yes."

CHAPTER EIGHTEEN

JACK HUNKERED DOWN over his horse's neck, trying to breathe air that wasn't filled with fine crystals of blowing snow. The storm had taken everyone by surprise. His friends had begged him to stay the night in town, but he didn't dare. He had too much to lose if something went wrong. He had to make sure Katherine was okay.

His horse knew the way and Jack trusted the animal's instincts. One hoof ahead of another and they finally made it to a clearing that looked vaguely familiar. A roofline. The faint scent of smoke.

He put the horse in the shelter of the barn and said a short prayer that he'd be able to find his way to the house—not sixty yards away. The barn door was yanked from his hand by the wind with a force that made his blood run cold. He squinted into the white wall of nothing.

He knew the general direction. He'd walked the same path every day for the past six months. But he'd heard stories of people frozen to death mere feet from their door. He lowered his chin, put his shoulder to the wind and took his first step. That was when he saw the rope tied to the hitching post.

He knew instantly who had put it there and why. Hand over hand, using the rope as a guide, he fought his way to the house. Without it, he might easily have wandered off course and died in a snowbank.

When he reached the porch, he stomped his boots and brushed off the thick, wet covering of ice and snow from his jacket. Despite the gloves he was wearing, his fingers felt numb. But his heart and mind were brightly alive with determination to make certain she was okay.

He opened the door and stepped inside. It took a moment for his eyes to adjust to the dim light from the fire in the hearth. Not the banked glow of embers one usually set at night but a well-tended cooking fire that held a kettle of bubbling water. A few feet away was the copper tub he'd bought her as a wedding present.

She was expecting him. Waiting. So in tune with him that not even the turbulent weather could keep her from sensing his intent to make it home—no matter what.

He looked around and spotted her. In her family's rocking chair she'd brought overland. She was watching his every move, but without missing a beat, she told the baby in her arms, "I told you your daddy was coming, little girl. No matter what, he'd get back to us, safe and sound."

Jack shrugged off his coat and hung it over the peg she'd asked him to install behind the door. A small triumph of civilization, she'd claimed. Her nod of approval went straight to his heart. He'd spent every day since they met trying to earn her respect in every way that counted.

In two strides he crossed the room and went down on one knee beside the rocking chair. He blew on his hands to warm them, then touched the schoolmarm's face. "Hello, wife."

Their kiss was tender, but it sparkled with the heat and desire they'd both found had grown in their union. He touched his baby girl's hand. The child's delicate little fingers wrapped around his.

He started to pick her up, but looked down a moment and thought better of it. "Maybe I better remove this first," he told his wife. "Don't want our darling Daisy to get scratched."

With a twist and a tug, his hand came away with a shiny star-shaped badge nestled in his palm. The gunslinger had gone legit. Love had changed him.

Jack looked at Katherine, the schoolmarm. So beautiful. So strong and compassionate and forgiving. So…Kat. She rocked forward and kissed him. "I love you, Jack."

THE WORDS ECHOED outside his dream and Jack opened his eyes. The woman of his dream was there, just inches away from him. Eyes wide. A knowing smile on her lips.

He blinked, trying to recall the images that had felt so very real. "I was dreaming. A snowstorm. We had a baby. I mean, Mad Jack and Katherine had a baby." If he closed his eyes, Jack could almost smell his child's scent. "I don't know what I mean."

Kat snuggled close, her head fitting just under his chin. "We'll have our own someday, Jack. You heard what the doctor said. Stress. That's why my body was so screwed up. But you're here now, and everything is going to be okay."

He knew that. He did. But there was still a lot to do. And even though it was still considered summer, winter would arrive before they knew it. His dream reminded him of that. He kissed her long and hard, then scooted out of bed. "I have to meet the pool crew at the house this morning. The solar-heating unit arrived yesterday. So much to do if we want to get you and the boys moved in before Christmas."

She groaned, but he knew she understood. Sitting up, she watched him dress. "I think they're happy about us, don't you agree? Really happy."

He looked around for his work boots but could only find one. "Who? The boys?"

She shook her head. "No. I mean, Mad Jack and Katherine. If we have a girl, can we name her Daisy? It's old-fashioned but sweet."

He stopped dead in his tracks. "You were there just now?"

Kat nodded. "I never doubted for a minute that you'd find your way home to us."

Jack believed her. He couldn't explain it, didn't even want to try, but he no longer questioned their subliminal connection.

She stretched. In the two weeks since Jordie's accident and their subsequent return to the Hills, she'd made peace with the fact that she wasn't pregnant. She actually seemed happy that she had a choice about whether she wanted Jack in her life.

Thankfully, she'd decided that everything happened for a reason—and the reason was love. She loved him and wanted to marry him as soon as they had time.

"By the way, the first piece of furniture we buy for our newly remodeled home has to be a rocking chair," she said. "I want one just like Libby's. The next time we have a book club there, you'll have to check it out."

Jack had been staying in Hill City while he supervised the remodeling of his newly purchased home. He spent every night that the boys were with their fathers in Kat's bed. Where they used protection. This time, Kat said, they were going to do things right.

That was fine with Jack as long as they sealed the deal soon. He was pushing for a Christmas wedding, but Kat wanted to make sure she didn't spread herself too thin by student-teaching and planning a wedding. Jack was hoping to convince his sister to move to Sentinel Pass—even temporarily—to help him set up his new office and help Kat plan a wedding. Rachel had learned a few days earlier that her job had fallen victim to the downturn in the economy.

Jack looked around once more, but still didn't see his boot. With a sigh, he started toward the door. "Maybe I left the other one on the deck," he muttered.

He'd only taken a couple of steps when he felt a sharp prick on the sole of his foot. "Youch!" he exclaimed.

Hopping around until he spotted something shiny partially buried in the old loop carpet, he reached down and picked it up. A cheap tin star. The kind a kid might wear while playing an Old West sheriff.

But it looked a little bit like the one… No. He shook his head and handed it to Kat. "Jordie's?" he asked.

Her eyes were big as she looked it over, front and back. "Umm…sure. If you say so. Who else could it belong to?"

Their gazes met, and even though they both did their best not to smile, within seconds Jack was back in bed with the woman he loved, rolling with mirth, laughing their heads off.

Who, indeed?

* * * * *

Single titles coming next month

THE PREGNANT BRIDE WORE WHITE

by Susan Crosby

When Jake McCoy came home to Chance City, he found a whole new family waiting for him. Was the adventurer ready to become an honest husband?

SOPHIE'S SECRET

by Tara Taylor Quinn

For years it's suited Duane and Sophie to keep their relationship a secret. Then Sophie becomes pregnant – and Duane proposes. Are they ready to make their private affair public news?

HER SO-CALLED FIANCÉ

by Abby Gaines

What possesses Sabrina to tell everyone she's going to marry Jake Warrington? She's sure her ex hates her! Sabrina needs Jake's help – and he might give it. But it comes with some conditions attached…

DIAGNOSIS: DADDY

by Gina Wilkins

Connor Hayes had just started to pursue his dream of being a doctor when he found out he was a father. Mia wanted to help, but was she up to multitasking as best friend… nanny…and love of Connor's life?

On sale 16th July 2010

Available at WHSmith, Tesco, ASDA, Eason and all good bookshops.
For full Mills & Boon range including eBooks visit
www.millsandboon.co.uk

0410_S0ZED

2 FREE BOOKS
AND A SURPRISE GIFT

We would like to take this opportunity to thank you for reading this Mills & Boon® book by offering you the chance to take TWO more specially selected books from the Special Moments™ series absolutely FREE! We're also making this offer to introduce you to the benefits of the Mills & Boon® Book Club™—

- **FREE home delivery**
- **FREE gifts and competitions**
- **FREE monthly Newsletter**
- **Exclusive Mills & Boon Book Club offers**
- **Books available before they're in the shops**

Accepting these FREE books and gift places you under no obligation to buy, you may cancel at any time, even after receiving your free books. Simply complete your details below and return the entire page to the address below. You don't even need a stamp!

YES Please send me 2 free Special Moments books and a surprise gift. I understand that unless you hear from me, I will receive 5 superb new stories every month, including a 2-in-1 book priced at £4.99 and three single books priced at £3.19 each, postage and packing free. I am under no obligation to purchase any books and may cancel my subscription at any time. The free books and gift will be mine to keep in any case.

Ms/Mrs/Miss/Mr ________________ Initials ______________

____

Surname ____

Address ____

____

______________________________ Postcode __________

E-mail ____

Send this whole page to: Mills & Boon Book Club, Free Book Offer, FREEPOST NAT 10298, Richmond, TW9 1BR

Offer valid in UK only and is not available to current Mills & Boon Book Club subscribers to this series. Overseas and Eire please write for details.. We reserve the right to refuse an application and applicants must be aged 18 years or over. Only one application per household. Terms and prices subject to change without notice. Offer expires 30th June 2010. As a result of this application, you may receive offers from Harlequin Mills & Boon and other carefully selected companies. If you would prefer not to share in this opportunity please write to The Data Manager, PO Box 676, Richmond, TW9 1WU.